MW01028487

EPHESUS

JUDAH'S JOURNEY

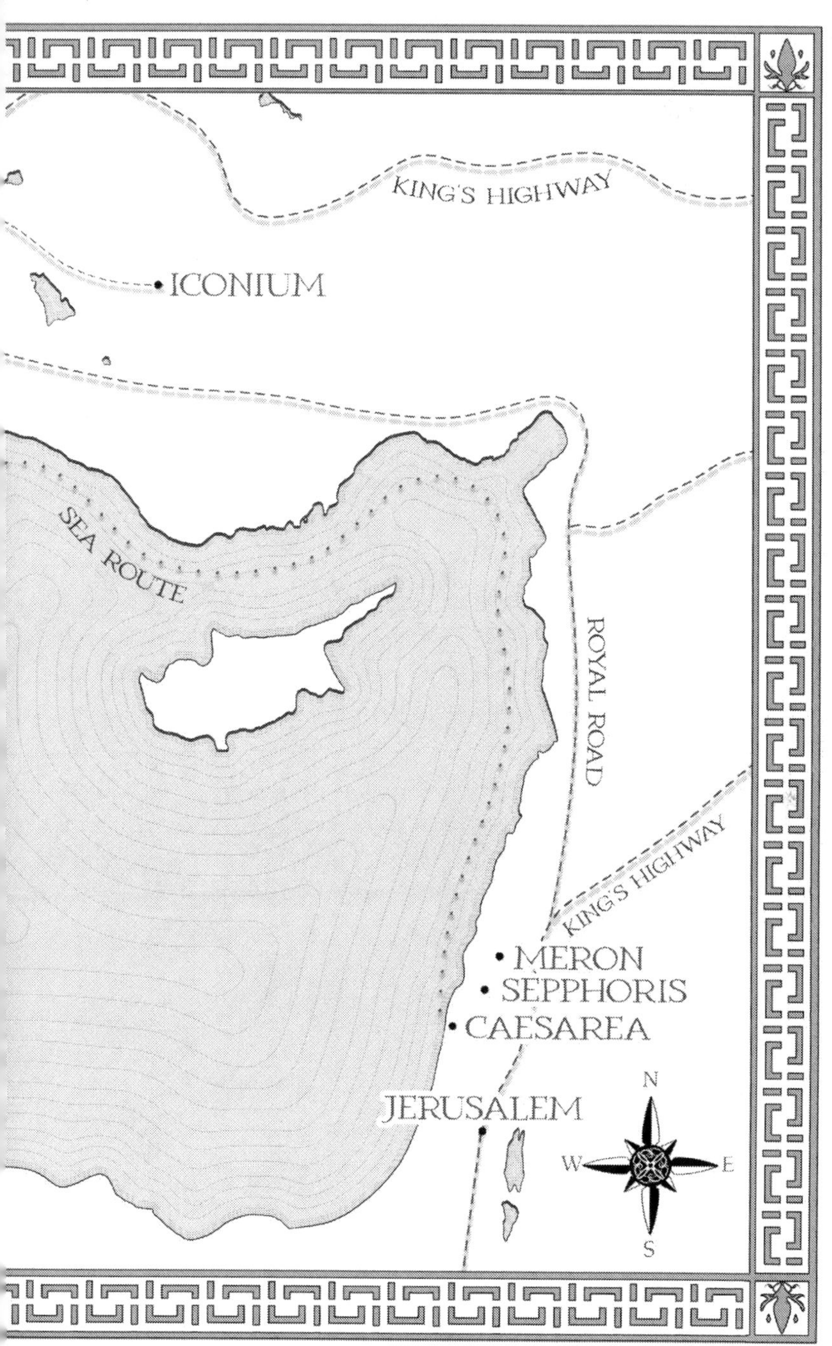

To my earthly parents, Jim and Diane Kleypas,
who have consistently and persistently displayed
unconditional, merciful, and welcome-home love

FINDING HOME

SUSAN K MACIAS

SM

Susan Macias

For more information, address: susan@susankmacias.com

First paperback edition February 2024

Cover by Serhii Myshkovskyi
Map by BMR Williams

ISBN 978-0-9993085-5-4 (hardback)
ISBN 978-0-9993085-6-1 (paperback)
ISBN 978-0-9993085-7-8 (ebook)

www.susankmacias.com

GLOSSARY OF 1ST CENTURY TERMS

Abba and Eema- Hebrew for Dad and Mom

Amphora, Amphorae- container with two handles and a long skinny body that ends in a point. Used to transport liquids.

Bet-hasefer- Hebrew early education akin to elementary school.

Bet-midrash- Hebrew upper education in the Talmud akin to high school.

Bimah- an elevated platform in the middle of the synagogue from which the Torah was read.

Bris- the ceremony in which the rabbi performs the rite of circumcision on male babies, performed on the eighth day.

Caravansary- inn built along well-traveled roads and at the edge of cities to house caravans. Usually included a large, walled area to protect animals.

Cistern- large receptacle for collecting rain water.

Chiton- basic tunic worn by men and women.

Mezuzah- Small parchment with the Shema written on it. The scroll is enclosed in a small protective container or box and affixed to the doorpost of the entrance in order to fulfill Deuteronomy 6:9: "You shall write them on the doorposts of your house and on your gates."

Mitzvah- a mitzvah is a command but also means a charitable deed or generous act.

Salve- Latin greeting

Shema- the declaration of faith from Deuteronomy 6:4-9 traditionally recited morning and evening proclaiming that God is One.

Taberna- a Roman tavern

Tallit- a prayer shawl used for prayer with the tzitzit attached to the corners.

Tannur- oven made of clay

Tepidarium- the warm room in a Roman bath before entering the very hot or cold rooms.

Thermopolium- equivalent to today's fast food, this commercial enterprise served drinks and hot food.

Tzitzit- knotted tassels worn to remind the person of the 613 commandments of Torah.

Then you will call upon me
and come and pray to me,
and I will hear you.
You will seek me and find me,
when you seek me
with all your heart.
I will be found by you, declares the LORD,
and I will restore your fortunes and gather you
from all the nations and all the places
where I have driven you, declares the LORD,
and I will bring you back . . .

Jeremiah 29:12-14a

CHAPTER 1
JUDAH

Ephesus
Sivan (May) AD 20

Many are the sorrows of the wicked, but steadfast love surrounds the one who trusts in the LORD.

PSALM 32:10 ESV

"Get in the cart, slave!"

He said slave. He means me.

When I'm pushed from behind, my leather sandal catches and I land face down on the dirt packed square, a loud pop echoing in my head. Fiery pain shoots straight through my nose, as jeers and whistles from the crowd inform me that at least they find amusement in my misery. Dancing lights parade across my closed eyes. Searing grips my tied wrists. Throbbing intensifies in my hurt shoulder.

Just when I think the pain can't get worse, I'm yanked upright from behind by the rope. As the wounds on my wrists rip deeper, my arm wrenches farther from my shoulder. Blood pours from my nose, staining my chiton and pooling at my feet.

"Please, let me die." But to whom does my guttural cry plead?

"Be careful!" Gallus, the man who purchased me, yells at my pusher. "You injure him, you'll work in his place!"

More gently, I'm guided toward a crude wagon. Other slaves, dirty, despondent, and also bound, peek from every available space between barrels and crates. One clear thought echoes through my mind: don't get on the wagon. Don't get on the wagon. Once there, I'll belong to someone else. Forever.

It seems half of Ephesus pushes their smelly bodies into this small market square. Catcalls and trash descend from the windows of second and third story apartments. Laughter circulates amongst the varied workers of every nationality, their dirty clothing signifying workers of the lower trades. What draws them to this display of human misery? Does seeing someone else's doom make them feel better about their own wretched existence?

Tasting blood, I spit out a red glob that lands near a heckler's sandaled feet.

"Watch it!"

His neighbor laughs. "You hungry?" He waves a bowl of foul-smelling broth beneath my nose.

"That's too good for him!" The heckler shakes bloody mucus from his foot. "How about some of this?" With a flick of his foot, he sends animal dung toward me. Raucous laughter erupts from the crowd.

Attempting to sidestep the dung, I double over in pain. Sweat stings my eyes, but my aching ribs scream at the quick movement. At least the kicker had poor aim.

"Make way! Make way!"

"No," I groan. That voice belongs to Aldric, Apollon's henchman, the same man who delivered the kick that probably broke my ribs. If Aldric is here, that means . . .

"Oh, Jude!" Frankincense mixes with dung. "Look what you've done to yourself. All that blood!"

Of course, Apollon wouldn't miss one second of my suffering. Straightening as much as possible, I face his hooded eyes, almost lost in the fleshy face I once venerated. In the year I've known him, he's never once looked happy. Yet now, he almost appears giddy.

What drew me to this man? His full jowls flow directly into his curved torso, swathed in lengths of blue silk intricately embroidered in gold. Had opulent clothing and heady perfume blinded me to his true character? Was I that stupid? My bound arms confirm: Yes. Yes, I was.

Just past his right shoulder, auburn waves blow in the breeze, and I catch Kassandra's gaze. For a moment, my eyes plead, even beg. *Help. Please!* But she withdraws behind her master.

Apollon's eyes narrow. "Come, Kassandra. Say goodbye to your plaything."

She coughs.

"Say goodbye," Apollon commands.

Stepping toward me, she keeps her eyes to the ground. Even now, with all my dreams of us destroyed, I grasp at one final memory. I drink in her curves wrapped in sheer, purple fabric, her hair, even more vibrant in the setting sun, and her long neck encircled with delicate gold chains.

"Kassandra?" I gasp.

"Now." Apollon's low tone issues an order.

"Goodbye, Jude." Kassandra lifts her eyes, revealing sorrow and resignation. Even if she did care for me, she's as powerless to change this as I am. With a toss of her head, she pivots and disappears into the crowd, taking my last hope with her.

Gallus signals my pusher toward the wagon. But when he prods me, Apollon places a hand on my shoulder. The pusher swears under his breath.

I don't blame him. Gallus scares me too. Maybe it's that scar running down his left cheek, or the way his muscles ripple under his ebony skin. Or maybe that his deep voice reminds me of a growl. When he bought me, he informed Apollon that he is an estate manager for an extensive country villa. The way he'd puffed out his chest, you'd think he owned the place. But the patrician who owns it, and now me, is named Valerius.

My owner. I'm owned.

Gallus turns to Apollon. "Sir, we must reach the caravansary before dark."

His fingers like pincers, Apollon grips my injured shoulder, sending lightning bolts through my body. He leans close. "You're dung under my feet. Remember that, each day of your miserable existence. You. Are. Nothing."

"Yes, take him, Gallus." Apollon sweeps his arm wide. "And give my best to Valerius."

Gallus bows then jerks me away from the man behind me. "I'll do it!"

Panting with pain, I ignore Apollon, one of the few choices that remain, and hobble to the wagon.

"Make room!" Gallus's command sends the occupants wedging into space that didn't seem to exist a few seconds ago. He grabs my rough chiton and hefts me like a sack of grain. Agony courses from my nose, through my shoulder, and lands in my ribs. I can no more hold back the cry of anguish than stop the incoming tide.

Little by little, I push myself upright and gaze west toward Ephesus's harbor. Was it just a year ago that I arrived there with such hope? Rosy clouds float across the western sky. Glowing on the horizon, the sun paints a golden path across the water. How I wish I could discover any other path than the one I'm on.

But there's no escape, so I turn my eyes east up the long, straight road that will take me out of this detestable city and over the mountains beyond. Orion peeks through the dusky sky, oblivious to my future. Unbidden, Abba's voice echoes from deep within me.

Look at Orion, son. The Holy One, who created the stars, created you.

Oh, Abba. Why do I think of you now, of all times? At least you, and especially Seth, will never know how I failed. Maybe you two sit on our balcony, eyes on the heavens. Maybe you see Orion too. Do you think of me, Abba? The son who is dead to you? The son who wishes he were dead?

As the driver whips the oxen into action, the milling onlookers step back. The cart bumps over the rugged street, wrenching my mind back to this sultry afternoon.

Apollon sends a final arrow. "Farewell, Jude. May your god treat you more kindly in slavery than he did in business."

My god? I have no god. I angle my face away from Apollon and brace myself for the jolting journey to the caravansary on the outskirts of Ephesus.

Each lurch brings fresh anguish. Nausea swells and despair consumes. Pain, however, overwhelms and I slip into the welcome embrace of unconsciousness.

Seth
Meron, Northern Galilee
Tammaz (June) AD 20

GRAVEL CRUNCHES under my feet as I pace across the courtyard of our family compound, turn, stride back, but never stray far from our room. Each time I pass our window with its billowing curtain, I beg Adonai to end this interminable wait.

A servant scurries from the room Hadassah and I share with a load of cloths. Are those red stains? My heart catches. Hadassah must survive this night. She must.

"Excuse me, sir." Our servant Tova sidesteps me with yet another lamp. How many women can fit in that small space? And how much light do they need? And why is this taking so long?

When I received word that the baby was coming, I rushed home anticipating meeting our child for the first time. Certainly, the baby will have brown eyes and hair like both of us. But will the hair flow in thin curls like Hadassah's, or be straight and thick like mine? I hope our child won't have Hadassah's short stature with my solid build. My height gives my muscles somewhere to go. I'd actually chuckled picturing a pudgy baby wreathed in thick curls—a strange combination of the two of us.

But that was at the eighth hour, with the sun just past its high point. Now the sun sets, and I still haven't seen Hadassah. And the furrowed brows and hushed tones of women flitting to and from the birth room reveal that something is wrong.

At first, Abba had assured me, "She will be fine."

An hour later, "Naomi is an excellent midwife."

An hour after that, "Would you like to pray with me?"

I found his efforts at comfort irritating, and my nerves wouldn't allow stillness. So he retreated under the arbor and I began pacing.

I make yet another circuit around the large courtyard of our family compound, striding pass the kitchen, servants' quarters, and barn. But every time I come to the family rooms and pass Judah's dark window, I curse under my breath. We shouldn't keep this space vacant for a fool who will never return, brother or not. Not even my fear for Hadassah drives away the disgust his memory provokes. In fact, I despise him even more.

"You need to toss it higher." Eli's voice draws me to the threshing floor where he instructs a new servant on how to effectively toss wheat to send chaff away with the breeze.

Manure, hay, and livestock join to create the distinctive atmosphere of our barn. In the adjoining pen, Methuselah, our brindle donkey, chews hay after a day of dragging his grinding wheel. Sheep jostle to enter their pen, herded by Timaeus, the local shepherd. Strange how normal life continues on.

When I sneeze, Eli looks up. "Any news?"

"Not yet."

His drawn eyebrows confirm my fears. Though he and his wife Miriam have been Abba's bondservants my entire life, I've rarely seen him display emotion.

"Don't worry, Seth." Eli clasps my forearm. "My Miriam is with her and will lay down her own life for Hadassah if need be."

Blinking, I give a terse nod.

"Seth!" Abba waves me over.

Glad for an escape, I join Abba at his favorite spot, a cedar table under a grapevine-covered arbor spanning the alcove between the kitchen and his room. In the corner grows an ancient oak, its limbs providing shade. So many arguments over scripture or discussions of the latest rabbi's teaching have occurred in this space.

He hands me a clay cup of wine. "I know it's difficult, but try to drink something."

I stare into the red liquid. "I can't stand this."

"I know, son. The woman's part is much harder, but the torment for husbands—unendurable. To be forced to wait, with nothing to do?"

"Did you fear?" I try to imagine Abba, absent his graying beard and wrinkles, as the nervous young husband awaiting his own child's arrival.

With a knowing smile, he says, "Certainly. You'll never forget tonight."

"And when your second son was born? Eema died that night."

"The saddest of nights." He sighs deeply. "Life accompanying death. But the Holy One proved a 'refuge for the oppressed and a stronghold in times of trouble.[1]' Then and now."

"What a waste. She died giving birth to a fool."

Abba clears his throat but allows silence to settle over us. Hanging my head, I thrust my hands through my hair. I've never felt so helpless.

"Seth, you can only cling to Adonai who gives life and ask Him to help your wife."

"That's all I can do?"

"And trust. Trust Him to do as He wills and that His will is good—even if it's difficult."

"You can say that? After what you went through twenty-one years ago?"

"Yes, I can. And mean it."

I rub my face and groan. "So, be helpless and trust, even though this could end in tragedy? That must be the definition of torture."

"And faith."

Grimacing, I lean on the table, my fingers drumming.

Abba chuckles. "Go pace the courtyard, son. More room to move."

"I just want her to be okay," I whisper.

"So do I."

Crickets hum their evening tune, as our neighbors' conversations filter over us. They get to enjoy their evening meal, while my life hangs in the balance?

Suddenly, a scream rends the night. I bolt upright, the cups spilling.

Abba grips my shoulder. Our neighbors' conversations halt. Every eye in the courtyard stares at our room. No one dares breathe.

I feel my future drain away. I've lost her.

Miriam

Meron, Northern Galilee

Tammaz (June) AD 20

"MIRIAM, she's growing weak. We must get this baby out."

"You can do this." I bathe Hadassah's face with a cool rag. "Not much longer now."

Naomi shakes her head at that, but the last thing Hadassah needs to think is that this will go on and on.

"Tova, take my place." I hand her the rag and then pull Naomi aside. "You've helped hundreds of Jewish babies be born and I trust you completely."

"You've assisted me at many of those."

"That's why I'm worried. When you clip your words and knot your brow, like you do now, the situation is dangerous. What's wrong?"

"It's taking too long and she's not progressing as she should by now."

"What should we do?"

"Let's get her walking." Naomi grabs my arm. "You're too good of a friend for me to lie to you. I'm very worried."

Hadassah groans in agony as I wipe blood and fluid from her legs and try to pull her up, but she resists.

Without a hint of her usual gentleness, Naomi commands, "Hadassah, you must move!"

With Hadassah's arm around our shoulders, and ours around her waist, Tova and I help her walk about the room in the yellow lantern light until I've lost all track of time. Contraction after contraction wracks this girl I've grown to love like she's my own.

"I'm so tired," Hadassah rasps.

Tova and I exchange anxious looks, as Tova wipes Hadassah's sweaty forehead and I give her a sip of water.

"That's okay," I say. "I'm asking the One who created you and this child to do it for you." If it were possible I would will this baby out of her.

Suddenly, Hadassah's legs give way and she lets loose a scream that sends any remaining hope out the window and into the starry sky.

"Sit her on the birthing stool, Miriam!" Examining her, Naomi cries, "The feet! This one's coming the wrong way. You must relax, Hadassah!"

Stroking Hadassah's clenching stomach, I say, "Relax, my dear. Breathe."

I lean close to hear her ragged response. "I . . . can't . . . do . . . this."

"Yes, you can!" Too frightened to be gentle, I shove her forward and kneel behind her. As she lays against me, I try to pray strength into her. "If you're strong enough to live with that husband of yours, you're strong enough to deliver this baby. Now push—push!"

CHAPTER 2
JUDAH

Outskirts of Ephesus
Sivan (May) AD 20

Oh that my vexation were weighed, and all my calamity laid in the balances! For then it would be heavier than the sand of the sea; therefore my words have been rash. For the arrows of the Almighty are in me; my spirit drinks their poison; the terrors of God are arrayed against me.

JOB 6:2-4

"Judah, the Lord has made a new day. Greet it with joy, my son."

"Abba?" I reach through swirling mist for his hand. Why won't he answer?

Shivering, I wake up. How is it that I haven't actually left Ephesus, yet my time there feels like another lifetime?

All night, I remained cramped in this wagon with nine other humans, eight men and one woman, all bound at their wrists. Their rumbling stomachs, hacking coughs, and low moans confirm they're also miserable.

The man across from me moans. While both of our eyes, hair, and skin are brown, his skin is darker, and he appears leaner and stronger.

"Morning's coming." His accent sounds Egyptian. "Maybe we get water soon."

"Maybe. If anyone considers the needs of slaves."

Last night, we joined the rest of the party at this caravansary on the outer edge of town. If my count is correct, there are five more wagons of various sizes, plus four camels and seven or eight donkeys, all heavily loaded, headed to Valerius's estate. Most of the servants dress in quality cream colored chitons with blue stripes at the hem. Those caring for animals and loading the carts wear coarse brown garments. Gallus, in a blue chiton with a cream stripe, struts and orders them all, berating every mistake.

"He scares everyone."

I nod.

"I'm Khafra."

"Hmmm." I turn my head as far away as I can.

Two men, dirty and in brown chitons, lug a bucket toward us.

"Get off and eat!" yells the short one. "We leave soon."

Gingerly, I edge from the wagon. As soon as the men untie us, we rush to the bucket, but my stomach turns at the brownish gruel, smelling like something we fed the dog in Meron. But, my comrades plunge in grubby hands and shovel it into their mouths. I hesitate a moment before I abandon whatever pride remains and extend a dirty hand. It's shocking, really, that I work to continue living. To keep breathing. What compels me?

After drinking from another communal bucket, we look around the walled caravansary for somewhere to relieve ourselves. All sorts of travelers mingle about the large enclosure, and with all the donkeys, oxen, and camels, there is no shortage of puddles and dung piles.

Khafra approaches the lone female and points at the wagon. She slips behind as he turns away and guards her. The rest of us find the best spot we can.

"Load up!" Gallus's baritone resounds and everyone scurries.

"What are you waiting for?" The short man who delivered the food herds us to the wagon. For a moment we hesitate. Isn't someone refastening our bonds? Then again, where would we go? Back to Ephesus to starve? Or into the hills to be eaten by jackals? One after another, Valerius's new slaves climb aboard the creaky wagon.

With everyone else loaded, I attempt edging up while clutching my ribs. Aldric's oversized leather sandal caused real damage. With a gasp, I fall back on the ground.

"Try again." Khafra grasps under my good shoulder and lifts me—the first kind touch I have felt in days.

"Thank you." Panting, I lean against the side of the cart, lay my head back, and wrap my arms around my middle.

Atop a magnificent black horse, Gallus calls, "Head out!"

The axels grind as the wagon transports us toward a new life. A life with no options.

"You hurt?"

I nod at Khafra but turn my gaze toward the sky. Palm trees rustle in the breeze. Black and white swifts soar above as the gray sky warms into blue. Lacey pink clouds lounge on the Great Sea's edge, still visible far below us. How does beauty still exist?

Look up my son. Whenever you feel despair, obey the Most High's words to Abraham and look to the heavens.

Oh, Abba. I wonder if your voice will ever leave me.

ON THE THIRD day after leaving Ephesus, we halt at a muddy watering hole from which slave and beast drink. I take a moment to evaluate my condition. My left shoulder and ribs throb, and a purple and green bruise covers my left side. Trying to untangle my hair with my right hand, my fingers catch in curls matted with blood and dirt. Gingerly, I touch my nose, swollen and forever crooked. Maybe forever isn't long. I grasp at life and crave death.

"Feeling better?" Since Khafra helped me onto the cart, he seems to think we should talk. He ignores my ignoring him. But I will never trust anyone again. Too dangerous. Too painful.

Then again, so is loneliness. "I wonder how much farther."

"I hope far," he says, patting the wagon as we reload. "Riding in this is better than what—" And he points his finger in the direction we will travel.

"True."

The only others who speak are two scrawny young men, darker even than Gallus and speaking a guttural language I've never heard.

"Next stop, the villa of Valerius Calidus!" The driver mounts his seat and turns to survey us. Then he laughs, as if it's all a joke.

Another servant hurls a few burnt loaves of bread into the cart. "Eat!"

Like we need telling after two days of starvation. Ravenous, I reach for bread—I groan as my left side constricts and my eyes clench shut. By the time I open them, all bread is claimed. Tears threaten. I've never known hunger like this.

"Here," Khafra hands me a piece of his loaf.

One of the youths taps my knee, offering me a second bite. When he smiles, hope flickers in my breast. For a moment, I feel human again.

AFTER TRAVELING through the city of Iconium, our caravan passes countless desolate fields to arrive at the villa just before sunset. When a servant opens the front gate of the enormous stone-walled compound, a Roman-styled, columned, white house with a red tiled roof looms in front of us. As we pass the multi-storied edifice, I think back to wealthy Ephesian homes and imagine mosaic floors, tapestries on the walls, couches to lounge on, and a beautiful inner courtyard. My new master is obviously prosperous, though swirling dust and the absence of green plants makes the opulence still look desolate.

But we head toward a cluster of outbuildings and barns. All the servants, whether dressed nicely or coarsely, immediately unload wares or care for animals to the tune of Gallus's commands. Unceremoniously, my nine comrades and I stand outside the large barn. Eventually, everyone else drifts off to buildings that must be their quarters. No one says a word to us. I try to remember feeling warm. Full. Loved. At some point I finally drift into sleep.

"He's coming," Khafra whispers hoarsely, waking our huddled mass.

Gallus sneers as we struggle to stand, the jagged scar on his left cheek vivid in the brightening dawn. "As property of my master, Valerius, you must work to make his purchase worth it. Drought means you must earn your food, your water, your clothes, and even your sleep. The animals of this estate deserve life more than you do."

Now, I'm less than an animal.

"What harvest remains must be gathered before the wind blows it away."

Brown chitons are passed out to the men, which we layer on top of whatever we already wear. A big, blond servant, who reminds me of Aldric back in Ephesus, joins Gallus. Tired of mean Germani, I shuffle to the back of the group. He and Gallus confer and then he points to five men standing in front of me, including Khafra. They follow him to the fields.

Gallus leers at the lone woman. Young and thin, she spent the entire journey curled in one corner of the cart. I suspect she's pretty, though she's kept her stringy, black hair over her dirty face and avoided all eye contact. There's nowhere to hide now.

"Name?"

"Prisca."

"Go to the back of the main house. They'll get you clean."

Without looking up, she walks toward the white villa.

I stand with Cali and Kato, the two young men who, if I understand their hand gestures and broken Aramaic properly, come from a country south of Egypt. Gallus sends us to the low sheep barn. Its disorder would horrify Abba.

"Clean this, and I mean every bit," Gallus orders. Locating shovels and tools, we remove dirty hay as if our lives depend upon it. When I observe the lads slipping dried grain from the floor into their mouths, I do the same. I'm sure we'll be beaten if caught, but survival demands it.

When darkness descends, Gallus returns and jabs me in the chest. "Our swineherd died last week. You know anything about pigs?"

I nod. I know that they're filthy, that they're hated by the Jewish people, and that handling them will render me unclean from now until the Messiah shows up. I also know my brother, Seth, would hate me even more if he knew I worked with them.

Gallus strides out of the barn, and I sprint to catch up. My trail of broken Commandments strings from Meron to Ephesus, from devouring tasty pork dishes to enjoying any willing woman. Herding swine shouldn't bother me. Anyway, the last time I cried out to Adonai, He remained silent.

As we pass the villa, I avert my gaze from the soft light streaming through gauzy window coverings, but I can't avoid the sounds of home. Pots clatter. Children laugh. A lilting female voice sings. On the breeze, aromas of cumin and sumac waft over me. My stomach growls and cramps. My heart protests more.

I try to focus as Gallus spits out instructions, but I miss most of them.

". . . and you'll sleep by the swine. When I send you to the hills with them, you'll sleep outside." He halts at a wooden hut that's alive with grunts and squeals and that leans so far to the left that I fear a good breeze will knock it down. "Remember—you lose one pig, you lose your life." Without looking back, he stalks away to berate another unfortunate servant.

As wind rustles palm leaves on the trees surrounding the estate, I examine my future. Filth. Hunger. Slavery. Sleeping with pigs. For the rest of my life. A withered life, like the plants surrounding the house. A bleak life, like the swirling dust that assaults each breath.

No longer conflicted, I want to die. I command my heart, *stop beating*. Its thumping mocks me.

With nowhere else to turn, I look up, just like Abba always told me to do. But clouds hide the stars. The God of my youth feels just as cloaked.

"Oh, Yahweh! Are You there? Help me!"

Falling to my knees, I wrap my arms around my aching ribs and let every racking sob I've suppressed for the last five days escape into the silence that answers.

CHAPTER 3
JUDAH — OVER A YEAR EARLIER

Meron
Nissan (March), 19 AD

Hear, O heavens, and give ear, O earth; for the LORD has spoken: "Children have I reared and brought up, but they have rebelled against me."

ISAIAH 1:2

"Judah, load up!" I hate Seth's bossy voice.

Roosters echo around Meron as I avoid my brother and dodge servants scurrying about our courtyard. Preparing our amphorae of prized olive oil for market in Sepphoris gets everyone excited. I have to admire Abba. No other man in Meron has such loyal, hardworking servants.

I suck on a lemon and put a little ginger in my water skin. I've discovered the usefulness of these remedies to ease the effects of too much wine. And as long as I smile and don't reveal that the sunlight feels like it's stabbing my brain, no one will know.

Climbing into the back of the cart, I shove aside goatskin tents so I can lie down beside the amphorae.

"Getting comfortable?" Seth snarls as he climbs to the driver's perch.

"Better than walking to Sepphoris like poor Matthias."

"I'll be fine." The servant, just a few years younger than me, smiles and grasps the lead rope to a heavy laden donkey.

"Better you than me, Matthias!"

The wagon's wooden wheels rattle down the streets as we snake out of Meron. I rest my head on a bag of barley.

Above me, Abba sits beside Seth on the bench. I scowl. Seth's back is as unbending as his personality. Eli, Abba's estate manager and bond servant, walks beside the oxen, who already protest the day's heavy work. The donkeys, led by servants, bray in agreement.

I sigh. Usually the bumps rock me to sleep, but this morning I can't settle, so I throw my arm behind my head and sigh once more. Like an old man.

The last stubborn star fades into the morning sky. Swallows swoop and soar. I crave the freedom their wings allow.

To be free from disappointing my family.

From the burden of opinions.

From the shadow of failure and guilt.

From the ache of a broken heart.

Last night at dinner, Abba informed me that Rachel would soon be betrothed. I've felt off balance ever since. Maybe that's why I drank so much last night, though the news shouldn't have shocked me. At twenty years old, she's past the age for betrothal.

Of course, I was supposed to lead the procession to her home. Another dream denied, though, I killed this one on my own.

If only I could believe accurately, at least according to Seth, and behave the way everyone in the synagogue expects . . . but I can't be that man.

That's not true. I could. But I desire some things so much that even my love for Rachel cannot redirect my heart. Why can't I live the way I want and marry Rachel?

Or at least, she remain unwed?

If I could just convince Abba to try new things.

New. What a word.

What if I could introduce Abba to Meoklis on this trip to Sepphoris? When I met the finely dressed Ephesian merchant, and he explained how Roman control allows unprecedented movement of goods, I knew this was the type of opportunity I had searched for. I could buy cloth from across the Great Sea and resell for great profits.

My heart quickens as I ponder the possibilities. If little Meron could support Ravid, the fine-cloth merchant, how much more could a city like Sepphoris or Jerusalem or Tyre? What far-off place would give me wings?

I sigh again as I watch a bird fly off. To start in trade, I need money. And I have none.

To leave olives and sheep and Meron, I need more than wings. I need a miracle.

"HE'S SLEPT the whole journey! He hasn't helped Eli or me—"

Seth's irritation awakens me, but blessedly the creaking wheels drown out the rest. Anyway, I know his criticisms by heart.

I abandon work. Whenever possible.

I get drunk with friends. At every opportunity.

I disappoint the family. Over and over.

I muffle my cough caused by the dust of the road. Slowly, I shift, relieving the ache in my right shoulder. Sleeping in the cart feels confining after two days on the road, but I don't want them to know I'm awake. I'd like to hear Abba's replies.

"Don't you realize how his actions affect the family?" Seth continues. "The village gossips joke about his unfinished tower, a job you assigned to him. Why don't you hold him accountable?"

Abba doesn't respond.

"His inaction places hardship on the servants."

Abba's chuckle surprises me. His tone conveys a question, even though I can't decipher his words.

"I'm always concerned for the servants!" I stifle a laugh. "With your stature as an elder, people in the village look to us. Judah's slothfulness damages our reputation and decreases our wealth. And worse, much worse, his disregard of Torah brings shame on our household."

Abba responds. Why won't he speak louder?

"So you don't care that he doesn't keep Shabbat? That he drinks too much? That he gambles? And you know there's more."

Abba knows most of my failings. But that doesn't mean I want Seth to list them.

"Can't you face reality?" Seth's anger challenges his usual reserve.

This time, Abba responds clearly. "Seth, I can demand that Judah change his behavior, but his heart will determine the course of his soul. He's been taught Torah and the Prophets. Remember what Joshua put before our people: 'Choose this day whom you will serve! ... As for me and my household, we will serve Adonai!'[1]"

"He's of your house!" Seth shouts. He actually *shouts* at Abba. "You *can* force him!"

"He's a man. He must choose for himself."

The finality of Abba's tone silences Seth, but my heart pounds. Abba said I must choose. Does that mean there's more than one option? If so, I need to find it.

"JUDAH, COME HELP ME," Abba calls.

Behind the curtain two stalls down, I hide and quell my guilt over not staying in the market to help sell oil. But I can't waste this rare opportunity to scout out business opportunities. I hope to connect again with Meoklis. Peeking around the curtain, I watch Eli move amphorae around the cart.

"Have you seen Judah, Eli?" The crease between Abba's eyes deepens.

Eli lifts his eyes to heaven, mouths something, and shakes his head. "No, Master."

Abba assembles the scale and weights. "Well, until he returns, it's like the old days—you and me handling business."

"I thought Judah would stay after Seth left," Eli says.

As did Seth. He detached himself from our group before the wagon stopped rolling, announcing his intent to visit the synagogue to hear some uppity rabbi from Jerusalem. I guess he stole my trick: disappear and leave work to the brother.

"Judah's heart is far from us, so it's no surprise his body follows suit."

More guilt rises, but I push it away by envisioning my desired future, a future I will never achieve if I remain where I am.

"Master, selling isn't your job. Please, go to the city gates or the synagogue. Matthias and I will man the stall."

Peering around the curtain once more, I spy Abba unstopping an amphora. "Aah, the aroma conveys life, health, and flavor." He claps Eli on the back. "Today, I prefer to be here, meeting new people and selling our excellent olive oil."

A few customers mosey toward the stall. Now's my chance. As I make my escape, Abba's laugh cuts through the buzzing market. Most men of his wealth and standing would rather spend hours in the synagogue than sell goods on the street. But not Abba. He enjoys talking with each shopper, taking pride in what we produce.

I bolt across the market square, almost running into a woman toting a stack of baskets for the market. I want to feel proud like Abba and find joy in my work. And if I can find Meoklis, maybe he can help me.

For the first time, I ignore the temptations Sepphoris offers. No time for the theater or games. By the time I reach the tavern in the cloth district, I'm panting.

"Jude, my friend!" Boisterous and cheerful as always, Meoklis waves me over to his outdoor table, offers me a stool, and pours me a cup of wine. I like how this wealthy merchant calls me "friend" and uses the Greek version of my name. I think he's close to Abba's age, but he looks younger with no beard and his gray-flecked hair cropped short in the

Roman style. Someday, I want to dress in a green-striped linen cloak and wear rings on my fingers, just like him.

"I'm glad to find you here, Meoklis. What's the news?"

"For businessmen, it's outstanding. We've never seen such days. You passed through markets boasting goods from all over!" Meoklis points to Roman soldiers patrolling the street. "All because of them! In fact, they look like money to me because they allow opportunity. Opportunity!"

How I long to profit from this opportunity. I have tried, yet Abba remains unconvinced. It's so frustrating.

"Ah, my friend. You're young and handsome. Why so glum?"

Why must everything I feel show on my face?

"My father refuses to invest in trade this year. I tried and tried." I risk honesty. "Meoklis, I have no money."

That admission hurts. I cross my arms, a deep frown accompanying my memory of last Shabbat when Abba, Seth, and I reclined on the rooftop balcony after our evening meal. I dared ask, "Have you thought more about investing in the cloth trade, Abba? The merchant I met with in Sepphoris says his contacts will help us."

"What's this fascination with trading?" Seth sneered. "We don't do business with heathens. Besides, when have you followed through on anything?"

"I'm not talking to you, brother."

Abba laid his hand over mine. "Rome's taxes keep increasing. Several dry winters have hurt all our crops, from the olives and grapes to our flax and wheat. Many people depend on us. Our tenants and servants."

"That may be—"

"I'm not finished. Your constant need for something different raises a question. Why, when you're blessed beyond measure, are you restless and discontented? What do you search for?"

My eyebrows knit together as Abba's question haunts me days later. I'm not sure what I search for, but if it existed in Meron or Judea, I would have found it by now.

Meoklis waves over a server. "Bring us bread and cheese. And some dried figs." Then he refills my cup. "Jude, you remind me of another young man I know. Such a man of means! But he didn't begin that way. No! His family couldn't understand his vision either."

A gulp of wine soothes my nerves. I wipe my mouth. "Tell me more."

Meoklis smiles, his normally loud voice dropping to a purr. "He acted with courage and determination. He let nothing stop him. Now, he reaps the rewards."

Heart pounding, I shift on my stool.

"He acted in his own best interest!" Meoklis bangs the table with his fist.

Why does this man use so many words to say so little? I muster all my patience. "Meoklis, what did he do?"

Like a fisherman about to haul in his net, Meoklis leans in. "I'll tell you exactly what he did."

CHAPTER 4
SETH

Sepphoris
Nissan (March), AD 19

Direct your steps to the perpetual ruins; the enemy has destroyed everything in the sanctuary!

PSALM 74:3

Ridiculous. Shameful. Delusional.

Every day, Judah strays farther from Jewish precepts. When Abba announced this journey to Sepphoris, Judah grinned and nodded. Suspicious. At least I bested Judah at escaping a morning selling oil. Remembering his disgruntled face almost brings a smile. Almost.

Crossing the street, I stay as far from the pagan theater as possible, turning just past a tavern full of rowdy patrons preparing themselves for the day's onstage debauchery. While this city still rebuilds from Roman destruction almost fifteen years ago, it still boasts a lucrative market for our products, along with providing opportunity for any sin imaginable. Theater. Greek philosophers. Prostitutes. Diviners. Pagan worship.

Without the purifying gift of Torah, these heathens can't resist such pervasive temptations. No wonder Judah loves this place. Thank You, Adonai that I am not like them. Or him.

Whatever Judah's hidden schemes are, I'm here to sit under Rabbi Yakov and hopefully invite him to visit Meron, after Passover. That is if these milling crowds don't keep me from reaching the synagogue before morning discussion ends.

I manage my way around donkeys loaded with wares and head toward the Jewish quarter. I don't understand Abba. He's taught me to honor Adonai my whole life, so why doesn't he correct Judah? He should demand obedience, and, if that doesn't work, drag him into the street and beat him for all to see.

I glance up to insure no heathens are dumping liquids from the apartments above. I wouldn't dare question the Most High, but I can't help wondering why He has allowed so many Gentiles to rule this city in the middle of Galilee. First Greeks, then the Herodians, and now the cursed Romans who demand complete control and tax us for the privilege. Forever naming things after themselves, our current oppressors changed the city's name to Diocaesarea. Judea might be Jewish, but it doesn't belong to us.

Shaking my head, I pick my way around ox droppings and dodge a woman carrying a water yoke, liquid sloshing out of the swaying containers with her every step. I emerge into a square teeming with shoppers of multiple ethnicities. The breeze is rich with savory spices and merchants hawking their wares. Grubby children hold out thin hands and beggars loiter around the perimeter. Hiking my hem to avoid the uncleanness, I navigate the mass of bodies.

I will not miss Rabbi Yakov. He always attracts Pharisees from various schools. While our local Rabbi Akiva follows the House of Hillel, Yakov sides with the House of Shimmei, whose pupils interpret Torah far more strictly. I know I'll receive good counsel. Or at least affirmation that I'm right and Abba is wrong.

Gaining speed, I shove my way forward until—

"Oof!" All thoughts of Abba and Judah scatter as I stare into the broad back of a Roman soldier. He turns with a glare.

"Watch it, Jew."

Bumping me with his metal, breastplate-covered chest, the centurion bestows a pompous smile. Watching me fall back, the soldiers behind him guffaw.

Dropping my gaze, I dip into a shallow bow. "Forgive me." *Infidel!* "I am sorry."

Head down, I sidestep the soldiers and walk away, barely resisting the urge to run. Cursed Romans. Cursed, cursed Romans.

Exhaling slowly, I turn the last tight corner before the synagogue.

"You showed them."

"Gideon?" I whirl around to find a beaming face. "What are you doing here?"

"Hello to you too, cousin. I'm fine, thanks for asking. And you?"

"I'm in no mood for jokes."

"Obviously. Is Uncle Ezra with you?"

"Not yet. Why are you here?"

Light streams through his sandy hair. "To listen to this rabbi we heard in Jerusalem. But I'll also take some of your excellent oil home to Elizabeth. Do you have a wife to deliver gifts to yet?"

"You know I'm betrothed."

A group of women turns at Gideon's roaring laugh. "Are you ever going to advance from betrothal to marriage? Adonai is generous to design such a union. 'He who finds a wife finds a good thing.'[1] That is written. My Elizabeth is a blessing."

"It's also written, 'a friend loves at all times, but a brother is born for adversity.'[2] Why, today, do you act more like my brother than my friend, bringing adversity when I need encouragement?"

"Ah. But my rabbi in Cana doesn't think the brother brings adversity. Rather, he is an ally ready to stand with you when adversity comes."

"Does your rabbi have a brother?"

"Judah's been adding adversity to your life?"

"Adversity. Work. Shame. Yet Abba refuses to chastise him."

"Well, he's no longer a boy."

"Then he shouldn't act like one! He should honor his family and Adonai."

Gideon places a hand on my shoulder, slowing us to a halt outside the synagogue. His tone grows serious. "Which matters more to you?"

"What?"

"Your family's honor? Or Adonai's?"

"How can you ask such a question?" Displaying my tzitzit, I say, "Like the blue and white threads in these tassels, the two are inextricably linked. If Judah tried honoring one, he'd honor the other. Really, you should know what I mean."

My cousin wraps an arm around my shoulders, something few others dare. "Seth, maybe Adonai placed me in your life to help broaden your own understanding." He sweeps his other arm wide. "Aren't you grateful for me?"

I raise an eyebrow.

"You and I study because we love Adonai, right? I seek to understand Torah so that I can best obey it. But does obeying Adonai mean we cannot enjoy Him? Or each other?"

"With so many rabbis and schools of thought, what draws you here to Rabbi Yakov?"

Three murmuring men hurry into the synagogue, while two black robed pharisees gesticulate on the front patio.

"Your preference for him influences me," Gideon answers. "He seems very devoted, but do you ever worry that in his pursuit of correctness, he forgets Adonai's lovingkindness? Does he ignore mercy to achieve righteousness?"

"First you joke, and now you sound like you're writing a psalm." One side of my mouth creeps up involuntarily. "I don't comprehend you at all."

Throwing back his head, Gideon laughs his hearty laugh and the two pharisees scowl. "And yet you like me. Admit it! You're glad to see me, and you're no longer so gloomy. I'm an exquisite example of Adonai's goodness to you."

"Ha! You're a thorn in my side." I struggle to not smile.

"By today's end, I'll make you laugh. But that smile will do for now. Be warned, however," Gideon jerks his head toward the synagogue. "I'll be asking hard questions today. So you might not want to sit next to me."

A cloud covers the sun. "Of course you are."

THE AFTERNOON HEAT has passed its zenith by the time Gideon and I make our way back through the market.

"What a satisfying afternoon listening to Rabbi Yakov. And thank you Gideon, for not making trouble even though you disagreed with many points."

Drawing his full lips into his mouth, and narrowing his eyes, he points a finger to me. "Is your purpose to nullify what Adonai clearly teaches?"

"Rabbi Yakov's voice is not that high." But I laugh at his impersonation anyway.

"I told you I'd make you laugh." Gideon bumps me with his shoulder as we enter the market. "And I hear Uncle Ezra's laugh! His joy is infectious."

The vegetable merchant next to Abba already packs her wares, as well as the basket weaver on the other side. But a crowd gathers around our stall. By the wagon Eli, Matthias, and other servants load empty amphorae.

"Eli, where's Judah?"

He shakes his head. Curse it all. Judah probably abandoned his duty before I made it across the square. I clamp my mouth so my anger won't form into words I'll later find shameful.

"Out of the way, cousin." With a grin and a wink, Gideon holds a clay container with a stopper. "Shalom, Eli. If I missed out on your oil, my wife wouldn't forgive me."

"Shalom. First, I have something for you." Eli retrieves a small, wooden box. "Elizabeth praised Miriam's date cakes so highly the last time you visited, you'll likely never be rid of them."

"Well, no complaints!" Gideon laughs. "As our little one's arrival approaches, my Elizabeth grows weary. But I should confess now, there'll be at least one fewer cake when I get home tonight."

"I believe Miriam assumed you'd eat one or two on your journey."

"Two! I heard you say two, and I'm holding you to that."

"Try it." Abba converses with three Roman dogs as though they're valued customers, offering each a piece of Miriam's bread for dipping. "You'll taste the quality."

Even the servant boy lingering in the back receives a bite. With collarbones that pronounced, he needs all the samples he can get. He smiles and Abba sneaks more bread into his pocket.

"Now," says Abba, turning to the soldier in charge, "other merchants may haggle, but their oil is more diluted and bland than ours. For this quality, we set our price. And we always sell every drop." Nothing antagonistic. Always smiling. And confidence that our product is worth the expense. I've never understood why he enjoys talking with customers, or how he sells so much.

I also don't understand why he stayed here instead of accompanying me to the synagogue. Even without Judah, we brought enough servants to man the booth. My spark of admiration dies.

Passing the Roman's glass bottle to Eli, Abba finally notices me. "Ah, Seth. How did you find the good Rabbi Yakov's discussions?"

"Excellent. You should have been there."

Gideon clears his throat. I ignore him because I know I'm right.

"And Gideon! How good to see you." Abba's smile never falters. "How's your charming bride?"

While they exchange news, I scan the thinning crowd.

Gideon punches my arm lightly. "You're gloomy again?"

"We're packing up and Judah is yet to return."

After giving me a sympathetic smile, he says, "Shalom, Uncle Ezra. May the Holy One bless you and keep you. And Eli, please tell Miriam thank you from us." Then he stares straight at me, holding my gaze. "Shalom, Seth." Leaning close, he whispers, "May you find more shalom than you feel right now."

He saunters into a side street and I can hear him singing a psalm long after he disappears from view.

"Eli?"

"Yes, Seth?"

"Is that Judah in the corner over there? He's talking to some Gentile wearing rings and a garish tunic. Where does Judah meet such friends?"

Eli shields his eyes against the setting sun and looks where I point.

"Do you know that man?"

"A Greek merchant named Meoklis. I know him a little," Eli pauses, "and trust him less."

The pair ducks under a striped awning, too far away to hear. But Judah's gesticulating arms and bobbing head worry me. Suddenly, the two men clasp right forearms, Roman style, before the heathen departs. Glancing at Eli, I note his tight lips and drawn eyebrows.

Judah turns to discover us watching him. He freezes. Is that worry on his face? Or fear? Before I can decide, he flashes an exaggerated smile and waves. "Hello, Abba! Eli! Seth!" He rushes across the square. His flushed cheeks leave no room for doubt. Whatever happened between Judah and that man, it included wine.

Abba's smile fades. "Have a good day?"

"Great day. I learned more about investing in the cloth trade. Opportunities exist like never before."

"We're not traders." I turn my back on Judah and begin loading the wagon. I'd rather do anything than listen to his wild plans for becoming rich.

"Seth, I'll handle this," Abba says.

"You do that." I lift empty amphorae onto the wagon where servants secure them.

Abba grasps Judah's shoulders. "Judah, we've discussed this over and over. We cannot invest in trade."

Judah nods. "Okay."

Eli and I look at each other, then at my brother. Judah has made underhand suggestions and outright requests for months. He's coaxed and pleaded. Now he doesn't argue when denied?

Abba raises his eyebrows. "Son, you've never agreed so readily. Is something besides wine causing this?"

Judah laughs a little too loudly. "No, Abba. I just thought I'd try. No reason to argue." Stepping around me as though I'm not here, he hefts supplies Eli bought for home, a barrel of salted fish and a cask of honey, onto the cart before tying a bag of dried fruit to the donkey's saddle.

Abba, Eli, and I exchange glances. Judah, being helpful? Something is off.

After he and Matthias lift the refilled water jar onto the cart, he climbs in and gets comfortable. Looks like he'll sleep the whole way home, the sluggard.

Widening my eyes at Abba, I point to Judah's napping figure. Will he do nothing? Abba looks from Eli's grim face back to mine, drops his shoulders, and pulls himself wearily onto the cart.

CHAPTER 5
MIRIAM

Meron, Galilee
Nissan (March) AD 19

The beginning of strife is like letting out water, so quit before the quarrel breaks out.

PROVERBS 17:14

Job would feel right at home with today's troubles. A hole in the barn roof. Bugs in my ground barley. A field worker injured. And at the market this morning, Lavinia made jokes about our uncompleted tower. I bet Jezebel was kinder than Lavinia.

I tried to hold my tongue. Truly. But words jumped out. "You do realize that Ezra ben Lavi pays for that tower to benefit the village? Maybe instead of criticizing, people could pitch in and help."

"Oh Miriam, don't take everything so personally." Lavinia winked at her friend.

How else should I take it, I'd like to know? Just because she's Barak's wife and drapes gold necklaces atop her lilac linen, she thinks she's something special.

After tying lavender to the storeroom beam to dry, I climb to the rooftop work area above the storeroom and servants' quarters. First, I check the ladies weaving on the loom, then I inspect the figs and raisins spread on a cloth. With this dry wind, they are about to shrivel into inedible rocks.

"I don't suppose anyone thought of checking these?"

"Sorry, Miriam," resounds through the three women weaving.

"Store them quickly or we will lose the whole lot!"

Back in the courtyard, I check on Tova. The silly young woman seems more interested in warming herself by the fire than stirring the pot of simmering lentils.

"The bottom will cake and burn. Mind your work, girl."

Tova jumps. "Oh, Miriam! Yes, ma'am."

I inspect the soup. "It's done. Get it off the heat and ready to serve."

"Yes, ma'am."

I don't know why Ezra hired this meek, gangly thing to assist me. All arms and legs but barely a voice. Just because gray hair escapes my headscarf and I move a little slower doesn't mean I need help. Training an eighteen-year-old takes more effort than just doing the work myself. Not that I'm hard to please.

Muttering, I grab my basket and head for refuge in the garden behind the kitchen. It's the one place I can work undisturbed and enjoy a few free moments. Neat rows of melons, onions, and garlic nod in the breeze as I pray aloud, grateful for the absence of noisy servants staring at me like I've lost my mind. It's not like I think the Most High will answer me audibly as he did Moses. But we often hash out the family's problems together, whether here or in the kitchen, and our partnership works best when I speak my end of the conversation out loud.

Ezra's home supports many workers, and it is my job to oversee their duties and fill their bellies. I hardly remember not being Ezra ben Lavi's bondservant. When Eli and I married, he owed Ezra money, so we worked to pay off our debt. Accomplishing that, we chose to tie our lives to his, and Ezra welcomed us into the household, treating us more like family than servants. His home became our home. His welfare became our welfare. I'm proud to enhance the family's reputation and affluence. It's a good life.

I weed, prune, and choose some early lettuces and herbs for tonight. I work my way down a row of onions, pulling six small ones until I reach the almond trees, inhaling the sweet scent of a thousand pink blooms. I stretch my aching back and rub my stiff fingers. Maybe I'm not as young as I once was.

Turning, I survey the servants working in the courtyard. One draws water at the cistern while another hammers away in the workshop. Several others haul barley into the storeroom. At the tannur, our large outdoor oven, a neighbor withdraws her loaves with a wooden paddle.

Laundry snaps in the spring breeze, scattering the chickens, whose squawking mingles with the squabble of roofers unsure where to place new beams. The rhythmic shuttle weaving back and forth on the loom mixes with the plod, plod of old Methuselah dragging his millstone around his short circuit. He's one of the few beings who have lived here longer than us, and we've been here thirty years.

I love this compound. From the shared dwellings enclosed by the rock and mortar wall that creates our courtyard, to the second story running above the family rooms, to the rooftop balconies on the other side. My gaze halts at the boys' rooms.

"Oh dear." I shake my head and return to my weeding. "You're creative, Adonai. I'll say that. Opposite as Cain and Abel, those two."

I pinch off sprigs of dill and tug a thorny thistle. "Life would be more peaceful around here if You'd made them a little more alike."

I glance skyward. "Sorry. Didn't mean to criticize. You can do what You want."

Returning to the thistle, I yank it from the ruddy earth. "I wish I could uproot their arguments as easily as these weeds."

Oh, those boys. Every time Master removes one barrier, they build another. If Seth and Judah spent as much energy on that tower as they did quarreling, they'd finish the silly thing. I attack another weed.

"You know how much they hurt their abba. So, if You want to change one or both of their hearts, I won't complain."

"Excuse me? Miriam?"

Straightening, I immediately regret it. Pressing one hand to my lower back, I wave with the other. “Hello, Rachel.”

Rachel adjusts the basket of cheese balanced on her head. “Are you hurt? Do you need help?”

“Oh, it’s just my back. You’ll understand someday.” Rachel is one of my favorite people, despite our twenty-five-year age difference.

“If I’m disturbing you, I can leave the cheese with Tova.”

“Of course you’re not.” I can’t help wincing.

“What beautiful lettuces! You have the finest garden in Meron—but please don’t tell Eema I said that.”

“Oh, they’re small, but it’s still spring.” My cheeks warm. “I’m glad you brought cheese. The men return soon from Sepphoris and they’ll be hungry.”

Pink blooms on her cheeks. Turning quickly, she glides ahead of me. Tall and thin, she’s the most graceful woman I know. I like her anyway.

In the kitchen, I pour Rachel a cup of water and examine the herbed goat cheese, her family’s specialty.

“Which would you like?” She glances at the doorway.

“Is something wrong, Rachel?”

“I need to make more deliveries.”

“Nothing else keeps you from a moment at my table?”

She draws a deep breath through pursed lips.

“You can tell me anything. I’m not a gossip.”

“I know.” She wrings her hands. “Someone from Nazareth approached Abba about us becoming betrothed.”

“Ah.”

“Abba may have spoken to Ezra. I’m not sure.” She eyes the door again. “And no contract has been signed yet.”

“Asher did visit Ezra this week. I always hoped you and Judah . . .”

“Yes.” Her voice drops to a whisper. “And I’d rather leave before he returns.”

I take her hand. “Congratulations, my dear.”

“Thank you, Miriam.” Her brown eyes don’t sparkle the way an expectant bride’s should. “Shalom. I must deliver the rest now.”

As I escort her to the gate, a long-held dream slips away. Judah is a fool for letting this girl go.

Rufus's bark breaks the afternoon quiet. Tail beating, the red beast scampers right under my feet, nearly tripping me. A moment later, I hear wooden wheels rumbling. Our men are back.

"Thank you, Rufus. You're occasionally useful. How about you guard the sheep with the same enthusiasm?" I cup my hands around my mouth. "The master's home!"

All around the compound, heads jerk up. Then the roofers' hammering accelerates and next to the loom the raisins are finally stored away. I rush into the kitchen.

Where's Tova? I hope the quiet mouse prepared the men's basin for washing. "Wouldn't it be nice if I didn't have to remind everyone what to do? Oh, Adonai, please help her get busy." On a wooden platter I stack fresh flatbread next to some olives. In a bowl of olive oil, I mix in the dill and add a pinch of salt. After I fill a pitcher more than halfway with water, I add wine, and in an earthen jug of fresh water I grate some ginger.

"I hope those boys didn't vex their father too much. Why can't they see how lucky they are and try to be more like him? Instead, Seth follows the strictest of Pharisees, and Judah acts almost like a Gentile." Loading as much as I can on a tray, I pause. "Adonai, in my opinion, Judah needs a kick in the backside and Seth needs a slap upside the head. Because if they keep running in opposite directions, they will tear this family apart."

Still deep in thought, I deposit the food on the arbor table, next to which Tova stands ready with pitcher, bowl, and towel.

I nod. "Good."

As our wagon rumbles into the courtyard, I force a smile. "Welcome home!"

Ezra joins us. "You're an oasis in a dry and weary land, Miriam." Though there's dark circles under his eyes, his voice sounds jovial. "The older I get, the more my bones complain. And here's Tova with cleansing water. I'm blessed. Thank you."

While Tova pours water over Ezra's hands and feet, Seth appears, tossing his headscarf onto a stool. "I'll update the ledgers before I go to

Uncle Daniel's for prayers. Will you join me?"

I suppress a desire to pinch him. Seth can say the right words yet convey judgment with his tone better than anyone I know. Tova moves to wash his feet, and he barely looks at her.

Ezra tears off a piece of bread. "Would you like me to join you, Seth?"

"Why wouldn't you come? What's more important than your prayers?"

My jaw clamps tight. It's not my place anymore to correct Seth, even if he deserves it. But what a thing to say to his pious abba.

"Nothing is more important. That's why I prayed the whole way home. But I ask again, would you like me to join you?"

"Don't you want to fulfill your obligation to Adonai?"

As if Seth's faithfulness or prayers could exceed his Abba's!

"What concerns you? That I won't pray or that I won't be seen praying?"

Ha! Good answer.

"I'm concerned for your influence in the village." Seth clenches and unclenches his hand. "I believe the other elders should see you at prayers more often. Do you find fault with that?"

"I'd rather you desired fellowship with me, but I appreciate your worry for my reputation. Tonight, however, I wrestle with deeper problems. I prefer that my prayers be uninterrupted by men trying to outdo each other's holiness."

Seth's dark eyes flash as I fill his cup. "That's how you see our friends? And me? An empty show of holiness?"

Seth picks at the bread like he's afraid I put worms in the loaf.

"Look at me," Ezra says.

Seth lifts his gaze.

"I don't judge your intentions or anyone else's. Perhaps I spoke harshly, but it's difficult to focus on prayer when those around you seem to be speaking to their neighbors instead of Adonai. Have you never sensed that?"

Seth eats without responding. He wouldn't dare insult his friends like he does his own Abba. I bite my tongue to keep silent.

Judah bounds up. I pour him some wine.

"Where have you been?" Seth asks.

Judah throws back his drink. "I just put my things in my room. Shalom, Miriam. A refill, if you don't mind. What long, bumpy roads." Flashing his toothy smile, he pops an olive in his mouth.

I glance at Master, who nods, and I fill it halfway.

"How would you know?" Seth's voice rumbles. "You drank so much in Sepphoris you slept the entire journey home."

"It did seem a short trip!" Judah roars with laughter.

"You're not washing before you partake? Or is that another law you plan on ignoring?"

"Look," Judah hiccups. "Tova's here to wash away the stench of my sins. But what concerns you more? My feet or my soul?"

"Both. Equally."

"Your brotherly affection is more than I can bear."

Seth jumps to his feet, his stool toppling. "It'd be best if you couldn't bear the shame you bring on our family and your soul!"

Judah lunges toward Seth, almost knocking Tova over. "It'd be best if you'd mind your own soul and leave mine alone!"

Bang! Ezra's fist pounds the table "Enough!" His voice, hard as granite, fills the courtyard as he jumps to his feet.

Mouths agape, both boys stare at their father, and I ask Adonai to dissolve whatever retorts sit on their forked tongues. Ezra rarely gets angry. But when he does, it cannot and should not be ignored. Tova grabs the basin and towel and scurries out as Ezra turns to his oldest.

"Seth, replacing mercy with condemnation brings only shame."

Throwing his bread on the table, Seth turns away.

Ezra moves toward Judah. "Foolish and sinful behavior, like drunkenness, stains your heart more than the dust of a thousand miles dirties your body."

Judah's face flushes, and he can't hold Ezra's gaze.

"And we all disgrace our family when we attack each other. The enemy celebrates when we welcome division, rancor, and selfishness like old friends."

Seth stiffens. Judah slumps onto his stool.

As Ezra's shoulders sag, an abnormal quiet envelops the courtyard. A few of the servants linger near the arbor, trying to hear what isn't their business. I shoot them a warning look and they scurry away.

The lines in Ezra's face deepen. "You each have a decision to make. What kind of brother will you be? You can either build on the foundation I've laid, or tear us apart. Your bickering grieves me and dishonors Adonai. Your brother's sins don't justify your own. One day, you will answer for your actions. Are you prepared?"

Seth plops on a stool, flicking breadcrumbs off the table. Judah stares at his feet. If only I could force these four blocked ears to open and two hard hearts to soften.

"The rage and rejection you hurl at each other hurts everyone around you."

Still no response.

"And breaks my heart."

Tears well in my eyes. This valiant, loving man deserves sons who make his life better.

"Miriam, I—" He offers me a soft smile. Curse my tears! I can't help but share his pain. I'd take it all if I could. "Thank you for always taking good care of us."

He turns to the boys. "After Shabbat, work on the tower resumes. You'll accompany me to the site after morning prayers."

He waits until they face him. Peering from one to the other, he places a hand on their heads like when they were children. "May Adonai's shalom pervade our sleep and fill the gaps in our hearts tonight." Exhaling, he shuffles to his room, looking older than I've ever seen him.

The second he disappears through the doorway, my words burst. "How can you hurt your Abba so? You take pride in attacking each other, when you should feel shame! Shame and disgrace." Drawing a deep breath, I gather Ezra's half-full goblet and barely touched bread. "I realize I'm not at liberty to speak this way anymore, but my heart is too broken to stay silent."

Judah puts his head in his hands.

Seth crosses his arms. "You're right, Miriam."

Seth admits I'm right? Well, that must taste like vinegar. Hope rises. "You may not address me in such a way. Judah can decide what he will and won't allow. But you're a servant in our home. I'm no longer a boy for you to scold. Never forget that again."

Judah's head snaps toward me, his mouth agape. A dozen retorts rush from my mind toward my lips, but I allow only one to escape. "So long as you don't forget the respect and love you owe your Abba."

Nodding, I flee to my kitchen, head held high. But my mind races. So, I'm just a servant to boys I practically raised? I can serve them, but no longer speak to them? I've attempted to honor our changing relationship, but now, when I view myself through Seth's eyes, a place deep within shatters. Something irreparable. Once again, I am barren.

Swiping uneaten food into a bucket, I stack platters on the wooden counter, but my vision blurs. Sniffing, I sink onto a cushion at the low table, light an oil lamp, bury my face in my arms, and cry.

"Stop it! There's no time to wallow," I tell myself. Sniffing and dabbing, I gather my errant emotions and try to stand. But I can't.

Light enters the dark kitchen when Eli pulls back the coarse brown fabric covering the door.

"Sitting? You never sit. What's wrong?" My husband's questions begin before he makes it through the doorway.

What a bother. The last thing I want him to see is my wet face. I force myself up and turn away, swiping my sleeve over my cheeks. "Shalom. Let me get you wine and bread. Have you washed?"

"Don't you have a better greeting for your old husband?"

On a clean platter I place bread and cheese. "Isn't refreshment what you need?"

"Your smile and tender greeting are more refreshing."

Just when I think he's forgotten how to say sweet things, he goes and says something like that. I try to remain under control, but can't.

"Miriam?"

I turn slowly, revealing my tear-stained cheeks.

"Oh, my dear." Compassion exuding from his deep brown eyes, he opens his arms wide, and I rush in. Nestling into his shoulder, I find my resting spot, the one place I'm taken care of in a life of taking care of others. His gray beard tickles my cheek, and I place my hand on the brown and green striped tunic.

"Seth and Judah?"

I nod.

"I fear you adopt their sorrows as your own."

"You? Fear?" That makes me chuckle. "Why would you fear about me?"

"If they end up destroying each other, I don't want you in the middle, their division dividing you. I still need you, Miriam." His hand rubs my back.

When's the last time he told me that? While never cruel or unloving, he rarely expresses his emotions. Hearing him now feels like a balm.

Running my finger along the lines of his face, I reach his coarse beard. "I'm grateful you still need me after all these years."

He kisses my forehead, releases me, and reclines on a cushion.

Open-mouthed, I give him my what-are-you-doing face.

"I can sit a few minutes. It will test how the younger servants work without supervision. Now tell me what's wrong."

"You couldn't have missed the argument." I hand him a bowl of dates.

"Yes, I heard it. But what was worse than the ones before?"

I repeat Seth's words to me, and the ridiculous tears return. "I know I shouldn't have said anything. But after his cold speech and easy dismissal. . . I'm not his eema, but . . ."

My words hang in the air. Disappointment at never having children of our own dwells eternally with us, dulled over the years, but never gone.

"You've acted like one since their eema died."

"They're men now. They no longer need nor want my input. But when he told me not to forget that I'm his servant, I realized our past is just that—the past."

Stuffing bread and cheese into his mouth, Eli nods.

"I don't mind being Seth's servant, and I'm proud of our life. But his coldness provides a glimpse of our future with him as the master."

I sit opposite Eli, grasp his hand, and whisper, "I'm sorry I could never give us sons." Tears drip from my cheeks onto our interlaced fingers.

"Miriam, where is this coming from? We settled this long ago.

Adonai knows what's best. We trust Him with what He has and hasn't given us, including children."

He lifts my chin, and I stare into his gentle grey eyes. "Miriam,—"

"Oh—sorry." Judah halts as quickly as he enters, coughing uneasily.

When I jump up, the dates spill. We shouldn't be seen touching each other, and here Judah finds us with our hands and emotions tightly woven.

"I didn't know you two were in here. I didn't—I—" Rubbing the back of his neck, Judah grins sheepishly. "I didn't mean to interrupt anything."

My mouth opens and closes, but nothing comes out. I'm not sure where I stand with him.

"Miriam, silent?" Judah laughs. "When does that happen?"

"Rarely, in my lifetime." Eli sips his wine.

"Or in mine." Judah snorts.

Hands on hips, I glare from one man to the other. Eli winks.

My young master clasps his hands and bows his head. "I came to tell you that, while I don't always like what you say to me, I'm still glad you say it. I may be flawed, but at least I'm not a stiff, prideful donkey." Bowing, he continues with mock gravity. "I am yours to correct."

I resist hugging him. "That's a big job. What if I take you up on that?"

"Well, I didn't say I'd listen!" He plants a kiss on my cheek and bolts from the room.

Oh no. More tears. Have I ever cried four times in a single hour?

"Well," I sniff.

"Well," Eli echoes, stretching his back with a groan. "Why they prefer anything over their honorable father, I don't understand. Staying with Ezra was the best choice we ever made."

"I agree." I retrieve the dates from the floor. "Was Judah as drunk as Seth claimed?"

Rubbing his forehead, he says, "He's a puzzle. Foolish and pleasure-seeking on one hand, gentle and kind on the other. There's a good man in there somewhere, but he seems determined to never let him out. In Sepphoris I saw him talking with a merchant I don't trust. Something happened while they were together; something that changed Judah.

He's been so sullen lately. But after meeting with Meoklis, he's seemed carefree. Why? I wanted to get home as quickly as possible."

Whenever my restrained husband gives a long speech, I know he's troubled. "So now we worry because he's happy? Do you fear that tonight's disaster could get worse?"

"Miriam," he takes my hand. "I don't know how, but I'm afraid it could get much worse."

With that, he departs, leaving me alone to worry away the evening.

CHAPTER 6
JUDAH

Meron
Nissan (March) AD 19

Many are the plans in the mind of a man, but it is the purpose of the LORD that will stand.

PROVERBS 19:21

Outside the kitchen, I snicker. Eli and Miriam, embracing? I mean, I know they're husband and wife, but it's strange to imagine them . . . Best to not dwell on that.

As I head across the courtyard, Meoklis's bold suggestion rolls around my mind, crashing into reasons it won't work. Excitement tangles with doubt, and I crave the solace of my room to think and plan.

"Hello, Judah."

I stiffen. Seth leans his back against the wall beside my door, arms crossed, gazing to the sky.

"I'm headed to Uncle Daniel's." Sarcasm drips from every word. "Care to join me?"

"Asking me to prayers? I don't know what to say." I tap a finger against my chin. "So many options! But I promised myself, for Abba's sake that I wouldn't argue. At least not tonight."

"I saw you sneak into the kitchen."

"I didn't sneak. I walked. Anyway, why do you care what I say to an old servant?"

Seth still doesn't look at me. "An affluent household requires order."

"Aren't we a family?"

"One you'd rather dishonor than serve."

What would he say if he knew what I'm contemplating? I can't imagine. "What do you want?"

"I'm here to warn you—don't come between me and Abba." Seth continues to stare upward. Why won't he just get mad? I detest his self-restraint. "Don't undermine my ability to direct Miriam or any other servant. And stop dishonoring the family."

"Oh, that's all? Anything I should do?"

"Well, yes. Quite a lot, actually—"

"So you're taking Abba's place?"

"As the eldest, it's my job to protect the family's honor and his position."

"You mean your position, don't you?"

"I mean exactly what I say. But yes, our decisions affect each other. It's honorable to pursue leadership. Why can't you see that?"

I step toward him. "I guess your pretension and hypocrisy block my view."

Pushing off the wall, Seth, jaw clenched, vein in his forehead pulsing, faces me. "I'm warning you, Judah." He jabs my chest with his finger. "Your ways must change."

"Careful, brother." I ball my fists, but glue my arms to my side.

"Your ways will change, Judah," he repeats, as if his proclamation makes it so.

Boy, do I want to push him off his self-righteous pedestal. "You're right. They will—but how and when I want. Right now, I wish to change my position from standing to reclining. And to change my eyes from open to closed. Now move before I knock that arrogant smirk off your face."

Seth smiles but keeps his finger pointing at me. I tighten my right fist.

At last, he drops his arm and steps back. "I prefer prayer to argument. But mind my words, Judah. Stop bringing shame on us."

Watching his inflexible back march away, I imagine tackling him from behind like when we were kids. His five-year advantage meant he usually got the best of me, but I still tried. And now his four-inch-taller height and his more muscular build give him the edge. But I miss the satisfaction of hitting him when he least expected it. Being a man entails too many restrictions.

An oil lamp bathes my room in golden light. Abba built me and Seth our own dwellings when we reached marrying age, choosing not to make us wait until betrothal. Seth became betrothed last year. Poor girl. I wonder if Hadassah realizes what a hard man he is.

I hang my cloak on its peg and look around my cozy room before plopping on a stool. Of course, I hoped to bring Rachel here. To continue the family. To build a legacy. Tonight, I would have cherished her welcome. Her warm embrace. Her willing—

"No!" I chide myself, shoving the thought of her aside. "No more childhood dreams. Stick to the plan."

When Asher, Rachel's father, declined my proposal last year, it felt like one more failure. But now I'm grateful. If married, I'd be tied to home like Methuselah to his mill, walking in circles and getting nowhere.

After sipping from the bucket of cool spring water, I splash some on my neck. Fingering the tassels on the corners of my undergarment, words from a lifetime of repetition echo through my mind. "And it shall be a tassel for you to look at and remember all the commandments of the Lord, to do them . . . and be holy to your God.[1]"

How do I both remember Adonai and pursue my plan? A plan that requires leaving everything behind?

Sighing, I extinguish the lamp. It is better that I'm not married, but I can't help longing for Rachel—her face, her heart, and her belief that I can accomplish anything. How will she respond to this idea?

Lying on my striped blanket, I brush away memories from today. Abba's crumpled forehead. Miriam's glistening cheeks. Seth's curled lip. Then I banish the image of Rachel's eyes so I can think about the worrisome details.

Sleep refuses to come. I can't fix my problems and sleep at the same time. Abba always says, "'He who keeps Israel will neither slumber nor sleep.[2]' Since the Holy One is awake, taking care of the nations and handling your worries, you can sleep."

Crawling under my blanket of brown, green, and tan wool, I roll over. "I doubt Adonai will spend tonight working on a plan He doesn't approve of. Although if He would convince Rachel to wait for me, I would be grateful."

Finally, I drift off to sleep. But into my dreams sweeps a black-haired, olive-skinned beauty who slips off her pink headscarf revealing shiny black hair, and who nestles into my arms. Some dreams refuse to die.

In the third hour, Abba asked, "Judah, did you get an accurate account of the barley?"

"Yes, Abba."

Halfway through the sixth hour, "Did you ask Timaeus of our concern about worms with the sheep?"

"Yes, Abba."

As the ninth hour started, "Judah, don't forget to sharpen the sickles."

"Yes, Abba."

Finally, as the sun begins its descent, I make my escape. Ascending Mount Meron, I try to work through the complications and consequences of Meoklis's suggestion.

Frustration fuels my legs, and I run until a stab clutches my side and sweat rolls down my back. Panting, I lean against the boulder that camouflages a ledge above a deep ravine. Here, as a boy, this vista of the valley became my refuge. I still come here to think.

My eyes trace the small road that wanders southwest from Meron.

That road intersects larger roads traversing Galilee, around Samaria, on to Jerusalem, and eventually to Caesarea's port. From there, boats sail all over the world. To Alexandria. Athens. Ephesus. Even Rome. What adventures do those distant places offer?

But how do I reconcile my colliding desires? I can't respect Abba and flee his constraints. Am I brave enough for this irreversible action?

"What should I do?" I yell into the abyss.

What should I do? echoes back.

"What do you want to do?"

I swivel violently. Joseph, the one person besides Rachel with whom I can be myself, steps around my boulder, his scant beard, mischievous grin, and freckled nose making him look younger than he is. We've spent our lives side by side. First as disobedient, undisciplined boys at bet hasefer, where we were told to "get fat on the Torah like oxen get fat in the stall." Next as students at bet-midrash, skipping class to play on the mountain. Then as restless young men, side by side in the synagogue on Shabbat, then gambling and drinking with the local undesirables the next night. And, finally, as I stood by his side a few months ago at his wedding. I've shared every dream with him. Except this one.

"You need something?" I turn away.

"What's got you so cheerful?"

"I am Seth ben Ezra's brother."

"Well, you're lucky there." Joseph sits beside me.

A breeze ruffles his hair and cools my sweat. Joseph bumps my shoulder with his. I bump him back.

"What did he do this time?"

"Acted like Seth." I shrug. "Arrogant. Critical. Like it's his duty to teach me how to be a better son." My voice catches. I may soon prove him right. "As if his judgmental looks and responses don't hurt Abba. Holy and respectful outside, but rotten inside. He praises Abba at the gates but challenges him at home. And he tells me how I should live?"

Scraping a pile of pebbles into my hand, I hurl them over the cliff, one at a time.

"If you're trying to hit him, you'll need to throw harder."

"My own personal Goliath." I examine my remaining pebbles. "I need bigger rocks. And a sling. I definitely need a sling."

"Taking him out would probably create more problems."

"Yeah. I know." I dribble the pebbles through my fingers. Should I share? Once I release the words into the world, I can't take them back. But if I'm to move from thinking to doing–from dream to action–then I must speak openly.

"I think I'm leaving."

"You're going on a trip?"

"No. Moving. Away from the groves and Seth. From the synagogue, the expectations, and the Law. That's what I mean."

"But where would you go? How would you live?"

"I've discovered a way—"

An eagle glides overhead.

"How? Where?"

The eagle dives, snatches its prey, and soars toward the mountain top with a resounding shriek.

Joseph grabs my arm. "Judah, explain yourself!"

"You must vow to not breathe a word to anyone." I face him. "Not a soul, Joseph. I mean it."

Joseph's eyes narrow. "You need a vow for that to be understood?"

"Do you swear?"

Joseph nods.

Sucking in my breath, I gaze across the valley. "I shall request my part of the inheritance."

"I don't understand."

Standing, I pace as much as the ledge allows. "I don't want sheep, or vineyards, or having to live in Meron. If I receive my portion now, I can enter business."

"But not here?" Joseph's eyebrows draw together.

"In a larger city."

"But Judah," Joseph whispers, "your father's not dead."

I kick the dirt. Joseph's father died last year. "I realize that, and I don't wish Abba dead. But last week in Sepphoris, I spoke to the trader Meoklis. He told me about someone who received his inheritance early."

"Meoklis? That's not a Jewish name."

"No."

"Such a thing might be common among Gentiles. But from childhood, we've been taught to honor not only our parents but also the land Adonai gave us. We are to possess the land despite Roman occupation. You think you can run away from that?"

"Why be tied down when I'm full of energy and have no family to support? The Romans have built roads and established peace that allows trade. Business opportunities exist everywhere."

"You're telling me there's no one here you want to make a home with?"

"Apparently, she'll soon be betrothed." I kick a rock over the side and sit beside him.

Joseph turns toward the valley and I give him time to absorb all I've said. Besides, I'm tired of talking. Locusts call to the diminishing light, and the breeze carries muffled sounds from the valley below.

When I stand, Joseph grabs my arm. "Please! You can't leave me like this."

"I don't want to hurt you—or anyone, for that matter. But there's no other way. If I move without any money, I'll become a beggar on the street, like those who plague Sepphoris and Jerusalem. Besides, I need money to make money and become a wealthy merchant in a city, instead of a crude farmer in a village."

"Thanks."

I sigh. "You know I don't mean you. But here, there's one God and one way. There's no room for anything else."

"So you're running from Adonai too?"

"This coming from you?"

"I have doubts. But not enough to consider Adonai so small that I can avoid Him by running from Meron," Joseph says.

"I promise I won't end up like Jonah."

Joseph's laugh sounds hollow. "Where are you moving to?"

"Ephesus." Revealing this feels liberating. My doubts fade with the sinking sun.

Running his fingers through his hair, it stands on end.

"Have I actually shut your big mouth?"

Joseph looks at his feet.

"Come on, tell me I'm stupid. Tell me I'm a heathen. Just say something."

I squat in front of him, but he hangs his head lower.

"When I succeed, I'll bring money back to my family. But I can't live Abba's way and accomplish my goals."

"What should I say? That you'll destroy your father? That you'll alienate your friends? That you could still end up a beggar? That you don't know how to become a merchant? Come on, Judah! You'd rather spend denarii than save them."

"But you also struggle with Torah's restrictions and our ways that never change. Just imagine when I'm a rich merchant. You'll come visit, and I'll feed you the choicest meats and wines."

"When will you tell your father?"

"Soon. I'll need to sell my holdings before the yearly caravan arrives." His stillness unnerves me. "Joseph, you're my oldest friend—and more of a brother than Seth's ever been. Moving away won't change that."

"I'll never see you again."

"Yes, you will. I'll come home bearing gifts for you and your pretty wife."

"We'd better get home. The sun and Shabbat won't wait."

I stand and offer him my hand. He stands on his own and moves toward the path home. Pivoting suddenly, he seizes my shoulders. "Judah, I've never been able to talk you out of anything. But think about this. Think hard. Or you'll destroy more than you realize."

"It'll be fine. Let's race down the mountain. I ran up here, and it felt amazing."

"Run?"

"You want to be late for Shabbat?"

"Mara would be horrified if I did something so undignified. She's trying to make me respectable."

That's exactly what I want to escape.

"Then don't let her see you!" I charge toward freedom.

CHAPTER 7
JUDAH

Valerius's Villa, Outside Iconium
Sivan–Tammuz (May–June) AD 20

I will be to him a father, and he shall be to me a son. When he commits iniquity, I will discipline him with the rods of men, with the stripes of the sons of men, but my steadfast love will not depart from him.

2 SAMUEL 7:14-15A

Dawn releases me from a miserable night spent outside the shed. Rubbing my shoulder, I move to the warm morning sun, close my eyes, and imagine myself anywhere but here. Even my dingy apartment in Ephesus, the lumbering camel, or the rolling ship.

When Miriam's table laden with goat milk, pomegranates, and olives swirls through my mind, I smell fresh bread. My mouth waters, but the pleasure ends when my stomach growls. Dreams make everything worse. To chase away the vision, I observe my new home. Within the estate walls, dozens of lean, almost hollow servants and slaves, all dressed in brown, lug water, carry wood, and herd animals. No one looks up. No one smiles.

Squeals and snorts remind me that I'd better figure out what to do. I'll treat the pigs like sheep. How different can they be?

Inside the ramshackle shed, the pigs mill about in their own filth. All animals produce waste, but they seem to enjoy it. At least sheep want to be clean.

"You know, my people have a poor opinion of you, and I'm beginning to understand why." Then I recall succulent pork dishes I savored in Ephesus. "You taste good, though. I'll give you that."

Holding my left arm against my body, protecting my shoulder and ribs, I wave my right arm and attempt to drive the animals outside. They don't even look at me. Great. What now? I grab a stick and start poking at them. "Go on. Shoo." The swine snort, some with alarming ferocity, but don't budge.

"Out. Out!" I yell. "You miserable vermin, get outside!"

"Who are you talking to?" A resonant voice interrupts me. For one blessed moment, I imagine Abba has arrived to rescue me and I turn to the doorway.

The voice might sound like Abba's, but the speaker looks nothing like him. I peer down into dark eyes, shrouded by one long, gray eyebrow. Even more startling is the wiry hair atop his head, each long, gray strand poking in a different direction. Bent to one side, the short, weather-beaten man looks as if he's spent his whole life outside. Limping closer, his broad smile reveals half the teeth he has a right to. He's one of the ugliest men I've ever seen.

"Come. Talk to ol' Pavlos. Who do you speak to, boy?"

"The pigs," I mumble.

"You're honest, at least. That holds possibilities. Now tell me why you're chatting to pigs. They don't understand you, you know."

Life is carved on his face as if by a stylus, but there's kindness in his eyes, something I haven't encountered much since leaving home. At least not that I could trust.

"I'm trying to drive them out so I can clean this."

Pavlos sniffs. "Bad idea. Pigs are mean. Ever herded them before?"

"Who are you?"

"Being careful, I see. Well, I'm Pavlos. I serve Valerius and, among other things, manage the animals' care under Gallus who oversees everything. Now, pigs like mess. There's no point in cleaning this. It'll just agitate them. Anyone familiar with them would know that."

My mouth clamps shut.

"Don't worry. I won't reveal your secrets." Pavlos smiles.

"I haven't got any secrets."

"Don't you now?" Pavlos's brown eyes twinkle, and he chuckles. "Then tell me, Master Honest, where did a Jewish boy learn to take care of pigs?"

My heart pounds.

He turns my right hand palm-up. "Your hands don't look like a worker's."

Crossing my arms, I stick my hands in my armpits, but the quick movement sends a wave of pain through my body. My breath catches, and I sink to the ground.

"Gallus told me you're hurt. Let's go outside." Pavlos reaches into a bag slung over his shoulder. "I've come to wrap you."

Before I can react, he supports me and we move outside. Removing my brown chiton and the one underneath, he prods and examines me in turns. Humming a familiar tune I cannot place, he wraps my ribs and shoulder with lengths of bandage, giving immediate relief. "I told you my name, so tell me yours."

"Jude."

"Jude? Your father named you Jude?"

Refusing to meet his merry eyes, I nod, reaching for a shovel.

Pavlos laughs again. "Well, Jude, the secret you don't have is safe with me. Lucky for you, taking care of pigs isn't hard, though this drought means food is scarce. For now, you'll bring them scraps from the house, along with any other feed you can find. Pigs eat just about anything."

"In a few weeks, you'll have to drive them to the hills to feed. Until then, I'll teach you how not to kill them. You don't want the master taking his prized dinners out of your hide. You've got little more than parchment covering your bones. I doubt you'd survive."

I don't have to trust this man to learn from him. "What do I need to know?"

"Not a talkative fellow, but to the point. Have you always been quiet? Or has life dried up your words? Well, let me see . . ."

Pavlos rattles off detailed instructions about herding swine. I try to absorb what he says until my vision blurs and my ears buzz. I lean against the shed wall, commanding myself not to faint.

He pauses. "You don't look so good. How about I get us some water?"

When he hobbles away, I slide down the wall and lean my head back. A few moments later, Pavlos forces a ladle into my hand and I drink. Having something in my belly helps, even stale water.

"You'll get a small piece of bread in the morning and at night." His voice is soft and slow. "Sometimes a cup of soup. Enough to survive. Barely. Not enough to fix your scrawniness. You see that tannur by that lean-to and tables? When I whistle, food is ready so get over there. Don't be late, or someone hungry will eat your portion. And everyone's hungry."

I hold my good arm over my eyes. "Thank you for the water."

"Ah, someone taught you manners. Well, you're welcome, Jude.'"

"Actually—" I draw a deep breath. "You can call me Judah."

Pavlos nods. "Judah it is. The work never ends, and yours will involve more than pigs. Until you take them to the hills, you'll help me wherever needed. Work hard, and maybe you might earn extra rations." The old man pats me on the head.

Anything sounds preferable to pigs. "How did you know?"

"What?"

"That I'm Jewish?"

"Anybody ever told you that you talk in your sleep?"

"What?"

Pavlos chuckles. "Well, I passed by here last night. You dream in Hebrew. Don't be late for breakfast."

I haven't spoken Hebrew since leaving Judea, and even in Meron only to recite Torah or pray. Does that mean I pray in my sleep? I stagger to my feet and shake my head. Why dream prayers when no one listens?

Limping away, Pavlos whistles the same haunting tune. I've trusted people before. People who charmed me with kind words and enticing eyes, only to betray me.

"No!" I yell.

A passing servant looks my way. I scowl.

No, I repeat silently. No trusting people. No replaying the past. No memories of home. No rehashing what I should've done or who I shouldn't have trusted.

This is my life. Caring for disgusting pigs. I'll learn all I can from Pavlos, but I won't trust him.

A sharp whistle pierces the quiet. Breakfast. I do my best to run toward the tannur surrounded by crude tables and stools. I won't be late. Not for anything.

During my first week, Pavlos asked, "Any questions about the swine?"

Gulping my pride, I whispered, "I need to know anything you can tell me."

Pavlos threw back his head and bellowed with laughter as heat crept up my cheeks. "Don't worry. Pigs aren't so tough." He proceeded to pour pig husbandry into my muddled brain.

So far, my opinion of the animals hasn't improved. Their stench resides permanently in my nostrils.

How long have I been rising early and laboring until I fall on my straw mat, exhausted, hungry, aching, just to wake and repeat it again? And again? There's no Shabbat here to mark time. Of course, I never observed Shabbat in Ephesus either, but parties, theater acts, and chariot races structured the days.

Now, my days run together. Just as well. Why track misery? But today, drawing water for my masters, at least I realize the pain in my shoulder and ribs is almost gone.

Every evening, near the eating area, the slaves in brown chitons gather. Finally, Khafra stopped trying to converse with me and found others more willing. My fellow slaves are just competition for food. I don't need friends. I don't want friends.

Last night, Pavlos handed me some dried figs.

I grunted.

"You're welcome," he laughed. Nothing deters that man.

What would he say if he found out that I'm actually glad to hear his uneven steps approaching and these snatched conversations with him brighten my days?

In contrast, I'm *not* happy to hear Gallus approach. "Aren't you finished yet" is often followed by, "Move faster" after which comes a push if I don't move quickly enough. But the worst is the snap of his whip. One crack sends us all scurrying. And Gallus grows surlier as the drought deepens.

I pull the rope and empty muddy water from the well into each wooden bucket on my yoke. How will we survive if the well goes dry?

"How's the water?" Pavlos exits the stucco barn.

I shake my head slightly. Grinning, he hobbles over, and I return a half-smile.

"Aha! You do know how to smile, after a sort."

I duck my head, heft the heavy yoke onto my shoulders, and shuffle back toward the shed, careful to not slosh one precious drop as the buckets swing.

"You'll work with me when you're done," he tells my retreating back.

"All right. I must fetch the kitchen scraps." I don't bother adding that scraps lessen by the day.

"Meet me at the barn afterward."

I maneuver around the goatherd as plumes of dust coat my clothes and lungs. His herd looks skinnier this week than last.

When I finally meet Pavlos at the barn, one of his hands rests on a gaunt boy's shoulder while the other extends a small loaf of bread. "Here, Lucius. I'll try to have more tomorrow."

Lucius stuffs half of it into his mouth. Hearing my footsteps, he whirls, hiding the other half behind his back. I step away. I'm not desperate enough to take food from a child. Not yet.

"It's okay." Pavlos pats him on the head, and the boy rushes out.

Stowing something under his cloak, Pavlos points to a wooden handcart. "Push and follow me."

I trudge behind until his whistle pauses and he says, "That ground corn will serve us well, Maya and Aneta." They sit on stone steps in the shade of the barn, relentlessly grinding.

"Thank you, Pavlos," Maya says, her skin tanned near the color of the chiton.

"She's also from Egypt," Pavlos whispers as we move on.

"So?" I reply.

"Slaves can marry."

"You want to marry her?"

"Oh, Judah."

"Then who?"

When Khafra, face concealed by crates he's toting, almost runs over him, Pavlos says, "Such strength! You and Judah arrived just in time." The Egyptian smiles, but I turn away and adjust tools in the handcart. After he walks off, Pavlos says, "And Khafra's Egyptian."

I just shake my head. "If you arrange marriages as well as you talk to each person we pass, we'll never arrive at our task. And then I'll be in trouble with Gallus!"

"One more stop!" He knocks at the villa's back entrance. Prisca, the female slave who traveled with me from Ephesus, surveys us vacantly. Though I pick up scraps from her every day, she never speaks or looks at me. From a recess in his cloak, Pavlos produces two kittens. "These should help the cook with the mice problem. But their mother died, so they'll need care. Can you do that?"

"Oh!" She strokes them tenderly as they mew, before nuzzling her face into their tawny fur. Suddenly, she jerks upright and scurries inside.

"Let's go!" Pavlos leads me to the large garden plot behind the house, where deep cracks split the surface into tiny canyons punctuated by dehydrated plants. This infertile ground looks like my life. Once full of promise, now barren.

Handing me a hoe, Pavlos points toward the far corner. "You start there, and I'll start here." He elbows me. "We'll see if a skinny young man is faster than a crooked old one." His whistling resumes as he hacks clods into dust.

"Why?"

"Why see who's faster?"

"Why work this barren ground?"

"Something more pressing to do? A business meeting, perhaps?" The soft chuckle isn't unkind. "First, we do this because Gallus ordered us. Second, and more importantly, we do this so that one day the ground won't be barren."

I slam my hoe into the ground and let out a bellow.

"With that out of the way," Pavlos dips into a low bow, "shall we begin?"

I drag my hoe behind me. The parched ground, hard as stone, foretells a day as interminable as my existence.

Pavlos's whistling resurrects a dusty memory. "'So teach us to number our days that we may get a heart of wisdom.'[1]" His melodic voice rises above the crunch, crunch of crumbling dirt. "'Return, O Lord! How long? Have pity on your servants!'[2]"

Pavlos knows Psalms?

Wiping sweat from my brow, I belt out a song from my days at The Crow. I miss that Ephesian taberna. Besides, heaven has no pity. If Pavlos believes differently, he's a fool.

As I swing my hoe over and over, blisters riddling my hands, the sun burns my neck, and my mind wanders from my drinking song to Pavlos's familiar words.

"'Let the favor of the Lord our God be upon us, and establish the work of our hands upon us; yes, establish the work of our hands!'[3]"

CHAPTER 8
SETH

Meron
Nissan (March) AD 19

For you save a humble people, but the haughty eyes you bring down.

PSALM 18:27

Judah cocks his head toward Abba and raises his eyebrows. I don't know what Abba's thinking either, but I recline on my blue wool cushion and eat another melon slice. For me, Shabbat dinner is the most tranquil moment of the week, with the oil lamps flickering, the remains of the meal still on the painted pottery, and the anticipation of worship tomorrow. I won't let Judah ruin it.

After I do nothing, he asks, "Anything else, Abba?"

"Do you ever wonder at the Almighty's power and wisdom in naming each star? Look at the multitude, my sons. He formed, named, and knows each one."

"Yes," Judah responds.

I stifle a laugh. Judah, wondering about the holy? I change the subject to a more practical one.

"Judah, I whistled three times this afternoon," I say. "I needed your help. Did you not hear me?"

"Nope. Sorry."

Of course not.

"Abba," Judah draws a deep breath. "I know you declined to invest in trade in Sepphoris," Abba leans his head on his fist, "and I know you have concerns, but I wanted to try one more time before . . . before . . . "

"Before what?" My hands slam the table, rattling the plates.

Abba raises his hands. "Let's maintain Shabbat peace," he glances at me, "regardless of the topic."

What reaction besides contempt does Judah's foolish obsession deserve?

Abba leans toward Judah. "On Shabbat, we should concentrate on the goodness the Most High showers on us."

"Amen," I say.

Abba says, "Be content, my son. Be grateful." Judah's straight mouth and stiff body should inform Abba that he'll never be grateful. Why keep trying?

I walk to the edge of the balcony, stretching to release a day's hard work and inhaling Shabbat's shalom. With our village built on the slope of Mount Meron, I can scan across the valley to the mounts on the other side where Safed, a village on a hill, twinkles in the descending darkness. I imagine I see the light flickering at the table in the house with the red door just right of the market square. There, Hadassah celebrates Shabbat with her family. When her father and I signed the marriage contract over a year ago, I never planned for the betrothal to stretch this long. But I keep finding one reason after another to delay.

"Did you hear me, Seth?"

"No, Abba. Sorry."

"Why don't you quit staring at Safed and go marry your bride?" Judah sneers. "You know, people have begun to talk."

I rub my forehead.

Abba extends one hand toward me and the other to Judah. "Let's end our Shabbat dinner in prayer, not conflict.

After a quick glance back at Safed, I join Abba in prayer. Shabbat, from tonight's sundown until tomorrow's, would be more enjoyable with Hadassah in my arms. Maybe it's time to plan the wedding. Maybe.

"How much longer?"

"Be patient, Seth," Abba says.

It might be difficult to judge the hour on this gray morning, but the shofar has blown. We must depart for synagogue because one shouldn't hurry on Shabbat—too similar to working. Yet, here at the front gate, I shift from one foot to the other as Abba mouths a prayer. I hope he asks the Almighty to pick Judah up by the scruff of his neck and shake him.

Judah delights in avoiding his responsibilities. Yesterday, I stood whistling for him in the wheat field. Judah knows that means, *I need his help, so get here now.* Three attempts returned nothing more than an echo.

Neighbors' heads swiveled my way as they paused their harvests to see what problems lay in Ezra ben Lavi's fields. After a swig from my waterskin, I stalked back into the grain field. At least my frustration fueled my swinging sickle.

Has Judah ever considered that I'd rather study Torah? Or return to Sepphoris while Rabbi Yakov visits from Jerusalem? Or travel to Safed to visit Hadassah?

How about Judah work and I leave?

But I control my desires—good desires—because duty comes first. I complete my work because I should.

Eli and Miriam nod as they pass, but Abba's too engrossed in his prayers to notice. As the breeze blows the morning clouds away, I squint at the sun. Why won't Abba tell Judah to hurry?

Yesterday, Eli answered my third call with three extra workers.

"What are you doing here?" I'd said.

Eli's mouth twitched, and the wrinkles around his eyes deepened. "Shalom, Seth. We're here to help."

"Aren't you a bit too old to harvest wheat?"

Still lean and strong, albeit slower, Eli outworks many younger men, but I didn't care.

"Master only asked me to supervise." After sending the workers into the field, he added, "We heard you from the vineyard, and suspected . . . the usual. We were on our way before your second whistle."

"Abba shouldn't have to send workers to compensate for Judah's laziness."

"Maybe. But we're your father's servants and it's his field, so we're at his disposal. And we're happy to work."

And I admit the added workers changed everything. We increased our pace and raced the sun. As they sang psalms to set the rhythm, my heart began lifting. I couldn't sing praise and nurse grievances against Judah at the same time, even though my indignation was righteous.

But waiting here, our tardiness on display, my heart feels anything but lifted. Neighbors hurry on the street outside our gate. Deep breath in. Deep breath out. The calming exercise helps. I need that because today I will discuss Rabbi Yakov's proposed visit with the elders and leaders and I don't want to be flustered.

Maybe I should just leave—

"Good Shabbat, Judah." Abba drops his tassels with a smile.

I cough. That's all he has to say?

Abba turns a kind gaze to me. "Ready to go?"

"I've been ready. That's why I stood here among the clucking chickens waiting for Judah to join us."

"Ah, brother, you're too kind."

Another deep breath. I gesture for Abba to exit the gate first before touching the mezuzah and following at a leisurely pace. Judah won't dictate our morning or ruin my worship in the house of prayer.

"Uncle Daniel, Rabbi Yakov brings strong teaching. His Torah understanding challenges everyone who hears."

When Eema died after Judah was born, Uncle Daniel took a special interest in me, and we've always been close. He says, "I'm happy to support you in this."

We exit the synagogue's shady entrance as our neighbors file past, chatting and gossiping. In the sunlit courtyard, I shield my eyes and spot Judah off to the side, joking with Joseph. At least Judah laughs. Joseph looks like he's eaten bitter grapes.

As I'm about to turn toward the group of elders, Judah's face turns serious. He stares at Rachel, who stands by Asher, trying to corral her three younger sisters while staring straight back. Has she no modesty? When her eyes shift and meet mine, she colors, wraps her headscarf over her face, and walks away, dragging a sister with her. Judah glares at me, but he's the one who ruined his chances with a girl far superior to him and now reaps what he sowed.

I move toward the men from whom I hope to secure an invitation for Rabbi Yakov. Uncle Daniel chats with Abba, Rabbi Akiva, and Mazal the physician about the hope for winter rain, taxes on wheat, and new babies in the village. Barak, a judge and wealthy land owner, joins them.

At a pause, I jump in. "I met Rabbi Yakov from Jerusalem in Sepphoris. He might include Meron in his circuit north if we'll host him."

Uncle Daniel and Mazal nod, but Abba glances to Rabbi Akiva with drawn brows.

Rabbi Akiva clears his throat. "He's a Pharisee from Jerusalem, correct? Many of them hold unfavorable opinions of the regions of Zebulun and Naphtali, what with our Galilean ways and accent."

The circle of men chuckle.

"True." Abba adds. "They can often sounds disrespectful. Did you find that with him?"

"He teaches clear obedience to the Law. Abba, you've always loved King David's words, 'To obey is better than sacrifice.'[1]" When I realize my hands gesticulate wildly, I clasp them in front of me.

"Obedience matters," Abba nods, "as does a pure heart full of lovingkindness. I'm sure your rabbi will present much for us to discuss."

"He's not *my* rabbi."

Abba pats Rabbi Akiva on the back. "Of course not."

Uncle Daniel envelops me in a side hug. "Ezra, what a wonderful nephew I have! Bringing us teachers and keeping us straight."

"So you'll support his coming?" I hold my breath as the men look one to the other.

"Rabbi Akiva, what do you think?" Abba smiles slightly. "Will our small village survive a Jerusalem Pharisee?"

Why does Abba, who loves Torah more than anyone I know, hesitate about a Rabbi with superb devotion to its application?

Rabbi Akiva raises his right gray eyebrow. "I welcome all teachers who challenge our thinking about Torah. Although, given the busy harvest, we can only discuss with him as much as work allows."

I wish Abba would voice similar approval, but for now I can welcome Rabbi Yakov to Meron. That's all that matters.

CHAPTER 9
JUDAH

Meron
Nissan (March) - Iyar (April) AD 19

I spread out my hands all the day to a rebellious people, who walk in a way that is not good, following their own devices.

ISAIAH 65:2

Though I'd rather do anything than what lies ahead of us, I follow Abba, Seth, and a group of builders in the morning light. Meoklis's scheme fanned my hopes into flame, but leaving feels impossible to figure out.

We join others streaming from Meron, like ants from their mound. I kick a rock.

"Ow! Who did that?" A man hops to face me, holding his foot.

"I'm so sorry, Asher. I didn't—I didn't mean to." My cheeks feel hot as I curse my ill-fated life.

"Are you sure?" He glares.

My mouth hangs open.

"Something wrong?" Abba approaches.

"Nothing, Ezra," Asher grunts. "Shalom."

As he stomps toward his field, I surge ahead to avoid Abba's questions.

Great. Now, Rachel enters this morning's thoughts. Though I'm afraid of what she will say, I long to discuss my plans with her, even though they can't include her. She would complicate everything. But what if I succeed? Maybe then?

Yesterday after synagogue, I'd felt her not looking at me until I captured her gaze and refused to let go. I know Rachel's eyes, and those ebony windows revealed sorrow. Maybe she isn't eager to become betrothed. Of course, Seth spied us. He looked as stiff and judgmental as the Pharisee he wants to be.

Seth. Always ruining everything.

After a five-minute walk, we reach the hilltop where Abba builds this lookout for the benefit of the village. Because the location offers surveillance in all directions, a watchman can spot any incoming trouble, from bandits to approaching storms. At least if I complete it.

"This project will help you develop responsibility," Abba had said.

Sorry, Abba, but the precision required, the figuring and measuring, bores me. It's excruciating to supervise workers as they choose a stone, file it into shape, determine the best placement, and make little visible progress after a day's work. Which explains why I ignored it. After all, Reuben, the village builder, could complete it.

But Reuben wasn't the boss, I was. And when I repeatedly failed to order materials and pay wages, the workers stopped coming. The village gossiped about the half-done work. A few months ago, Reuben went to Abba, asking what to do.

When Abba asked me to join him under the arbor to discuss the tower project, I felt like a boy being scolded for neglecting my Torah studies. I tried again. I did. But there were just always better things to do. I hate how meddlesome villagers, happy to benefit from Abba's generosity and not encumbered with the work, gossip and find fault. What right do they have to judge me?

"Well, at least we know you can begin something," Seth gloated. "You just leave the finishing for others."

"Judah, I hoped you would learn to apply yourself," Abba said. "The Most High gifted you with energy and ingenuity, but neither will benefit you unless you finish things. A foundation without walls is useless."

Last week, face like stone, Abba declared, "Judah, you will complete this." So once again, I face this cursed tower with dread. Abba assured Reuben that this time will be different, and now they circle the tower's foundation, examining and commenting on the progress. The foreman points out issues and the measuring rod and plumb line appear.

"Excruciating," I mutter and search for somewhere to sit during the endless discussion of details. Just one more reason to leave.

Seeking the shade of the large sycamore tree, I lean against the trunk and close my eyes. The morning sun, pleasant and warm, bodes a hot day before too much longer. I might as well enjoy the cool while I can.

"We haven't even started and you already need a rest?"

I open one eye. Seth glowers down at me. Apparently, the girls consider him handsome. Something about his thick brown hair and serious eyes. They might appreciate that he's tall and strong, but they don't know him.

"Would I accomplish more if I stood and scowled like you?" I yawn and stretch. Seth ruins everything. The urge to wrestle him to the ground returns. If I ambush him—grab him around the knees—I could take him.

But I've brought enough shame on Abba, and I am about to bring much more. Besides, I'm a grown man. I can't wrestle my brother. But I can do the next best thing and imagine tackling him. Grinning, I picture his smug disapproval transforming into shock as he hits the dirt.

"Dreaming of wine?" Seth prods me with his sandal.

In my mind, Seth lands on his back, eyes bugging out.

"Did you drink even more of Abba's last night?"

My imaginary knuckles smash his nose, spattering blood onto the ground.

"The memory give you pleasure?" Seth crouches beside me and lowers his voice. "Or do you dream about some whore in Sepphoris?"

My smile broadens as I envision smashing Seth's nose with my other fist.

"You disgust me," Seth whispers.

I imagine my knee heading where it could inflict real damage.

"Judah!" Abba calls.

I pop my eyes open, stare straight into Seth's, and whisper. "You have no idea what I'm thinking." Then, louder than necessary, I answer. "Coming, Abba!"

The telltale pulsing in Seth's forehead proves I've threatened his restraint. I whistle on my way to Abba.

"Judah, you'll be Reuben's assistant."

Reuben tries to cover his groan with a cough. My satisfaction evaporates. I feel no more desire to build this tower than harvest grain.

"Let's gather around and thank Adonai!" Abba's voice rings out. "Then Reuben will instruct everyone on the plan. If we work hard and cooperate," he stares at me, "we can achieve significant progress today. One of our Proverbs tell us, 'The name of the Lord is a strong tower; the righteous man runs into it and is safe.'[1] Let's call on His name for help to build." Abba prays as if Adonai stands among us. I feel like I'm eavesdropping on a conversation between my father and Someone I don't know.

"Amen!"

Reuben begins to delegate duties, and I stare at the infernal tower that I once again find myself building. Abba and Seth circle the structure, Abba's arm around my brother's broad shoulders.

If Seth oversees me overseeing the workers, I'm leaving. But Seth departs.

"He gets to leave?" I cross my arms as Abba approaches.

"The wheat harvest isn't complete. He's making sure we end well."

"End well? Good one, Abba. Not like me and this tower, right?

"That's not what I'm saying, though I agree. Even the Creator didn't rest until He completed the work. 'And he rested on the seventh day from all his work that he had done.'[2] Shabbat is holy because we follow the Creator by resting. The other six days, we follow Him by working. And once you begin a job, don't stop until it's finished."

"As you've told me my whole life. You have a passage for everything."

"Actually, Torah does. I'm still learning which ones apply to which situation. Don't resist the life His Word can give or the protection it offers."

Abba gazes so deeply into me I'm afraid he'll discover my scheme.

"Yes, sir," I mumble and move away. I almost wish I had time to complete this job just to prove I can. To show Abba. To spite Seth. To silence the village gossips.

Thoughts of Rachel, unbidden but welcome, block Reuben's voice. Maybe she will wait for me if I can find a moment alone with her to explain. Could I convince her? I must. Because now, more than ever, I am determined to leave.

"GRAB THE OX!" At Rueben's panic, I scramble.

Crack!

The gray ox bawls in complaint as the yoke breaks and drags the beast to its knees.

"Beelzebub! Only three days of work and already this!" Rueben kicks a dirt clod and scowls at me.

"It's not my fault."

He looks unconvinced.

"I'll see if Malachi has one to purchase!" I sprint into Meron before Rueben can stop me, joining people from the surrounding areas arriving for market day. Between vendors and customers, I bet our population has doubled. The market means I might catch Rachel where I can finally talk with her. But first, I rush to Malachi's carpentry shop.

"Our yoke broke. We can't heft stone for the tower without a new one!"

"Why are you always in a hurry?" He hefts a yoke on his workbench. "Come back at the seventh hour. This still needs a bit of sanding."

Perfect. With a wave, I navigate crying children and scolding eemas, to the market square. Miriam chats with Salome, Rachel's Eema, at the family's cheese stall.

"Shalom."

Both women look at me cock-eyed.

"I thought you were supposed to be at the tower." Miriam gives me her what-are-you-up-to-now look.

"Broken yoke. Don't worry." I flash them a smile. "I'll be back at work as soon as Malachi has the replacement ready."

"Hmmm."

Rachel is nowhere to be seen. Not behind the table of cheese or under the woven awning above that allows dappled light on the disapproving women. All I can do is hope she appears before I must return to work.

With time to kill, I decide to prepare for my trip. The trip no one knows I'm taking.

"I need some rope for binding bundles—for travel."

"Certainly," the squatty man at the rope stall extends several options.

Scanning the crowd, I don't see Rachel.

A Syrian merchant sells leather goods. I try on hats with wide brims, good for traveling. "Do you have any more of this darker color?"

"Over here, sir."

"And I need a larger satchel, one with a hefty shoulder-strap."

Stowing the rope and hat in the satchel, I take another circuit of the market, as if I'm shopping. Where's Rachel? Cumin and sumac at the spice stand cause my stomach to rumble.

Will Rachel understand better than Joseph? I pick at a few vegetables, trying to imagine her response. "She won't understand," I lament to a melon.

"What?" Gilah, the vegetable merchant questions me as she mounds peas for display.

"Nothing," I mumble. Thoughts always jump from my mind to my mouth. It's so irritating.

"Right." She brushes frizzy gray hair behind her ear and reveals a missing front tooth when she smiles. "I may not understand either, but if you're waiting for a certain someone, would you move to the next stall? Ehud won't mind if you block his carpets. Shoppers need to examine my vegetables."

“Sorry, Gilah. I’ll take some dried figs.”

Wandering around the mass of shoppers with their baskets and bags, I toss and catch the figs over and over.

Still no Rachel. And I must return to the tower. I turn to leave when pale pink fabric flutters in my right periphery. There! At the wine merchant, the vendor fills Rachel’s amphora. But that only solves one problem. I shouldn’t approach a single woman by myself.

But why? Why do our customs keep me from talking to her whenever I like? I stride toward the wine merchant but trip over a boy.

“Watch out mister!” Above a wad of dirty, patched clothing, the boy’s flashing hazel eyes and balled fists condemn me. I admire his spirit.

“I’m so sorry, sir.” I hand my figs to the street child. “Enjoy.”

“Really? Thanks!” Judging from the speed with which he escapes, he must worry I’ll have second thoughts.

As I approach Rachel, who hasn’t noticed me yet, I hear giggles. Lavinia and her daughter Sapphira glance from me to Rachel, widen their eyes at each other, and giggle again.

Gilah calls out, “Hope she understands.”

Miriam and Salome, with arms crossed over their chests, glare at me, Miriam shaking her head.

Why does everyone think they’re allowed an opinion about my life?

Turning to the left, I escape the square, the wine stall, and the villagers’ curiosity. It feels like a victory until I realize I still need to talk to Rachel. Hurrying through alleys, I rush to a perfect place along Rachel’s path home where we can speak unseen. If I can convince her to stop.

At the bend in the empty street right before Rachel’s home, I duck into a thin alley beside a stone barn. Concealed behind a large myrtle bush, I throw my bag to the ground and command my breathing to slow. Her eyes always muddle my mind, and lack of air won’t help.

Finally, her soft steps approach. I call quietly, “Rachel.”

Rachel gasps, almost dropping the amphora.

“In here.”

She peers into the bush. “Judah? What are you doing?” Her whisper sounds angry.

“I didn’t want to speak to you while the whole village watched.”

"So you decide to meet in the shadows? Alone?"

"Please, I must speak with you."

"Then ask Abba." Rachel shifts the amphora on her shoulder and glances up the empty lane.

"I don't think Asher would let me past the front door."

She sighs. "Yes, he would."

"With your sisters next to us? Or your whole family? We need privacy."

"That's not proper."

"Please, Rachel. I'm facing big decisions. I've discussed things with you my entire life."

"We're no longer children. We shouldn't talk alone."

"For a year, I've striven to banish you from my mind and heart. But I can't. Have you forgotten me?"

"We're so different, Judah. I prefer serious conversation, you like joking. I'm content in Meron, you're always trying to envision some plan so you can leave. Abba's decision was for the best."

"Maybe. Or maybe our differences draw us to each other, because I still desire you more than any other thing."

She steps back. Her breathing accelerates and her eyes glisten.

"I have an idea that can change everything. I want to know what you think. And"—I step closer, resisting my desire to touch her—"if it all works out, I want to know if you'll marry me. As we always hoped."

Rachel blinks, mouth agape.

"Please." I grab the amphora, but she won't let go. "Please!"

She moans softly. "You have one minute." Glancing around, she lets me take the container which I lean against the wall, and joins me behind the myrtle, standing an arm's length away.

"I've discovered a way to become a merchant. I'll trade luxury material and become wealthy, able to buy my family—our family—a fine house, full of luxuries."

She blushes, but her tone remains hard. "How?"

"I'll purchase cloth to sell here and in other villages at a profit."

"No. How will you get the money to begin? Your abba will never agree to such a risky venture."

"I don't have time to explain. But trust me—"

"Rachel!" A young voice calls from the courtyard.

"My family is looking for me. I must go."

"Give me a year to go make my fortune. Asher will have to accept a man who can care for you so well." Drawing breath, I dare my riskiest request. "Please don't become betrothed."

She bites her lip.

"Please don't accept some son of a dog who will never love you like I do." Impulsively, I grab her hands and pull her close. "Wait for me?"

"How long? For days? For years? And for what? I don't covet fancy things or servants to do my work. I like work. You offer me luxuries you don't possess and I don't desire."

"Rachel!" sings the child's voice again.

Rachel pulls away. "I must go. If Keren finds us here, not just my family will know, but the whole village." She deftly swings the amphora to her shoulder, holding my gaze the entire time. "Goodbye, Judah."

"Please answer. Will you wait for me?"

"How do I answer that? Everything you've said only raises more questions. How will you get money? Do you know how to run a business? You have many strengths, but your plan requires commitment. Patience." Rachel's urgency increases. "When have you ever been patient in your life? What have you ever persisted with?"

"You."

Afraid to breathe, I attempt to read her rigid posture, the only movement her headscarf flowing in the breeze and the light dancing through the bushes across her face. If she closes this door to us, I can never reopen it.

"You could've had me. I've wanted you since I was old enough to dream of my own family and have never seen myself with any man besides you. But in my dreams, we're here, attending synagogue, raising our children in the teachings of Adonai. But something's changed." She steps closer. "You no longer desire these things. The man in my dreams is the man you used to be."

If she had slapped me, I would hurt less. "So you wouldn't marry me if I returned with wealth and position?"

"I might. In spite of those things, not because of them. But Judah, you ask me to sit in Abba's house, grow older, and wait for you?"

"Could you marry another?"

"I gave you my heart long ago. I shouldn't have, but I did. Even so, yes, I could marry another. I might never love him like I love you, but I desire a home and children. I cannot remain with my parents, waiting for you to grow up."

My dreams yank me one direction and Rachel the other.

"Rachel!" The voice calls again, sounding worried.

"I must go now." She steps toward the street.

"Please, please wait for me."

Rachel looks at me and slowly shakes her head. "Coming!"

My heart rends completely.

Keren and another sister join her with questions about where she's been and why she's emerged from the bushes.

I can't watch her walk away. In the shadows, I lean against the wall and sink to the ground, head in my hands. A lark trills above my head, mocking me.

After a year of pushing her out of my heart, why had I opened myself to hope?

She won't wait for me? Fine. I won't wait either.

I stand and shake out my cloak. For a moment, I stare at my travel supplies, and then I know. It's time.

I'll demand my inheritance tonight. No more fear. No one, not even Rachel, can stop me.

"You're a coward and a fool!"

I reprimand myself while I shovel hay into the manger for some pregnant ewes. What's wrong with me? Another Shabbat has come and gone and still I haven't talked with Abba. I awaken with determination, but Abba looks tired. Or Eli needs my help. Or Seth glowers nearby.

As I walk out of the sheep pen, I feel the familiar squish under my foot. Sometimes I really hate sheep. At least when I'm at the tower, there's no manure.

Seth demands exactness for our tithe, so I measure the dill and mint harvest. As if Adonai actually cares about every herb's leaf.

By the end of the day, I'm filthy. So before evening meal, I wash myself, don a clean tunic, and tie on clean sandals. An unusual quiet hovers over the compound. Maybe Seth isn't home? When I reach the rooftop, I find only Abba reclining at the table.

"Are we dining alone tonight?" I try not to sound hopeful.

"It appears so."

We each speak our nightly blessing, "Blessed are you, O Lord our God, King of the Universe, who brings forth bread from the earth," and scoop lentils with the bread. As I dip hard-boiled eggs into garlic-infused olive oil and answer Abba's questions about the sheep, my insides knot and palms sweat. How do I begin? How do I ask Abba for what I have a right to only when he dies?

Abba discusses tenant properties and details about the renters like they genuinely interest him.

I appreciate our tenants more than Seth, but their lives bore me.

"Over in Cana, John and Jehudit just delivered an eighth son."

I place both hands on the table.

"So many boys, all dark haired—"

"I want my share of the estate now."

Abba's egg drops to the table.

"What?" He blinks at me. "What did you say?"

I stare at my white knuckles. "Abba, I'm requesting my inheritance now. Opportunities exist today—ones never before seen! I'll sell the property so I can invest in business. The yearly caravan west arrives soon. I'll travel with them to a trade center, work hard, and become a merchant. If all goes well, and I know it will, I'll bring money back. I'll help you in the end!"

Nothing will ever be the same. Either Abba will refuse me or grant my wish. Either way, my life changes now.

The oil lamps sputter and moths dance in the light as I raise my gaze. Shock, anger, and hurt mingle on Abba's face.

Jumping up, I pace the rooftop. Letting my plan escape my mind, my arms flap about with the energy of pent-up hopes. If I explain enough, certainly Abba will understand. Perhaps even agree.

Finally, I drop on the cushion beside him.

His same expression remains, only deeper. Sadder. Hasn't anything I said resonated?

We stare at each other.

"Sorry I'm late!" Seth ascends the stairs two at a time. "A wheel fell off the cart and—" He looks from Abba to me. "What's going on?"

"You'd better sit. Judah has something to tell you."

CHAPTER 10
ELI AND MIRIAM

Meron
Iyyar (April) AD 19

A wise son makes a glad father, but a foolish son is a sorrow to his mother.

PROVERBS 10:1

Eli

Outside of Master's doorway, I stretch and rub a crick in my neck. I may be too old to sleep sitting up. Sometimes I'm up all night during lambing time or if a freeze threatens. But the last time I slept outside this doorway was twenty years ago.

I stretch to the left and then right, easing my tight back. Dawn's gray just now pushes back the night and I walk slowly across the courtyard toward Methuselah.

Yesterday, as I returned from the fields, yelling and arguing reached me before I made it through our gate. Seth hurled words like *dishonor*, *shame*, and *disgrace* as if they were daggers. Villagers peeked out from doors, craning their heads from their own rooftop dinners. Once the boys stormed off, I helped Master to his room and he told me what Judah requested.

Methuselah stamps at a fly as I join him at the small mill barn. Morning mist and sunshine stream through slats of his pen, and the sheep bump about their enclosure next to him.

"Hello, old friend." Methuselah leans into my hand and I scratch his head. "Sorry. No food this morning. I'm avoiding the kitchen." Usually I pilfer treats while Miriam is distracted.

Sighing, I pray. "Oh, Most High, I ask for Your help. I must tell Miriam, and I don't know what to say. I must help Master Ezra and I don't know what to do."

Out of my side vision, I see Miriam across the courtyard staring at me. Without looking her way, I turn toward the barn. I'll help milk the sheep and goats. I'll assign tasks to servants in the barley fields. I'll inspect the flax to determine when to harvest. I'll stay busy and away from Miriam.

I'll tell her what's going on. Eventually. As soon as I have the strength.

Miriam

Certainly Eli will tell me what's going on. He might delay as long as possible, but he'll tell me. So I'll just wait. I'll be fine—as long as I haven't dried up like a raisin from the glare of my worry and fear.

Neither Ezra nor his sons ate this morning. In fact, all three are yet to be seen. We servants keep our heads down and hands busy, waiting for whatever comes next, heaven help us. I fetch eggs, tend my garden, and chop vegetables.

"How can I know when to put out meals if no one leaves their rooms?" I check the stone water jars and then start chopping leeks. "I wish someone bothered to inform me of what's happening. Not that I matter."

Sighing, I pour water on the barley flour and mix. "Adonai, I know Eli works out problems internally. It took me years to learn that he needs time, like grape juice fermenting into wine. It's frustrating, but that's my husband." I add more water.

"But Adonai, those brothers last night! So angry." I add leaven. "They're as opposite as Esau and Jacob, who also stayed at each other's throats, now didn't they? Jacob cheated Esau and ran off. You know Adonai, I've always wondered how Jacob wound up being who we admire when he cheated and lied and such. But we place him right there with Abraham and Isaac, so I guess everything worked out for him. I've always felt a little sorry for Esau, though."

"You feel sorry for Esau? Do I need to send for Rabbi Akiva?"

I startle at my husband's voice after such a quiet, stress-filled day. My doughy fists plant on my hips, and my lips purse.

He grins. "You don't want anyone to hear you denigrating one of our fathers."

"Who has time to bother with me? No one tells me what's happening, even when I live with the results. I'm walking on eggshells around here, avoiding the family but preparing what they might require just in case." With the back of my hand I wipe sweat from my forehead and glare at this infuriating man.

Eli's countenance falls as he draws the curtain across the doorway, darkening the room. Finally! After wiping my hands, I light the oil lamp on the table, and the glow illuminates his furrowed brow. He sinks to a cushion and his back curves as if carrying the world.

From my own cushion, I reach across and squeeze his hand. "Tell me."

He squeezes back and presses his lips together. I try to not fidget. He'll speak when he's ready. Certainly.

"Judah requested his portion of the estate last night."

"What?" My ears buzz. "No. He can't do that, can he?" I put my hand on my chest, afraid my heart might leap out. "You must be wrong. Judah couldn't do something so unthinkable. He wouldn't!"

"He told Master he wants his inheritance now so he can become a merchant in a faraway city where he'll be happy, wealthy, and free." He rubs his temples.

"He said that? Did he also say, 'I tried to wait, but you wouldn't die fast enough'?"

Silence fills the dim room. The oil lamp, seldom lit during the day, casts dancing shadows on the wall, but I barely notice. I can't make sense of this. Doesn't Judah understand the shame he will bring on his father? On all of us?

"How could he do such a thing? Is there no hope?"

Eli shakes his head. "I doubt we can stop this. Ezra could've banished him last night, if he wished. He could still throw him out or have him beaten."

"I can't imagine such a thing, as much as Judah deserves it."

"Even knowing Master for so long, I don't know what he'll decide. He tried to reason with Judah, explaining how rejecting the family rejects Adonai. But Judah refused to listen."

"No wonder Seth yelled with such fury."

"Yes. Judah spoke with Master alone first, but then Seth came home. I've never seen him so angry. This affects him too."

"How did Ezra react?"

"He's as broken as when Anna died."

Oh, the overwhelming sorrow when our mistress died. The months after her passing cloaked the home in darkness. Eventually, Ezra forced himself to rejoin life for the sake of his sons.

"At least Anna grieved her own leaving. On her death bed, she apologized, as if death gave her a choice. She'd wanted to stay, but the Holy One had written the number of her days. Death hurt, but everyone trusted the Almighty with what He allowed."

Eli says, "Well, while the Almighty might determine life's length, He never limited the days a son should honor his abba. Ezra leaned on my arm and told me what Judah had asked, and then all I'd heard made sense. He asked me to pray that he'll know how to respond."

"Oh, Eli."

"I slept outside his room last night. Just in case he needed anything."

"I saw you this morning. You were talking to Methuselah."

Eli moves to my cushion and embraces me—a rare occurrence during the day. "I was also praying."

"I heard you praying," I continue. "Did you get an answer?"

Eli stands with a chuckle and draws back the curtain. Leaning against the doorframe, he surveys the compound. "After I pleaded for help, I realized all I *must* do is love Adonai, serve Ezra, and care for you. I can't fix Judah or keep Seth from making matters worse. You and Ezra provide plenty of responsibility."

"Has Judah been so happy lately because he figured out a scheme to escape what he considers confinement?"

"I suppose so."

"And here I was, thinking he had matured! But he's the same boy, always looking for the next thing instead of enjoying what's staring him in the face. And now he pains his father and shames his family."

"He sees himself and no one else. Can't he imagine the ramifications? I keep thinking, 'A foolish son is a grief to his father and bitterness to her who bore him.'[1]"

"And to her who raised him!" I grab the dough from its wooden trough and knead, even though it isn't ready yet. How could Judah be so selfish? How? And poor Ezra. I ache for him. He does not deserve such a son. I slap and pound the dough.

"You know that bread didn't do anything wrong."

Flour coats my tunic and apron. "What do we do Eli? What do we do?"

"Keep your eye out for Master. He's praying, and I imagine fasting as well. I think he slipped out to the synagogue, but I'm not sure. You might take him food, though I doubt he'll eat. No one else should take anything to him, though. Only you."

I'm grateful for a task to busy my mind. "I'll make a tray and put it where he can find it. Some fresh water and a little wine, which he might want even if he doesn't eat."

"You're a good woman."

"I'm a foolish woman who succumbed to that rascal's winsome smile and warm hugs." I dash away tears. "How could he do this?"

Eli rubs my shoulders. "That's why I've avoided telling you. With as much as you love him, I knew how devastated you would be."

I lean back on him, grateful that Eli understands me.

"I don't know how he came to this either," Eli says. "But we must hide our frustration and grief so as not to make things worse. Say whatever you want to me, but we must support Master completely."

"Well, of course." I nod curtly. He really thinks I need to be reminded how to act?

Eli caresses my cheek before he leaves.

I sigh. I'll need to guard against taking my frustration out on Eli, the one person I can depend on no matter what happens—even if he does tell me what I already know.

CHAPTER 11
JUDAH

Villa of Valerius
Av (July) AD 20

If they violate my statutes and do not keep my commandments, then I will punish their transgression with the rod and their iniquity with stripes, but I will not remove from him my steadfast love or be false to my faithfulness.

PSALM 89:31- 33

I've rarely bumped into Cali and Kato since being assigned to the pigs, and I keep my distance from Khafra. Really, I just avoid everyone, as much as possible.

But, this evening, the aroma of simmering soup attracts me to the servants' fire like an oil lamp draws moths.

The two boys wave. Cali extends a clay cup. "Water with wine! You want?"

"And soup!" Kato slurps from a bowl.

Their Aramaic sure has improved.

"Thank you," I mumble to Cali, accepting the cup of reddish water. Even the touch of wine improves the flavor.

"It speaks!" Prisca's hard face and bitter eyes take away from her sultry beauty.

I sit by Kato who flashes his big smile. Maybe he'll give me some soup so I can leave. But Prisca continues. "Your accent isn't Ephesian. So where's home?"

"Judea."

"God's chosen people, I hear. Tell me, did God choose you to be a slave? To feed pigs and live on bread?"

"Apparently." Too bad Pavlos accompanies Valerius on a trip into Iconium. I could use his help.

"Prisca, he's probably too hungry to talk," says Khafra. "Soup might loosen his tongue."

I'd do almost anything for hot soup instead of dry bread.

"The cook gave me scraps today"—Prisca lifts a wooden spoon—"and Erastos procured goat bones."

Erastos, the goatherd, shrugs. I assume procure is another word for steal.

Prisca stirs the pot, releasing a savory aroma. "Soup for your story."

Anonymity or soup? Food wins. Besides, I don't have to tell much. "All right. But I eat first."

Though it burns my tongue, the hearty broth can't get into me fast enough until a sudden stomach cramp makes me stop short. "I might be sick."

"You ate too fast. But that won't get you out of telling your story. We have all night."

I hug my middle as my insides revolt. Retching would waste the first warm food I've tasted in months, and if willpower matters, I'll keep this meal inside.

A sip of water eases my nausea.

Someone throws dung on the fire, and Prisca goads me. "Well?"

I'd best get this over with. "I come from a small village in north Galilee. My family owns sheep and grows olives. My Abba—" My voice catches. "My brother—" A stomach cramp seizes me again, but I push through and describe home. And once I start, I, surprisingly, can't stop, until—

"I no believe," interrupts the donkey handler on my other side, his rancid breath erasing the soup aroma. "If you was rich and had so big vineyards, how be you sitting with us, looking like one day from feeding vultures?"

"Yes. How did you wind up here?" Prisca challenges.

How can I explain? I describe Seth's anger, Meron's expectations, and a girl named Rachel who'd never be mine. Nausea returns, but this time from regret. "So I took my inheritance and went into business," I conclude. My whole body heaves a sigh. "Between corrupt businessmen, wrecked ships, and a drought, I lost everything. My debts landed me in"—I choke on the word—"slavery." Flinging my empty hands out, I say, "Now I have nothing. Not even an interesting story."

Prisca's angry face flames more than the fire. "Your father loved you? Provided for you? No one beat or abused you? You woke to food? And you ran away? From that!"

I swallow.

She hugs her knees. "My father, who only knew how to be cruel, sold me to pay his debts. I've been used from then until now for whatever my master wants, whenever he wants." Her voice rises. "I work all day, but never enough to please anyone. Then, at night, I'm called to Valerius's bed unless I'm lucky and he desires his wife or another servant. This will be my life until they throw me onto the rubbish heap. For that's all I am. Trash."

Her face, dappled with firelight, looks carved from stone. "How could you walk out on so much love?"

Why hadn't I guarded my words? I have no answer for her question.

Slowly, people pair off to discuss tomorrow's work. No one speaks to me. From my filthy body to my dirty clothes, labor's stink surrounds me. But my soul smells worse. Quietly, I drag myself to my home with the pigs, where I recommit to avoiding everyone.

How could you walk out on so much love? The question haunts me. I hadn't just walked. I'd run, ripped out hearts, stomped on my heritage, taken from my family, kept what I wanted, and discarded the rest.

Huddling in my thin blanket, I attempt sleep, but every time I close my eyes, I only see Abba's back. I spend a restless night trying to remember his face.

"GALLUS WANTS you ready to leave in three days." Pavlos hobbles up as I clean the barn.

"No!" My vehemence shocks both of us.

"You knew this was coming, Judah. You've known from your first day here. The pigs always go to the hills this time of year."

"What will they eat?" I protest. "Everything's dead."

"They'll survive on whatever they find."

"Well, I won't!"

Pavlos nods. "It'll be difficult for you. You're expected to forage and thankfully the hills contain many insects."

"Insects! I don't eat 'swarming things', as you probably know."

"Like you never ate pork in Ephesus? Anyway, I believe locusts are allowed."

Driving my fingers through my curls, my finger catches on a knot. "Ouch!" I let go a string of curses I learned at The Crow. I experience enough pain without hurting myself.

Pavlos just laughs. "Listen, I'll try to hold back bread before you go, but that won't last long. You must eat anything—*anything*. That's the only way you'll survive."

"Well, what will I drink?"

"In the early morning lick the dew off the plants. You must fill your skins at any well you come across. Consume any liquid you can. Do you understand?"

"No, and I don't want to."

"Throw out all your standards. In a drought like this, do what you must to survive."

For the next two days, my anxiety and hopelessness hang around my neck like a millstone.

At least it's summer, though nights in the hills can be chilly. Tonight, my last night here, I build a fire in the courtyard, absorbing the security that walls and gates provide.

Pavlos's familiar limp invades my gloom. "Shalom, son of Abraham. Everyone else staying inside?"

"Or away from me." I poke the fire with a stick as he sits beside me. I haven't made eye contact with or spoken to anyone since the other night.

"Ah, yes. I'm sorry I missed that. Someday, you must share your tale with me."

"Not unless you ply me with hot soup and a touch of wine."

"I rarely have either." He extends a bundle. "But here's an extra cloak—old and mended many times. Still, it'll offer protection. I also gathered what skins I could, though they may require repair."

As I inspect the gifts, gratitude breaks through my despair. I stroke the coarse, brown wool, a luxury in a life of minimal sustenance.

"Thank you, Pavlos. This might be the grandest garment I ever possessed."

Pavlos's eyebrow lifts.

I laugh bitterly. "Yes, I've fallen from the fine silk and linen I wore in Ephesus to calling this"—I stick my finger through a hole—"beautiful. Still, it'll warm me."

"Ah, life gives perspective." Pavlos lifts the hem. "When this scratchy, ill-woven cloak represents survival, it is transformed. Neither silk nor linen would protect you on those hills. 'One who is full loathes honey, but to one who is hungry everything bitter is sweet.'[1]"

"How do you know Hebrew?"

He tosses dung on the fire. "I know many languages. I've heard and seen much in my seventy years."

"Why didn't you tell Valerius I'm a Jew?"

"You're a slave. All he cares about is your ability to work. Besides, I don't tell other peoples' stories. We have little else left."

A distant howl sends a chill down my spine, and I move closer to the fire.

"Now let me ask you a question. When you left home, were you running to or from something?"

"Both, I guess. The hungrier I get, the less I remember."

"What once seemed unbearable can become a mere inconvenience compared to how bad things can be."

"I felt so . . . so . . . I just . . ." What? That if I had freedom, if life looked like I wanted, if I had a successful business, I'd no longer be unhappy? "Tell me, Pavlos, since you know so much, why is finding happiness so hard?"

"A question for the sages, yet they have no answer. Why do you think happiness is something you can find?"

"What do you mean?"

"It's not bread or gold. You can't possess it."

"Well, you seem happy." His smiling face reflects golden in the firelight. "I've never met a man so content. I don't understand."

His gappy smile broadens. "Do you mean how can I, a man with a bum leg, bent spine, and no freedom, be joyful?"

"Yeah, something like that."

I add fuel to the fire and sparks dance into the night.

Pavlos closes his eyes. "I've lost so much and I am now trapped in a life I would never choose, but, 'For God alone, O my soul, wait in silence, for my hope is from him. He only is my rock and my salvation, my fortress; I shall not be shaken. On God rests my salvation and my glory; my mighty rock, my refuge is God.'[2]"

Wind whistles through the courtyard, stoking the fire. But, I feel more warmed by the words.

"How do you know the Psalms?"

"There's more to my story, as there is to yours. But that's enough for tonight. Tomorrow I'll guide you to the hills astride my trusty steed. I'll meet you at the back gate right after I distribute the morning bread."

"And you'll tell me more?"

Pavlos grunts and hefts himself up, in his awkward way, wincing. I wonder if he always hurts. He seldom shows it.

"Maybe. For now, Judah, don't wonder at my knowing these words. Wonder at the words! You have access to a hope that's as steady as a rock. You can hide in a refuge as unshakeable as a fortress. Your situation doesn't change that. Isn't that a reason to be happy?"

I look away.

"Tomorrow, then. Sleep well." Pavlos hobbles off to bolt the gates.

The cloak smells like dirt, barn life, and hard work. I shake it and trapped dirt joins the smoke swirling upward. Miriam would never approve.

I add the last bits of wood and dung to the fire and wrap myself in the crude garment. Under its filth, I smell wool. It reminds me of home. For the hundredth time, I wonder if anyone misses me.

The thought of Seth missing me evokes a bitter laugh. He'd rejoice at my humiliation. He was right. I was wrong. I'd rather die in the wilderness with the swine than crawl back to him. Not that I have that option.

Trailing after the pigs, I leave the compound. The estate, which once felt like a prison, now seems like a haven compared to the approaching unknown.

At least Pavlos accompanies me astride his mottled, lop-eared donkey, Gaidoros, who obeys Pavlos without hesitation. Maybe repulsive exteriors hide beautiful hearts.

All morning we trudge the dusty road, dodging pig waste. Pavlos breaks the monotony. "A story will help pass the journey."

"How far are we going?"

"Farther still. Master Valerius ordered me to stay with you tonight." He leans closer. "He doesn't want to lose his pigs."

I'm more expendable than swine. I scowl.

"Oh, Judah." Pavlos laughs. "Stop wasting time being offended and be grateful. I brought extra food. We'll have time to relax by a fire tonight. See the good."

"Fine. Tell me your story."

Looking toward the horizon, he smiles faintly. "My story—yes. Though my memories seem like a mist fleeing from the sun."

"Whatever that means."

"You'll understand when you're old."

"Are you Jewish?"

"Yes, I'm a son of Abraham, and blessed to be so, though I can't live as the Law prescribes."

"How'd you become a slave?"

"When I was young, about twelve-years-old, Parthians attacked my village in Syria." His voice becomes serious. "We tried to fight, but we were farmers, not soldiers. A horse trampled me, breaking my leg and back. I couldn't move." He slowly wipes his eyes. "I couldn't protect my family. The raiders killed my grandmother with all the other elderly. They—" His usually jovial face is pure sadness. "They ravaged my sisters along with all the other young women."

"I'm sorry, Pavlos."

"Yes. I am too. They took the ones who survived to the slave market." He slaps his bum leg. "Being damaged goods, I was sold cheap from one master to another, most of them cruel and difficult. Finally, I landed with Valerius, who's kinder than many."

"He's kind?" I snort.

"Compared to others. For him I've worked hard to learn and become a blessing. Even here, even like this, Adonai has plans for me."

"Did you ever see your family again?"

He shakes his head slowly.

What comfort can I offer? I voluntarily fled my family. "What was your name?"

"What?"

"As a boy—your name?"

"That name belongs to someone long gone."

I squint against the glare of the relentless sun and cough as the dust the pigs stir up dries my throat.

"How did you survive?"

He rocks from side to side atop Gaidoros. "By remembering the Words. My father drilled me as a boy and I feared forgetting them, so I repeated them as I worked. Every law, psalm, and prophetic proclamation became my food.

"When I had no bread, I became like Jeremiah. He ate the Lord's words[3], and they became the delight of his soul. They were, and are, my delight, because they taught me to endure.

"When brokenhearted from never hearing one kind word, I remembered, 'How precious is Your lovingkindness, O God!'[4]

"When cruel men abused me, I remembered"—he lifts a fist and yells to the hills—"'The Lord is my strength and my shield; in him my heart trusts, and I am helped!'[5]"

"Why did you not despair?"

Pavlos chuckles. "Who says I haven't despaired?"

"You never seem sad. I'd rather—" I turn away.

"What? Die?" Shifting his weight, Pavlos takes a swig from his waterskin before passing it to me. "Don't assume I haven't wished for death. I'm an old man who's had many chances to despair. But I'm not dead, so I live. You'll face the same decision. What will you choose?"

What will I choose? How long can I live with these animals as my only companions? I scoop small stones from the road and throw one at a pig's backside. It squeals and runs off the path, the others careening after him.

"Come back, you stupid pigs!"

Pavlos howls with laughter. Wiping his eyes, he looks into my angry face. "Don't be mad at me. You started this. Go round them up!"

Already tired and hot, I run after the spooked animals. Why do I always make my life harder?

CHAPTER 12
SETH

Meron
Iyyar (April), AD 19

May he send you help from the sanctuary and give you support from Zion!

PSALM 20:2

H*urry*, I urge myself. Usually I'm not late for morning prayers. But usually a foolish brother hasn't turned my world upside down by attempting to destroy our affluence and rip apart our family.

This morning, I crave the peace inside the synagogue. I need it. I wonder if I can pray enough for Adonai to change Judah's mind?

"Oh—sorry!" I almost run over a woman carrying a baby.

She answers me with, "Humph."

I force my feet to slow. After straightening my tunic, I tighten my belt and smooth my beard. Inside the cool stone interior, shafts of daylight from the high windows slice between the shadows. But I'm not yet ready to join the men already gathered.

Standing in a shadow, I mutter a prayer, "Adonai, Isaiah said, 'You keep him in perfect peace whose mind is stayed on you, because he trusts in you.'[1] Peace seems impossible. Please help me anchor my mind on You, because now all I have is anger."

Something moves in the shadowy corner. Abba? Any hope of peace flies out the windows. He displays his grief, rocking back and forth, arms crossed, head covered by his cloak. I cough, but his swaying never wavers.

Uncle Daniel approaches. "Shalom, Seth. Is your abba—?"

Abba's rocking form catches Daniel's eye. "Ezra?"

No response.

"Ezra, prayers are beginning. Will you join us?"

"What?" Abba, his voice cracking, looks up with red-rimmed eyes. "I'm coming." Kissing his tassels, he heaves himself as though carrying a full sack of grain.

Men exchange glances. Curious eyes examine me. Shoulders shrug, but I hold my head high. Today, for the last time, I stand untainted by scandal.

Uncle Daniel also raises his eyebrows at me, but I shake my head slightly. He and everyone else can stew. They'll know the truth soon enough.

With Abba on my right, I draw my cloak over my head.

"Let us begin." Rabbi Akiva lifts his hands.

In unison, we chant the Shema. "'Hear, O Israel: The Lord our God, the Lord is one! You shall love the Lord your God with all your heart and with all your soul and with all your might!'[2]"

For a few blessed moments, I abandon reality and immerse myself in the words.

CHAPTER 13
JUDAH

Meron
Iyyar, (April) AD 19

All the ways of a man are pure in his own eyes, but the LORD weighs the spirit.

PROVERBS 16:2

"Woah!" When my gray donkey, stumbles, I grab the pommel with one hand and pat his neck with the other. "I know it's been a long trip, and I'm uncomfortable too. But home is near!" Well, my soon-to-be former home.

The condemnation I've endured since my announcement made me glad to flee. Even Miriam ignored me.

These past three weeks traveling to find buyers for our farthest holdings has proved more difficult than I'd hoped. My biggest problem? I need hard coin. Bartering holds no value. Since only the shrewd keep coins, the price dropped quickly. If I'd been patient, if I'd taken my time, if I'd been willing to walk away from the bargaining table . . .

But I don't have time for potential purchasers to gather funds. The yearly caravan arrives soon. I must be ready.

So, with Abba's ring to give me authority, I sold my third of Abba's estate. Mine. My decision. My business. On one hand, I should have sold it for more. On the other hand, I now possess more money than is safe to carry as I travel alone. What if someone robs me before I start?

I urge my ride to an uncomfortable trot.

Finally, Mount Meron looms on the horizon. What a relief to jostle up the road running through the fields to the village. Kefir turns from his wheat field. That man always wants to be the first to know who approaches so he'll have a story to tell.

"Shalom, Kefir!" I wave.

He shields his eyes against the descending sun, drops his hand, stares a moment longer, and deliberately turns his back to me. That's odd.

"Shalom, Asher," I nod as I pass him on the road. He strides into the field, away from me.

Joseph faces me, but with sad eyes. When he visited me before I left for this trip, he tried to talk me out of leaving. Our conversation dissolved into argument. Now, nothing remains to be said. He nods and goes back to work.

After Malik gives me his back, I understand. They think I broke faith with them all. Leaving my family means I'm abandoning the community. Fine. Let them keep their backward ways. I don't care.

To my right, Reuben directs a few men building the tower, now at least six cubits tall. I hope sunburn covers the shame tinging my cheeks.

When I ride through our gate, only Rufus greets me. Miriam ducks into the kitchen. Eli heads into the barn. And the other servants follow suit, leaving me to fend for myself.

I unload my heavy bags into my dark room with an empty water bucket. Rufus whimpers at my doorway.

"At least you still like me," I whisper, petting the dog's head.

Leading the donkey to the barn, I toss the reins to Matthias.

"Get Eli," I instruct the young servant.

"Eli," he calls out as he tugs the protesting donkey into the barn.

After a few moments, Eli approaches. "Yes?"

I remove the ring with the family seal and thrust it at him. "Please return this to Abba."

While he stares at the ring in his palm, I fill my bucket. In my room, I light two lamps, and close my door.

Emptying every bag and pocket, I stack the coins, from mite to denarius, and start counting. My smile grows. I lace my fingers behind my head and tip my stool onto the back two legs. Even poor deals have accumulated to an impressive sum. And I still have a few local holdings to sell.

At a quiet knock, I slam down and sweep the coins into a large leather pouch. "Enter!"

"Sir." Without looking at me, Tova places a tray on my table and departs. Wine, bread, olives, dates, and one of Miriam's spiced date cakes. I inhale the cinnamon and cloves. No one but Miriam hands out her cakes. Though I haven't dared face her since requesting my inheritance, at least she hasn't forsaken me.

Like a dam breaking, a laugh escapes, releasing deal-making-tension, road-weariness, and community-shunning sorrow. I drink deeply and plop a date in my mouth. My dream, though costing me, draws closer and will be worth every painful step.

"That completes our transaction. I congratulate you on an excellent trade." Crispus pats his large stomach.

Not as satisfied, I attempt a smile. Crispus, one of the few Gentiles in Meron, doesn't shun me, but he also knows I must leave with the caravan tomorrow. Again, I'm in a poor position to make a good deal on land sales or animal purchase. Tucking my money pouch into my belt, I shake the merchant's hand.

"Please deliver the camel to my home." While I hate the stubborn, spitting animal, it carries more than a donkey, so I need one for my trip to Caesarea.

I exit the dim building into blinding sunlight. I wait under the flapping burlap awning for my eyes to adjust. I'd hoped for more, but still I have enough. Enough to leave. Enough to venture. Enough.

As I walk down the street, friends turn away upon recognizing me, like I'm a leper.

Deborah, Samuel's wife, points at me as she bends to speak to her three sons, probably warning them not to grow up like me. Well, good luck. Catching the eldest's gaze, I wink.

When I reach home, a crowd congregates at our gate. Too drained to face them, I detour onto a narrow side street that spills out on the hill, to circle around and enter through the back gate.

Near the back gate, young Ben-Timaeus counts.

". . . Sixty-one, sixty-two. . ." Jockeying for position, the sheep enter the gate one by one.

"What's the commotion at the gate?"

". . . Ninety-seven, ninety-eight, ninety-nine." He latches the gate and wipes his brow. "A young lamb went missing. Abba's been searching since last night."

At the sound of Timaeus's singing, we both look to the mountain. "'For you have delivered my soul from death, my eyes from tears, my feet from stumbling. I will walk before the Lord in the land of the living.'[1]" He pats the creature laying around his tall shoulders and strides up.

"You found him!"

"Yes, son. He likes to run away, if one can presume to know a renegade lamb's mind."

I ruffle the lamb's wooly head. "He looks secure on your shoulders."

"Join us, Judah-ben-Ezra, in celebration! My family waits at the front gate."

"These days, I dampen joy."

"Yes, I've heard," Timaeus says. "Safe journey, and may Adonai bless your steps and your days. And may He bring you back to us."

"I don't want Adonai to bring me back, but thanks anyway."

"Then may you receive what He wants and desire His will most."

I wait for a smart retort. Nothing comes to mind, and he and Bentimaeus have walked off anyway.

Stealing through the back gate, I edge across the bustling courtyard and into my shadowy room. Lighting a lamp, I check my belongings one more time.

I slap my forehead. "I should have said, 'As long as His will is that I succeed.' Why can't I ever think of the right response in the moment?"

It's early to retire, but I don't want to see anyone. After months of dreaming about my future successes, those dreams become reality at sunrise. Some difficult goodbyes face me in the morning, but I won't have to confront Seth. We've avoided each other for weeks. How will I say farewell to Miriam and Eli? And how can I face Abba?

CHAPTER 14
SETH

Meron
Iyyar (April) AD 19

Weep not for him who is dead, nor grieve for him, but weep bitterly for him who goes away, for he shall return no more to see his native land.

JEREMIAH 22:10

I storm across the courtyard that buzzes with preparations for the caravan's departure tomorrow. Servants walk away from me as I approach, chickens scurry for their roosts, and Rufus slinks whining toward the barn.

"Eli! Where's Abba?"

He doesn't look up from the wax tablet where he records the number of wool bundles. "I believe he's in the gathering room."

He calls something else, but I'm already halfway across the noisy courtyard.

"It's done?" I ask, barging into the room.

Reclined at the three-sided table, Abba doesn't flinch. "Seth, please greet our guest. Hasan, you remember Seth, my older son?"

On the right couch, Abu Bakkar Hasan, the caravan manager, bows his head in greeting. Set with glass dishes, the table looks like a celebration when we should be mourning. Can't Abba offer this heathen hospitality without inviting him to our table? I cannot feast with such a man.

Wrapped in orange silks with green embroidery, the Arab smells like sweat and myrrh.

"Seth-bar-Ezra. So wonderful to see you."

"Hasan," I say, shifting from one foot to the other.

"Will you join us?" Abba points to the left couch.

Hospitality rules become such an inconvenience when this type needs lodging. Most Jews would never host an Arab, and certainly never eat with one. Rabbi Yakov certainly wouldn't approve, so I remain standing, unsure what to do with my hands.

Abba asks Hasan about wheat prices, his children's health, and the Roman prefect.

Eventually, Hasan stares at me. Clearing his throat, he says, "I'm afraid I need to attend to business. Wouldn't it be nice if servants did their duties without supervision? I hate to cause you more work, but could you possibly have food delivered to my room?"

"Certainly, my friend." Abba smiles. "Whatever you prefer." After several more pleasantries, the oriental barbarian bows and exits.

"With all the tragedy within our walls, you're entertaining such a man!" My voice shakes.

All pretense of cheerfulness falls away, and Abba sags. "It'd be shameful to turn him away, regardless the excuse."

When Abba wrings his hands, my anger fades. However, I won't assure Abba that all will be okay, because that's a lie. We're one-third poorer than we were a month ago. And we stink of Judah's disgrace.

As he slumps on his couch, Abba buries his head in his hands. "And to answer your first question, yes, it's done. All transactions are completed, though I haven't asked for details. Judah has converted all he could to cash and must be wearing a weighty money belt."

Seeing Abba devoid of his normal strength and joy jolts me back to the night Eema died. I was just five years old and his abject pain terrified me. I can't recall any time, other than after Eema's death, that he has cried like this. I sit beside him, encircling his trembling shoulders.

"Oh, Abba, I'm sorry—"

Miriam and two servant girls bustle in with trays overflowing with cheese, date and fig cakes, fresh fruit, and other delicacies. They halt and I jerk my arm away.

"Why didn't you knock, Miriam!"

Miriam's eyes narrow and she stands ramrod straight. As boys, when we got into mischief and she drew herself up like a Roman spear, we knew we were in real trouble. Thankfully, when she observes Abba's slumped shoulders and bent head, her stance softens.

From outside, a joyous cry invades the somber room. Abba doesn't seem to notice.

"I'm sorry," says Miriam in a gentle tone. "I didn't mean to disturb you." For me, her face and words harden. "Sorry, Seth. I didn't know you were here. As directed, we brought refreshments for Ezra and the Arab. Has he stepped out or left all together?"

Of course, they would serve Abba's guests as quietly as possible. But I won't apologize. "He's left for the evening."

Miriam looks from the three trays of feast Abba special-ordered and back again.

"Leave the food here so Abba and I can eat."

"Fine." She directs the girls hiding behind her to set out the food. Succulent aromas fill the room, turning my stomach. I can't eat. I doubt Abba can either.

"Thank you, Miriam." Abba doesn't lift his head. "You prepared a beautiful feast."

"Please let me know if you need anything else." Miriam's voice cracks.

"Why are people celebrating outside?"

"Timaeus found the lost lamb and his family and a few others have gathered."

Abba attempts a smile. "Finding what's lost brings great joy. Why don't you set aside food to take to Hasan's room? And some for Seth?" Abba squeezes my hand. "Give the rest to the party."

Considering others when his own heart lies in pieces? I can't decide if I admire or disdain that.

"As you wish." Miriam begins gathering food. "Seth, would you like us to make you a plate now, or would you prefer to eat later?"

"Um, I—" I can't make a simple decision? "Later. I'll eat later."

"Fine. I'll leave some wine, bread, and cheese just in case." Once finished, she whisks from the room.

After refilling Abba's goblet, I pour some wine for myself and raise the goblet to my lips when—curse it all! I forgot to wash! I slam the goblet, making Abba wince. I return to find Abba's lips moving as he rocks. A fly buzzes around the fruit bowl, and the sounds of celebration filter through the windows.

"Amen," Abba whispers.

"Amen," I echo, though I'm not sure I would agree with all his prayers.

Another cheer resounds outside. Miriam must have delivered the food. Someone sings, others join in, and the volume and energy swell.

"Abba, please drink." I push his goblet closer.

"Thank you, Seth, for your presence and care."

Foolish Judah. Does he even realize how he hurts our family?

Abba sips his wine. "I don't want to be with people tonight. Your interruption saved me from a long night feigning interest in Hasan's meandering stories." Another cheer resounds outside, and Abba gives a weak smile. "They celebrate finding the lost lamb. I grieve the son who is about to be lost. Could you help me up?" Rising with a grunt, he envelops me in a fierce hug. "Thank you, my son," he whispers, kisses my cheek, and leaves.

I'm never alone in this room we use for guests and groups. Reclining in the quiet solitude, I try some bread, but it tastes like straw. For a long time, I sip wine and stare into the oil lamp's dancing flame. Slowly, a tear slides down my cheek. Crying? Why am I crying? I dash the tear away, grateful I'm alone. But another soon follows, and another.

Sadness I've pushed away since Judah's betrayal demands release.

Sadness for Abba's pain. For losing part of our fortune. For the decrease in our respectability. For—

I take another drink and realize I weep for something I never imagined I'd grieve: the loss of my little brother.

CHAPTER 15
JUDAH

Meron
Iyyar (April) AD 19

Where shall I go from your Spirit? Or where shall I flee from your presence?

PSALM 139:7

Finally, streams of sunlight announce the day. Excitement prevented deep sleep, but I don't care. I'll sleep next year, when I'm prosperous.

"I don't have to wear these anymore," I remind myself as I wrap my tzitzit in a scrap of blue linen and plunge them deep into a bundle. Around my waist, I tie on my money belt—my future depends on its bulk. Next comes my new, blue chiton, over which I layer a cloak, the tan, brown, and blue stripes a perfect compliment. I'll buy Roman looking clothes in Ephesus.

"Matthias?"

He rushes across the busy courtyard.

"Load these last bundles on my camel." I hate camels. Yesterday, when I bought her, she spat at me.

"Yes, sir. Anything else?"

"Would you fill these waterskins?"

"Yes, sir."

That just leaves food. Which means I need to go in the kitchen. Which means I must see Miriam.

Drawing a deep breath, I duck through the doorway. The table overflows with wrapped packages and new wineskins. Miriam's back remains stalwart as she chops food on the counter. How do I say goodbye to the woman who's cared for me my whole life? She's always been more family than servant. I shift my feet and rub my sweaty hands on my cloak.

"Ezra ordered provisions for your journey," Miriam doesn't turn around. "But keep them separate. I don't want any Gentile food contaminating your supplies."

"How did you know it was me?"

"You've rushed into this kitchen the same way your whole life. I know your sounds as well as your face."

Someday I'll send her an expensive gift, but now I must flee before I lose my confidence.

"Thank you. I'll need something to pack this in."

"Here, my dear—" Eli rushes through the door.

I lock eyes with him.

Handing a satchel to Miriam, he hurries out.

Silence fills the room's corners. I hand her food packets that she stows in the bag, stuffing it full. I wouldn't have packed so much. I hope I can take care of myself.

Our hands brush as she stuffs in the last bit.

"Thank you, Miriam." My voice cloudy, I grab her hands. "I'll remember you with each meal."

"Don't forget to wash and thank Adonai."

"I won't."

After I kiss her worn hands, I grab the bag and bolt into the courtyard. Her sob breaks as I leave, but I'd go hungry before I'd go back in there.

One goodbye remains. I spot Abba under the arbor with Abu Bakkar Hasan, and I stride over.

"Shalom, Abba." I say as naturally as possible. "Shalom, Hasan."

"Salaam, Judah." Hasan stands with a grunt. "I hope you're prepared for the journey. We leave any moment."

"Yes, the servants have loaded my bags. And Miriam's packed enough food to travel to Rome and back. Thank you, Abba."

Abba twirls the signet ring on his finger. "You're welcome, son."

Son.

I grasp at words to fill the chasm between us. "I'll enjoy her date cakes."

A wan smile responds.

Hasan says, "I'm sorry to cut your goodbyes short, but we must depart. Ezra, thank you for your business and hospitality. I always anticipate my visits to your home. You're a good man."

"Thank you, Hasan." Abba stands. "May Adonai bless your trip and prosper your business."

"And may Hubal bless yours." Hasan grabs a few more dates on his way out.

"I must leave now." What a ridiculous thing to say.

Rising, Abba places his hands on my head, and presses his forehead to mine. "'The Lord bless you and keep you; the Lord make his face to shine upon you and be gracious to you; the Lord lift up his countenance upon you and give you peace.'[1]"

As Abba's voice resonates, I grasp his forearm.

"Remember Adonai's word to our father Jacob. 'Return to the land of your fathers and to your relatives, and I will be with you.'[2]" His voice grows husky. "Judah, my son, you can always return."

"I will someday. With wealth."

"You may return without it."

I pull away. "Shalom, Abba." With a single nod, I walk away. Emotions knot my insides—frustration at Abba's last words, regret for hurting Miriam and Eli, sorrow over losing Rachel, excitement as dreams become reality, and anticipation of future success.

I stay to the perimeter of the caravan, opposite Seth, who oversees the wool's loading. To him, I'm dead, and dead men can't say goodbye.

"Where is that beast?" I scan the melee.

"Where do you belong?" Hasan's caravan manager sneers.

"With my camel. I can't find her in all these stinking creatures."

"You'll smell the same soon enough. You going all the way to Caesarea?"

"Yes."

"Ever ridden a camel?" He sizes me up.

I stand straighter. "Do you know where my beast is or not?"

"Oh, this ought to be good. Let's find your mount. She might stink, but she's better than walking—though you might prefer walking after a few days."

Just one more obstacle to endure.

The Arab points out Veru. As I attach my bag of food, I resist the urge to pull anything out. I didn't eat this morning, but I won't partake until we're beyond the house. Then I'll own the food, not Abba.

Other travelers already sit on their camels, awaiting departure.

"Looks like we're starting, my ugly lady," I whisper to Veru as I ensure all my baggage is tied on well. "I'd appreciate a smooth, pleasant trip, with no temper tantrums. Okay?"

The manager calls out from the front, and I mount just in time for the camel driver to coax Veru to stand. Lurching forward, the animal straightens her long back legs. I clutch the pommel to keep from sailing over her head. Then I lean back as her front legs unfold. Six cubits off the ground, I sigh. This will be a long journey. The camels align, nose to tail, waiting for the signal.

I'm leaving. I'm actually leaving. Glancing to the balcony where I watched caravans depart as a boy, I find Abba there. Our eyes lock, and I raise my arm without thinking. Abba brushes his cheeks. He's probably swatting at the flies that always accompany camel trains in hordes.

I won't search for Miriam's farewell. I'll ignore Seth. And as the caravan departs Meron, I won't check if Rachel stands on her balcony.

The caravan plods forward and turns right out of the village. We approach the spot where, if I glance back, I have a perfect view of Rachel's home. Don't look. Don't look. Don't look.

I disobey.

There she is. Arms crossed, and headscarf wound about her face. I tighten my grasp. I can't pursue my plans and her. But, still, I drink in the sight for as long as possible.

With a shrill whistle, the caravan manger guides our menagerie from Meron. When a building blocks my view of Rachel, I set my gaze west. Away from home and the past. Toward my future.

CHAPTER 16
JUDAH

Galatian Wilderness
Elul (August) AD 20

For my life is spent with sorrow, and my years with sighing; my strength fails because of my iniquity, and my bones waste away.

PSALM 31:10

"It's hotter than Sodom and Gomorrah when it rained fire." Desperate to hear a human voice, I talk to myself. But that story causes me look up to make sure bolts of fire aren't coming for me.

In these hills, I occasionally run into another herder, but there's no trust in these desolate stretches where we compete for sustenance. So I keep my head down and take care of my charges. For over a month, I've roamed the hills with the swine. We cover great distances and get nowhere.

The landscape's browns and grays paint a picture of death. Persistent hot days wither vegetation, leaving little to forage. I wonder what death from starvation feels like.

Tonight, I settle on a carob tree's branch, a precarious but safe place to sleep. I wrap my cloak tight against the cool desert night, expertly folding it to avoid holes.

My companions snuffle in the leaves below me.

"Soon, I'll dry up and blow away. Then where will you be?"

Too hungry to sleep, I shift away from a branch poking my back and lean against the trunk. On this moonless night, constellations paint their way through a milky river of greens and blues. The sky looks more alive than anything I see during the day.

I find Orion and remember the ancient words. *He who made the Pleiades and Orion, and turns deep darkness into the morning and darkens the day into night, who calls for the waters of the sea and pours them out on the surface of the earth, the Lord is his name.*[1]

"The earth could use some of that pouring water right about now, if You don't mind."

Funny how I still speak to Someone I don't believe is listening.

I turned my back on Yahweh when I left Abba. In Ephesus, I agreed when Cosmas called believing in one god unsophisticated. I prayed to other deities, even worshipped in Artemis's temple. I told Apollon I had no god. Yet, sometimes I still cry out to Him. I confuse myself.

And now, I don't stem the words trickling through my mind, like a stream in the desert.

When I look at your heavens, the work of your fingers, the moon and the stars, which you have set in place, what is man that you are mindful of him, and the son of man that you care for him?[2]

"Do You see me?" I ask He who made the stars.

An owl hoots, and the swine snort.

"Do You still care about me after all I've done?"

My stomach grumbles. Crickets chirp.

And I wait—but for what? A voice?

I drift in and out of sleep, haunted because if there is a God, He's apparently too busy for a starving, blasphemous swineherd trying to sleep in a tree.

"PLEASE DON'T LEAVE TOMORROW," I plead, petting Gaidoros's grazing nose.

Two days ago, the clop, clop of hooves announced the arrival of Pavlos and his brimming bags of food. I don't know how he found me, but I don't complain. After a month of only pigs for company, I cherish our long chats around the fire at night. His presence might satisfy me more than the bread he brought, but I don't tell him that.

"Sorry, I have to go back," he says. After a few pipe puffs, he adds, "Tonight, I want to hear your story."

I shift on my mat. "Not sure I want to tell."

He puffs, coughs, and sips some water. "I told you mine, so fair is fair. Besides, this peaceful spot could use an entertaining tale."

"Peaceful? All I see is terror and desolation."

He smiles. "Depends where you look."

"Why does everything you say sound like it holds more than one meaning?"

He grins.

"But, I suppose it's my turn, though I'm not sure where to begin. I didn't get the best response last time."

"Tell me where you're from. Describe home."

Home. The word stirs memories I prefer buried. Leaning my head against a boulder, I allow the past to emerge from the shadows.

"I grew up in a small village called Meron, in the district of Galilee in Judea."

"Aah."

"Nestled at the base of Mount Meron—"

"Where it got its name?"

"You're brilliant. There's a spring with the best water . . ." Suddenly, I crave cold spring water with such ferocity. To combat that, I envision the village's meandering streets crowded with people and livestock.

"Like other villages, the houses look like stucco boxes stacked by a child. Streets spike off small squares and weave around buildings—nothing like Ephesus's long, straight avenues. If you don't know your way, you'll get lost. On market days, locals come to buy and sell. And on Shabbat, everyone gathers at the synagogue."

My voice thickens, probably from the smoke. I certainly don't miss the mundane agrarian life I worked so hard to escape. Then again, in Meron, no one cheated me. No one robbed me. No one set out to destroy me.

"And your parents?" Pavlos prods. "Tell me about your mother."

I stare at my crusty feet. "I never knew my Eema. According to my brother, I killed her."

Pavlos puffs harder.

"She died after I was born."

"I am sorry, Judah. What about your father? What's his name?"

"Ezra ben Lavi." My heart aches.

After a pause, Pavlos asks softly, "What's your house like?"

Another deep breath. "My house stands on the front edge of Meron, just inside the village gate. We have a large compound with lodgings, barns, and storerooms. Even a well. Neighbors come to us for water and bake bread in our tannur."

"Sounds like your family has money."

"Yes, though Abba never flaunted it. He prized industry and generosity." My smile returns. "Abba's baritone voice always filled our compound with psalms. You two would have been friends."

"You speak of him in the past."

"I'm dead to my family, so I suppose they're dead to me."

"Assume nothing, Judah. They may miss you as much as you miss them."

"I don't miss—"

Crickets chirp and Pavlos coughs several more times.

"You don't sound good."

"My pipe dries my throat." He winks. "But it's worth it. Now keep describing. I miss the joy of home life more than anything. Belonging to place and people."

"Don't you belong to someone now?"

He rolls his eyes and adds dung to the fire. "Do ol' Pavlos a favor. Tell me what tonight would be like there. I want to picture it." He settles back against Gaidoros's saddle and tugs at a blanket.

"You want to torture me?"

Grinning, he nods.

I chuckle. "All right. We enter our compound and touch the mezuzah. As we pray, the smell of Miriam's bread hits us."

"Who's Miriam?"

"The bossiest, most efficient woman you've ever met. She's good at everything except understanding that things she finds easy can be difficult for others. She and her husband, Eli, are Abba's bond servants. Eli is the steward."

"And she cooks?"

"Like a dream. But before we can eat, she reminds us to wash. Then she points us to the balcony on top of the gathering room, where one of her hearty meals awaits."

"What will we eat?" He smacks his lips.

"Bread, lentil soup, fresh vegetables, dried fruit,"—my mouth waters—"olive oil with herbs floating on top, and goat cheese. Wine from our vineyard. We recline on pillows, eating slow and talking long."

"Wonderful. Wonderful! Tell me more. What do we see from the rooftop?"

"Well," I close my eyes and picture the life I ran from. "We can see the street below, a few people milling about, coaxing animals home. A friend yells shalom to Abba from the gate. Neighbors wave from their rooftops. Lamplight bathes the streets in yellow patches. On the hills circling the valley, distant villages sparkle. But you won't be looking at the horizon."

"No? Why not?"

I snort. "Because you and Abba will argue long into the night about Torah and the prophets."

"I'd like that," he sighs, patting his stomach as though stuffed.

My stomach grumbles.

"What about your brother? Is he married?"

"Betrothed to a girl too kind for him who's from Safed, a village on another hill. I doubt he's married her yet."

"You're not close to him?"

I laugh dryly.

"And what about you? Is there a girl waiting for you in Meron?"

"Rachel," I whisper. I picture the woman in a pink headscarf draped around shiny, straight, black hair that enhances a face bright with conviction, energy, sincerity, and . . . something else. Something unnameable that runs as deep as Mount Meron's crystal springs. No paint. No guile. Just—

The vision fades. I rub my eyes with my fists. "That's enough for tonight."

Wrapping my cloak around me, I turn my back to Pavlos.

"Good night, Judah. Sleep well." He mumbles his nightly prayer and is snoring in moments.

I would love to sleep, but pain and regret plague me. I should never unleash the past. It harbors too many dreams, dry and dead as this wilderness. No path back exists.

CHAPTER 17
MIRIAM

Meron
Sivian (May) AD 19

Be gracious to me, O LORD, for I am in distress; my eye is wasted from grief; my soul and my body also.

PSALM 31:9

"Master wants to speak with everyone." Eli disappears from the kitchen doorway before I can turn around.

"Adonai,"—I rub my aching temples—"couldn't You delay this summons until my eyes aren't the color of pomegranate seeds?" I've hidden in my kitchen for a week. Tova delivered messages and food to the household. I even handed off my kneaded, formed dough to younger servants to bake. They returned beautiful, golden loaves. Not a blackened one in the bunch. Maybe I can delegate more than I thought.

I don't want to leave the seclusion of this room, but Ezra

commanded and I always obey. Dusting off my tunic, I wrap my headscarf tight, and force myself into the fading sunlight to join everyone clustered in front of the arbor.

The household servants gather close to Ezra. I hide behind the field workers hired for the harvest, who stand at the back. They better not carry gossip back to their wives.

Eli beckons me to join him next to Master. As if I want to be on display? I shake my head defiantly.

"Thank you for gathering." The murmuring quiets. "I know you're tired from a hard day's work. It's best to be . . ." Ezra pauses. ". . . It's best to be honest. Our household suffered a blow that affects everyone. At the moment, we are Meron's main source of gossip, and until something wonderful or terrible happens, that won't change."

I refuse my feet's desire to escape to my kitchen.

"I ask for your loyalty. Please don't stoke the fire."

Some people nod, while others display red cheeks.

"Because Judah sold a third of our estate, we've had to dismiss workers."

The crowd buzzes with nervous whispers and I yank my headscarf over my face.

"Seth is currently assessing our remaining land. We'll retain whatever laborers and servants we can. But I exhort you—remain dignified."

"Did he say dignified?" Tova asks.

I jump and grasp my heart. "Shhhh," I hiss. When did she join me?

"Like tares growing in the field that we can't sift out until the harvest, we must tolerate the gossip for a season. If you feel tainted by affiliation, you may leave. But if you stay, please do so with a loyal heart. Hold your heads high, do your work well, and help our neighbors. Though we bear Judah's shame, we haven't sinned. The less we react to gibes, the sooner the winds will die down."

Tova whispers, "He's very brave."

"Yes. He is."

"Thank you, all. Sorrow is easier when friends carry it with us. Please let me bless you." Ezra grasps his tzitzit and prays.

In my heart, I beg. "Oh, Lord, help me bear this. I feel as shameful as Judah's actions. But to honor this man, please help me trust You."

MUTTERING, I gather baskets and duck into the cool, quiet storeroom. On the shelves sit jars of honey, baskets of dried grapes, and almond containers. Stringed figs hang beside dried lavender.

"You know, Adonai," I say, rubbing the leaves to release the calming scent, "I'll need more than lavender to behave as Ezra requested. Dignified, of all things, and until the winds of discord die out? Some people in this village bite and devour like it's sport."

"Who are you talking to?"

"Oh!" Jumping, I collide with the table and nearly send a pile of bowls and flasks cascading onto the floor. Quickly, I grab wobbling containers on my end of the table.

"Sorry! Sorry! Sorry!" Tova steadies the vessels on her end, eyes wide.

"Who do you think I'm talking to? Myself and Adonai— Whhaattt!" I shriek, when, without warning, something rubs against my ankle. Screaming, I leap from the unknown invader and knock a just-settled bowl onto a ball of black fur. Yowling, a cat tears from the room as more containers crash.

Through a barley flour cloud rising from shards of clay, Tova gapes at me.

"Miriam?" Rachel rushes in.

Hands on my head, I look from Tova to shattered containers to Rachel.

"What's wrong? What happened?"

"The flour—that cat—I just—" I turn in a circle.

Rachel covers her mouth and starts shaking.

"Are you laughing?"

She doubles over and a few guffaws escape.

"Well, I like that."

"I'm sorry," she hiccups. "But between your scream, that black cat screeching out of here, and flour everywhere—" Full laughter bursts forth.

Brushing flour off my tunic, I chuckle which grows into good, hard belly laughs. My eyes squeeze shut, tears escape, and I sense my tension running out like that cat from the storeroom.

Tova remains like a statue. The only things moving are her eyes, which bounce from Rachel to me and back.

"Oh, dear," I wheeze.

Rachel hugs me. "I haven't laughed since . . ."

"Me either."

Together, we savor the first mirth in weeks.

"I'll . . . I'll clean the mess?" Tova stammers.

"And I'll help." Rachel grabs a broom.

With one last giggle, I pat Tova on the shoulder. "Well, this is what happens when I think about everything besides the job at hand."

We pick out the large urn pieces, sweep the flour, and put it aside to sift and clean later. Nothing will be wasted.

"Thank you, Tova."

"Oh. Well . . . I, um, am glad to help."

Rachel smiles at her.

With a clap of my hands, I say, "Well, let's try this again. You take the baskets there, and I'll grab this one."

We exit the storeroom into the bright morning. "I suppose we should buy another urn."

Tova tries to cough over a small laugh, but I snort and Rachel giggles.

"Checking the storeroom sounds like fun," Eli says, and I smile. "I haven't seen that happy face in some time."

"Well, don't get used to it." I wink.

He tries to straighten his mouth but the edges refuse.

"We're on our way to the market—that is, if you'll let us pass. Don't you have work to do?" I turn to Tova. "Come, let's confront the day of judgement."

"You're braver than I," Rachel says. "I came to check what cheese you want this week, but only because Abba forced me out of the house."

"I understand completely." After she takes my cheese order, she departs.

"Don't let those old gossips scare you," Eli whispers in my ear. "Remember, we only answer to the Most High. Return their pettiness with kindness."

"I'll try." My forehead presses into his cheek for a moment. *Thank*

You, Adonai, for this good man. And for a silly cat, and for shared laughter.

Eli clears his throat. "About the missing eggs—there seems to be a thief. I'll keep an eye out."

"What a disgrace. Nowhere is safe."

"The problem may get worse. The drought up north is driving more and more foreigners our way. More hungry people means more theft."

With my headscarf straightened, I roll my sleeves. "Well, I'd like to hang on to our eggs. Find the thief, Eli." Heading out, I call back to Tova, "Come on, girl, keep up."

MERON'S MARKET hums with hagglers and flies. Awnings flap in the breeze, shading women who chat over vegetables and men who argue about the price of livestock. Roman soldiers, looking bored and misplaced, weave through the crowds. How far from home they must be. I bet their mothers miss them. I never considered that before Judah left.

Slipping past one stall after another, Tova follows me like a shadow. Whenever I spot a friend, I smile, nod, and dash past.

At least we are not as bad as Ari, who I do not smile at. Instead, I curse the bad eye of greed.

At last we reach Ravid's cloth shop. While we hire women to weave most of our cloth, today I need fine linen to sew Ezra a new formal robe. Since sewing is my least favorite activity, I've put it off. But now I want to bless him.

"Ohhh," Tova exclaims over the materials on the outside table.

"Miriam! Shalom!"

I halt in the doorway, and Tova bowls into me. *Dear Adonai, have mercy.*

"I didn't expect to see you out so soon!" Lavinia bustles toward me, her daughter Sapphira cowering behind her.

Stay dignified. Stay dignified. "Shalom, Lavinia."

"So," Lavinia whispers, leaning in, "how is Ezra coping?"

"Oh, fine. Just fine. Good life and peace to you on your betrothal, Sapphira."

Sapphira blushes. "Thank—"

"We worry about Ezra with this loss and shame!" Lavinia presses a hand to her heart. "I can't imagine how he must feel!"

This woman has no understanding of shame.

"What neighborly concern," I gush. "As Job needed friends, so do we."

Lavinia's smile freezes. She's probably trying to decide if I've complemented or insulted her.

Recalling Master's exhortation, I add, "We must all find consolation in the Most High."

Her eyes blink rapidly.

My triumph at hushing the village busybody wanes as I realize the potential consequences. Corking Lavinia here means her opinions will spill out everywhere else.

Swallowing my pride, I lower my voice. "You, in your wisdom and understanding, realize how little we want to discuss our family in the streets. We appreciate your discretion more than you know."

Her eyebrows puckered, Lavinia says, "Of course?"

"Come, Tova. We must buy Ravid's cloth before it runs out."

"We purchased beautiful pieces for Sapphira's wedding garments." Lavinia's eyes sparkle with renewed energy. "And I'll try to keep a lid on the gossip. Though you know the ladies."

I sure do. And she leads them all. Her husband, Barak, must spend much time on the corner of their roof.

"I appreciate that."

Sapphira, catty and conniving with her friends, always seems unsure what to do in her mother's commanding presence. How will she ever turn out, having been raised by such a woman?

I take her hand. "May the Most High grant you a happy home full of love and encouragement."

Her smile broadens.

"Well," Lavinia steps between us. "We must be on our way."

As they depart, Sapphira looks over her shoulder and mouths, "Thank you."

"I wouldn't be that woman's daughter for all the denarii in Jerusalem," I mutter.

Tova giggles. "Me neither."

I look up at the girl beside me. "Those aren't words to repeat. Understand me?"

"Yes ma'am," Tova's eyes dance. Maybe there's hope for her after all.

Inside, we examine cloth just imported from Persia. Tova strokes the silks and linens with admiration.

"You like to sew?" I ask.

"I made all the clothes for Eema and my older sisters."

"And this?" I point to the sleeve of her dress with its pleats and decorative edging.

"Yes."

"What would you do with a complicated project, like Master's robe?"

"Well, I would . . ." As she describes where she'd place tucks on the shoulder and how a certain fabric would provide the perfect border, my mind wanders.

I interrupt. "And can you do embroidery?" At a vigorous nod, I say, "I don't have the patience. You've got the job. I've been dreading this."

"Oh, Miriam, thank you!" She claps. "I'll do my best work. I promise!"

"All right, all right. Ravid?"

"What can I do for you?" Even shorter than me, Ravid bows.

"We'll take these." I hand over Tova's favorite materials, on a deep green wool. "Master needs a new cloak."

"Good choices, Miriam. Very nice. I'll cut them for you."

I run my finger over smooth silk. "Cloth looks like work to me," I confess.

"It gives me pleasure," Tova says. "So many possibilities."

If she takes over the household sewing, she might prove useful yet. Smiling, Ravid slides me a neat package.

As I turn to go, he grasps my hand. "We're praying for you all."

"Thank you." I feel my shoulders relax. "Shalom, Ravid."

"Shalom."

Standing in the doorway, I survey people ambling across the street.

They greet each other, laugh at jokes, and argue about this year's wheat compared to last. A man prods a stubborn donkey as boys race through the crowd.

"Shalom, Miriam," Naomi calls from across the street. "I hope you are well."

Others nod or say hello. Maybe some delight in our misfortunes. But others display compassion.

"It's a good day. Don't you think, Tova?"

"A very good day."

"Let's go home. We need to bake the bread."

CHAPTER 18
SETH

Meron
Sivan (May) AD 19

Be not quick in your spirit to become angry, for anger lodges in the heart of fools.

ECCLESIASTES 7:9

Dark clouds scud across the valley, barely drizzling. We've had little rain for months, and now we face summer, which is always dry. I feel just as dry, like a grape that's become a raisin. After the week I've had, I look forward to working outside today, if just to release tension which now energizes my trek up to the vineyard.

Immediately after Judah's grand exit, Abba sent me to visit our remaining holdings to assuage our tenants' fears and make an accurate accounting of what remains. Abba expanded our family holdings from what he inherited from his own abba. With an excellent eye for stock, he increased our herds—or maybe the Holy One blessed him like He blessed Jacob. Either way, with Judah's portion gone, and even though we retain reasonable assets, the losses cut deep. And while Abba still controls everything as long as he lives, the ownership transferred to me at the division of the inheritance. I feel the full weight of that responsibility.

And then, as if the evil eye is trained on us and no one else, when I arrived home yesterday, Meron buzzed with excitement over Rabbi Yakov's arrival. I planned the rabbi's visit, but why must he and his disciples arrive now while the stench of disgrace surrounds us?

"Hurry!" I command the laborers behind me.

I planned to host him. With the largest compound in Meron, we offer the best accommodation. But the rabbi can't reside with such contamination. Instead, he and his disciples stay with Barak, where gossips surely exposed Judah's scandal to him, describing Abba's odd response in great detail.

Though still morning, sweat drips into my eyes as I ascend the last climb to our vineyard, my hoe laid across my shoulders. Even if the clouds refuse to rain, they could at least stay and provide shade. But they scuttle quickly south to deliver their precious water to some other land.

Panting, I arrive and strip off my cloak. The laborers, heads lowered and faces red, eventually draw near, one or two clutching their sides.

"As soon as the cart arrives, we'll apply fertilizer. We can't afford for the blossoms to wither."

They gulp from their waterskins and wipe their brows. "Yes, sir."

I stalk into the vineyard, hiding from possible conversation, and drop my satchel. After driving my hoe into the dry ground for an hour, I'm coated with dust.

"Shalom, Seth."

I startle.

"Rabbi Akiva?" His blue eyes sparkle, like he knows some hidden joke, just like when he taught me in bet midrash, though now, his hair and beard are completely white. "You have no vines. What are you doing here?" I rustle twine out of my bag.

"I came to see you, actually."

"Me?"

"I thought you might need someone to talk to."

"Thank you, but I must work." I tie grape vines to their supports.

"Everyone must rest for a moment now and then." He winks as he sheds his cloak and grabs my discarded hoe. "Besides, 'two are better than one, because they have a good reward for their toil.'[1] I'll work beside you until you take a break."

"Rabbi, I—"

"I've helped my neighbors all my life. Don't worry, I know what to do." Then he starts singing. I learned this trick of his in school. There was no interrupting him when he started singing a psalm, so I lash a vine and move to the next plant.

After working steadily, he asks, "How is Ezra?"

Abba. My heart, already beating fast, speeds up. I grunt and hold my hand out. "I need the hoe."

He nods and takes my twine. Just when I get into a good rhythm, he says, "I'm sure you two disagree on how he handled Judah's departure."

I hit a rock with my hoe, and the handle jerks abruptly in my left hand, tearing open a blister. "Hades!" I throw my hoe to the ground.

"Let me look at that." Rabbi Akiva leads me to a pile of logs and makes me sit. After he pours water on my wound, he wraps it with a bandage that a neighbor brings over.

"Drink some water, Seth."

With my good hand, I take the waterskin and drink.

"Now, tell me how you are."

"Rabbi Akiva, I don't think—"

"I've known your abba most of his life. I performed your bris and I taught you and Judah all the way through bet midrash. It's unlikely you can surprise me."

I poke at a scarab beetle with a stick while I try to unravel my conflicts with Abba, but, I have no words.

"Then tell me about your journey to your tenants. How did that go?"

"It was painful. Most of them had already heard about our family from their neighbors. Judah asking for his inheritance while Abba is alive—well, nothing so scandalous has happened in a long time. I assured them we won't raise their rents or sell their properties."

"That must have relieved them."

"Yes, but I also met former tenants from land Judah sold. Many of them have had to leave because of higher rents, or because their new landlord kicked them out. It's not my fault Judah sold their land to disreputable Gentiles, but I'm the one they complain to!"

"These are hard times for you. And for Ezra." From a small bag fastened to his belt, Rabbi Akiva draws out some dried figs and hands me two. "But I fear that your theological differences will keep you two from comforting each other."

Smacking the fig, I lick stickiness from my finger.

"You're both men who love Adonai's Word, and love to sit with others to examine the text and argue its application. Start there."

"I do admire how Abba pursues nuance and connects one idea to another—" Under the beating sun, I wipe my forehead. "—how he searches the text for how the Holy One, blessed be His name, values mercy and lovingkindness."

Speaking around the fig in his mouth, Rabbi Akiva quotes, "Oh give thanks to the LORD, for he is good; for his steadfast love endures forever!'[2]"

"But what of the commands? How will we obey without building hard fences around each law, staying as far as possible from breaking one?"

"But what of Hosea's words?" His eyes twinkle again and I await his challenge. "'For I desire steadfast love and not sacrifice, the knowledge of God rather than burnt offerings.'[3]"

"Oh yes, one of Abba's favorites to quote. In fact, last night he recited that to me to explain why he studies."

"Which is?"

"To quote Abba, 'To know the Most High better, because the more he knows Him, the more he loves Him; and the more he loves Him, the more he obeys Him.'"

"Beautiful thought. He must share that the next time he comes to synagogue."

"But does that explain his response to Judah's betrayal? Why he didn't declare Judah dead? Even David said, 'I hate the assembly of evildoers, and I will not sit with the wicked.'[4]"

"Is that what you think he should have done?"

"Oh, I don't know!" I crush loose dirt clods with my heel. "Why didn't he at least turn his back on that foolish, selfish, disrespectful, sinful, dishonoring . . . ?"

"Run out of words?"

I try to laugh, but can't. "Rabbi, is this what hate feels like? Judah and I might never have been friends, but I don't know what to do with how I feel toward him."

"Troublesome questions."

My head sinks into my hands. He allows me time to breathe.

"Thank you for not rushing in with answers."

"There are no easy ones. But, I pray these issues between you and Ezra will ease as your pain over Judah's actions dulls, as it will, in time."

"Actually, the distance between Abba and me began growing before Judah ran off. Now it's widened into a canyon." My voice drops to a whisper. "I don't know how to reach him anymore."

"Do you want to?" Rabbi Akiva waits until I lift my gaze again. "And now Rabbi Yakov has arrived, whose opinions align with yours much more than Ezra's. That doesn't make this situation any better."

I stand and offer the old rabbi my good hand. "No, it doesn't."

Rabbi Akiva's smile crinkles his eyes into tiny slits. "Give Ezra time. And listen to him. You can't hope to understand someone you've already decided to disagree with."

My mouth quirks to one side. "Like you and Abba have already decided about Rabbi Yakov?"

"Good point!" His hearty laugh echoes. "How about I promise to listen to the good Rabbi and you promise to listen to Ezra?"

"Hmmm. I'll try."

"As will I. Shalom, Seth."

The unrelenting sun scorches my skin as I ponder what I will say if Rabbi Yakov asks me about our situation. I'd better figure it out fast, because I face him tomorrow.

I WOKE this morning anticipating to finally sit under Rabbi Yakov's teaching and present myself as an eager student. Maybe ask a few probing questions.

Today, however, seems attacked by demons. Sick sheep. Quarreling servants. Confused laborers. Disappearing eggs.

Finally, I head for the gate.

"Seth?"

What does he need now? Since Abba refused to join me, I'd think he could take care of whatever is next.

"Eli is waylaid by problems in the grove and I need to help Matthias bandage the cow's hurt leg. Such a day! Please, on your way to synagogue, can you deliver the food basket to Samuel and Deborah?"

"Abba, please have someone else deliver it."

"I would never ask you if someone else could."

"Fine," I mumble.

Finding no basket in the kitchen, I return to the courtyard. "Miriam, where's the basket for Samuel's family?"

Where is that confounded woman?

"On the arbor table!" She sounds irritated.

Swiveling from side to side, I scan the grounds. "Where are you?"

Her glaring face emerges from a patch of leeks in the garden.

I wish I could say something to restore our relationship while still maintaining my position. For now, I grab the basket, nod in her direction, and head out the gate.

"Seth!" Uncle Daniel joins me. "Ready for more teaching?"

"I was." I hold up the basket. "But I must first deliver food to Samuel's, which could take a while, this being market day."

"That's kind."

"Abba's generous to a fault. When Samuel broke his leg, everyone helped, but now it's mainly us."

"Well, it's difficult to keep up with all who need help."

"I think one reason Abba still does this is because Samuel and I used to be good friends. I celebrated with him and Deborah when they married."

"How many boys do they have now?"

"Two. No—three, I think." We stop in front of the synagogue. "If

Abba had asked earlier I could have already delivered and returned. But now I'm delivering soup instead of learning from Rabbi Yakov."

"I'll ask the Most High to part the market crowd like He did the Red Sea." He bounds up the stairs. "Good luck!"

Gritting my teeth, I sidestep a kicking donkey and narrowly avoid a stampede of dirty children running away from the crowd.

As I veer toward Samuel's home, I'm confronted with a man built like a bull tromping toward me, his face shielded by a heavy amphora.

"Watch it!"

Wham!

Run over by him, I tumble onto the dusty street, my basket landing at my feet. Grabbing the crock, I save Miriam's broth from spilling, but the fruit and bread roll into the gravel.

"Fool!" I bellow at the man's retreating back. Cursing this horrible day, I reach for the runaway food, appalled to be crawling through the dirt.

A grimy hand threads between sandaled feet and snatches Samuel's bread. I trace the arm to a scrawny boy.

"Give that back!"

Tucking the bread under his cloak, he darts into the crowd.

"Thief!"

Abandoning the basket, I give chase. I'll catch him if it's the one thing I accomplish today. But as I turn a corner, a rock wallops my shoulder.

"Ow!" I clutch my arm and stumble forward. The thief has vanished.

Rubbing my aching shoulder, I remember the basket and sprint back into the market. The contents are pilfered. Even the crock is empty. Panting, I curse and spit onto the ground.

"Looks like a rough morning, Seth. Cursing anyone in particular?" Ari, the Jewish traitor, smirks in his tax collection booth.

"As someone who regularly steals from our people, you couldn't possibly understand."

Several heads turn toward his laughter. "Well, at least that little thief didn't pilfer your self-righteousness."

An old man in line to pay taxes snickers. I shake dirt from my cloaks, pick up the basket, hold my head high, and stride toward the synagogue.

Before entering, I stash the basket at the base of a tree. When I return home, I'll dispatch a servant to deliver more food. Samuel and Hannah will remain hungry until then, but I refuse to miss any more of Rabbi Yakov's discussion. Beggars can't be choosers.

Wiping my forehead, I tighten my belt, and banish my scowl.

Then I enter the synagogue. "Shalom, everyone!"

"What an amazing two weeks." Barak joins me in the corner of the synagogue.

I glance sideways as the bald man with the paunchy middle. Though I respect Barak's standing as an elder, he's not a man I've admired in the past. "Rabbi Yakov's long visit has been amazing. I've learned a great deal."

"He exposes so many details of the Law's application. Rabbi Akiva's arguments against his interpretations surprised me. But your responses have been enlightening." He glances around and leans in. "I think Rabbi Yakov appreciates your enthusiasm."

I cross my arms over my chest. "Do you think so? Often, in my excitement, I must remind myself not to discuss too loudly."

"I never would have known!"

Before we approach the men clustered around Rabbi Yakov, Barak says, "I'm glad that—well—that you haven't let your family situation keep you from this."

When Barak departs, I stand beside Mazal, the physician. In the middle of the doctor's sentence, Rabbi Yakov turns to me. "Excellent questions today, Seth."

I bow my head since I can't help but smile. Rabbi Yakov personifies virtue, from his long tassels almost dragging on the floor, to his black and white chiton and cloak, to the serenity on his thin face. Naturally, I'm proud he noticed my thoughts.

"Many speak of Ezra ben Lavi's prayers, how the Word fills them. Why doesn't he join us?"

Pride evaporates. "He urged me to come even though domestic matters prevented his attendance." I'm not lying. Not really.

"I see." Rabbi Yakov smiles, but his eyes are cold.

"He'll come once some estate issues are resolved." Also not a complete lie.

"Life is full of problems, Seth. We must examine our priorities."

My cheeks warm, and I clear my throat. "You're wise, Rabbi. I'll share your insight with him. Hopefully, he'll attend tomorrow."

"Rabbi, thank you for your insights," Uncle Daniel chimes in. "With your many disciples, we amassed quite the crowd today."

Rabbi Yakov purses his lips, one eyebrow raised. "Is it normally difficult to find more villagers? I understood Meron to be devoted."

I clear my throat.

"Well, yes"—Daniel shuffles his feet—"we're devoted to the Most High. But during the wheat harvest, gathering people is difficult. And dry weather makes tending to crops more time-consuming."

Stroking his beard, Rabbi Yakov says, "Many things challenge devotion. Galilee is known for its lax application. I observe this everywhere I go."

Uncle Daniel and I glance at each other as we all depart the synagogue.

The rabbi continues, "And when even your elders can't make time, your community will follow their example."

Uncle Daniel's lips tighten. I bite my tongue.

The rabbi flashes another enigmatic smile and sweeps from the courtyard, his tassels flowing as his disciples scurry behind.

Uncle Daniel breaks the silence. "Oh, my."

"Yes."

Uncle Daniel puts an arm around my shoulders. "I'll walk you home." He lowers his voice. "We need to talk." When we're out of earshot of our friends, he says, "Has Ezra's grief lessened?"

I snort. "Instead of disowning his foolish son, Abba prays for him."

"He should censure Judah's betrayal, and no longer mourn over it."

"You think I don't know? That I haven't pressed him?" We make our way through the narrow streets, ducking under laundry. "Just yesterday, he spent all day praying on the mountain. When I asked if it helped, he replied, 'I now understand how Jeremiah felt when he said his grief had no cure. I too am sick at heart.'[5] Then he went to his room and ate alone."

"Would it help if I spoke with him?"

"Maybe. He must attend Rabbi Yakov's discussions. We've endured enough already. Abba compounds the problems."

We pause at the cross street leading to Uncle Daniel's home.

I point to our front gate, down the street to the right. "What a burden, our home forever known for dishonor and foolishness."

"It's not just Rabbi Yakov. Other village leaders wonder at Ezra's behavior. It's all very . . . unexpected."

"That's a word for it." I shake my head. "But I must warn you, he probably won't listen."

Uncle Daniel scratches the top of his head. "We've been friends our whole lives—like brothers even before he married my sister." His hand moves to my shoulder. "I've always admired your father. He loves the Torah better and applies it deeper than anyone. But you never know when that will make him"—he looks to the sky and shrugs—"unpredictable?"

"Adonai help us!" I turn toward home, back to my unpredictable Abba with his unexpected actions. If we can't convince him to move past his grief, then I'll have to do something drastic. But what?

CHAPTER 19
JUDAH

Mediterranean Sea
Tammuz, (June) AD 19

O LORD God of hosts, who is mighty as you are, O LORD, with your faithfulness all around you? You rule the raging of the sea; when its waves rise, you still them.

PSALM 89:8-9

Clinging to the side of the undulating wooden merchant boat, I will my roiling insides to quiet. If the water would calm for a moment, I might conquer this nausea. But one wave sweeps into another as gulls screech and sails flap in the wind.

Meoklis claps me on the shoulder. "Not a seaman?"

I'd throw him into the sea if I had the strength.

"Dreams are expensive things, Jude. Now, you're paying with your stomach, but, misery is a small price for opportunity."

From his raucous laughter, it seems Meoklis finds himself hilarious.

If I ever laugh again, it will be at my naive, Galilean self.

When I arrived in Caesarea a few weeks ago, I'd stood on the walkway above the circular port and marveled at Herod's engineering wonder, where more ships than I knew existed rocked at the dock.

In the salty warmth of the Great Sea, I'd closed my eyes, leaned into the breeze, and rejoiced as it blew away the interminable miles on Veru.

No more sleeping under the stars.

No more flea-bitten, smelly caravansary.

Certainly the worst lay behind me.

First, I procured lodgings and buried my money belt deep in the recesses of my bags.

Then, I rushed to a Roman bath, and had my hair cut and face shaved, Roman style. Refreshed, I sold Veru, and replenished my supplies. I couldn't wait for the next leg of my journey.

I'd expected to find a captain, pay for my passage, and set sail without a hitch. But after querying boat after boat, I realized securing a berth could take weeks.

I even asked Adonai for help.

After another frustrating morning at the port, I'd eaten well, drunk enough wine for three men, and visited the theater. The debauchery on stage made me flush, but I welcomed the entertainment. When the crowd roared with laughter, I laughed too. If four thousand people enjoyed the play, why shouldn't I?

"Jude!"

I scanned the crowd to find Meoklis sauntering forward. "What a surprise!"

"My friend!" I clasped his forearm. "I haven't seen a familiar face in weeks!"

"Tell me, what brings you to Caesarea?"

"I have my inheritance, Meoklis, and the will to make my mark."

His smile broadened. "A man with the world at his fingertips, partaking in Caesarea's pleasures."

"I'm trying to get to Ephesus, where I planned on looking for you. But I didn't realize how difficult it is to secure travel."

He slapped me on the back so enthusiastically that I stumbled forward a few steps. "You must have performed a ritual to make a god happy, because I'm sure there's space for you on the ship I'm taking."

"To Ephesus?"

"To Ephesus! What a city. A jewel, a wonder! And we depart within the week."

The next day, I descended to the harbor following Meoklis as he snaked through the crowded dock. Gulls dove, fishermen unloaded their pungent catch, and porters of all nationalities lugged heavy crates, barrels, and amphorae.

At a grain ship, Meoklis introduced me to Captain Narmer, who stood tall and thin like his mast.

"Three days, we leave," said the captain, looking me up and down. His Egyptian accent was impossible to miss as he spoke broken Aramaic. "No be late. No too much baggage."

"Whatever you say!" I was ready to abandon everything—save my money belt—to get on his ship.

Now, as our creaking ship plunges, briny water sprays down my front. Cursing sea travel, I inch back to the perch I created by tying a tarp to crates and barrels secured to the deck.

I swelter in the day, shiver at night, and feel queasy during both. Last night, a storm soaked me through. This morning, I tightened my money belt again.

Meoklis sits beside me, his face to the sun. "Now, Jude, don't despair. I have high hopes for you. The Roman Empire loves to create young businessmen. Why, I know former slaves who are wealthy beyond imagination."

Afraid to open my mouth, I lean my head on a crate.

"Once you get settled in Ephesus, I'll make a special introduction. I know a man who cultivates a few new businessmen a year. You'll be perfect." Meoklis rubs his hands together.

I draw my knees to my chest, trying to keep my insides inside.

"Just hang on. We're almost there."

Moaning, I close my eyes and rest my head on my knees.

My dreams lie on the other side of these waves. If I survive this voyage, I'll reach them.

"It's glorious!"

Turquoise water and a cloudless azure sky set off the white city rising up the slope from the harbor. Larger than three Jerusalems, Ephesus extends further than I can see. I understand now why Augustus recently dubbed the city the "First and Greatest Metropolis of Asia." Sailing into her port makes the voyage worth the pain.

I wobble and halt on the gangplank.

Around us, boats of all sizes vie for a berth. So many people—slaves, merchants, travelers. So much cargo—crates, bags, amphorae. So many languages, clothing, ethnicities, skin tones. The tumult assaults my senses. And I love it. I will make my fortune here.

"What's the holdup?" booms a voice from behind me. "Move it!"

"Sorry!" I scurry onto the wharf, scanning for Meoklis, who disembarked with the other first-class passengers. Why does solid ground continue to rock? Ahead, I recognize his deep blue silk and jog after him, trying to convince myself that beginning a new life in a huge metropolis isn't unusual.

"Follow me!" Meoklis turns before I can speak. "Let's remove ourselves."

"My baggage—"

"Don't worry. Narmer will include your bags with mine. They'll be delivered to my warehouse shortly."

"Thank you."

"Stay close. Before you know it, we'll be sipping wine in my office. And I imagine you're hungry." Meoklis laughs. "Haven't kept much down since we left Caesarea!"

In response, my stomach growls. Solid ground, a goblet of wine, good food, and a prospective business partner. This city holds promise.

CHAPTER 20
MIRIAM

Meron
Tammuz (June) AD 19

Father of the fatherless and protector of widows is God in his holy habitation.

PSALM 68:5

"Stop fighting!"

Is that Eli yelling? A chorus of screeching hens and angry voices crescendo from the chicken coop and spill into the courtyard.

"I'm not letting you go!" Eli's rare angry tones shock me. This must be bad.

"Eli? What's going on?" I drop my vegetable basket and rush over to find Eli and Matthias rolling in a dust cloud.

"Ow!" Matthias recoils, clutches his nose, and lays across a squirming mass.

With a burst of youth, Eli grabs at the legs. "I've got him!"

The three combatants lie in a panting heap, surrounded by half the household.

"What is going on?" I repeat.

"What?"

He shouldn't sound angry. We all wonder the same thing.

"Let me through." Ezra examines the heap of bodies. "Well, this ought to be an interesting story."

"I caught him stealing eggs." Eli pauses to swallow and nods his dirt-streaked face toward the whimpering mass. "But, he fought like a hyena. Matthias got the worst of it."

Blood trickles from Matthias's nose.

"Back to work, everyone." Ezra waves a hand and I shoo everyone away. And stay right where I am.

With equal parts firmness and gentleness, Ezra says, "If you agree not to fight anymore, we'll let you up. But you must promise not to run off."

"Yeah, okay," squeaks the thief. Eli and Matthias gingerly arise, though Eli retains a firm hold on the culprit's shoulder.

"Why, it's just a child!" I cluck my tongue and shake my head. "And his clothing has more patches than original material."

The boy squirms under Eli's grip. "You said you was gonna let me go."

Ezra smiles. "Seeing how you're no longer pinned with your face in the dirt, I'd say your lot has improved. When we know we can trust you, Eli will release you."

His curls are so dusty I can't determine their actual color.

Grabbing a stool, Ezra sits and points to the yolk river running down the child's cloak. "I don't think you can claim you were not stealing the eggs. Too much evidence otherwise."

No response.

"Look at me," Ezra orders softly.

His hazel eyes flash.

"What's your name?" Ezra asks.

"Samson," the boy mumbles.

"A fine name of a great warrior of the Lord. You're Jewish?"

"Yeah, I guess so."

"You guess?"

"Well, I got no parents. But, mostly all the poor people rounds here are Jewish."

"Do you know how old you are?"

"Wellll . . ." His shoulder rise to his ears. "Ten maybe?"

Ezra leans close. "How do you live, Samson?"

"I work and I glean." Samson digs his toe into the ground. "I beg when I hafta." He looks straight into Ezra's eyes. "And I take a few eggs sometimes. I never take all of 'em."

Grasping Samson's upper arms, Ezra draws him gently from Eli's grip.

"You're strong, like your namesake."

"I guess."

"You look like a hard worker."

"Yeah, but people think I can't do nothin' cause I'm too young. And small." He spits the last word.

"Well, I believe your mind is as strong as your body." Master gives Samson's biceps a squeeze.

Samson shrugs.

"Samson, you owe someone an apology." Ezra points to Matthias. "You made his nose bleed."

"Ain't my fault. He was grabbin' me."

"If you hadn't been stealing, he wouldn't have grabbed you."

"If I hadn't been starvin', I wouldn't have stole nothin'."

"If you'd asked, we would have given you bread."

Samson chews on a dirty nail and I barely hear his, "Sorry."

Matthias stops pinching his nose. "I forgive you?"

"There. Doesn't it feel wonderful to apologize and clear the air? How much better the world would be if we all owned our misdeeds. Now, Samson, there are a few more apologies you need to make. Can you think of any?" He tilts his head in Eli's direction.

With his chin on his chest, he mumbles "Sorry."

"For what?"

"Fighting?"

"What else?"

I point to Samson's eggy cloak with shell still stuck there.

"I'm sorry for stealing the eggs?" He doesn't sound sorry.

"Thank you." Eli nods toward Ezra. "But they're not my eggs."

Samson stomps his foot. "You want me to apologize to everybody?"

"Just the people you wronged," Ezra encourages.

Samson sighs, eyes darting from the front gate to the back, like a trapped bird, searching for an opening. "Well, who owns the stupid eggs?"

"I'm considered the owner, but in fact, the Most High owns everything." Ezra points at the sky.

"If He owns everything, why'd He give so much to you and nothin' to me?"

From this child's viewpoint, what with his matted hair, unpleasant odor, and shoeless feet, I suppose our compound looks grand. Because it's my home, I forget its abundance.

"Torah tells us to help those around us." With Ezra's hands on Samson's shoulders, his fidgeting ceases. "And yes, I'm blessed so I must give. You have little, but you're not alone. The Holy One looks out for you."

"How's He lookin' out for me?"

"He brought you here."

"To get caught!"

"If we hadn't caught you, you'd continue stealing. Adonai doesn't want you to be a thief anymore."

Ezra glances from Eli to me with that look in his eye. My husband shakes his head and I think, *no, no, no.*

"Tell me . . . how would you like a job?"

Samson rolls his eyes. So does Eli. "You'll hire me?"

"I need someone to deliver messages and assist where needed. In exchange, you'll have a home, meals, clothing, and—if you do a good job—a shekel each week."

"A shekel? For me?"

"But there are conditions." Samson's shoulders sag. "First, you must submit to a thorough cleaning and then keep yourself clean."

Samson wrinkles his nose at the word cleaning. I join him, knowing who will be blessed with that job.

"Second, you must respect those in authority. Third, if you decide you no longer want the job, you must come tell me like a man."

"Well, I guess so."

"Good, but I'm not done. Finally, you must attend school."

Samson's face changes to horror.

"To live by the Word, you must know it. First, Torah study, then work. You'll be too busy to get into mischief." Ezra crosses his arms.

"School? Do I hafta?"

"When our people entered this land, Joshua gave them a choice: the blessing or the curse. You have the same options. Do you still want the curse?"

"But it's hard!" Tears glisten in his eyes.

"Yes, blessings are hard sometimes. But they're also good."

"Well—" He sounds defeated. "All right. I guess."

"And Samson, you may call me Ezra."

With his grimy thumb, he points back to Eli. "What does he call ya'?"

Ezra's quirked-to-the-side smile, absent since Judah left, adorns his face. "Eli decided long ago to call me Master, though I've told him it isn't necessary. But then again, it's his choice." Ezra points to me. "This is Miriam, Eli's wife. She calls me Ezra."

Samson looks uncertain. "That's weird."

"I imagine we are somewhat peculiar. But, I'm glad you'll stay with us anyway. Well, Miriam," he winks and leans toward me, "what do you think? Is there hope?"

Crossing my arms, I stare at the mess of a boy and point to my kitchen. I bet Rome's pagan games are nothing compared to the coming spectacle. "You might as well know, I don't appreciate thieves who take my eggs. Now go."

Eli snorts. Master coughs. Samson looks helplessly back as I march him toward the kitchen.

"I just hope I have enough soap."

CHAPTER 21
JUDAH

Ephesus
Av (July), AD 19

Do not enter the path of the wicked, and do not walk in the way of the evil. Avoid it; do not go on it; turn away from it and pass on.

PROVERBS 4:14-15

"Just follow the boy," Meoklis had said, as if it would be easy.

Even in this Roman city with its straight streets and square corners, I struggle to keep up. Now and then he catches my eye, nods, and takes off again. I wipe my forehead and follow hard after him.

Locating housing in Ephesus proved difficult. And living at an inn for three weeks proved expensive. When Meoklis warned he couldn't store my belongings for free any longer, I complained about my struggles to secure an apartment. He introduced me to a friend who owns multiple buildings. We discussed details, laughed, drank wine, and before I knew what had happened, I'd agreed to a lease.

Miriam's voice kept nagging me. Slow down. Be careful. Her advice felt unnecessary in Meron where I trusted everyone, even villagers I didn't like. Maybe here I should take her word to heart.

However, whatever this room looks like, it will suffice. Soon I'll live in a classy apartment near the garment district. And someday, I'll own a fine home on the hill.

Grasping a small parchment in one hand and my satchel in the other, I spot my guide ahead. After the boy makes three wrong turns, I start to worry. If a local can't find this spot, how will I ever make my way? Finally, he points to a wooden gate, chatters in a lilting language, and holds out his hand. I place an assarius in his palm, and his eyes grow wide. Guess I overpaid, but that's the smallest coin I have.

I stride past the lopsided gate, through an arched walkway, and into a courtyard surrounded by two-story buildings. Staircases and balconies connect the haphazard construction, which suggests one room after another being built as time or money allowed. A patch of blue sky peeks through overhead.

To receive my key, I must hand my parchment, now crumpled and sweaty, to a Balbina. Against the left wall, under the lone tree, sits a small hut. A smoke puff draws my attention to someone beside it.

"Hello?"

No response.

"Do you know where I can find Balbina?"

An old woman turns and stares at me suspiciously. Hobbling over, she pokes me. "Who are you?"

"Judah—I mean Jude." That came out louder than I meant it to. "Are you Balbina? I arranged for a room here. Already paid my rent."

"Got proof?" I think she has more hairs on her chin than most young men, and wears more veils and robes than three women combined.

She examines my parchment with care and me with suspicion before shuffling to her hut. Returning with a large key, she points to a staircase.

"Second story, to the right."

I get lost in the wrinkles on her face.

"You expecting a grand escort?"

"Um . . . no . . . I mean, thank you. Some porters will deliver my baggage soon. Could you point them to my room?"

She grunts. "No cooking in the building."

"Alright."

"And no waste in the courtyard."

Current aromas defy the fact that such rules exist. But, I simply head to my room. Stains paint the sand-colored walls, and the wooden steps are thin and smooth in the middle.

With a click, my door opens to a musty room with mottled stucco walls. A few dusty shelves, a wooden bed frame, and a small table with a stool make up all my furnishings. High on the wall, a window barely wider than me not only lets in air and light, but also provides corners for multiple spiders to make their homes.

The apartment in my dreams looked brighter and smelled better.

When my baggage arrives, I hang clothes and my water bucket on pegs, smooth bedding on the bed frame, place two oil lamps on the table, and organize my parchments beside the lamps.

Holding my money belt, I turn in a circle. "Where am I going to hide you? You're too heavy to wear all the time." I feel like Miriam with this new habit of talking to myself.

"Isn't there an odd-looking brick up here?" Moving aside my dried fruit on the shelf, I dislodge the brick. Behind it, I discover a cavity. I stack my precious coins, replace the brick, and move parcels in front of it.

What do I need to purchase before dark? Oil for my lamp. Food that is not dried fruit. And some wine. The food at the thermopolium across the street smells delicious so I grab the few coins I kept out of my bank, lock my door with my key, and race down the stairs.

PING! Ping! Ping!

Groaning, I rub my temples and push myself to sitting. My head pounds in unison with incessant hammering outside my window. Leaning against the cool stucco, I try to orient myself. My stomach feels like it's back on the ship and I need water. I force my eyes open. The room spins.

An empty wineskin accuses me. *Wine is a mocker, strong drink a brawler, and whoever is led astray by it is not wise.*[1]

"Stop," I instruct my reservoir of memorized scripture.

Next time, I'll mix more water with my wine. Water. I crave water. I grasp the empty bucket, which slips and clatters onto the wooden floor.

Cradling my head, I let loose a few curse words I learned on the boat. At home when I didn't feel well, Miriam would fetch cool spring water and fresh herbs to soothe me. Now, if she knew that the reason I felt poorly was because of wine, she would only provide meager comfort and a lecture.

"As soon as I'm successful, I'll hire a servant."

Silence.

I bend to retrieve the bucket, and the throbbing intensifies.

"Fetching water," I mutter. "Women's work." After struggling to lock the door, I descend into stabbing sunlight. I'm not sure I'll make it to the well.

Balbina cackles on her stool, sending her chin hairs quivering.

"Would you fetch me water?" I rasp.

Her cackle grows shrill. "Do it yourself."

"If I pay you?"

"These old bones couldn't do your work if they wanted to. And they don't want to." I observe her crooked hands and know I'm on my own.

Emerging onto the crowded street, I almost retch. Ping! Ping! Ping! To the left stands a leather shop, the craftsman pounding nails into sandals.

I do *not* crave water from Meron's spring. I do *not* long to smell clean green fields or eat Miriam's bread. Wrapping my gauze scarf around my nose, I attempt to subdue the smells of hot people and rotting waste. Slowly, I advance toward the well in the next square to join a long line of people holding buckets. When I fill mine, I wrinkle my nose before gulping the cloudy liquid and splashing water on my face and neck.

"Hey! What you doing?"

I turn to face a broad-shouldered ruffian. Inspecting me, he says in an accent I can't identify, "You not from here?"

"No," I gulp, grateful I haven't replaced my Judean clothing yet.

"We no waste water on faces and heads."

Obviously. "Sorry."

The sun sits straight overhead by the time I'm back in my room, and now I must hurry to meet Meoklis. Shaking out my garments, I dress as best I can and stuff scrolls into my satchel.

First, I purchase bread and olives, and then I try to remember how many turns we took on the way here yesterday. For my first three weeks, I stayed close to the inn. Now, I must get to know this city better. If I head downhill, certainly I'll find the harbor.

My headache eases as my mind sifts through the variety this metropolis offers. Languages I've never learned confuse me. Spices I've never tasted lure me. Music from instruments I've never heard intrigue me.

A cacophony of street hawkers proclaim their products.

"Fine jewelry from Egypt!"

"Ivory imported from Ethiopia!"

And on every block of the city, "Buy your silver statue of Artemis! Finest quality."

When I finally turn onto Arcadiane Street, the huge avenue running from the city center to the sparkling port, I lean against one of the many columns lining the street and smile. I know where I am. From here, I set out for the cloth district where fine fabrics arrive from around the Great Sea.

"Meoklis!" I rush through the door of his office. "It's a relief to see a friendly face!"

"Greetings, Jude." Meoklis looks me up and down and wrinkles his nose. "How is your apartment?"

"Fine."

He pinches the edge of my green striped cloak between two fingers. "What is this?"

I jerk the homespun cloth away. "It's all that was clean. I plan on purchasing better clothes."

"Good!" Meoklis claps me on the shoulder. "I'll take you to the best shops, and later we'll visit the baths. I make more business deals in the baths than here in my office."

Questions crowd my mouth, but I clamp my mouth tight. I want to appear confident, not overeager.

"You Jews don't appreciate baths in the same way. Pity."

"All Judean villages have ritual baths." I'm surprised at my defensiveness.

"Interesting."

"I anticipate what Ephesus offers. The Roman baths in Sepphoris and Caesarea were amazing."

"Good, good." Meoklis winks. "We might not feel holy afterward, but we'll enjoy it."

I don't desire holiness. Just experience and success.

CHAPTER 22
JUDAH

Galatian Wilderness
Elul (August) AD 20

"Come, let us return to the LORD; for he has torn us, that he may heal us; he has struck us down, and he will bind us up.

HOSEA 6:1

"Ju—dah. Ju—dah!"

Are the hills echoing my name, or do I imagine it?

From the bottom of the ravine that the swine and I traverse, I scan the hilltops surrounding us. Only a vulture circles above. "Great! Now I'm hearing things!"

Then the clip clop of hooves makes my heart beat faster.

"Juuuuu—dahhhh!"

Rocks scuttle down the hill behind me. Whirling about, I spy Pavlos and Gaidoros cresting the hill.

"Down here!" I leap in the air and wave my arms above my head. Never have I been so glad to see a person. And particularly this person.

With his good-natured chuckle, he calls, "You're are as brown and thin as the trunk of a palm tree! I almost couldn't find you."

"I'm glad you did!"

Now, reclining by an evening fire with food in my belly, I gaze at the man I no longer find ugly. After he catches me up on all the news from the villa, he says, "I come with news. Master Valerius and a few of his associates have organized a caravan transporting goods south to trade for grain. You'll return in seven days to join it."

"My own personal Sheol is ending!" I lift my arms. "Yahoo!" My heart skips a beat as my shout echoes.

Pavlos laughs which turns into a lingering cough.

"Are you okay?"

With a flick of his hand, he dismisses my concern and changes the subject. "Tell me Judah, has your time under the stars, with only Adonai and the company of your snorting friends, changed how you think about your choice to move to Ephesus?"

"Well, the pigs don't tell me what they think. And Adonai has made no effort to help me, even when I've asked, be it here or in Ephesus."

"So Adonai should have blessed your venture?"

"Please, Pavlos. Examining how well my past choices worked out wastes your company and this warm food."

Again a cough incapacitates him.

"Have you told Gallus or Valerius that you need a physician?" I ask.

"I'm fine. Now answer my question, Judah. You think you should feast on the abundance of Adonai's house and that He will still give you drinks from the river of His delights[1] when you rejected Him in favor of evil?"

"You have a psalm for everything. And please don't mention feasts or rivers. Anyway, what evil am I savoring now?"

"Don't confuse lack of opportunity with commitment to the Most High."

I add dry brush to the fire.

"Do you still blame Seth for your bad choices?"

"He beat me over the head with how unholy I was. Who would want to follow his God?"

"You can't blame Adonai for someone who follows Him poorly or teaches His truth incorrectly."

"But if Adonai is all powerful, why didn't He stop Seth from acting like that?"

"Since creating the world, Adonai has given humanity a choice. But He also gave us His Word. His Truth. We study His teaching so we can know Him and learn how to act. It's your job to learn truth, no matter what your brother did."

"You don't understand what it was like, old man."

"Probably not. But Seth's failures don't keep you from knowing He who created heaven and earth, the One who has never left you, though you've done your best to run from Him."

"Hmm."

"Do you fear God yet?"

"Fear?"

"Love, respect, honor, obey, adore. Use whatever word you like best."

"Do I fear or respect the Hebrew God who ignored my pleas for help and now lets me starve as a slave?"

"How can you turn your back on Him yet still blame Him for what happens?"

"I don't know what you mean."

"Really?" He leans his head back. "'Yet they did not obey or incline their ear, but everyone walked in the stubbornness of his evil heart. Therefore, I brought upon them all the words of this covenant, which I commanded them to do, but they did not.'[2]"

"Sounds like an angry prophet."

"No, a weeping one. Jeremiah offered life to people pursuing death, and it broke his heart when they wouldn't listen to him. Because I fear, or respect, God, I don't reject the parts of His Law I don't like. I do things His way even when I don't understand. You confuse knowing about God with actually knowing Him. To understand what He did in the past isn't believing He acts now."

"You talk too much," I mumble. "Just like Abba."

"Until you believe Adonai, you won't trust Him."

When a jackal howls, the swine snort restlessly and I lie back.

"Judah, if the rest of your life involves slavery, injustice, and hurt—if you hunger and thirst until your dying day, will you trust Adonai anyway?"

"The rest of my life?" Starvation must have shortened my perspective to the present. I yell to the moon. "I curse the dog Apollon with all my heart!"

All my heart! The hills reply.

"Feel better?"

"No."

"Until you stop hating your enemy and start taking responsibility for your choices, you'll never be free to thrive."

"Thrive! Are you thriving? Limping around? Coughing all the time? Giving everything you have to the villa and getting nothing in return?"

"That depends on your definition of thrive."

"You're a slave. You're crippled and sound sick. You have no family. Define that!"

"Here's another psalm for you." He ignores my groan. "'God is our refuge and strength, a very present help in trouble. Therefore, we will not fear though the earth gives way.'[3] Selah—pause and consider that. Living in His power and by His help doesn't require money, position, or even family. Living a full, happy life here, like this"—Pavlos sweeps his hand down his deformed leg—"proves how safe my Refuge is. 'His steadfast love' isn't desiccated by this drought or altered by my infirmity."

"But we'll be slaves forever!"

"No one lives forever."

"So be a slave or be dead. Comforting thought." I stare at the stars.

"You remember when we broke up the dry ground though conditions weren't right for planting?"

"Yeah. Stupid waste."

"That prepared the ground for when the rain comes. It always falls eventually. So prepare your heart. Crush the hard places and pull out the weeds for when the Most High shows up. He always does. In His perfect timing."

"Look up, Pavlos. Another cloudless night. Rain isn't any closer than He is."

"Quit scanning the horizon. Examine the past for proof that every drought ends and Adonai remains. Faith remembers what He's already done. He's freed slaves before, if you remember."

"After four hundred years!"

Leaning forward, he says, "But what if they hadn't endured or remembered Him? Who would He have parted the Red Sea for? Or fed manna to in the wilderness?"

"Well—" No retort comes to mind.

"Maybe you'll be set free, maybe not. Maybe freedom awaits your son or grandson. Can you be faithful now, knowing that you may never see His fulfilled promises? Can you teach your children to do the same?"

"I . . . I've never considered them—the generations after me."

"That's because you don't see past the end of your nose." Pavlos coughs hard and draws his cloak around him. "When conditions improve, you'll find opportunities to earn money. You can save and buy your freedom."

I snort. "How long would that take?"

"I've saved all my years of slavery. Could you do the same?"

I hang my head.

"Adonai is not through with you. Maybe he brought you here so I can remind you who He is. Stop looking at your brother and blaming him if you misunderstand Adonai. Stop looking at those who cheated you and blaming them for your slavery. Look up, Judah. Look up!"

Laying back, multitudes of stars cover me like a tent, and I imagine Meron resting under these same white lights. Even if I managed to buy my freedom, I can never go back. I destroyed my life there.

"'Return, O faithless sons," Pavlos says, as though reading my mind. "I will heal your faithlessness.'[4]"

"I can't go home. Even if given the chance."

"That's your choice. But I'd give my good leg for family. Think on that." Pavlos turns his back to the fire. "Good night, my friend."

His wheezing snore, the humming locusts, and the crackling fire are now my company. Inside me, something ignites from the words. *Return, O faithless sons. Return.* They spark hope, and hope hurts.

"LET'S GO, my beauties. It's our last night in the wilderness. And my last night sleeping in a tree while you snuffle underneath."

I climb the carob tree in search of a perch as the swine snort through fallen pods. The bread Pavlos left ran out two days ago. As my stomach rumbles, I recall eating myself sick at Ephesian parties. Of course, Kassandra's dishonest eyes and Apollon's self-satisfied face always lurk in the same room as all that food. Maybe I prefer hunger.

At what moment did I turn right when I should have turned left? Which decision ruined everything? Maybe I just took one small step after another, away from the people who loved me. This self-reflection is uncomfortable, but if Pavlos's words are correct and freedom is for my children, then I have things to figure out.

My stomach growls again. While I surrendered pickiness long ago, I haven't stooped to the swine's level—until now. I pop a dry pod into my mouth and suck.

"Ugh!" I spit out the bitter husk.

A few carobs, small and withered, still cling to life on a high branch. If I could reach those, there might be sweet meat inside. My mouth waters. I inch up the trunk. Higher. Higher. Fighting dizziness, I extend a shaking hand. Just . . . a little . . . farther.

Crack!

I fall through the air and land with a thud. Pigs screech and run away while stars dance across my eyes and I struggle to catch my breath. Rolling my head to the side, I see the carobs, still clinging to the branch within reach. I also spot the largest, meanest pig heading toward them.

"I don't think so!" Lurching forward, I grab the fruit and scramble into the tree. The pig grunts.

The carobs aren't very sweet, but at least the meat remains and I suck out every tiny morsel. The swine snort through the downed branches looking for more. I don't dare return to the battle. They'd kill me. And though I sometimes wish for death, the thought of dying terrifies me.

Return, faithless Israel, declares the Lord. I will not look on you in anger, for I am merciful, declares the Lord; I will not be angry forever.[5]

Jeremiah was always Abba's favorite prophet. I wonder why? I crumble a dried leaf realizing that if I never see him again, I'll never know.

"Oh Abba." He used to add bread and a kind word to everyone's daily wages. He sent supplies to poor villagers. Even his lowliest servants thrived more than Pavlos does.

I sit up.

Is it possible? Could I return to Meron and become his servant? I have no idea how to escape slavery. But what if I could? What then?

CHAPTER 23
SETH

Meron
Av (July) AD 19

House and wealth are inherited from fathers, but a prudent wife is from the LORD.

PROVERBS 19:14

Touching the mezuzah, I return from three days of visiting with Hadassah. Except for her father pushing me to set the date, I found time with her mostly refreshing, though she does tend to bounce from one task to another. She reminds me of a Sunbird, hovering in flight and flitting from flower to flower.

Tova rushes up with water to wash.

"Where's Abba?"

"In the barn, sir."

"He's out of his room?"

"Yes, sir!"

When Abba's laugh rings from the barn, I head that way. I haven't heard his laugh since Judah left. I've miss—

Wham!

I clasp my chest and bend over, trying to find the breath that just flew out of me when someone or something barreled into me.

Rufus barks and jumps around a boy sprawled on the ground.

One hand still clings to my chest, and with the other I grab the youngster. Trying to squirm away from my restraint, a boy's hazel eyes stare at me from under a shining mass of dark, curls.

He drops his head. "Sorry."

"Seth!" Abba's bright face and happy energy seem opposite to the man I left. "Did your visit with Hadassah go well?"

"Uh"—I grip the wriggling child harder—"yes. Her family sends greetings." I jerk my head toward my captive.

"Oh, yes. Meet Samson. Samson, this is my son, Seth."

"Who named this wisp, Samson?" I release him.

"One day he'll be a mighty warrior." Abba's eyes quiet me, an ability he's never lost. "For now, he's Eli's new helper."

Samson puffs out his chest, and Rufus licks his hand.

"Wait!" I stare at his face. "You're the beggar who stole my bread!"

"I'm not a beggar!"

"Well, how about a thief?"

Abba steps forward. "How about a created soul and a hungry orphan?"

"I'm being reprimanded? He stole Samuel and Deborah's bread and threw a rock at me!"

Abba steps closer. "Adonai's given us so much, more is required from us. This boy has nothing."

Then he kneels and looks Samson straight in the eye. "Did you steal from Seth?"

The boy plays with his belt. But Abba's unyieldingness recalls memories from my childhood. This kid has no idea who he's up against.

Rufus leans against his leg. After a big sigh, he says, "Yeah."

Abba cups his cheek. "Samson, if you are to live in this house, you must repent and never again steal. Do you understand?"

"He's living here! And the revelation that he's a thief doesn't deter you?"

"I already knew. Don't forget the Proverb, 'Men do not despise a thief if he steals to satisfy himself when he is hungry.'[1] Samson stays in the loft above the feed room until we find a more suitable place."

"It's the best I ever had," Samson mutters, not taking his eyes off Rufus. The dog's tail thumps up dust. "And I won't."

"Won't what?" Abba asks.

"I won't steal no more. I only did 'cause I don't like starvin'."

I shake my head.

Abba says, "Besides feeling sorry for your wrong, you must apologize to Seth."

Samson looks aghast. "You hafta apologize for everything around here."

"Only for our wrongs."

Samson pleads with his eyes for any other way, but a nod indicates the non-negotiable requirement.

"Fine," he sighs. "I'm sorry that when you called me names and kicked dirt on me I got mad and threw a rock at you. And I'm sorry I stole bread you dropped, just because I hadn't eaten nothin' for two days."

Abba ignores my fierce head shake. "Hopefully as you learn to love the Creator, your apology will transform to something more sincere."

"I have no more time to waste here."

"Wait, son. Samson, in the same proverb where the Holy One instructs us to not despise hungry thieves, He instructs the thief to repay seven times what he stole. You'll need to repay Seth."

"Seven times? That's not fair!"

"Stealing isn't fair either. I'll help you figure out how to pay back what you owe. Here, you will eat without stealing and learn Adonai's ways—they're always a blessing even when they feel hard."

"He doesn't know what you mean," I grumble.

"I'm poor, not stupid." Turning his back on me, Samson puts his arm around Rufus. "I'll pay Seth back. But I won't like it."

Abba tousles his hair. "Obedience comes easier when we like it, but it's not necessary."

Just when my life was returning to normal, an orphan crashes into it. Oh, Most High, will You ever smile on us again?

Boys released from Torah studies shriek with freedom. I wish I could be as carefree. As we leave the synagogue, men call "shalom," and I wave farewell without looking at them. Wandering Meron's narrow residential streets, I can't get Rabbi Akiva's admonition out of my mind.

"What's your delay in marrying Hadassah?" he asked. "Don't forget that Adonai gifted us with marriage as a blessing."

Like I don't know that. It's just that—

Whack!

Air whooshes out of me and I grab my side which was just impaled by an elbow. The culprit, one of the racing school boys, sprawls into a pile of baskets. From underneath, his muffled voice says, "Sorry. I was runnin' in one direction and lookin' in another."

"And look what happened!" Throwing off baskets, I uncover the boy. "Samson?"

"Why'd I have to run into you?"

"Is it your life's goal to cause me bodily harm?" Levi, the other racing boy, lurks off to the side. "Aren't you Samuel's son?" His grave nod looks scared.

Samson grunts, "Sorry."

I wait for more, but only receive a sour face. Then again, he's Abba's problem. "Watch where you're running."

"Sure, Seth," he looks back as he and Levi resume their chase, "See ya!" Then he almost runs over a woman with a baby on her hip.

I return to wandering the streets and considering Hadassah. My friends are all married, but after the initial joy, strife arises. Not that happiness is the purpose of marriage, but I'd think wanting to go home would make every day better.

I like Hadassah. But, when I visit, her entire family surrounds us, which, while proper, means I don't know what being alone with her is like.

What do women want? Before my betrothal, I'd never considered the question. I don't spend time with females other than Miriam. A sister would've been helpful. Or Eema. Life with females remains a mystery, and I dislike surprises.

Life's rhythm of work, study, and Shabbat creates peace, with the Feasts to provide variety. Applying the Law—to do the right thing day in and day out—this defines a good life. A wife could disrupt this, especially if she possesses strong opinions, a vivacious spirit, and curls that cascade down her slender neck.

On the other hand, with Hadassah I could start a family. Maybe with grandchildren, Abba would quit adopting light-fingered orphans.

"That's it!" I stop and smack my forehead. That's the drastic change Abba needs. I'll talk to him and set the date. Then we'll find somewhere else for Samson.

Looking around, I get my bearings and stride the shortest way home.

"Poor Kefir," Abba says. "He hurt his back today and it will make harvesting flax difficult."

Samson glances at me, probably afraid I'll disclose his disreputable behavior in the streets.

I lean back on my pillow at our rooftop table and dip my bread in honey. "Samson, I need to talk with Abba."

Mopping his third bowl of lentil soup with Miriam's bread, Samson pops the soggy bite in his mouth and speaks with the half-chewed food on display. "Okay." He grabs more bread.

"Privately."

Piece of bread in hand, he says, "Oh. Sure." After a last swipe, he stuffs it on top of the last bite, stores more bread in his belt, and rushes down the stairs without washing.

Abba chuckles. "Now, what would you like to discuss?"

"I'm ready to wed Hadassah."

"Hallelujah!" He claps me on the shoulder. "I was beginning to worry."

I stiffen.

"Forgive me. I rejoice at your good news. A feminine laugh and joyful spirit is just what this family of males needs. When? We must prepare the feast."

"Three weeks should be sufficient. Her father stands by the contract, praise be His name, despite Judah's scandal."

A shadow flits across Abba's face. But that's Judah's fault, not mine. "Do it while you have the nerve. Marriage can feel intimidating. I'm sorry your eema isn't here to help you understand women's ways."

"Do you still miss Eema?"

"Every day. I miss her smiling face when I walked through the gate. I even miss her irritated face when I returned late."

"Why?" Irritation in marriage scares me.

"She became unhappy because she feared for my safety or desired my presence. To be wanted is precious."

"I suppose." I play with my empty cup. Abba never even contemplated marrying again. Could I possibly ever love Hadassah that much? With so much of myself?

"I pray you and Hadassah will grow in love and friendship. Marriage can double your joys and halve your sorrows. But you must open your heart. Remember The Song. Yahweh gave marriage as a gift."

"I understand," I say. But I don't. Could I ever dare to be so vulnerable? To be so out of control?

"The Song describes more than just physical love. Our Creator desires deep connection between husband and wife. If they delight in each other physically, mentally, and emotionally, they reflect what Adonai designed marriage to be from the Garden." Leaning his head back, Abba closes his eyes and breathes. "'This is my beloved and this is my friend.'[2]"

I try to picture Abba as a young groom joyfully proceeding to claim his bride. Will I be able to find the joy that Abba describes?

"Go to her as her beloved. Speak Solomon's words. 'Arise, my love, my beautiful one, and come away, for behold, the winter is past; the rain is over and gone. The flowers appear on the earth, the time of singing has come.'[3] Bring singing back into our home."

Duty compels me to marry. Family obligation requires it. Physical longing demands it.

But if this is the right thing to do, why am I terrified?

CHAPTER 24
JUDAH

Ephesus
Elul (August), AD 19

I have seen everything that is done under the sun, and behold, all is vanity and a striving after wind.

ECCLESIASTES 1:14

"Oil, please." I hand the merchant my clay pitcher. Shading my eyes, I check and find the sun higher than I hoped. Mundane chores take way too long.

After I fetch clean clothes from Junia, the laundress in the stairwell across from me, I head to my apartment, taking the stairs two at a time before I change into the nicest clothes I've ever owned, grab more coins from the table, stuff scrolls in my satchel, and fill my skin with water.

As I rush out the gate, Balbina calls, "Is all this hurrying getting you anywhere?"

"Of course it is!"

After two rights and a left, I veer through a narrow alley. Skirting slow walkers, I avoid piles of waste and enter the market to buy enough salted fish, cheese, and bread for today.

"Jude! Today's batch is delicious!" I love Aram's skewers of sizzling pork and my stomach growls. But meat's expensive.

I display a brass sesterius. "I need this to last."

"Spend less on clothes and you can buy better food."

"I'll eat better once I earn denarii instead of only spending them."

Stuffing my dinner in my satchel, I enter a shop selling oriental silks and Egyptian linen. "Greetings, Demetrius. Any new fabrics?"

"Just look at this beautiful weave, Jude," he says as he holds out the end of his belt. Blue, red, and green interweave in a delicate pattern.

"Amazing! Where is this made?"

"You're always so curious." He leads me to bolts of exquisite cloth. "And I suppose you want to know how much I paid and how much I'm selling it for?"

"Your wisdom is always helpful."

He unrolls bolt after shimmering bolt, rattling off exorbitant prices at a dizzying speed.

"You look dismayed." He pats my arm. "But remember, I didn't start off selling fine, imported fabrics in a store, but cheap cloth from a cart. However, instead of spending the profit on myself, like my competitors," he nudges me, "I purchased a little higher grade cloth each time."

I nod.

"It took a long time, but look at me now."

"I don't have a long time!"

"You're young. How can you already be out of time? Find a good wife. Work hard. Grow slow, like a tree. And one day an impatient young man will enter your shop, and you'll tell him the same thing."

I wind a delicate pink ribbon around my finger. "Demetrius, do you know a merchant named Meoklis? He's helping me get started."

He pauses as he refolds fabric. "I've met him."

"And?"

He restacks the bolts of fabric. "You're a man and must make your own decisions."

"That sounds like a warning."

Demetrius turns to me. "I don't know you that well, Jude. But be careful. Men like Meoklis abound in this city. Maybe they will help you. Maybe they will help themselves to you. Only wisdom can tell the difference."

The hairs on the back of my neck prickle, so I change the subject to Egyptian linen. Eventually, I thank him and exit the shop. I value Demetrius's opinion, and he's been helpful, but I'm trying to grow fast, not slow. That's why I listen to conversations between businessmen and government officials in the State Agora. And at the baths, I talk to anyone willing to share. My big break is out there. I just have to find it.

Arriving at The Crow, I thread my way around raucous tables of men throwing knucklebones. I dodge the lanterns hanging from the ceiling, and make my way to the back right corner, where Meoklis's circle always congregates.

"Greetings!"

"Jude!" exclaims Otho from Athens, a pudgy man with straight, brown hair and dull eyes. From his slur I'd say he's been at the tavern several hours already. "Meet our new friend, Cosmas. I was just tell —tell—"

The fair-haired, athletic man next to Otho rescues him. "He was explaining how Meoklis has been helping him."

"Yes!" Otho falls onto his stool. "And even though this Greek Adonis is more handsome than all us put together, we're going to let him stay around."

I like Cosmas's genuine smile. "I'm Jude. Where are you from?"

"Corinth. My father sent me here to develop our trade route further. And you?"

"From Judea. I trade in fine textiles. At least, that's the plan."

Cosmas and I fall into easy conversation. We compare Corinth and Judea, finding vast differences and surprising similarities. It seems people are people everywhere. Fathers and sons. Dreams and obligations. Hopes and fears.

"Where do you live?" he asks.

"Meoklis helped me find an apartment in the leather district."

Cosmas blinks.

I lean in. "Took me weeks to figure out how to get around here. There are more streets and alleys in my neighborhood here than in my whole village back home."

"That makes me feel better. Corinth's big, but nothing like Ephesus. My room is close to the docks." He wrinkles his nose. "I always smell fish."

"Well, my place smells like people. A lot of people."

He knocks his shoulder against mine. "Ephesus. Some parts aren't as glamorous as others, but what a world we live in."

As if on cue, four soldiers barge into the tavern, demanding drink. Patrons scurry from a table they commandeer.

Cosmas winks. "To quote Meoklis, 'At least they're good for business.'"

I lift my goblet. "To being good for business."

He returns my toast, and we spend the afternoon bantering, sharing my lunch, and ignoring everyone else. Satisfaction fills me. For the first time, I've met someone I feel comfortable with. I finally have a friend.

FROM NIGHTLIFE, to food, to the baths, I enjoy everything more with Cosmas. Last night, we managed to get ourselves invited to a dinner party. Meoklis embraced us like old friends. "Come to The Crow at the third hour, tomorrow. Opportunity awaits!"

So here we sit while Meoklis beams. "Well, my friends, so many people pour into our fair city, and here you, a lucky few, gather. And what a treat today! What a treat!"

As we wait, Cosmas asks, "How do you know everyone?"

"I've met everyone here through Meoklis. He's helped me every step of the way."

"Hmmm."

"He's here!" Meoklis announces and trips over his own feet. "Sir, your presence honors us. My friends, please meet Apollon."

Frankincense wafts over us and all conversation ceases as a rotund man swathed in glimmering red silk approaches. His sandy hair is cut short, and his fleshy cheeks are lined with a trimmed beard.

"I bet the silver embroidery on his cloak costs more than a month's rent!" Cosmas whispers.

One man after another stands and gives his name. After each introduction, Apollon, whose nose points toward the ceiling, slowly closes and reopens his eyes, and then turns to the next man.

Waiting our turn, I whisper back. "I've heard merchants utter his name in tones somewhere between respect and fear."

"Cosmas, from Corinth."

"Jude, from Judea."

"Otho, from Athens."

Leaning back, I whisper, "He doesn't seem very glad to be here."

Cosmas snorts. "He looks like someone who's never glad about anything."

After the last introduction, Apollon bows his head slightly. "At your service." He then whispers to a short, sinewy, man behind him who scuttles away.

"I'm looking for a few select partners interested in serious business," Apollon declares. "And maybe—just maybe—it will be you."

Murmurs echo through the tavern until everyone, even the Roman soldiers, grows quiet. At the entrance, two blond Goliaths stand on either side of the door.

Cosmas raises an eyebrow and whispers. "Germanians?"

"Or ex-gladiators?"

Then a stunning woman saunters past the two sentinels and all attention transfers to her. Blue silk drapes her curves, with a gold belt accentuating her waist and gold chains encircling her long neck, while also intensifying the color of her extraordinary amber-colored eyes. Intricately braided auburn hair crowns the vision. She sinks onto the stool Meoklis offers.

"Kassandra," Apollon says, pointing at the woman.

"Maybe he doesn't appreciate competition for our attention," Cosmas says, behind his hand.

"Then he shouldn't have brought her!"

Apollon raps his knuckles on the table. "Opportunities wait right outside the door and I continually hunt for bold investors as partners. Let me tell you about others I've worked with."

The haughty man transforms. His nasally voice remains, but his passion builds as he spins story after story of brave men who risked everything before earning wealth beyond imagination. Elbows on the table, leg bouncing underneath, I lean forward. Last night I lost three denarii playing knucklebones here. Today, across this same table, sits the opportunity I've searched for.

Apollon surveys each of us that pant for the next word. When I think I might burst, he splays his hands on the table. "Before we go farther, I must determine if you're as qualified as Meoklis claims. I don't work with just anyone."

Apollon wants to be sure of me? Well, I'll be whoever he needs me to be.

IN THE WEEK since Meoklis introduced us to Apollon, Cosmas and I have conversed with Apollon twice. Our first meeting occurred when he invited us to his salon and fed us delicacies like I've never tasted. I hoped to steal another glance at Kassandra, but she never appeared.

"I like you two. You show more promise than the others," Apollon said. I pounded Cosmas on the back and toasted him. He didn't appear as flattered as I felt.

Today, we accompanied Apollon to the three-story Varius Baths, the finest in Ephesus. It made the facility I use look like a horse trough. We talked, met contacts, and consumed wine for hours in the warmth of the Tepidarium. I'm still fuzzy on the exact details, but Apollon's scheme screams opportunity.

"So what do you think?" I ask Cosmas as we wander back from the baths. "Are you interested?"

Glancing around, he mutters, "Yes. But wary. Let's have dinner somewhere far from our friends. And where we can feel a breeze to cool this late summer heat."

Twenty minutes later, we grab food from a busy thermopolium.

"Let's find somewhere to sit."

"Is something wrong?"

"Sorry, Jude." Cosmas sighs. "I'm just struggling. How do I know who's honest and who's scheming to part me from my money?" He slurps some broth. "I never knew how hard being on my own would be. People are different here. I wish my father could advise me."

I choke. "What do you mean?"

"You're telling me you have no doubts about these men or this plan?"

"Do you?"

"I—I'm not sure. How did you meet Meoklis?"

"I met him in Sepphoris. He's the one who gave me the idea . . ." I haven't told anyone how I got my money. "We sailed here together, and he helped me get settled. I might live on the street if it weren't for him. And you?"

"I met him in the tavern under my room. The next day, he reappeared and invited me to meet his other young friends. How long have you known him?"

"Feels like a lifetime, but only since last Iyyar—I mean Aprillis."

"You're Jewish?"

I nod.

"I have Jewish friends in Corinth. We got along despite their peculiarities."

"Peculiarities?"

"The list of dos and don'ts. What to eat and not eat. But mainly the one God. My family seeks favor from many gods and goddesses. Jews seem to look to their God for how to live. I even remember something about my friend being forbidden to mix fabrics."

"Yes. 'You shall not wear cloth of wool and linen mixed together.'[1]"

"Sorry, but I think it's weird to have such specific instructions. Did you follow all that?"

"Abba used to tell me that we assume that Adonai knew why He told us what to do and not do. Sometimes we understand, and sometimes we might not, at least not yet. So, until we do, obey anyway." I shrug.

"I prefer to not risk making any of the gods angry, so I cover every possibility."

"Yes, well, our God doesn't allow for any others."

"Rather selfish of him." Cosmas winks.

"He's jealous—at least that's what He calls Himself."

"So, you only worship Him?"

"Not anymore. I don't want to miss out on what the others have to offer."

"Have you visited the Temple of Artemis?"

"Not yet."

"What? How can you live in Ephesus and not pay homage to her?"

"Well . . ."

"Have you at least bought her statue?"

"I—I will!" Scratching my head, I say, "I can't explain what I don't understand. If I embrace new ideas, will I turn my back on my people?"

"But Jude, to live in her city and be successful, you must honor her."

I bring us back to what I care about. "Let's discuss business. Why were you afraid to talk before?"

"There's something about Apollon that I don't trust—not to mention his entourage, like those two guards?"

"Leuthar and Aldric."

"They belong at Circus Maximus, not beside a businessman. And his assistant Haman lurks in corners, eavesdropping on conversations."

"I think he looks like a jackal."

Cosmas laughs. "That might insult jackals."

"Will you attend Apollon's party tomorrow?"

"Yes, at least to find out more."

I attempt confidence. "I think Apollon might be who I've been searching for."

"Maybe. Or maybe he's something else entirely. But if we don't go, we'll never know. Besides," Cosmas flashes his toothy smile, "I want to see Kassandra again. Now she might be what I'm looking for."

"Don't you think she's Apollon's?"

"That's another thing I plan to find out."

CHAPTER 25
SETH

Meron
Elul (August) - Heshvan (October) AD 19

The LORD is my chosen portion and my cup; you hold my lot. The lines have fallen for me in pleasant places; indeed, I have a beautiful inheritance.

PSALM 16:5-6

"He's come! The Bridegroom is here!"

I stride the ascent to Safed as my heart pounds and my temples pulse. My ears buzz. My fingers tingle. I'd swallow my nausea if my mouth weren't so dry. Why did I choose the hottest month of the year for our wedding?

Gideon pounds me on the back. "Smile, cousin. Your wedding day is a good day. I didn't travel from Cana just to observe misery."

I attempt as big a smile as my parched lips allow.

"Don't worry, Seth," he whispers, putting an arm around my shoulders. "You'll be grateful tomorrow."

Gideon steers me until our procession of singing friends and family arrives at Hadassah's home. There's no escaping now. The disgrace of abandoning my wedding would be worse than a lifetime of regret.

Hadassah's family escorts her, crowned and beaming, to the door, her tiny frame bedecked with as much finery as it can hold. I admire the brown curls cascading down her back, our wedding the last time it will flow in public. Her loveliness unnerves me.

We avoid each other's eyes as we descend the hill, her family following. Everyone climbs into carts and wagons to drive to Meron for the wedding feast. Neighbors and relatives join the procession.

When we finally reach our home in Heron, Abba greets the crowd which pushes through the gate of our compound. "Shalom! Enter. Gather around!"

The crowd adds their own instructions.

"Keep moving."

"Quiet!"

"Sit down in front. We can't see!"

Abba finally quiets everyone. "A new family begins, which means Israel continues, so we must all celebrate." Joining our hands, he places his on our heads and continues speaking. Hadassah's delicate hand trembles in mine and makes me deaf to his words.

Facing each other, I dare to search her eyes.

". . . When You began marriage in Eden . . . "

They exude the same love and joy I observe in Abba when he talks about Eema.

". . . So we ask You to grant . . . "

Could she love me already? My world tilts.

"My love," she whispers, sending my stomach roiling, though this time pleasure accompanies the nausea. I step closer to her.

Rabbi Akiva prays, "May they be fruitful like . . . "

With one finger I place a curl behind her ear.

"Amen!" Rabbi Akiva proclaims.

"Amen!" the crowd repeats.

Cheers, music, and Abba escort us to seats of honor. I hold Hadassah's hand tight and wonder at the joyful throng. As a boy, I had asked Abba, "Why are guests so happy when they aren't the ones getting married?"

"New families mean new life," he had said. "And if guests are wise, they will go home more dedicated to cultivating love and comfort inside their own families."

Hadassah's laugh reels me back to my wedding.

"Why are you laughing?"

"I always laugh when I'm happy."

"I see." I laugh when something's funny, not just because I'm happy. But the conundrum slips away as her coy eyes awaken new feelings—not unpleasant, but perhaps hard to control.

She whispers, "And your nervousness brings me joy."

"I'm not nervous."

"Your hands are shaking."

I draw them back.

Tightening her grasp, she laughs again. "Please don't be vexed with me already, Seth. I'm grateful. I was afraid I'd be the only one nervous." Her gaze drops. "And the only one happy."

I squeeze her hand. "I'm pleased, Hadassah."

She rewards me with an ecstatic smile. Maybe Hadassah is fierier than I realized. While that fire will warm, I hope I'm not scorched.

The crowd congratulates us from all directions, ending our private moment. As I covertly finger one of her curls, her giggles shower us like spring rain. How will I stay in control married to this woman?

THE SMELL of myrrh in Hadassah's hair calls me to a new day. I nestle closer to my bride and inhale. Some Pharisees disdain perfumes, as had I before discovering this delight. Solomon was wise when he wrote, "Your anointing oils have a wonderful fragrance."[1]

These quiet weeks devoted to the beginning of our life together have been an oasis after the extended wedding feast. Yet, I also find aspects of marriage disconcerting. Her laugh ripples through my day, challenging my propriety. Intimacy offers deep pleasure, but it also demands profound vulnerability. The mental and emotional connection scares me. Do I want her to know me that well?

She's proved more than I expected. More energetic. More opinionated. More desirable. Like now, as her soft curls spill over her straight nose and smooth cheeks. Encircling my waist with her arm, she leans into my chest and drifts back to sleep. I run a finger along her slender, almost fragile, arm. Such a small body to hold so much woman.

And she loves touching me—caressing my shoulder or tracing her finger down my cheek whenever she's near. When she put her arm around me in front of Miriam yesterday and I saw Miriam's amusement, I almost instructed her to never touch me in public. But I didn't want to upset her with correction. Not yet.

"Good morning, my husband," she mumbles blearily.

I am her husband. She is my wife.

I kiss her forehead before rising to begin my morning washing. After I don a fresh tunic I find her sitting, messy hair framing her beautiful face, blanket drawn around her bare shoulders.

"Good morning."

"Good morning." She mocks my serious tone and face. Then she giggles. "Oh, don't frown at me!"

"Sorry. I know you're not laughing at me, but I . . ."

"When happiness makes me laugh, I don't know how to stop. Please don't let it anger you. You only need to worry if I stop laughing."

I turn away in case my skepticism shows on my face. "Will you be okay? Do you feel comfortable here? I'll be gone all day."

She holds out her arms and the blanket slips off. I shake my head slightly.

"Come. I want to send my husband off with a hug."

I hesitate.

"Just a hug." Her voice quiets. "I promise."

I sink onto the bed and envelop her, my finger tracing her spine. I need to leave now or I'll stay another hour. Burying my nose in the hollow between her neck and shoulder, I sigh.

After a quick squeeze, Hadassah pushes me away. "Off with you. I'm here to help, not keep you from your work."

This woman keeps me so off balance. I move to the other side of the room and knot my belt. "Today I'll be in the grove preparing for the olive harvest."

"I have duties too. I must get to know how things work. I'll spend the day with Miriam, and she's delightful, so don't worry about me."

"Miriam? Delightful?"

"Yes! She's wonderful!" Rising on her tiptoes, she kisses my cheek.

Now I'm certain I'll never understand her. I pause at the door. Though I want and need to work, I dread the effect of normal life on our union.

"I love you, Hadassah," I whisper without making eye contact.

"Oh, Seth!" she laughs. "I love you too. So much."

Blushing, I make my escape.

"WHY IS EVERYONE SO EXCITED? How do we get the olives down? How will we get the oil out of the olives?" Before Samson can ask another question, Abba grabs his hand and laughs.

Hadassah trots ahead and grabs the boy's other hand. "It's my first olive harvest as well, Samson! You and I must stick together."

Abba says, "We use every drop of oil pressed from these olives. It burns in our lamps and tastes delicious and provides money for our household. Some trees are hundreds of years old. They've seen many generations harvest their fruit and press out the oil that represents life and prosperity. And today, you will help us."

Carts toting empty amphorae rumble up the mountain. All around us, Meron's villagers stream to the olive groves, filling the air with song. Strong men strike the branches of the trees with long sticks, sending olives raining onto cloths laid in the dirt. As we gather the fruit, Samson runs from Ezra to Eli to me with messages.

Rabbi Akiva wanders from grove to grove, reminding every one of Yahweh's injunction. "'When you beat your olive trees, you shall not go over them again. It shall be for the sojourner, the fatherless, and the widow.'[2] Don't forget to leave some for the poor."

"Hey, orphan!" jeers Barak's youngest son Hevel, a boy around Samson's age. "We left olives for you."

Before Samson can respond, Hadassah marches up to Hevel, her shaking finger almost touching his nose. "Go find your Eema so I can tell her what you just said." After the bully runs off, she looks Samson eye to eye. "You work for Ezra and Eli. You wear sandals and clean clothes. You're part of our home. You are *not* an orphan anymore." She ends with a kiss to his sweaty forehead.

When he grins and runs off toward Abba, she turns to me with satisfaction. I don't know how she connected so quickly with Samson, but they just keep growing closer.

"You seem happy." I tuck a curl into her headscarf.

"Oh, Seth, Abba's so loving and generous. And I adore Samson. Don't you?"

"Hmmm. But please be careful whose child you chastise. Barak and Lavinia won't appreciate it."

"Then they should teach their son some manners!"

We work for hours. Eli directs activity at the press where Samson stands beside Abba, shovel in hand. Families wait in line to press the amber oil from this season's crop into airtight stone jars. Hadassah sits with the other women sorting olives.

"Seth," Miriam calls, "my clay canisters are still on our cart."

"Okay," I sigh. Judah always oversaw the fruit being properly separated, pressed, and stored, and he set aside the olive remains that Miriam uses for medicines and cosmetics. Yet again, Judah's selfishness doubles my workload.

"Matthias, Miriam needs help. And don't forget to gather the hulls and pits for our fires."

"Yes, sir."

"Ezra, who is collecting the olive pulp for the animals?"

"I've got it."

"It's going well!" Abba joins me.

"Really? With no Judah, the job seems to drag on and on."

"What's next?" Samson runs up.

I must admit that he's given his all. "Good work today."

"Thanks, Seth!" He sniffs his sleeve. "I smell like olives. It feels like I belong—oof!"

"You do belong!" At Abba's enveloping hug, Samson laughs and I shake my head. If I leave it up to Hadassah and Abba, Samson isn't going anywhere.

"YOU SHOULD WEAR this warmer cloak for today's trip."

With a kiss on her cheek, I put on the green wool cloak. "I just need to record our tenants' olive harvests from last month. Even with so little rain, this year looks like a decent yield."

"I'm sorry you must miss two days of teaching with Rabbi Yakov. Were you surprised when he arrived?"

"He seems to enjoy springing his visits upon us." I sling my leather satchel over my shoulder. "And if Judah hadn't fled with our wealth in his belt, this would be his job and I wouldn't miss anything."

"Yes, my dear. But now you have the opportunity to meditate on what he's taught this week and return with even better questions tomorrow! Here's your pallet."

With the neatly tied bundle under one arm, I kiss her again, but this time on her smiling lips.

"What was that for?"

"For not being a demanding woman."

"Let's hope you always feel that way. Now go so you can come home all the sooner."

Yawning, I emerge from my room. Well, *our* room. Mine and Hadassah's. So far, marriage's advantages outweigh its disruptions.

But, thinking about Judah feels like a thorn I can never extract. I stride to the barn, scattering hens foraging for grubs. I had ordered the servants to have donkeys ready at the third hour, but the barn seems empty.

"Matthias?"

"Matthias isn't here." Samson peers from the loft.

"You still sleeping? Aren't you supposed to be at chores or school by now?"

"I don't sleep here no more. I'm checking on the kittens that got born yesterday. They look lots better today—all dry and fluffy. But their eyes are still closed. How do they find their mama's milk?"

"Samson, where's Matthias?"

"I think he's gettin' food from Miriam."

"Then why didn't you say that before?"

Samson blinks. "You never asked."

Shaking my head, I leave the barn.

"Have a good trip!" Samson calls after me.

Across the compound, Matthias ties parcels onto the donkeys. Everything looks in order, so why do I feel irritated? And where does Samson sleep? And did Miriam pack enough food? And how do kittens find their mama's milk?

I mount my donkey and ignore the thorn of Judah. "Shalom, Matthias. Did you bring an extra cloak?"

"Yes, sir! Should be a chilly few days."

"Then let's go."

CHAPTER 26
JUDAH

Ephesus
Tishri (September) AD 19

Why then has this people turned away in perpetual backsliding? They hold fast to deceit; they refuse to return.

JEREMIAH 8:5 ESV

"Come on Jude! I don't want to be late." Cosmas beckons me toward the exit of Demetrius's shop.

"Be patient!" I hold up a gorgeous, deep red silk. "We haven't yet examined the cloth Demetrius bought from the Arab traders."

"Sorry, Jude, and I'm sorry, Demetrius. But, I'm in a hurry. An enchanting lady awaits, and she's more beautiful than anything here."

"But look at these silks!" I extend a dusky green one.

"That's okay, Jude," Demetrius says. "I understand. I was young once, too." He laughs and refolds fabric I've rifled through.

"Demetrius, I am glad Jude finally introduced us," Cosmas says.

"As am I."

"You have been very informative. Actually, you've answered some questions that have bothered me. So, thank you. And now Jude, I'm leaving whether you come with me or not."

"I'm coming!" I hand a folded piece of cloth to the merchant. "Thanks for helping Cosmas and me. I'll try to come back in the morning."

"And Jude," the merchant grabs my arm, "please be careful about Apollon."

"What do you know?"

"Only that you need to be cautious. But, we will talk another day. Cosmas is halfway up the street already!"

Rushing up Arcadian Street, I finally reach my friend, though Demetrius's warning reverberates.

"Hurry up!"

I struggle to keep up with him as we climb toward the extensive house on the hill. "I thought you don't like Apollon."

"I'm not attending for a creepy, fat man. Only for Kassandra." Even Cosmas is panting.

"Has she ever explained their relationship?"

With a head shake, Cosmas avoids talking.

Apollon's parties provide free drinks and flirting women. For the last few weeks, Cosmas and I have attended to learn more and connect with Apollon's business partners. Well, I do. Cosmas attends for one reason: Kassandra. She commands everyone's attention. Apollon watches her sashay through the room, working her magic on the men, and never flinches, even when she chooses a favorite. And for the past several weeks that lucky man has been Cosmas.

On Apollon's street we slow a little, and he finally answers. "I assume she belongs in some capacity to him. It's not like I plan on taking her home with me to Corinth. I already have someone there anyway."

"Then, why are you pursuing Kassandra?"

"Well, let me see. She's mesmerizing. She's willing. She's exotic. I can keep going if you want more reasons."

Still breathing hard, I halt outside.

"Don't worry, Jude," his arms encompasses my shoulder, "you'll understand someday. What's the name of your girl back home?"

I push his arm off.

"Look, someday you'll get back to her. But you're here now, so enjoy where you are and who you're with." With that, Cosmas races through the front door.

MY HEAVY WATER buckets slosh on each person I bump into, and I regret failing to fetch water last night.

Balbina cackles as I slog into the quiet courtyard, my sandals soaked. She spends her days sweeping, leaning against her stone hovel, smoking her pipe, and checking on tenants.

"Good morning, Balbina. Want some water?" Doing small favors for her seems to help our relationship.

"It's getting bad."

She's right. The water's color and smell deteriorate daily.

"I'll take a little." Balbina hands me a cup. "You're turning green. Don't drink so much stupid wine with your stupid friends."

Pressure builds behind my eyes. "Thanks for the advice."

In my room, I apply a cool rag to my forehead. "Stop treating me like the enemy." My body doesn't listen to my command.

For relief, I think about last night when Kassandra told me in her husky voice, "I like your Galilean accent." When Cosmas left the room, she whispered in my ear, "Tell me about yourself, Jude." She leaned close, filling my head with her scent. I've never seen a more beautiful woman. Her limbs are long, like a gazelle. But it's her eyes that hypnotize me the most.

Still fighting a headache, I shake out my new blue and red striped chiton, its linen softer than any homemade cloth, and the matching cloak from the clean laundry. Appearance matters to Kassandra. Maybe she'll appear at Apollon's office during my appointment.

Rachel isn't beautiful in a way people notice at first. But the more she talks or cares for others, the prettier she grows. Her sincere eyes, her kind responses, her quiet confidence, and her willingness to help people all merge into a loveliness that—

“Stop,” I reprimand myself. “No, Rachel.”

Last night the most alluring woman in Ephesus flirted with me, yet my mind still wanders to a Judean woman I will never claim for my own?

Like a rushing wind, more Meron memories ambush me. I crave Miriam’s bread, a few wise words from Eli, a question from Rachel, and a long walk with Abba. A compulsion drives me to grab a blue fabric bundle holding my tzitzit from the top shelf. Though I never tie them to my inner garment, the silken cords feel like home in my hand.

As I finger the knots of the tzitzit, I whisper the Shema. I try not to, but the words demand utterance. “‘Hear, O Israel: The Lord our God, the Lord is one. You shall love the Lord your God with all your heart and with all your soul and with all your might.’[1]”

Everyone here displays an amulet for luck. Abba would remind me that the Most High doesn’t work like that. Yet, here I am, twisting the cords and repeating the prayers. For luck? Or am I just not free of Meron’s clutches? I throw them to the floor.

I dress, periodically bathing my neck to still the headache, which I’ve decided is Adonai’s punishment for having a good time. Pleasing food aromas float in from the street below and mix with unpleasant smells of too many people living in too little space. Both my hunger and my nausea increase. Tightening my wool belt, I hesitate at the door.

Stop being foolish.

Locking my door, I urge myself down the first few steps but halt.

It doesn’t matter. Keep going.

I descend another step.

Stop.

Curse.

Sprinting back to my room, I grab my tassels from the floor and carefully wrap them and place them on the shelf.

I’m not free yet.

"Have you decided?" Cosmas asks as we make our way to The Crow.

I twist and untwist my belt.

"Well?"

"In the last week I've considered, counted and recounted my money, and tried to make up my mind."

"And?"

"I can't! It's your fault."

"Mine?" Cosmas scoffs.

"Your continued doubt concerns me."

"Apollon will want your answer."

"And yours."

Cosmas inspects his fingernails.

"And don't you mean, 'Do you think Apollon will choose us?' Just a few will gain his approval. You always seem to forget that."

"You actually think he'll turn away anyone's money?" I feel naïve when he laughs.

The Crow is crowded with sailors, merchants, and women for hire. All the men I've met through Meoklis crowd around our usual table.

"Jude, your opportunity!"

"Meoklis."

"All your sacrifices will be repaid at last."

"I hope so." Someone shoves wine into my hand, and I gulp courage.

"You've made a good impression. Apollon informed me."

"He's hard to read."

"Well, his invitations to parties, the theater, and the baths should encourage you. I think you will receive good news today."

"I hope so, because it's time to make money instead of spend it."

The patrons at the next table crane around at Meoklis's hearty laugh.

I pour more wine into my goblet. I can barely sit still, but I must project confidence and poise. Despite Cosmas's assertion, I believe that Apollon will choose only a select few to invest in this shipment of fine fabrics bound for Alexandria. The risky opportunity promises a big return, though I'm unsure how much Apollon will require us to invest. But as he says, "Little risk, little reward."

While my friends debate the plan's advantages and disadvantages across the table, I try to absorb their many opinions. Cosmas lists concerns and warnings, but Meoklis addresses them rationally. I hate my indecision. My big break should feel certain. Obvious. Not confusing.

In the back room of my mind, Abba's voice recites a proverb. *Without counsel plans fail, but with many advisers they succeed.*[2]

But what if the many advisers have conflicting opinions? I down another goblet. No fear. No quaint proverbs. I am a businessman.

Voices hush and heads swivel as Apollon approaches the table, his oriental silks rippling from his stout waist.

"Ah, my young friends. Such lively conversation. I heard you the moment I entered."

His smile doesn't reach his eyes. Kassandra stands behind him, a filmy lilac scarf around her head and shoulders. She winks at Cosmas, who smiles. I shouldn't envy him.

Apollon hands her money. "Go buy quality wine—whatever the cheating owner has hidden behind the bar."

As she nods, he grabs her arm. Cosmas rises from his stool.

"And make sure he adds no water," Apollon snarls. "I'm not paying for water."

"Don't I always?" Jerking her arm away, Kassandra tosses her head and sends perfume wafting over the table.

Apollon's heavy fist pounds the table. "Men, it's time to decide. I'm offering shares in my next venture for a bargain."

But when he states the number, a gasp circles the table. I'm one of the gaspers.

"I need to know who's willing to invest. But just because you want to, doesn't mean I'll accept you."

He scans the group, but no one meets his eyes.

"Come, come. You can't all be cowards."

Is anyone brave enough to voice our concerns? Or are we all afraid that if we prod too hard, we'll lose the chance to invest?

Arriving with a fresh pitcher, Kassandra mixes the wine and water in

Apollon's preferred ratio. He points to the cup beside his, which she fills.

"This excellent wine goes to the first man who bravely invests."

Cosmas clears his throat. "Our main concern regards safety. It's late in the shipping season."

"You want safety, run home to your mother. Aren't you serious about business?"

Stools scratch the floor, fingers drum, and we stare at Cosmas.

"I am serious," Cosmas says. "Serious enough to not jump into a risky scheme."

"You're wise." The compliments sounds more like an accusation. "Any other concerns?"

Theo, a Macedonian speaks. "How long after investing until we realize profits?"

"Well"—Apollon spreads his pudgy hands—"there are no guarantees. It depends on how long the voyage takes, how quickly the merchandise sells, and the length of the return trip. That's business, my friends."

"And the terms?" Cosmas leans forward. "How will profit shares be determined?"

"I discuss terms after the handshake. If you weren't such an amateur, you'd know that."

"So you expect us to decide with no understanding of the timeline or terms? This is how you do business?"

"With those I trust. And those who trust me."

Shaking her head, Kassandra stares crestfallen at Cosmas. When she backs away from the table, I know he's lost both the chance to invest and the woman he desires.

Cosmas flashes his disarming grin. "Well, that's just it. I don't trust you. So thanks, but no thanks."

A few men wince. No one speaks to Apollon that way.

Cosmas moves toward Kassandra. "Will I see you later?"

Something—sorrow?—flickers in her eyes, but she turns up her nose and looks away.

"I always suspected you were just bait."

Smack!

Her slap makes contact, but Cosmas responds with a kiss on her cheek. She rushes from The Crow.

We stare mesmerized as Cosmas lifts his goblet, still filled with cheap wine, and says, "May you gain wisdom and fortune. May Artemis turn her face to smile on you. And may your ships not go down in the storm." Draining his cup, he slams it on the table and strides out.

A few people cough, and from the corner of my eye I spy Theo slipping away.

"Not everyone is cut out for business." Meoklis's voice wavers and he pours more wine.

"Good riddance. People with no backbone are useless." Apollon rubs his thumb back and forth on the edge of his cup.

Abba's voice nudges me. *Wealth gained hastily will dwindle, but whoever gathers little by little will increase it.*[3]

But little by little takes time, as Demetrius told me. I'll never become rich sitting around and talking. Caution means failure.

"Now, who's ready to become a rich man?" He pushes the wine forward.

I swallow the lump in my throat, and grab the cup. "I'm in."

WHERE'S COSMAS? This past week, I've visited his room twice, scoured our old haunts, and asked all our mutual friends. Ever since he stormed out of The Crow, he's nowhere to be found.

This morning I should be figuring my accounts and conferring with Apollon. Instead, I'm searching the crowded Arcadiane Street toward the harbor.

As I peek through the window into the thermopolium we visited last week, someone barrels around the corner and runs straight into me.

"Cosmas!"

"Jude? What in Artemis's name are you doing just standing there!"

"I've looked for you every day for a week!" I push off his hand and straighten my new cloak. "So excuse me if I didn't expect you to run into me."

Cosmas strokes my silk attire. "Nice."

I swipe his hand away. "Yeah, so keep your fish smell off." His smirk reminds me of Seth, and I ball my fist.

"I'm sorry, Jude. Let me make it up to you."

After purchasing grapes and salted fish, we sit near the harbor and gaze out at the Great Sea. Leaden waves crash as storm clouds roll in.

"I wonder if it's finally going to rain," I say.

"I'm going home."

"We just sat!"

"No, I mean to Corinth. Home."

"What? Why? You've barely started in trade."

"My father can sell what I've purchased so far. But this"—Cosmas points over his shoulder toward the district of Apollon's office—"and these people . . ."

I swallow.

"You're investing?" He pops a grape in his mouth.

Around us, seagulls dive for scraps. "I need to take the risk, Cosmas."

"Well, Jude." Cosmas gives a half-smile. "May the gods bring you luck and prosperity."

"That's it?"

His lips purse. "You control your own money. What should I say?"

"Tell me what you think!"

He looks behind himself and to the other side. Then he grasps my arm. "Be careful, Jude. Don't trust Apollon."

I cross my arms over my chest.

"He takes and he breaks. He's not looking out for you. Just himself," Cosmas presses.

"And I'm only looking out for myself. It's business."

"Don't you understand?" He shakes his head. "He risks nothing. You risk everything."

As I survey our surroundings, I spot a man skulking behind a row of barrels—Haman. He ducks out of sight.

"See what I mean?" Cosmas whispers.

"I—"

"Congratulations on your investment!" Cosmas bellows. "Let's enjoy my last day. First the baths and then the theater!"

Realizing what Cosmas is doing, I force a laugh and suggest further entertainment. I might fool Cosmas and Haman, but I can't fool myself. My friend is leaving me. My business partner is spying on me. And if this business venture fails, I'll have nowhere to turn.

CHAPTER 27
ELI

Meron
Chislev (November) AD 19

Whoever has a bountiful eye will be blessed, for he shares his bread with the poor.

PROVERBS 22:9

My feet crunch gravel in the early quiet, and I rub my arms against the chill. Sheep nuzzle in their pen, and our rooster struts and puffs, preparing to crow. I love mornings when I have a few moments to myself. As I scratch Methuselah's forelock, the kitchen area hums with activity. Miriam rises before the rest of the compound. She claims her job is most important, saying, "If I don't prepare the food, how will anyone work?"

"She's probably right," I tell the donkey.

In the kitchen, I say, "Shalom. It's a cool morning."

"Sun's up already? Well, we're almost ready. Tova, hurry with the barley." She steps around me like I'm a stool in the way. "The rascal awake yet?"

"You mean Samson?"

She faces me, fists on hips.

"I told him to get dressed and fold his mat. He should be here any moment."

"Oh, you told him, did you?" She rolls her eyes. "Men."

"What do you mean?"

"I mean he's probably nestled under his covers, thanking the Most High you're the one in charge of getting him up."

I scratch my head. "So, I should check on him?"

"What an excellent idea!"

Her tone nettles me all the way to our room, where I find Samson curled in his blanket and snoring. Sighing, I rouse the boy and guide him through Morning Prayer and washing. Then I hurry him across the now active compound.

"Eli, are you available?" Ezra's voice rings out.

I steer Samson under his arbor, where the brazier burns.

"Shalom, Master." I prod Samson.

"Ow! Why are you poking me?"

"Say shalom to the master," I hiss through gritted teeth.

"Oh. Sha"—he yawns—"lom."

"Sha—lom!" Master gives the boy a bear hug and is rewarded with a crooked smile. "Why don't you go sit by the tannur and get warm. Tell Miriam—politely—that I request she feed you there."

"If you're the master, why do you request insteada just tellin' her?"

"Just because I can doesn't mean I should. I've learned lovingkindness from the Most High. Our world would be a better place if we modeled Him more."

Samson shrugs and runs off. Moments later, Miriam' voice pierces the crisp air then cuts off.

"I guess she received your 'request.'"

"He needs warmth and fattening up. And love." Master slaps his hands onto the table. "Eli, because of our situation, every time Rabbi Yakov has visited we haven't been able to host him as Seth had hoped. But with the Rabbi's last-minute stay in Meron, we have an unexpected opportunity. I'd like to have a banquet this evening. Seth returns today, and he'll find the rabbi and his disciples good company."

"Good company?"

"Seth, like Samson, needs love and support."

And warmth. I hope his kind wife can eventually soften him.

"How many guests would you like to invite?"

"The rabbi, his inner circle, and the elders—but just the men. We don't want to ruffle the venerable rabbi's sensibilities."

"About thirty?"

"Maybe forty. I know it's a difficult task, but I don't want to miss this chance."

"Yes, sir."

"We must inform Miriam."

"Yes, sir." I stand straighter. "I'll go get her."

Samson huddles by the tannur with three barley loaves on his lap and a smile on his face. With a wooden paddle, Miriam withdraws more bread for the servants.

"Miriam, Master would like to speak to you."

"Now?" She turns her flushed face toward me.

"Yes, my dear."

"I'll take over," Tova offers quietly.

Miriam scowls but hands the paddle to Tova. "Don't let any burn."

"Ah, Miriam!" Master waves us over. "Every morning you bless us with something warm and tasty. Thank you."

Miriam smiles. "It's my pleasure, Master."

"I have a colossal idea," he continues. "Unfortunately, pulling it off will destroy your schedule. But I wouldn't ask unless I felt it essential."

"I'm afraid to ask." Miriam looks from Master to me, but I refuse to make eye contact.

"You're a wise woman. But I won't hold you in suspense. Rabbi Yakov will move on soon, and I'd like to invite his group plus a few friends to dine with us. For Seth."

Miriam blinks. "When?" Her voice quavers.

"Tonight, if possible. But I don't want to overburden you, Miriam, even for Seth's sake."

"Well,"—her eyes gain a stony resolve—"with Adonai's help, anything's possible."

"Thank you. I hope you understand why this matters."

She picks up Master's empty platter. "Unless there's anything else, I should get started."

I say, "I'll instruct some servants to set out boards for tables. And with the temperatures, we should build some extra fires and put some blankets with the seating cushions."

He puts his arms around us. "You two—I'm grateful. Eli, let's slaughter a young goat and get it on the spit quickly."

"Yes, sir!"

"You do realize that an invitation from Ezra ben Lavi is a compliment?"

"Of course." Kefir says before ducking behind Malik, who, along with our other friends, huddles around Rabbi Yakov atop the entrance steps to the synagogue.

The rabbi's uncommonly long tassels sway in the brisk wind. "As I have said, building fences around the Law allows us to remain obedient."

"Well said." Mazal nods.

"Where and with whom you dine matters in order to remain pure."

Does he think the Holy One hears him better because his fringe can be seen from the city gates? I lift my hand to catch Daniel's gaze, but he shakes his head and walks away.

"You must maintain proper boundaries with diligence." Rabbi Yakov says and a fire burns in my core, though I keep my face impassive. Why did Rabbi Akiva pick today to visit his daughter across the valley? His gentleness and reason would've countered Rabbi Yakov's influence.

I cough and shift my feet. Jair, one of Rabbi Yakov's disciples, swaggers toward me. "Please thank your master for the honor, but I'm afraid our Rabbi cannot join Ezra tonight. We're gathering to pray and our devotion to the Most High comes first." With a smarmy smile, he bows and walks away.

While Jair distracted me, the other villagers slunk out. But, if they plan on insulting Ezra ben Lavi, then they can look me in the eye and say it. If Rabbi Yakov's influence can undermine decades of love and friendship, did that friendship mean anything in the first place?

RUFUS BARKS, the first to notice my return. In the courtyard, torches sputter, musicians tune their instruments, and servants place cushions around the low tables. The smell of the roasting meat makes my stomach turn. Master, dressed in his fine new robe, directs the setup. Judah always ran into the hills to avoid unpleasantness. I wish I could do that.

But I must deliver the news that Rabbi Yakov uses the Almighty's name to reject the most reverent man in the village—and that our friends follow his lead. I hope the meat's aroma wafting over the village makes their stomachs ache with longing all night.

"Eli, you're back!"

Oh, Adonai, please help.

"How many guests can we expect tonight?" Master looks out the gate, confusion clouding his face. "Did no one follow you?"

"They aren't coming."

"Who isn't coming?"

"I invited Rabbi Yakov and the city leaders. The rabbi smiled, but his disciples claim they're praying and send their apologies," I look at my feet, "as do our friends."

Master's eyes flash. "What excuse could they all make?"

"First was Barak, who fawns over the rabbi and leads this foolishness. You know he bought Kefir's field last week. He said he's sorry, but he's inspecting it."

"As if he didn't do that before buying it?"

"It makes no sense. But he asked me to consider him excused."

"Excused, indeed," Ezra grumbles. "And the others?"

"I caught Sapphira's new husband by the arm. I told him how fortunate it is that their visit coincides with our feast."

"And he said?"

"That since he's newly married, he can't join us. I reminded him Torah protects the first year of marriage from battles, not banquets. He at least had the decency to blush."

"But not the decency to attend."

"No."

"And Daniel? Certainly my brother-in-law is coming?"

"Remember the five yoke of oxen he purchased?"

"I was with him."

I can barely bring myself to tell him. "He said he must try them out."

"He insults me like this? Why now?"

"I asked that, but he just shook his head and walked away. I'm sorry."

Master paces and mutters. "He must really be angry that I didn't take his advice. But this? It feels so petty."

Servants scurry along the courtyard, stealing glances and whispering back and forth. From a banquet table, Miriam raises her shoulders and lifts her eyebrows at me. I shake my head slightly, trying to reassure her.

For several moments, Master stares at the goat roasting on a spit, then he turns in a circle, surveying the courtyard. Food is spread on tables and fires are lit. "We've prepared a feast, and the streets are full of hungry people." He strides up to me. "Let the satisfied feed themselves. Go find anyone who is poor or lame. Servants can help carry the crippled."

"What? Master, I—"

"I'll inform Miriam." He marches toward my gaping wife.

At least I don't have that job. But I must lead the servants.

"Come, you three!" I call to men arranging wine jars. "And Matthias! There's work to do."

The men exchange worried glances but obey.

"Go wherever the poor and sick gather." I ignore their furtive glances. "They will be guests at our feast. If any cannot walk, help them."

Master stands beside Miriam, who has one hand over her heart and one on her forehead. He rocks from his heels to his toes and taps his mouth with his finger. What is he thinking now?

"Eli?"

Here we go. "Yes, Master?"

"Invite Tirzah. Being blind, she'll need assistance. I'd like for her to sit on my left."

"Yes, sir."

Miriam slowly shakes her head.

"And Eli—"

What next?

"Invite Ari and seat him to my right."

This feels further than I can stretch. "The tax collector? In the place of honor?"

"I doubt he receives many invitations."

"I—" Several times Daniel has visited with Ezra, urging him to get along with Rabbi Yakov and to mollify the elders. This will accomplish the opposite.

"Something else?" Master asks.

Confusion emanates from gawking servants. Animated conversations occur in every corner. Miriam looks like she might cry or scream or run from the courtyard—maybe all at the same time. Part of me feels like joining her.

"All will be done as you asked!" At my loud proclamation, the courtyard falls silent. "Don't stand there. Master Ezra is throwing a banquet! Get to work." I turn to my wife. "Miriam, please make sure Tirzah is seated on Master's left. Your date cakes are her favorite."

Her mouth opens and closes a few times. "I know they're her favorite. They're everyone's favorite." She stomps toward the kitchen.

Poor Miriam. If I feel stretched, she must feel ripped down the middle. She prepared special dishes to impress the village leaders, hoping to restore Master's reputation. Now her efforts will serve outcasts. And Ari? She hates him. Vehemently.

"Tova!"

"Yes, sir?" Arms full of cushions, she rushes up.

"Assist Miriam. I advise you to say little. Better yet, say nothing. And for your own safety, don't get in her way."

Her eyes shine with doubt and understanding.

I lower my voice. "This will be difficult for her, and I'll be busy elsewhere. I'm counting on you."

"Yes, sir," she whispers, nodding conspiratorially.

I locate Master talking to Samson, who pats Rufus. "Could you explain how to find the orphans and homeless so the servants can invite them to dinner?"

Samson shakes his curls. "Doubt they'll come if a stranger asks 'em. They don't trust nobody."

"Hmm." Master strokes his beard. "Good point. Would you accompany the servants?"

"Yep."

"But you must stay with them at all times."

"Why? I lived there. Nobody hurt me. They're nicer than them old bullies in the village."

Ezra bends to eye level. "I imagine so. But I protect the people I love. Do you understand?"

Samson steps closer to Rufus. "Uh, well, sure. I guess."

Samson doesn't look like he understands. I wonder if he's ever heard the words, "I love you."

Ezra turns to me. "Send two strong servants with him."

"Yes, sir."

"This might not be the night we planned, but nothing will go to waste. Now get to business—we're running out of time!"

CHAPTER 28
MIRIAM

Meron
Chislev (November) AD 19

Whoever brings blessing will be enriched, and one who waters will himself be watered.

PROVERBS 11:25

I've lost count of how many times I've traversed from my kitchen to the courtyard and back again. Meal preparation for the village's leaders seemed impossible. Now, I'm cooking for street rabble? Inconceivable.

"Matthias, can you—"

"Sorry." Tova squeaks.

"Tova, that's the third time you've run into me!"

She takes a big step back. "Just trying to help."

Patting my heart, I take a deep breath. "Follow me."

"Yes, Miriam."

"But not too close."

"I'll try," she says as we enter the kitchen.

"We'll have more people than originally planned so we need more bread—a lot more bread."

"Barley loaves don't take long. Would you like me to start now?"

"No. Tomorrow, after everyone's come and gone."

She blinks. "Right away."

With quick movements, she measures milled barley into a large pottery bowl.

"Let's just do what's necessary and get this night over with."

Eli's head pops in. "Miriam, may I speak with you before I leave again?"

"I know I must maintain a good attitude and try to make this disaster better by working cheerfully, despite what I think and feel. I do *not* need to be told by you!"

"Miriam, please."

I hold my breath for a moment. "I'm busy. Go invite the honored guests we get to host."

Whirling around, I discover Tova and Eli exchanging questioning looks. "You two"—I waggle my finger from one to the other—"stop it. Everyone has work to do. Get busy."

Hadassah bursts into the kitchen as Eli exits. "I just returned from Rachel's and heard what's happening. What can I do?"

"You could talk your father-in-law out of this foolishness."

"What? Why? It's a wonderful generosity!" Her face glows and she pings about the room.

"Wish I had your energy. You can help Tova bake bread." How this angel wound up with Seth, I'll never understand. Seth! How, will he respond?

Serenaded by Hadassah's laugh, she and Tova form loaves which they take outside to bake.

Finally alone, I pray. "Well, Adonai, I suppose You see what's happening? You wrote on a wall once. Maybe You could give Ezra a message? Steer him away from angering the whole village? Do You really want me to serve my finest food to the lowest people? To give my best efforts to the least deserving?"

In response, the lyres and pipes begin.

"Well, fine. There's no way but through. Like Jeremiah, I will say 'so be it, Lord.'[1] But if You're forcing me to do this, I could use Your help."

"So be it," I whisper. Then I storm into the courtyard. "Is the bread ready yet?"

DELIVERING MORE loaves to the tables, I hum with the musicians, whose tune makes the banquet feel like a party. The dirty crowd of vagrants recline on cushions and blankets, their hard edges softened by torchlight.

My feet complain and my back begs me to sit, but I'm not too tired to admit I was wrong. I felt sure these hungry masses would storm the tables and raid the storeroom. Instead, they behave with restraint and gratitude—awed by Master's status, no doubt.

"Here's the last barley cakes," Hadassah whispers as she deposits a large basket on the table. Her cheeks flushed, she places a hand over her stomach.

"Thank you. You've been a great help." I give her a quick hug. If I'd had a daughter, I'd want one like this girl.

Hadassah's smiles wanly. "I wish I could do more. I'm afraid I'm coming down with something. The food smells started bothering me." Wrinkling her freckled nose, she takes a deep breath. "It's better out here."

"You've felt bad for a while?"

"Off and on for the past week. Maybe my body's adjusting to my new home."

"Maybe," I say doubtfully.

She leans her head on my shoulder. "Abba's amazing, isn't he? Few men would dare to perform such a loving and generous act."

Not your husband, that's for sure.

Hadassah glances toward the gate, "I wish Seth were home. The sun's setting. I'm worried he's out so close to dark."

"How do you think he'll feel about this?" I ask as I stack empty platters.

Hadassah's gaze clouds and she bites her lip. "I'm a little worried. He might not understand at first. But I hope he will."

"You're a good girl, Hadassah. I'm glad Seth has you."

Laughter echoes through the courtyard, Master's the loudest. Samson wrestles with ragtag boys his age, and Eli stands watch at the gate.

I massage my back, surveying the contented crowd. Cleanup will be another big job, but for now, I take in the gratitude shining on each face, even the dirtiest ones.

Chances are Seth's will look quite different.

CHAPTER 29
JUDAH

Villa of Valerius and King's Highway
Elul (August) AD 20

A voice cries: "In the wilderness prepare the way of the LORD; make straight in the desert a highway for our God.

ISAIAH 40:3

"Welcome! Here's fresh bread and water!"

"Pavlos," I croak. After a long swig, I stuff a huge bite in my mouth. "This villa looks like an oasis."

Grabbing my staff and satchel, he helps me herd the swine inside the walls. "Eat all you can for the next few days. You are too thin for your skin! And we have a long journey ahead."

"Who are all these people?" I stop short. Not only humans, but carts, wagons, camels, donkeys, and horses crowd the interior. After the solitary desert, the noisy crowd feels overwhelming.

"They join us for the caravan and began arriving this morning. More will be here tomorrow."

"Jude!" Khafra joins us. "Valerius is glad you're back!"

"Really?"

"He wants to roast two of the swine for his guests, and if you'd been any later, we would have had to cook something else."

"Two that I guarded with my life?"

"Good job."

"Humph."

Pavlos laughs.

As Khafra drives two of the younger ones away, I gulp more water. "Who else from our household goes with us on the caravan?"

"Valerius, obviously. You and I. Gallus."

"Gallus? Why?"

His laugh ends in a cough. "Prisca to cook, and Kato for the animals."

"Not Cali too?"

Pavlos shakes his head.

"At least the King's Highway takes us south."

"Which matters because . . . ?" He winks.

"No reason." I herd my remaining companions back to our hut.

Soon, the smell of roasting pork tortures all of us slaves. We know we won't get any meat, but maybe, if we're lucky, we can suck on the bones and fat.

"Slave!" Gallus bellows from his horse.

"Sir?" He never uses my name, but somehow, I know when he calls me.

"Do you know weapons?"

"Uh"—lying about something this crucial would be foolish—"no."

The big man looks disgusted. "Well, if we run into bandits, you'll fight anyway."

Unsure how to respond, I nod.

"Get back to work," he barks as he wheels his horse.

"I'm not the one who started the conversation," I mutter.

I'd hoped to rest before the next trek, but for two days I load supplies and tend to animals, as those who will join us on the caravan continue to arrive, and set up camp outside the compound walls.

Nervousness over what we will face grows inside me. I'll miss Veru, my old camel. This time I'll walk the whole way. And we might face bandits? My fighting experience consists of verbal wars with Seth and wrestling with Joseph. I became proficient with a bow and arrow as a boy, but it was only a toy with dull tips. However, I'm a slave and I'll do what I'm told. Even use weapons. Kill or be killed. I shudder and get back to work.

Heat dances in waves, blurring the horizon which blends into sun-drenched sky. The noises of the caravan permeate deep into my brain. Plodding of camels. Braying of donkeys. Cursing of drivers. Sighing of travelers. We all crave relief from the interminable sun.

There's been little wildlife in the last week, except for vultures. Daily, they circle in lazy orbits above the train.

Shielding my eyes from the glare, I think there might be more today than yesterday. "One, two, three—"

"Argh!" Tripping on a rock, I grab the nearest wagon.

The driver jerks around. "Keep your grubby hands off my wagon."

I suppress several sarcastic retorts. "Sorry," I limp away.

"Careful, slave!" Gallus's voice barks from behind. His black horse slows to a walk and snuffles in my ear. I don't bother turning around.

"You fall here and you'll be a feast for vultures before you can stand."

I trudge on.

"That's why this road's so clean. Never a rotting body here."

Picturing vultures scavenging Gallus's decaying body brings a smile, so I keep my head down.

"You hear me?" Gallus clicks his horse closer, bumping my shoulder.

"Thanks for the advice," I hiss through gritted teeth.

"You'll need more than advice to survive this march."

Food and water would be helpful, but I keep that idea to myself.

Gallus laughs, mean and hollow. Urging his horse forward, he swerves my way and runs into me. For the second time in a few minutes, I trip and catch the same wagon's side.

"Hey!" The driver growls and raises his whip.

Gallus's chuckle fades as he trots away. At least someone enjoys my misery.

"Sorry."

"You're gonna be sorry when my whip finds your back!"

I slow my pace so I'll no longer walk beside this guy. What a miserable day. I wish I could find Pavlos in this big caravan. My waterskin is empty and my bread long gone. But I must keep moving my feet. One step. Then another. Walk one more mile. Be that much closer to home.

CHAPTER 30
SETH

Meron
Chislev, (November) AD 19

For the LORD reproves him whom he loves, as a father the son in whom he delights.

PROVERBS 3:12

Matthias and I urge our donkeys to a trot. To the west, gold and pink silhouette the Galilean hills. After a day of constant delays, we will arrive home much later than is safe to be on the road.

"I see Meron!" Matthias points ahead.

"A welcome sight!" Fear of bandits no longer pushes me as much as Hadassah's welcoming embrace pulls me. "I look forward to a warm meal." I slow the donkey to a respectable walk.

As we near the town gate, I cock my head. "Do you hear something?"

"Is that music?" Dismounting, we lead our donkeys through the town gate and toward the smell of roasting meat and the sounds of celebration.

A pack of dirty boys tears from our front gate as if a wolf hunts them. Then the wolf appears—a wolf with a curly head atop a soft blue tunic.

Of course.

"Samson!" I grab his arm. The boy's momentum almost bowls us over. I grasp the harness and the donkey protests the halter yank, adding more noise to the cacophony.

"Whaddya do that for?" Yanking free, Samson crosses his arms. "I almost had him." He nods to a boy lurking in the shadows.

"I don't care who you nearly had." I point to our home. "What is going on here?"

Samson looks from the gate to me and back again.

"Oh, this? Well, Ezra wanted to throw a dinner for your stuffy rabbi and his disciples. And he invited all the city leaders, but none would come."

"What? Why?"

"Because they're stupid?"

I point at the crowd again. "Well, if they wouldn't attend, who did?"

"Your abba didn't want to waste the feast." Samson answers like I'm the child in this conversation. "So, he invited other people who needed food. They're here now." He leans close and grins. "I've never been to a party like this before. It's the best time I ever had!" With a howl, he resumes the chase, and hollering fades into the dark streets.

Rabbi Yakov won't enter our gate? Our friends and neighbors insult us like this? And if Rabbi Yakov won't even come to our home, will he ever consider me as his follower?

I approach the open gate and gasp. Our courtyard teems with tattered vagrants of all ages. Where did they find this lot? The alleys? The dung pile? Blind old Tirzah, cackles and pats Abba on the shoulder. When a servant moves, I spot the man on Abba's other side. Ari? Abba invited him?

"Matthias!"

He runs to my side. "Yes, sir?"

"Inform my father that I demand to speak to him."

Matthias stiffens. "Um . . ."

"Did you hear what I said?"

"You want me to ask the master to leave his guests and come to you?"

I glare at the young servant. "Since you stated precisely what I instructed, I know you understand. Deliver my message!"

"Yes, sir," he mumbles.

Stepping around partiers, Matthias glances back at me before bending and speaking into Abba's ear. Abba's head jerks toward the gate, before he turns back to Matthias and pats his shoulder.

"Hurry up," I mutter.

But Abba speaks to Ari and leans over to Tirzah before he makes his way toward me. He pauses with one person after another, each responding with a vigorous nod and enthusiastic smile. He must be asking if they want more wine.

"Seth, Shalom!" He finally exits the gate with open arms. "We were worried about you. Did our business conclude as you hoped?"

"Do you display your concern by throwing a party for every beggar within a thousand leagues? Do you honor our home by defiling it with the unwashed?"

"Oh, son, this wasn't the night I planned."

"Your street boy said Rabbi Yakov wouldn't come. That no one would come."

"Yes." Abba's back stiffens. "That's correct."

I await his explanation. But he just sighs, deep and long, and rubs his forehead.

Laughter reverberates within our walls. "Then who do you entertain?"

"Those who needed the meal more. Sharing with those who have little feeds my soul."

"You dishonor our home!"

He takes a step closer and we stand eye to eye.

"You're offended by people who accepted my invitation?" Abba places his hand on my shoulder, but I step back. "Seth, I invited your rabbi, though I don't agree with him or his interpretations. And I invited the village leaders—lifetime friends. None would come. Not even Uncle Daniel. Do you think I should've sat in my home, penitent and forlorn, letting good food go to waste, praying they will someday approve of me?"

"What an excellent idea."

"I disagree." A rare edge enters his voice. "These hungry people accepted with gratitude. I will not be cowed by men who set themselves above Torah, which repeatedly commands us to care for the poor and orphans. You're telling me it's better to use Torah to intimidate others and demand conformity to lists and standards they create?"

"I know your opinion of Rabbi Yakov."

"And what do you suppose he'll think about my mitzvah?"

"That you defiled our home." I keep my voice quiet though I want to scream. "Because you disobeyed the cleanliness laws that protect our people."

"And what of the proverb that says, 'Whoever has a bountiful eye will be blessed, for he shares his bread with the poor'[1]?"

"You've brought dishonor upon our home!"

A few people near the gate turn toward us.

He leans close. "Did you not feel that you also brought dishonor when you summoned me out here? Where is it written for a son to treat a father in such a way?"

"How could I enter our courtyard when it's filled with such people?" Pacing, I rub my hands together. "After a difficult journey, I can't even get to my room."

The donkey brays as if to agree with me.

Abba summons Matthias. "Take the animals around back to the stable and Seth's belongings to his room."

Matthias tugs the ropes, and urges the animals to a trot as if he can't escape fast enough.

"How will you enter our home—through the front gate with a hospitable spirit, or through the back gate to avoid my guests?"

I cross my arms. "I'll go around back."

"Very well. I'll let Hadassah know you're home."

Her laugh drags my gaze to the courtyard. "Where is she?"

"She's helping Miriam, whose opinion of tonight reflects yours, by the way. Hadassah, on the other hand, thought this a beautiful act of generosity."

"Never involve my wife in such matters again," My thumbs pressing into my temples, my fingers rake hard across my forehead.

"I'll let you discuss that with her. I hope you sleep well tonight, and then we can speak more calmly tomorrow."

"How, when our thoughts oppose each other?"

"Seth, as your thoughts tonight accuse me, also remember the proverb that says, 'Whoever is generous to the poor lends to the Lord, and he will repay him for his deed.'[2] While this generosity"—Abba points to the feast—"feeds the poor and sick, it's actually all for Him."

In the courtyard, he stoops to assist a fallen child, speaking to its mother. "Probably a prostitute," I mutter, cursing my need to skulk around back of my own home.

LAST NIGHT'S event will be today's gossip, so I climb to the olive grove earlier than usual, hoping to avoid neighbors' questions. Thankfully, so far, only my yawns accompany me on the hike.

At first light, I fled our room, but tiredness hangs like a heavy cloak. Worry and anger make poor bedfellows, and an upset wife doesn't offer peace. I replay our first married argument.

"What a beautiful generosity. And everyone was so grateful," she had said, bouncing around the room in excitement.

"He brought disgrace on us!"

Her fluttering halted. "But Seth—"

"I won't discuss it," I responded.

"Don't you think—?"

"No more!"

"I want to discuss this with you."

"Do not speak of it again."

Then she sunk to our bed, laid her head on her arms, and cried. I would have kissed away her tears, if I hadn't feared her thinking me weak. All night, Hadassah slept as far from me as she could, her sniffles my companions. Just before dawn, she bolted from bed to vomit in a clay pot. I bet the unclean got her sick. As soon as she fell back asleep, I escaped.

The gray dawn warms with the sunrise, and I stop to draw breath under a cedar tree. After a long swig from my waterskin, I eat dried fish and try to pray, but find my mind recalling all that Abba has to account for.

All day I labor. When workmen arrive, I ignore them. And after they depart, I continue working. Finally, as the sun begins its descent, I emerge from the silvery olive trees. My neighbors who worked in their groves all day descend to the village ahead of me.

Closing my eyes, I face the evening breeze that portends winter soon. "Please, help me, Adonai. I must face home and—"

"Shalom, Seth!" Abba calls.

What is Abba doing here? As a boy, I adored his voice's rich power. Now it's just irritating. "That's because now he adopts orphans, invites beggars to our table, and gives away a third of our fortune," I mutter as I lean down and grab my satchel.

Panting, Abba grasps my upper arms and looks full into my face.

"Shalom, Abba."

"I wanted to join you this beautiful evening."

"Then let's go."

Abba's hand remains around my shoulders, and the last of our neighbors scurry home. As boys, Judah and I kept a lookout for Abba returning from long days in the field. We raced for the first embrace, thrilled to be in his presence again. We fought to climb onto his back or take the tools from his hands, each wanting to be the closer one. Abba laughed, tousled our hair, and asked about our day.

When had we begun running from instead of toward his presence? Putting myself in this condemnation with my brother startles me.

"Did you hear me?"

"Sorry. My mind wandered for a moment."

"To a pleasant place?"

"To childhood, when we ran to greet you." Why did I say that? It will just stir memories of Judah.

Abba's sigh expresses contentment, not sorrow. "Ah, yes. It fills a father's heart for his children to rejoice at his coming home. I remember once walking back with Kefir. When he saw you two racing to me, he said, 'I wish my children ran to me like that.'"

"Well, if he hadn't always been angry, they might've run to him instead of away."

"That's the challenge. He wanted a relationship without first winning their hearts."

We walk a few moments, warm memories easing tension, as the locusts begin their evening song.

"Seth, we seem to be on different paths, but I want to win your heart back. After Judah left, our divide increased. And after last night—well, I don't want this gap between us. I want to be your abba, to whom you still run."

"I'm a man now. I no longer run."

"Yes, and an intelligent man. So, I believe you know what I mean."

I do. And if Abba wants to discuss an issue, there's no squirming away. So be it. He shall receive the honesty he asks for.

"Abba, since Judah left, you skirt propriety."

"Possibly. But first let's discuss last night. The disrespect of our friends hurt you *and* me. I'm sorry my response made their rejection even harder on you, but filling our table with the needy and hungry . . . meeting needs that would be met no other place . . . giving respite and warmth to those ignored and shunned . . . Do you not understand how this fulfills the Most High's commands? How many times does He instruct us to care for the poor?"

"You use the Law to justify defiling our home?"

"I don't seek justification any more than approval. But you must know, I always desire obedience to Adonai. I never intentionally break His Law. Please, tell me which law I broke."

"How could bringing uncleanness into our home not be disobeying Torah?"

"All the guests cleaned themselves properly and had their feet washed."

"Those people's feet mustn't have been washed for years, if ever. You burdened a servant with such a lowly job?"

"I washed their feet."

I stop dead. "You?"

"Yes."

"You washed the lowliest beggars' feet?"

"I wouldn't ask my servants to do something unless I was willing to do it myself. And they had worked hard all day."

"Isn't that the point of servants?" I yell.

"No, Seth. Servants aren't a way to avoid discomfort. I share life with them. Their service allows our family to prosper."

"Prosperity you allowed to be cut by a third,"—I point west—"and disappear over that hill, never to be seen again!"

"I know you don't understand why I allowed Judah his inheritance." When he slaps his legs with his hands, I jump. "Yes, I could have declared him dead and preserved our wealth and reputation. Do you think then the elders would've dined at my table?"

I turn my back on him.

"But your disapproval of me began long before Judah left. Yes, you appear to respect me. But it often seems like the whitewashed tombs, which appear clean and beautiful on the exterior."

"Doing the correct thing makes me like a tomb?"

"If you do what's right, but on the inside your love and affection decay, what is that?" Abba steps around me and places his worn hands on my cheeks. "And now I'm afraid you'll close yourself off from Hadassah, who emerged from your room subdued and red-eyed. Just like you turned from me earlier on this road, so you've done in life." He takes a step back. "In our relationship, you've replaced love with actions that signify respect to every observer except me."

"You're saying I act disrespectfully?"

"I know and feel your disapproval. I call to you, Seth—turn your face and your heart back to me. Turn them back to Adonai."

"Back to Adonai?" My voice echoes through the groves. "I've never turned from Adonai. That reproach falls on Judah and even on yourself, but not on me. I live my life pursuing Him and His laws—"

"Then why do you loathe my mercy or generosity? Do you not understand that they flow from my devotion to Him?"

"How can you say such things? Your actions shame us."

"You wonder why I avoid Rabbi Yakov? Because his interpretations consistently leave out the cry of Adonai's heart for us to be His people and that He will be our God, because He desires relationship with us!"

"Stop!"

Abba grabs my forearm. "Yes, for our good, He gave us Torah to teach us what to do, what is healthy to eat, and how to behave with one another. Torah guides, directs, and teaches us. It preserves our people. But remember the Lawgiver loves us with an everlasting love. In the Psalms, He calls us to run to Him, abide in Him, find our shelter in Him, and allow Him be our rock and our fortress![3]"

"You verge on blasphemy!"

Wrenching free of his grasp, I slip and stumble, banging my knee on a rock. Gravel scatters and I groan.

"I've spoken no blasphemy." Abba sinks beside me. "Certainly you recognize my words as Adonai's own?"

I grab my throbbing knee and lay my head on it. Yes, I recognize the words. But I also know Abba acted incorrectly, even if I can't cite a passage to prove it.

"Son, your heart has moved far away—as far as Judah's body. I no longer speak openly with you, as I do now, because of your resistance. But this time, please let my words sink in. Don't listen in order to formulate an argument. Line my words up with the truth you know, pray about them, and then decide what you think."

I know what I think. I feel as solid and immovable as Mount Meron on which we sit.

"Can you do that?"

A response is my only way out, so, I nod weakly.

"Thank you. You've heard my concerns about Rabbi Yakov before. So while there's nothing new in my words, I hope there might be something new in your response."

Aromas of villagers' dinners rise on the breeze and make my stomach growl.

Abba says, "Don't substitute anything for being Adonai's child. If you examine each situation to find what Law's being broken, you'll miss the people Adonai places in your life. You'll argue over man's opinion about how to obey Torah, but miss Adonai's smallest, plainest instruction and ignore His requirements for justice and love. 'So you, by the help of your God, return, love and justice, and wait continually for your God.'[4]"

"Abba, I beg you. Please stop. I can't listen anymore." I stand, wincing. "We should get home."

"Would you give an old man a hand?"

When I pull him up, Abba clasps me close.

"Seth, my love for you lasts forever. Neither your disdain nor your judgment will change that. But in order for us to enjoy fellowship, you must let me back in your heart."

"I'll never agree with your actions regarding Judah. And I'll never share a table with vagrants."

"Then we seem to be at an impasse. But I'm not going anywhere. I'm here. You can either love the father I am, or long for the father you wish I were."

I limp toward the path. "I'm exhausted. Can we please go?"

"Yes. Let's go home. The one we share physically. But, I want to share it relationally as well. I'm your abba. Please be my son."

Adjusting my cloaks, I lean on my walking stick, grateful for the stability it gives my knee.

And then we head back to the village. In silence.

CHAPTER 31
SETH

Meron
Chislev, (November) - Tebeth (December) AD 19

A man of many companions may come to ruin, but there is a friend who sticks closer than a brother.

PROVERBS 18:24

"Seth, wait!"

I ignore Joseph's call as I depart the cold of the synagogue.

"Seth!"

I can't tolerate his cheerfulness. Besides, he's Judah's friend. Why does he keep reaching out?

"Seth!" Uncle Daniel calls.

"Yes?" I turn. "Ouch!" Hopping on one foot, I grab the toes Joseph just smashed.

"Sorry! I was trying to catch up."

My smallest toe already swells.

"Are you okay?"

It's bruising!

"Your face looks like a storm over the Sea of Galilee. Come, I'll treat you to something warm."

"I haven't time." I limp a few steps. "Where's Uncle Daniel?

"He already left. Look, you can't go home to your bride like this. Have a drink with me and relax a bit."

"Fine." Hadassah's been so grumpy I don't want to go home.

As we meander through the maze of streets, my toe feels better until, at old Malachi the carpenter's shop, I overhear Abba's name.

"Did you hear of Ezra's good deed? Last week, he fed all the poor in town," Malachi says.

"I never knew a man more generous," adds his customer.

They probably hope to get a free meal next time. Well, there won't be a next time.

"What did you think about today's commentator?" Joseph asks. "In my opinion, old Nathaniel should leave expounding to someone younger."

"His thoughts were as life-giving as the Dead Sea."

"Don't hold back. Say what you think." I glare, but Joseph smiles. "Seth, I've always appreciated your dry wit, and it's nice to hear you joke a bit. Is marriage helping usher your humor back in?"

"My humor never went anywhere." I march straight ahead.

Silently, we make our way around market booths to reach a small stall where Joseph orders tea. Crossing my arms, I lean back on my stool and stare at the table.

"Such a man!" A woman at the vegetable stand beside us exclaims. "What Israel would be like if all men behaved like him. If anyone's ever had a good eye, it's Ezra!"

Her friend leans in. "But, do you know what he did?"

Out of the corner of my eye, I spy her two listeners shake their heads.

"A servant told me he washed the guests' feet!"

"No!"

She nods. "Can you imagine how filthy they were?"

There's no escape from hearing about this nightmare? I turn my face from the three clucking hens so they won't recognize me.

"Well, his proud son must've hated that. But have you ever known anyone so benevolent?"

"One son lost to the world and one son drowning in his own self-importance. Did you hear that Seth refused to attend the banquet?"

Which servant shared all this?

"Well, he won't get any credit for that good deed, now will he?" They titter.

Heat invades my face, and my fingers dig into the wooden table.

"Sorry, Seth," Joseph says. "I'd hoped to give you a distraction and ease your mind. Now these gossips make everything worse."

"They're uneducated women who don't understand Torah and its requirements." I hate Joseph's pity.

"Were you able to talk with Rabbi Yakov before he moved south?"

"Oh, yes."

"What did he say?"

"Let's just say his condemnation of Abba's banquet was complete. I'm tainted by my father's and brother's choices."

A server delivers hot mugs, smelling of spices, with steam curling in the breeze. Joseph leans back and crosses his arms.

"What, Joseph? What are you thinking?"

"I doubt it's anything you'd care to hear."

"Then keep it to yourself."

"I already was. You're the one who asked." Joseph slurps his drink. "How do you think the wheat will fare with this dry weather?"

"What?"

"Wheat. If we endure another dry winter? And what about the terrible drought up north? It's devastating everything. Nothing grows, and I hear people are dying in droves."

"What are you talking about?"

"Come on, Seth." Joseph nudges my shoulder. "Let's talk crops like old married men. Let others discuss good deeds and feasts and who has a good eye or a bad one. We have more important matters."

For the first time in a week, my mouth curves enough to break the hard line that had begun to make my teeth ache. "I think the decrease in the harvest will be offset by its value increasing. Other sources have been harder hit."

"Very true. Less grain everywhere means higher prices here."

"Speaking of wheat, I'm going out to inspect our fields." I drain my cup. "And maybe not go home at all."

"Remember how you feel about running away."

"True." I lift my face toward a bit of sunshine breaking through the gray. "Thank you, Joseph. For the perspective."

Joseph gives me his lopsided grin. "Anytime."

I turn to the three gossiping women behind us. Realization and blushing cheeks replace their confident talk.

"Ladies," I say. Then I enter the teeming street and move toward the gate out to the fields, feeling better than I have in days.

"'. . . who can stand before His cold?'[1]" Uncle Daniel recites as frigid winds ricochet off Mount Meron's crest, stirring the dust in front of his house.

"If winter's chill would bring rain, I wouldn't mind so much."

"This year's dry cold worries me." Abba, on my other side, wraps a shawl over his cloak. "Will crops grow? Will we lose sheep and goats?"

"What do you think, Seth?" Uncle Daniel asks.

I want to say, I think you and Abba should stop putting me in the middle. But, their relationship remains as nippy as the weather. At least Abba joined us for prayers this morning. Now if he'd just direct his words to Daniel instead of everyone else.

"We can't wring moisture from the skies," Barak says.

"Ezra," Malik calls from another group, "could you come help me? I can't correctly recite a passage."

"On my way." Abba joins him.

"How are things at home?" Barak raises his eyebrows.

"Fine."

"No more dinner parties?" When Barak laughs at his own question, I try to formulate a stinging retort. Nothing.

"Let's not rub salt in the wound." Uncle Daniel pats him on the shoulder.

After Barak departs, Uncle Daniel asks, "How are things really?"

"Well, Hadassah always seems unhappy, and the only time Samson isn't asking a question is when he's making a mess."

Uncle Daniel pokes at the flame in the brazier.

"Discussions in the synagogue feel tepid, and the arguments are shallow with Rabbi Yakov gone." I rub my hands over the flame.

"Today's prayers did feel rather uninspired."

"And you and Abba—"

Uncle Daniel clears his throat.

"Are you ready, Seth?" Abba walks out the front gate without saying goodbye to Daniel.

When my uncle sighs, I turn toward him. "One of you needs to take the first step. 'Whoever covers an offense seeks love, but he who repeats a matter separates close friends.'[2]"

"And I've discussed his transgressions repeatedly, which he knows. But all of us have! I'm just unsure what to do."

"I hope you figure it out soon." I hurry out to catch Abba. We fall behind a neighbor's oxen and match their slow pace.

"You and Hadassah have seemed rather gloomy lately. Is there anything you need to talk about?"

Crossing my arms, I stuff my hands in my sleeves. "I can't figure Hadassah out. For weeks she's acted sullen, she doesn't laugh, and she sleeps later than normal."

"I've noticed she's seemed less energetic and has been absent from many evening meals."

"But she keeps telling me nothing is wrong." I kick a pile of leaves. "So I've stopped asking."

"Shalom, Ezra and Seth." Malachi calls out. "Eli ordered a new ax handle. It's ready." As Abba enters the work shed, I move on. He and Malachi could chat for an hour.

In our compound, the sound of laughter draws my attention. By the oven, women huddle together, blankets on laps, carding wool.

Looking restless, Hadassah sits beside Rachel who rubs her back. I distrust their friendship, if for no other reason than Rachel brings Judah to mind. Hadassah rubs her stomach with one hand and her head rests on the other. I don't care what she says, something is wrong.

"Hadassah, may I speak with you?"

A hush falls over the group. Hadassah adjusts her headscarf and attempts a smile. The ladies on either side wink. What's the matter with them?

Hadassah rises with Rachel's help, and my concern grows. "Let's go to the arbor."

There, I coax the brazier back to life and add fuel. Miriam appears with warm ginger water and date cakes. She says to Hadassah, "Try to eat one. You'll feel better."

What does Miriam know? She pats Hadassah on the shoulder before exiting.

"Hadassah, what's wrong?"

"I'm sorry if my weakness bothers you." She clasps her hands.

"Bothers me? I'm worried about you."

"You sound angry."

"Something's wrong, and everyone seems to know but me!" When she groans softly, I quiet my words. "But I'm not angry." I take her cold hand. "What's wrong?"

A chilly breeze circles us, and I force myself not to move or speak.

"I—" A sob cuts her word.

"Please! Tell me!"

She places my hand on her belly. "Can you not guess?"

I almost shift away from this intimate touch outside our room until I realize my hand covers her womb. I stop breathing.

"A baby?"

She gives a weak smile.

Joy like I've never known surges through me. What wonder. A child will call me Abba!

"A baby!" I hug her, no longer caring who sees. She melts into my chest. Her tears soak my cloak, and my joy turns to confusion. "Why haven't you told me?"

"Oh, Seth!" She wipes her nose on my shoulder. "You've been so angry. So distant. I wanted to share this with you." She looks deeply into my eyes. "But how can we share joy when we can't even talk without bickering?"

I lean my forehead against hers. Slowly, our breaths synchronize. As the brazier crackles, I search my pregnancy knowledge and find little. I remember Gideon describing how ill his wife Elizabeth felt.

"You feel poorly?"

She groans. "My mother continued with life with no problems when she expected. But I'm struggling so much. The smell of food disgusts me. That's why I haven't been at evening meal."

"Oh!" Stupid. Stupid! Signs were here, but I hadn't paid attention. I assumed her anger and disappointment in me had kept her away. "I'm sorry."

She lays her head on my shoulder. "No, I'm sorry. I'm weepy and grumpy, and I feel awful. The ladies all say it's normal, but I feel like my body's attacking me."

I stiffen. "They knew before me?"

"Don't be angry. I need my Eema." Another sob escapes. "Miriam's never been pregnant, so I can't ask her for advice. And today, the others guessed from my behavior. They just want to help. And I need help."

And I can't assist with this. I rub her back and she rests on me. I've missed being close to her.

"Are you happy, my husband?"

"I'm thrilled." Kissing her forehead, tenderness makes its way back into my heart. "And I'm sorry."

"I'm sorry too," she whispers back.

I lift her chin. "I love you, Hadassah."

Suddenly, a sound I haven't heard in weeks warms me more than a dozen braziers. Hadassah laughs. Faint and restrained, but a laugh all the same.

CHAPTER 32
JUDAH

Ephesus
Chislev (November) AD 19

The fool says in his heart, "There is no God." They are corrupt, they do abominable deeds; there is none who does good.

PSALM 14:1

My head propped on one hand, I brush the embroidered, red linen cushions. I can now discern differences in weave and quality. I understand value and profit. I'll be successful, for all Cosmas's warnings.

My friend ran home, and I invested with Apollon. Over a week ago, the Minerva, packed with silks, linens, and my future, sailed south. The Tyrians' appetite for beauty ensures profits, as Meoklis repeatedly assured me. He also warned with a smile, "There are no guarantees in business. Just opportunity, Jude. Opportunity!"

"And how do you enjoy the advantages of being my partner?"

At the nasally voice, I leap up. "Greetings, Apollon! Thank you for tonight's invitation and for seating me so close to the head table."

"I take care of my friends." Even though I'm taller than him, he manages to look down his nose at me.

"Today's games were amazing! I could see the sweat on the gladiators' faces! You were the only thing missing."

He waves his hand as if shooing a gnat away. "Kassandra saw to your needs?"

"Yes." Hopefully the dim candlelight hides my flushing cheeks. Several times she slipped her arm around my shoulder or whispered in my ear. I change the subject. "Where's Meoklis? I haven't seen him for weeks and hoped he'd be here tonight. Isn't he also an investor?"

"I believe he's traveling." Turning his head, he growls to a servant behind us, "Make sure his cup and plate never empty."

"Yes—yes sir." The young man refills my goblet, but his shaking hand drips some on the table.

"Fool."

"I—I'm sorry." He cleans the drip with the bottom of his one-shouldered, dark blue chiton, the same that is worn by all the servants, and ducks away. How does Apollon strike such fear in his people when he never even raises his voice?

"Your home is incredible." Scantily clad nymphs dance across every wall of the open-air courtyard. Mosaic floors portray stories of the gods, with intricate patterns framing them.

"I don't suppose you'd find this in Judea," he says.

"Mosaics, yes. But, no likenesses of people or animals in a Jewish home." I don't add that it would be too close to breaking the second commandment.

"How strange. Glad I'm an Ephesian and celebrate the human form." He moves on before I can answer.

As I recline and drain my goblet, Kassandra enters. The music combines with conversations around me to create a buzzing that reminds me of bees back home.

Kassandra's form certainly deserves celebration. Tiny braids interweave with auburn waves, which are all pinned up somehow. Her gold and jade bracelets clatter against one another as she works her way from one group to the next, moving closer to me. I lie back on my pillow and gape at how her green silk, the color of olive leaves, outlines every curve, glimmering in the torchlight as she approaches.

"Enjoying the wine?"

My eyes travel from her delicate sandals to her painted eyes. "Immensely, among other things." I try to act like I speak with a Greek seductress regularly. "In fact, why don't you refill my cup?"

She sinks down, her gown contrasting against the cushion's red. "I'm not your servant," her voice, husky and soft, is for me alone.

With a gulp, I run my hand through my short hair.

Kassandra rolls her eyes. "Fine. Let me help you." She fills my cup and hands it to me. "Maybe you'll gain courage to speak."

Maybe.

I encircle her hand that holds my cup and gaze into her eyes, trying to find the woman inside. I only see locked doors.

"I like you, Jude." She lowers her lids and kisses me, deep and long. "A lot." Fine. If she won't allow me into her heart, I'll settle for her body.

After two weeks of dinner parties, I noticed a change in atmosphere last night. A nervousness hung in the air and between courses I heard one businessman after another complain about storms out at sea.

As I became nervous and agitated, Kassandra urged me to remain calm and to have another glass of wine.

But this morning I woke up to fear and rushed to the port. The Minerva left three weeks ago—too soon for good news, but not for bad.

Other businessmen wander among the sailors, listening for information.

"What!"

I turn toward the desolate cry.

"The ship went down? By the gods, we're ruined. Ruined!" A finely dressed man pulls on his hair. Beside him another man bends over double. With a scream, the first man tears his hair and runs from the dock. The other faints.

I might be sick.

What if that happens to the Minerva? To me? I finger the softness of my new blue cloak. In fact, I need to talk to Meoklis—

"Endless opportunities exist, my friend. Endless!"

"Meoklis!"

The merchant, arm around a wide-eyed young man, scans the crowd and then sends his protege off with a servant. "Jude. What are you doing here? Another trip? I thought you'd never board a ship again!" His laugh sounds cruel.

"Have you heard anything of the Minerva? I'm waiting for word—" I stare west across the Great Sea.

"We came through fine." He points to the ship he just disembarked. "A bit rough, but why invite trouble? Go. Make a sacrifice. Buy an amulet." He strokes my blue wool robe. "Lovely. Did my tailor make this for you?"

"No—in fact, I've been wanting to ask you about why your tailor charged me so much."

He drops the cloak like it burns him.

"My new tailor charges half of yours." I've been wanting to ask him about this.

"I thought you wanted quality, so I took you to the best!"

Meoklis's servants lug supplies to a nearby ship.

"You're leaving again?" I have the whining in my voice. "I've been looking for you for weeks!"

"Yes, yes. You'll live the same someday, with offices and shops in different ports." Meoklis glances over his shoulder repeatedly.

"Am I keeping you from something?"

"I must introduce my new friend around before I leave."

"Why didn't you introduce him to me?"

"Oh, well"—Meoklis turns toward the city—"I will soon."

"When will you return?"

"Who knows? Who knows!" He hurries off.

Alone again. I despise loneliness.

I haven't seen Kassandra for three days. Even though I know I'm nothing more than a dalliance, when she's with me, it feels anything but. I curse the crowds that suffocate me and twist the fringe on my belt.

Stop it!

I've attained the life I desired, one with opportunity and risk. Besides, I know how to divert myself. I'll play knucklebones with my friends at The Crow. I'll forget my worries about the Minerva and Kassandra. And I won't be alone.

"I DEMAND TO SPEAK WITH APOLLON!" I step closer to Haman.

"Back up," the wiry man sneers as my angry voice draws Aldric and Leuthar out from the office.

I lower my voice as much as my panic allows. "At the dock today, rumors of the Minerva's calamity circulated."

Haman crosses his arms. "Apollon doesn't speak to rumors."

"Apollon doesn't speak at all! I've received no invitations to dinner or the theater. I need to talk to him."

I don't add that two nights ago, when Kassandra and I were finally together again, she avoided any discussion of the ship. That only increased every fear.

"When he wants you, he'll tell you. Don't come back until you're invited."

"Can I leave him a note?"

Aldric and Leuthar, muscles flexing, step forward until their chests are a breath from my face. I raise my hands in surrender. "All right, all right. Everybody calm down. I'm leaving."

"You're the one not calm," Haman says. "Now get."

Fine, but if the ship carrying my fortune lies at the bottom of the sea, I might need to join it.

"I DON'T UNDERSTAND." My fist pounds the table, scattering scrolls and upsetting a lamp stand. I ignore the pain shooting up my arm. Haman steps forward.

"No, you obviously don't." Apollon waves his man back. "As I told you, nothing's certain in business. Trading in fine cloth holds risks."

When Apollon summoned me to his office, I hurried with hope. "I just recall something about the quickest way to fortune."

"But when your goods reside at the bottom of the Great Sea?" Apollon shrugs.

Cosmas's warnings whisper in my thoughts as my gaze narrows and heat radiates through me, offsetting the cold in the marble room. Shifting, I turn where I don't face the orange tapestries encircling the room. The black pattern reminds me of a spider.

"Now, now, my friend!" Apollon uprights a small statue. "If every downturn causes table banging, you'll either break a hand or split a table, and we require both for business." Waddling around the table, he embraces me with his pillowy arm, his heavy perfume turning my empty stomach.

"These things happen—storms, droughts, robbers, wars. So many challenges to a merchant's success. Unfortunate, I admit, but more opportunities still exist."

After a deep breath, I say, "Tell me again what happened."

"Storms ravaged many boats just off our port. The weather's been unpredictable lately. Someone must have angered Neptune, eh?"

"You should've warned me."

Apollon returns to his carved wooden chair, resting elbows on its arms to reign over his scroll-laden table. "It's your job to know the risks. I'm not responsible for your decisions. You wanted the quickest return, and I gave you opportunity—something, I might add, not everyone would do."

"Opportunity? Did you and the captain enjoy splitting my money?"

"Don't accuse me, boy." Apollon plants his hands on the table, all cordiality gone. "Greater men than you have found that dangerous. You want to blame someone, blame your God. And don't accuse my captain, either. He barely escaped with his life."

I pushed too far. But my gut knows there's more to the story than an unlucky storm. Somehow, Apollon cheated me. But that makes no sense. If I make money, Apollon makes money. Why would he ruin me?

"I have no god," I mumble.

"You're a Stoic? No wonder you encountered such a loss. Who's looking out for you? Next time, sacrifice and wear an amulet the entire time your merchandise sails. No god, indeed." Apollon's friendly voice returns, but I know dangerous currents run under his silken exterior.

Haman fills two goblets with wine. Apollon extends one to me. "Come. Drink. Mourn your loss and move on. Business continues, my friend."

After gulping the wine, I bang the goblet on the table.

"At least the loss doesn't affect your thirst."

"Oh, it's affected. It's increased!"

More wine cascades into my goblet.

"Drink slower," Apollon warns. "We'll guzzle cheap wine after this. For now, savor the flavor. Besides"—and his menacing tone returns—"if your luck doesn't change soon, cheap wine is all you'll ever drink."

CHAPTER 33
MIRIAM

Meron
Shevat (January) AD 20

Thus says the LORD of hosts, "Render true judgments, show kindness and mercy to one another."

ZECHARIAH 7:9

"Tova, where's the ground wheat?" Shivering, I stoke the oven.

"Methuselah's barely moving the grinding stone," she says through chattering teeth.

"If he moved faster, he'd be warmer." Hurrying toward the kitchen, I collide into Hadassah at the doorway.

"Sorry, Miriam," Hadassah whispers.

"You're up early." My heart softens at her drawn face. "You're so pale. Come sit by my fire. Would you like ginger tea?"

"Please."

"Seth took you cold water this morning?" I ache for this wisp of a girl, trying so hard to be brave through the misery.

"He's trying to be kind, so I act like it helps. But nothing does." She lays her head on the table with a groan. Her muffled voice continues. "And with Rabbi Yakov back, he rushes to get to synagogue."

"Why that man keeps showing up . . ." I sigh.

Tova rushes in. "I have the flour for the rest of the loaves!"

"Hush. Can't you see your mistress here?" I point to Hadassah.

"I'm sorry." Tova moves to the counter and mixes leaven into the fresh ground flour. "When my sister struggled, the midwife in Nazareth blamed an evil spirit. Eema laughed in her face and began feeding my sister mint, lemon seeds, wheat porridge, and soft-boiled eggs."

"Did she get better?" Hadassah lifts her head.

Tova smiles. "Yes. After the baby came." Her smile fades when she observes my disapproval. With her arms elbow-deep in the dough trough, she raises her eyebrows.

"Oh, Tova." Hadassah chuckles. "Thank you. I forget this isn't permanent. No matter how bad I feel, this will eventually end."

"So, you have no actual help?" My fists rest on my hips.

"Oh, those things offered relief. Just not a cure."

I point to the door. "Well, go to the storeroom and fetch mint and eggs." Tova inspects her doughy hands.

"Oh, never mind. I'll do it." I wrap in my thick shawl and grab a basket.

Hadassah laughs again, this time a little livelier. "You both give more relief than tea ever will, though tea sounds helpful."

"You come to us any time, my dear. Men tend to be useless at times like this."

Hadassah places a trembling hand on my arm. "I've never needed more help."

"It's a pleasure. You remember that. Now, Tova, hurry with the dough. We don't have all day."

As I leave, the two giggle again, though I can't figure out why.

CHAPTER 34
SETH

Meron
Shevat (January) AD 20

As charcoal to hot embers and wood to fire, so is a quarrelsome man for kindling strife.

PROVERBS 26:21

"Gideon!"

When my cousin doesn't appear, I stomp my feet and rub my nose. As our large tannur bakes bread, it warms whichever side of me that faces it.

"Excuse me, Seth."

I move from the opening as Miriam withdraws twelve toasty flat loaves.

"Excuse me, Master Seth."

Tova totes another wooden paddle with more bread. With deft

movement, she deposits them on flat stones inside. Before she's finished, Miriam returns with more.

"I'm glad for visitors." She deposits the third batch. "But it makes the morning busy."

"At least Gideon and Elizabeth's visit enlivens our evenings." I warm my hands with the oven's heat.

"I know Elizabeth and her baby girl cheer Hadassah." She waits until Tova walks away to ask, "Did she eat last night?"

"Not much." Nor did she talk much, especially once Gideon, Abba, and I discussed Rabbi Yakov's interest in Meron. In my mind, I replay last night's discussion.

"Why does he keep visiting little Meron?" Gideon had asked.

Abba laughed and then said, "Probably for more funds from Barak."

"Abba!" At my warning tone, Hadassah turned from me. "We're grateful he seeks winter shelter here."

"Are you grateful, Uncle?" Gideon asked.

"I'd prefer some rain and more warmth in our days." Abba stared at me. "But if the lively conversations that seem to accompany each of the Rabbi's visits are our only source of heat, then yes, I am grateful."

When wind swirls cold air through my robes and around my neck, I edge closer to the oven, inhaling the bread's yeastiness. Where's Gideon? I want to get to Barak's for today's discussion. With Abba's banquet still fresh in Rabbi Yakov's mind, I must prove my personal stances. Being late is no way to start rebuilding with him.

"Ready?" Gideon stretches as he emerges from Abba's room, with a wink and a grin. He draws his cloaks tighter. "The wind's cutting straight through today."

"Yes."

"I tried to talk Uncle Ezra into joining us, but he thought it best that he doesn't."

"You've eaten?"

"Aah." Gideon pats his belly. "Miriam's bread and date cakes! At least my insides are warm."

I shake my head and head to the gate. "We're late."

Gideon matches my pace. "I bet Uncle Ezra and Rabbi Yakov could warm a room. I'd love to hear them discuss the proper way to hold a dinner."

I clench my fists and accelerate.

"Learn to laugh, Seth. If 'a joyful heart is good medicine'[1], you need a big dose."

"I don't need medicine. I need Abba to stop arguing Rabbi Yakov's every interpretation."

"You'd like him to stop being Jewish? All our discussions sound like arguments." He chuckles. "You can't blame Uncle Ezra for being better at discussing than anyone else."

Frost crunches under our feet and a baby's cry floats from a home we pass.

Gideon grows serious. "Elizabeth worries about Hadassah."

My foot catches on a cobblestone, and I cough over a curse. "She's miserable, can't eat much, and is always weary. If I could fix it, I would."

"Maybe it'll pass. Elizabeth struggled at first." Gideon blows on his hands, wraps his cloak tighter, and leans into the wind.

"Hadassah says by the time the almonds blossom, she'll have improved. But the midwife told me not to hope too much."

We arrive at Barak's courtyard as red-nosed servants tote stools and cushions into the room. I grab Gideon's arm. "Look, the last time Rabbi Yakov was here was when Abba threw his banquet for the unclean. Please don't cause trouble today. For my sake."

"Me?" Gideon grins. "I have no idea what you mean."

Must everyone in my family make life a challenge?

"Abba, what did you hope to accomplish today? Do you purposefully obstruct my relationship with Rabbi Yakov?"

"After Gideon left, you pestered me to join a discussion before the good rabbi moved on. So after three weeks of avoiding him, I did just what you asked. Did you expect me to not speak?"

"What Rabbi Yakov must think of me now!" I bound up the stairs to the balcony.

Trudging behind me, Abba says, "I wasn't trying to cause dissension, but to provoke thought. Discussions are rich opportunities to gain understanding."

Hadassah carries a bowl of steaming lentils up the stairs. "I'm glad it's warmed enough to eat here again. I do better in fresh air."

Tova places bread, cheese, and olives before us.

Crossing my arms, I frown at Hadassah's interruption, but Abba says, "Hadassah, your smiling face brightens our evening. Are you feeling better?"

"A bit. Enough to eat at least."

"And this meal smells delicious."

Hadassah beams at Abba. She didn't smile at me like that.

"Yes, thank you," I mumble.

She sinks to her cushion without looking my way. Why even try when she's so hard to satisfy?

Abba breaks the bread and offers thanksgiving.

"I wish Gideon and Elizabeth could have stayed longer." Hadassah takes a small bite.

"What about all your talk of mercy?" I shoot at Abba. "And the words from Jeremiah? 'For as often as I speak against him, I do remember him still. Therefore, my heart yearns for him; I will surely have mercy on him.'[2] You fooled no one."

"I'm glad I communicated clearly."

I fling my half-eaten bread on my platter. Hadassah's eyes bore into me. Last night she reprimanded me for being disrespectful to Abba. I then informed her that I didn't get married for my life to be examined.

"The rest of the village considers Judah dead, but I've seen you sneak to the top of the tower, a tower you had to finish I might add, and gaze to the horizons." I scoop lentils with bread. "Don't deny it."

"Why would I deny it?"

"And you pray for him?"

"Certainly!" Abba doesn't even sound sorry.

"Why is he still on your mind?"

"I'm a father. He's always on my mind. As are you."

"He's not coming back." Why do I even need to point this out?

Abba takes a long drink and then turns to me. "What would you do if he returned with riches?"

"I'd turn my back on him. His money would be cursed. He's dead to me."

Hadassah refills Abba's bowl, shaking her head.

"Thank you, Hadassah." He scoops a bite and chews thoughtfully. "All right. And what if he returned with nothing?"

"I'd let the village deal with him. They'd scourge, chasten, and humble him. Even then, he'd never again be my brother."

"Oh, Seth." Hadassah lays her hand on my arm, but I pull my arm away.

Abba leans on the table, getting as close to me as possible. "But Seth, you passionately pursue the Law—in order to obey. Right?"

"Do you mock me?"

"Then how do you read this Torah instruction? 'If your brother becomes poor and cannot maintain himself with you, you shall support him as though he were a stranger and a sojourner, and he shall live with you. Take no interest from him or profit, but fear your God, that your brother may live beside you.'[3] Doesn't this scripture apply to us?"

"It applies in the Year of Jubilee."

Hadassah jumps in. "My abba taught us Moses's words, which say, 'If among you, one of your brothers should become poor . . . you shall not harden your heart or shut your hand against your poor brother, but you shall open your hand to him and lend him sufficient for his need, whatever it may be.'[4]" She holds out her palms as if ready to give to any beggar that passes.

This is why women shouldn't be taught Torah.

She blinks at my glare. "It's one Abba recited whenever he gave to the needy."

"I'd appreciate my wife's loyalty."

"Always. And my honesty." She strokes her growing middle and drops to the cushion.

"I can address only one issue at a time. We'll discuss this later." I ignore Hadassah's hurt eyes and Abba's look of remonstrance. "Abba, would you expect me to welcome Judah back? You would ask me to give him shelter, food, and security after all he's done to us? After all he has cost us?"

"I wouldn't be the one asking, son. I didn't write the Law. But like you, I attempt to obey its goodness."

I stuff a large bite in my mouth and search for a passage to refute this reckless mercy. I recall nothing specific. "There're other laws to consider. Other ways to consider this issue."

"We can usually find an interpretation that offers escape from a direct command."

"Abba, he's not coming back."

"No, he's not." Abba stands and paces. "But think Seth, what does Adonai do with our sin? '...as far as the east is from the west, so far does he remove our transgressions from us.'[5]"

"Maybe Adonai can do that. I cannot."

"As a father, I can do nothing less. 'As a father shows compassion to his children, so does the LORD show compassion to those who fear him.'[6]"

"This discussion is fruitless! First, he'll never return. And second, Judah has committed too many transgressions!"

Abba halts. "Too many transgressions? How many times did His children profane Adonai's holy name and chase foreign gods? Did He ever limit forgiveness if His people repented?"

A cold breeze flickers the torch light. Looks like our warm spell is over.

Hadassah's soft voice says, "'I have blotted out your transgressions like a cloud and your sins like mist; return to me, for I have redeemed you.'[7]"

"Enough!" My wine spills and my voice echoes through the courtyard. "Enough, Abba." I regain evenness. "I cannot consider what you're asking."

Turning to Hadassah, I say, "And from now on, if you can't agree with me, say nothing. Do you understand?"

Her eyes flame and her arms cross. "No, I don't understand. Not even a little." Never taking her eyes off me, she wraps her headscarf tight and pushes herself up. Turning to Abba, she says, "Good night, Abba," and descends the stairs.

I stare after her. This. This is why I hesitated to get married.

"I'll leave too, son." Without turning around, he adds, "I don't understand you either. But like Hadassah, I love you deeply. Hopefully, you can come to value our love before it's too late."

I sit dumbfounded as the temperature drops. Too late for what?

SHABBAT SHOULD BE PEACEFUL. Restful. Holy. Instead, with Abba and Rabbi Yakov arguing point after point, I came home late this afternoon from synagogue with pounding temples and a racing heart.

"What an outrage! What a debacle!" I storm about our room. "Every time Abba refutes Rabbi Yakov, he shames me. Why provoke needlessly?" Jerking my cloak off, I fling it to the ground, plop on a stool, and drum my fingers on the table. "What's this?"

"A red glass vase from Sepphoris."

"And the dead stuff?"

With one hand rubbing her stomach, Hadassah hangs my garment on the peg with the other. "Dried herbs. No flowers grow in winter."

"I don't understand Abba!" I start pacing again, tripping over the green and red rug. "Why is this always in the way!"

Hadassah moves it under the bed, sits in the opposite corner, lights a lamp, picks up embroidery work, and sighs.

"You labor on Shabbat?"

"The sun's down, Seth." Another sigh.

I glance out the window. "So, it is." I move from complaints about Abba to our poor crops and lazy servants. Frustrations spill like a torrent.

Finally, I halt to catch my breath. Hadassah continues to embroider.

"Well?" I demand.

"Well, what?"

"What do you think?"

"You want to know what I think?" Her needle sits frozen in air.

"Yes."

"Why?"

"Why? Why! So I can quit talking to myself!" She flinches and I lower my voice. "So I can hear another person speak sense."

"I thought so." She takes a stitch.

"Are you going to answer me?" My jaw clenches.

Hadassah keeps her eyes on her work. "No."

"Because?"

Her lips move silently before she stares at me. "You don't want to know what I think."

Using all my self-control, I ask, "Then why did I ask you?"

"Because you want to hear that I agree with you. You don't want to know what I think."

"What's wrong with that? As my wife, isn't that your duty?"

This time her volume increases. "Do you think the Creator looked at Adam and said, 'I think Adam needs someone to agree with him? To always think he's right? To never offer advice?'"

I drop onto my stool while Hadassah throws down her embroidery and takes over my pacing. "You're blind, Seth. Blind to Abba's wisdom and the truth Rabbi Akiva speaks. Blind to Rabbi Yakov's arrogance. Your anger at Judah colors your judgment and imprisons you."

"Judah has nothing to do with this."

"Of course he does! Your bitterness blinds you to all you have." She faces me with arms extended. "Like me."

The room grows darker.

"You are so angry. Why? Because I think differently than you? Because I perceive more sides to a situation? My perspective should be a gift. Yet, you resent it."

She closes the distance, her cold fingers trying to loosen my clenched ones.

"Please, Seth." When she kisses my hand, her tears seep into my fist. "Don't push me into a corner to nod and agree. Let me offer the wisdom the Most High gives me. I want to share with you, to be one with you."

"You're just a woman." Jerking my arm away, I step back. "Don't presume to advise me."

She stares, unmoving.

Clueless as what to say, I stare back until the oil lamp sputters out. In the twilight I no longer see her face, but I hear her shudder.

"I'll get more oil." Grabbing the empty flask from the hook, I lurch out the door. I've not taken two steps before her sobs reach my ears. I caused such pain? Going back to comfort her would admit that I'm wrong. And I'm not. Besides, it's probably just pregnancy that makes her so emotional.

"Matthias!" I thrust the flask toward him. "Please have Tova deliver more lamp oil to the room. I'm going out."

Rushing out the gate, I head toward Uncle Daniel's where I hope to enjoy an invigorating evening with only men.

CHAPTER 35
JUDAH

King's Highway
Tishri (September) AD 20

Therefore my people go into exile for lack of knowledge; their honored men go hungry, and their multitude is parched with thirst.

ISAIAH 5:13

Dust shrouds my body and coats each breath. I no longer hate camels. They're magnificent creatures Adonai created for man's benefit.

Good thing that summer in the hills toughened my feet, because the distance walked in the past three weeks feels beyond calculation.

"Doing okay?" Pavlos's voice jostles from behind me. Our paths rarely cross during the day, and at night he has no energy left to chat. I miss talking.

"Better than a party in Ephesus with a breeze wafting over the terrace, cool wine flowing, and a gorgeous lady on each side," I snap.

From his mount on Gaidoros, Pavlos snorts. "Then I suppose you wouldn't want a ride on my noble steed?"

"Where would I fit?" I ache for a break from the eternal walking.

"We'll make it work. Ol' Gaidoros isn't pretty, but he's tough as bronze. Like me."

Grasping his hand, I swing a leg over the donkey's rump and cling to Pavlos's shoulders, grateful for the awkward seat.

"I haven't seen you much." I regret the accusation in my voice.

"My duties never cease on these trips. And—"

A cough racks his body.

"And what?"

"The dust makes me cough. I'm too tired at night for the fire."

Just as I begin to relax, Pavlos says, "Your price for the ride is a story."

"My price?"

"Everything has a cost in life—you should know that. Whoever rides Gaidoros tells me a tale. Makes the day go faster."

"I have no stories."

"Sure you do. Tell me about your childhood."

"My past comfort mocks my present misery. Maybe I'll walk."

"Come on, tell me another story about your brother. Or your father. Or that talkative woman whose bread would make me weep. I should meet her."

"She's married."

"Aren't they all, at least the good ones. Here,"—Pavlos pulls bread from his satchel—"I'll give you this, but you must tell me a story. Agreed?"

Grabbing the bread, I take a bite. "Fine, but I won't talk about Miriam's bread, or food at all."

Pavlos slaps his knee and laughs, scaring Gaidoros, who bolts toward the roadside. I grasp Pavlos, who continues to laugh as he reigns in our ride.

"Your laugh feels as good to my ears as this bread to my belly."

"Thank—" A racking cough interrupts him.

“I’m worried about you.”

After gulping from his waterskin, he continues as if I’d said nothing. “No food talk. Tell me another story about your brother.”

“You’re torturing me.”

“More than walking?”

“Fine. But it costs more bread.”

“Upping the price!” Pavlos pulls out another loaf. “You are a businessman!”

I chomp in quick bites and sigh. I haven’t eaten two loaves at one time this entire journey. The almost full feeling delivers a drowsiness I’m not sure I can fight.

“Tell me about growing up with your abba.”

“Hmm . . . as boys, Abba loved us no matter what. But he never allowed us to get away with anything. His rules were law. We were to trust his love and his protection.”

“He sounds wise.”

“Well, as I grew older, it no longer felt like protection, but a barrier to what I wanted.”

Pavlos coughs again. “And your brother?”

“He struggled with Abba, too. Only differently.”

“In what way?”

“Well...” I replay arguments between Abba and Seth, trying to pinpoint the why. “It’s hard to put into words. Seth cared so much about other people’s opinions, and Abba cared only about Adonai’s.”

We plod past baked grass and withered trees.

A lizard skitters across the path.

Somewhere a hyena cackles.

And I lay my head on Pavlos’s shoulder.

“No sleeping, Judah. I paid two loaves for this.”

“All right. Let me think.” Yawning, I search my past for a tale to keep me awake and decide on one that displays Seth’s stubbornness. Instead, Pavlos and I laugh at two foolish brothers. Grateful to not be walking this hot road, I share times we tried to fool Miriam and how she always caught us. Between laughs and Pavlos’s cough, the miles move by. I talk of home and sheep and olives and a brother I never understood. For the first time since I left home, I realize something. I miss Seth.

"OVER HERE, SLAVE!" Gallus barks, his dark skin glistening. I just watered the camels, the thirstiest creatures in the known world. Exhaustion rolls over me and hunger gnaws at me. If he names another task, I will collapse.

"Valerius wants an update on the camels."

I raise my eyebrows.

"Sometimes he wants to speak to a servant instead of me."

I nod, perplexed. I've only spoken to Valerius a few times since he purchased me.

The merchants gather around their fire, laughing and joking. Meat roasts on spits and flatbread bakes on stones, their delicious aromas rising with the steam. Men spear food from passing platters.

"Master?" I swallow, as a platter passes under my nose.

"Are the camels watered and happy?" Grease drips from the corner of Valerius's mouth.

I swallow. "Yes, Master. At least they looked happy—for camels."

He howls as he leans to his neighbor, hooking his thumb back at me. "They looked happy for camels!" Both men lay back on their cushions and laugh until tears flow. The wine must be good.

I shift from one foot to the other. "Anything else, sir?"

Wine sloshes in his cup as he hands me two loaves of warm bread. "Here."

"Thank you, sir!" My stomach grumbles as I make my way toward the servants' fire. Though small, our blaze provides warmth and security.

Clutching my treasure, I search for a secluded spot. I wrap my cloak tight, turn away, and eat my bread in anonymity.

CHAPTER 36
SETH

Meron
Iyyar (April) AD 20

Let the people of Israel keep the Passover at its appointed time.

NUMBERS 9:2

"Eli, is the Temple tax safely stored? Remember, only Tyrian shekels."

Samson runs up. "Why?" We haven't even left yet, and his tunic is covered in dirt.

"Because there's no image on that kind of coin."

"Huh," he grunts and runs off.

Eli says, "Yes, I double checked. And the travel funds are stored separately. And Miriam has a few more supplies."

"I'll check. Matthias?"

"Yes, sir?"

"Check the ropes binding the food cart. I don't want the amphorae to spill like last time."

"Already done. They won't go anywhere."

I wish Hadassah could be in charge of the food, but the smell makes her green. Yet, she insists on making this trip even though we've struggled through the entire winter with her being miserable. Frustrating woman.

I stick my head in the kitchen doorway. "You have extra supplies? And don't forget we travel for eighteen days."

Miriam whirls around, wooden spoon aloft like a sword. "As you have for the past twenty-five Passovers. Haven't I always packed enough?" Her spoon points to bundles and containers stacked around the table. "I also prepared teas and ointments for Hadassah. There's enough for eighteen days, but she might forget to use them when she feels sick. So someone needs to help her."

"Then tell Tova. I'm no midwife."

"Matthias!" I call as I bolt from the kitchen. "Miriam has more food!"

What have I forgotten? After a cold winter and dry spring, Passover promises hope. But traveling to Jerusalem gives me a headache. Relatives and villagers who join our caravan to the Holy City fill the courtyard. I thread my way through to the barn, where Abba directs Tova to bring more bedding for Hadassah's wagon.

"Son, thank you for your abundant preparations to help everyone travel. I know it's taxing."

"Our aunts, uncles, and cousins enjoy your generosity."

"Well, Passover started with a family meal, and so it continues." He attaches a pole to the corner of the wagon.

"What's all this?"

"Bind that last stick tightly in the corner like the three I've already secured." Abba drapes a canopy over the cart. "This should keep Hadassah comfortable. Considering how bad she feels, I'm grateful she wants to come."

"This what you wanted?" Samson clutches dried lavender. How does this boy get so messy and sweaty before the third hour?

Abba beams. "That's perfect. The fragrance will help Hadassah. Now go fetch the other supplies from Miriam."

Still panting, Samson dashes off in a swirl of dust.

"To ease your mind about your beloved, I have instructed Tova to care for her," Abba says.

"Maybe Hadassah shouldn't go."

"I want to go," a weak voice squeaks from behind me. Holding her belly with one hand, Hadassah props herself against the barn's rock wall with the other. "I want to go to the Temple and praise Adonai in the Court of Women—more this year than any other."

"I appreciate your devotion." I don't add that she feels like a burden. Instead, I put my arm around her and remind myself one more time that children are a blessing.

She leans her head against my chest. "I'm sorry to take you from your work." I help her into the bed of the cart.

"I'll help any way I can." Tova joins Hadassah.

"And I'm sorry to you as well." Hadassah settles back on the pallet.

"Why?" Tova giggles. "I won't have to walk. And I brought my embroidery."

Rising dust announces Samson's return, arms full of small containers. "Here ya' go, Hadassah. Miriam said somethin' about mint in the water and . . ."

Samson looks to the sky with his mouth squished to one side.

What a useless boy.

A grin sprouts. "Oh, yeah." He looks at the flasks in his right arm. "Mint in these"—he turns to the flasks in his left arm—"and ginger in these."

"Thank you, Samson." Tova stows the supplies in a crate. "I'll remember."

"You're such a help." Hadassah holds out her hand to him. "What would we do without you?"

What would we do without him? We'd clean fewer messes and break up fewer fights. How does this orphan make her smile?

"Well, praise be His name!" Abba claps his hands. "Adonai's always solving more than one problem at a time."

"It's time to leave." I state the obvious.

Hadassah's eyes droop. "I'm sorry I delayed you."

I calm my tone. "No more apologizing from you. Just get comfortable here."

She grasps my hand. "Thank you, Seth."

I squeeze back. "I'll check on you at the first stop."

Why is it that what I need to do, what I want to do, and who I need to serve always compete with each other? How do I direct this caravan and be gentle with my wife? How can I honor Abba and follow Rabbi Yakov? Loving is so hard and costly and time consuming.

Mounting my donkey, I call, "Up to Jerusalem!"

CHAPTER 37
JUDAH

Ephesus
Sivan (May) AD 20

The sorrows of those who run after another god shall multiply; their drink offerings of blood I will not pour out or take their names on my lips.

PSALM 16:4

I should eat well tonight. I finagled a dinner invite from a wealthy perfume merchant who didn't want any empty seats at his party.

"Right this way." The servant leads me past the head table.

"Greetings, Jude." Apollon smiles his not-very-happy smile from his seat of honor.

I halt. "Apollon." I'd rather not run into him, but I do wonder if Kassandra is here. When the servant clears his throat, I follow him. He finally deposits me at a table in the back corner. How embarrassing.

From across the room, Apollon gives me an enigmatic smile and raises his golden goblet. I raise my clay cup in return as if it didn't bother me. Then I lean back on a wool pillow and stuff food into my mouth.

Last week, Apollon offered me a loan for another venture, but I'm trying everything to stay out of his web.

Kassandra saunters into the room with the son of a Persian merchant panting behind her. She barely pays him attention. I haven't seen her in a week, and the sight of her in her lilac gown makes the food in my stomach churn.

"What's your business here?" The fat wine merchant to my right slurps his wine.

"I trade in linen and silk." It sounds official. Real. But to trade implies that I received something in return for the material now worn by fish. Anger makes the cheap wine taste more bitter.

"Ahh, yes. Better than grain these days." He leans in. "There's little to buy. The Romans try to keep cities fed with bread, but without rain, more and more will die. In the countryside, it's getting ugly."

"How do you know this?"

My dinner partner's jovial smile contrasts his news, and his waistline contradicts it. "I just returned from a caravan trip. No rain this winter. From here north, fields dry into wastelands. What will we eat? That's what I want to know." As if fortifying himself against future starvation, the man stuffs more olives into his mouth.

The longer I listen to his report, the faster my heart beats. How will I survive? My money won't stretch far if food prices keep rising.

The smell of jasmine dissolves my thoughts.

"Hello, Jude." Kassandra sinks onto my pillow.

"Why, hello, lovely lady." My neighbor effuses as olive oil dribbles down his chin.

She ignores him.

"What do you want, Kassandra?"

She plucks a grape from my plate and guides it slowly into her mouth, never breaking eye contact. I turn away.

"Oh, Jude, sulking's for children. You had bad luck. It happens."

"Bad luck? I lost everything!"

"But what will you do next?" Her finger strokes my arm.

"What do you care? My calamity meant your exit. Go back to your new catch. I'm sure he'll revel in your attentions, as I once did."

"Wouldn't you like to again?" She stretches out and snuggles close. Her toes rub my foot. "I miss you. Do you miss me?"

"Certainly not!" Curse my wavering voice.

She lays her hand on my chest. "Then why is your heart beating so fast?"

"Run back to Apollon." I move my foot and try to sound angry, but my husky tone reveals my desire. I'd give anything to experience her again.

"I'd prefer you." Her dangerous amber pools reflect the dancing lamplight.

My hand shakes as I reach for my goblet.

She moves closer, our bodies pressing together. "Don't give up, Jude. Try again. For both our sakes." With a light kiss, she whispers, "I'll come to you later tonight."

"Why would Apollon let you? I have nothing left."

"Well . . ." Kassandra looks almost vulnerable until she tosses her head. "Sometimes I serve his pleasure, and sometimes I serve my own."

"Be careful on the streets." Our fingers interlace.

"Aldric will guard me. But your concern and protectiveness—" She touches my cheek. "Try again. Try for me. For us."

She slides her hand away and moves on. By instinct, I check on Apollon who stares straight at me and my skin crawls at those self-satisfied eyes.

It's time I learned to consider my interests alone. Tonight, I'll enjoy Kassandra's arms. Tomorrow I'll figure out a new plan, without Apollon.

"So . . ." I turn to my gorging neighbor, who smiles at me with admiration. "You were telling me about your last caravan?"

AT MY LAST visit to the baths in search of contacts, I found a potential partner named Drusus. Everything went so well at first—until Drusus wanted specifics.

"How much can you invest?"

"I am still raising funds."

"Do you have special skills you can offer?"

"Well . . ."

"What successful ventures have you already been involved with?"

At that I hung my head. "None yet. My first investment sunk."

"I like you Jude." Drusus wrapped his towel around his shoulders. "But I need at least one reason to work with you."

One closed door after another steers me where I swore I'd never be again—partnering with Apollon. And with no money left, my risk feels immeasurable. The only collateral I have left is myself.

"SIGN HERE."

The stylus threatens to drip so I brush the tip against the ink bowl.

Don't do it.

Apollon drums his fingers.

I wipe my forehead, shift in my chair, dip the pen again, take a deep breath, ignore the internal warning, and dash my signature across the contract. Apollon's smile almost looks genuine.

"Good. You finish out our little band."

Swigging wine, I comb my fingers through my lengthening hair. I wish Kassandra would saunter through the back door.

Apollon bustles papers, rolls papyrus, and works figures on a wax tablet. Finally, he leans back and nods.

"You've made a wise decision, Jude."

"Why are you fronting me the money?"

"I want you to be successful."

I snort. "Come Apollon. You're many things, but selfless?"

Linking his hands over his middle, his mouth's corners raise just a bit. "No, thankfully, I'm not burdened with worrying about others. You want the truth? Let's just say it makes my partners happy to see more investors."

"That makes sense."

"And I enjoy keeping you under my thumb."

I shift in my seat.

"And there's little risk. Unless you die, I have a way to get my money back."

"How?"

Apollon's mouth twitches. "Let's hope you don't find out."

"WHERE'S MY SCROLL?"

I fling dirty clothes to the floor, push aside papers, and stack dried containers of ink. From my scruffy beard, my matted waves, now long and unfashionable, to my dirty clothes, I look like my neighbors who I previously disdained.

"Where's the contract!"

Hurling items to the floor, I knock over a goblet of last night's wine and red creeps toward my papers. The bottom scroll, the one I search for, contains a large red blotch.

Just like my life. So much damage and no solutions.

A peek behind my brick reveals the few coins that remain. If this deal fails, I'll slip to the wharf, buy a ticket on any ship, and sail away. Like Jonah, but hopefully without the storm and big fish.

Quickly, I exit to avoid Balbina's demands for rent. In the street, I hold my cloak over my mouth to protect myself from the dust clouds whipped up by the winds.

"Please!" I plead as I walk. The woman next to me, a basket of dried fish balanced on her head, turns and stares. But to which god do I send prayers? I'm not sure, but if just one listens, I beg that today will hold some small fortune. Some change. Some luck. Some help.

After wandering aimlessly, I find myself at the place I've avoided my entire time in Ephesus. Climbing the steps of the awe-inspiring Temple of Artemis, I keep my head down, though it doesn't matter if someone sees me. They don't care if I disobey the First Commandment. Besides, this isn't the first law I've broken, though I hadn't yet worshipped other gods.

"And," I whisper to myself, "I wouldn't be stealing into this marble temple if the God of my youth answered prayers or blessed my business or just once shone favor upon me."

"Great is Artemis of the Ephesians!" Voices proclaiming the goddess's wonder echo off the marble. My head swims from incense, and my cavernous heart collapses. For all I've turned my back on, somewhere inside, I still believe in Adonai, at least too much to ask for help from Artemis. And so I flee the magnificent temple, but it's so inconvenient. He leaves no room for another.

But where does that leave me?

I WANDER THE MARKET STALLS, looking for affordable food. Dried fruit and fresh bread cost dearly. Shoppers wear haunted expressions and gaunt bellies.

I reach toward some figs.

"Show me your money first." The peddler's angry tone surprises me.

"May I examine before I purchase?"

"First, prove you can buy." He yells at a boy behind me. "Show me money before you get closer."

The scrawny lad in a torn, faded green chiton flees.

"A bit harsh, friend." I display my coins.

"You think so? Well, *friend* I have a family to feed. But my merchandise keeps walking off in hungry pockets."

"How much do these cost?"

My eyes widen at the price, but he won't bargain. "That's what they cost, and you won't find this quality anywhere in the city. Now, do you want any or not?"

Fingering my few coins, I say, "I must pass, but I wish you luck on feeding your family."

"And I wish you luck on not starving."

What does it feels like to starve? I've experienced lean winters after a poor harvest. But even in difficult times, Abba shared with beggars who passed through the village. I recall Uncle Daniel chiding Abba, "You can't feed everyone."

"No, but I can feed the people at my door," Abba would reply.

Hunger intensifies old memories. Not helpful. So I search out more affordable, poorer quality figs and buy a string of twelve. Just eat three, I instruct myself as I stuff them in my satchel.

With no reason to go back to my dingy room, I munch and wander, and investigate narrow side streets into unknown parts of Ephesus. I try to plan my escape, but my hungry mind can't think. Maybe I should eat one more. Better to feel full now, even at the expense of tomorrow's hunger.

I reach for a fig—

Where are they! I grope in my satchel and my panic rises.

They're gone. Yahweh hates me. Once again, He allows me to be cheated and swindled through no fault of my own.

But when were they stolen? I scan the tide of people, and to my right, I spot a dirty green chiton sprinting away—the boy at the fig stand!

I run after him through narrowing streets. The twists and turns, complicated by merchants, barrels, animals, and people make it impossible to catch him. Gasping for air in an unfamiliar alley, I halt.

My ears roar and sparks dance across my closed eyes. Leaning against a stone wall, I hang my head, ignoring the dripping sweat. If I could just will away every terrible disaster. Reverse time. Unmake bad decisions. Guard the only food I owned from starving street children.

As my heartbeat slows, smells and sounds infiltrate my warring mind and I sense something familiar. Something safe. I refuse to open my eyes for fear the feeling will vanish.

"You all right, mister?" A girl's voice interrupts my trance. "You sick?"

Lifting my head, I stare into brown eyes wreathed in frizzy brown hair that refuses to remain in her braid. Her clothes look Jewish.

"No, I just need to sit."

"You need some water or somethin'?"

"Can you point me to a well?"

"Come get a drink from our bucket. My eema won't mind."

Eema. So, she is Jewish. I've landed right back where I ran away from—a Hebrew community. Fool. Act like a thirsty Gentile, get a drink, and leave.

I allow her to guide me to a low door across the alley that enters a small, dark room. At the doorway, my hand instinctively touches the mezuzah. The girl watches me but says nothing. Inside the smell of fresh bread assaults me, and the orderly home, bathed in yellow light, tugs at my heart.

"Eema, I found someone who needs help. He's thirsty, and he says he isn't sick, but I'm not so sure. He also said he just wants water, but he looks awfully skinny, don't you think?"

Looking unfazed, the young matron wipes her hands on a cloth. "Welcome. We help all who Adonai brings."

My stomach tightens as bread's aroma travels from my nose to my growling stomach.

Take a drink and leave.

She turns to her daughter. "Miriam, fetch water so he can wash."

Miriam. Naturally. If Yahweh exists, He's having a good laugh.

"Here you go, mister. We always wash our hands before we eat. My Syrian friend made fun of my washing all the time. My Abba said I shouldn't play with her no more."

Maybe the name Miriam endows its owner with talkativeness.

"Are you Jewish?"

"Miriam, hush," her mother scolds.

"Well, he looks Ephesian, but he touched the mezuzah, and look, he's washing his hands just like Abba. Why would he know how to do that?"

As I consider bolting, Miriam's eema hands me warm bread. Burying my nose in it, I inhale long, the scent like medicine. With reverence, I break the bread and take a slow bite, closing my eyes. Meron lays in my hands and mouth. I'm at my Miriam's table, surrounded by my family's warmth and Abba's laugh. A tear escapes.

"I think he's crying." Miriam whispers louder than her eema talks. "What's wrong with him? Do you think he doesn't like your bread?"

"Hush, child. Food carries memories. Let your friend be."

I savor another bite, allowing home to saturate my weary soul. "Thank you, ma'am. Your bread is delicious."

"My eema makes better bread than all the ladies on this street. Abba says she's the bestest cook anywhere and we're the luckiest family 'cause she's ours. Where's your eema?"

"She died when I was born."

Miriam gasps. "That's the worstest thing I ever heard. Did you hear that, Emma? He never even knew his eema." The girl pats my arm.

Everything feels too familiar, mocking me and intensifying my disappointment. I need to leave.

"Thank you, Miriam. Thank you for your hospitality, ma'am. Your bread is . . . perfect." I move toward the door.

The woman smiles and extends a small loaf. "I wish I could give you more, but times are hard." A shadow crosses her face. "Let this loaf remind you that Adonai's kindness follows you wherever you go." I try to grab the loaf, but she clutches my hand. "'Where shall I go from your Spirit? Or where shall I flee from your presence?'[1]"

I nod, stuff the bread in my satchel, and flee.

"Bye, mister!" Miriam calls. "Come back tomorrow if you want more bread."

I wave without looking back. Miriam's eema is wrong. If Yahweh is real, I was able to flee from His presence, because He is nowhere to be found.

CHAPTER 38
JUDAH

Ephesus
Sivan (May) AD 20

Why then has this people turned away in perpetual backsliding?
They hold fast to deceit; they refuse to return.

JEREMIAH 8:5

The gulls' screeches welcome me to the harbor, just like yesterday and the day before. My life depends on this enterprise, and I need news as much as I require air. Sailors discuss various storms and ships, but there are no reports of our ship.

Yesterday, I tried Meoklis's home, hoping he might have news. But he hasn't returned from Caesarea. What irony. I left Judea under the influence of a man who ran back there. More humor, Adonai?

As I mill about, I observe wealthy citizens boarding ships to flee the drought, either west to Rome or south to Egypt. Eventually, hunger forces me back toward the city for some food. I'm following the sandals of the person in front of me when a familiar perfume stops me short. I look into the face of the last man I want to see. His cropped hair and trimmed beard gleam with oil.

"Bad news, Jude?" Apollon asks.

"No news."

"Sunken ships tire me."

"Yes."

"You mustn't be sleeping at all, unless you can still afford wine."

"I'm fine."

"Check in with me tomorrow to discuss next steps."

It feels as if my life slips away like sand grains through Apollon's hand. I make my way to a shop that sells cheap wine. Tomorrow's hangover is a small price for a few hours of oblivion tonight.

"Rent's due!" Balbina croaks as I attempt to slip past her. I ascend the stairs two at a time. No lamp oil means I'll drink in darkness. But before I've made it halfway through the bottle, a soft knock sounds. I crack open the door to a dock worker.

"I have news," he says.

PAIN AND PING, ping, ping wakes me. Clutching my head, I struggle to sit. For one blessed moment, I can't remember why I drank so much last night.

Then it hits me.

The ship sank, and my life is worthless.

I crawl to my water bucket and stare at the brownish liquid. I brave a swig, which I immediately regret when I retch into the waste bucket. The vomit, plus my unwashed clothes and body, smells like despair.

The prudent sees danger and hides himself, but the simple go on and suffer for it.[1]

"Stop!" I retch again, but it's only bitter bile. Spent, I lie on the worn wood floor.

I thought I could drown the fact that I owe more than I'm worth? That my money belt weighs nothing? From my floor I look out my small window. Rainless clouds float past and I long for a mountain breeze, spring water, and the view from my rock perch on Mount Meron. Maybe there I could devise a solution. Instead, I lay in an empty, putrid room, hopeless and ruined.

The plans of the diligent lead surely to abundance, but everyone who is hasty comes only to poverty.[2]

"Shut up!" I roll over to a sitting position.

I must leave Ephesus. Now. Pulling myself up, I reach for my shelf—my things are moved!

My heart pounds harder than my head, and I sweep everything off, shattering clay containers on the floor. Removing the brick, I stare into the empty crevice.

A bellow like an animal caught by a jackal scares me until I realize I'm making the noise. I kick the waste bucket, splattering its contents across the room.

I search through every shard on the floor. I feel to the back of the crevice. I dump my satchel on the bed. Nothing. I can't even run away.

Balbina!

Ripping open my door, I trip and tumble down the steps, landing in a heap in the courtyard.

Balbina cackles. "Where's your rent?"

"You wretched hag! Where's my money!"

"Foolish boy."

I stumble toward her. "I'll report you."

"And I'll report you for not paying your rent."

"You do nothing! You smoke and laugh." My rage builds with each puff she gives her pipe. "Do you know how hard people's lives are?"

Her cackle halts and she points her crooked finger at me. "You have no understanding of how painful my life has been, and how generously Jupiter hurled trouble at me." Balbina's pipe rests in the corner of her mouth. "Yes, I sit and watch, because that's my job and that's all my broken body can do. You want to know what I see?"

My feet won't move.

"A stupid boy who thinks he knows everything. But you know nothing! Nothing but how to spend money, get drunk, and act important. You either strut about in fine clothes with scrolls under your arm, or stumble in drunk with a whore. But look at you now!" She inhales and blows smoke in my face. "Don't blame your foolishness on me."

"Did you steal my money?"

"You think these knees climbed those stairs?" Her eyes dance. "Nothing's safe in the city. An old cripple is the least of your worries."

"Who stole my money? You know everything. Who went in my room!" My voice reverberates around the courtyard, and a few doors creak open.

"I don't know and I don't care." Her call pursues me up the stairs. "Pay or get out!"

Why didn't I flee last night? I must escape, but how can I without a single coin? I've already sold everything valuable for nowhere near its worth. Maybe I can work on a ship? Or with a caravan heading out of town?

Layering my remaining clothing, I stuff my few belongings into my satchel. "I can't let Balbina see me," I mutter. My window! The table screeches as I shove it near and climb on top. Hoisting myself up, I squeeze out and onto the red tile roof of the single-story shop next door.

Below me, the sandal maker pings as crowds push by. Good. People provide cover. Scooting down, I peek around the corner of the second story. And I freeze. Leuthar skulks outside the gate as Haman enters.

Hurry, hurry, hurry.

When Leuthar looks away, I drop to the street and duck behind bolts of leather at the sandal maker's. Drawing my hood, I step from the shadows.

"Where you going?" A meaty hand wrenches me back and something in my shoulder pops.

"Please!" I plead to cold blue eyes.

Aldric grins. "Apollon say you run."

He pummels me with his fist, and I descend into darkness.

My arms bound, I'm pushed around the corner to Apollon's office. Twisting an ankle, I slam into the wooden post. I half-sink, half-fall to the ground, dizzy with pain and despair. Passersby duck their heads and hurry on.

"Get up." Aldric growls as he kicks me in the gut.

Air whooshes from my lungs. Drawing my knees to my chest, I gag.

"Get up!" Leuthar draws his foot back.

"I—can't," I cough.

"You'll already feel the master's wrath for spoiling him this much," Haman warns. "Beat him later, after the sale."

With Leuthar on one side and Aldric on the other, they drag me to Apollon's office. I hardly notice as 'after the sale' echoes in my mind.

Inside the hard marble office, the guards deposit me on a stool.

Apollon sips wine and drums his fingers on his chair's arm, like a king on his throne. I admired, then trusted, then suspected, then doubted this man. Now, I only fear him.

"Didn't I make myself clear? Look at him! I want to get as much as possible for him."

"Master," Haman says, "the fool tripped and your guards were overly enthusiastic in helping him."

Leuthar and Aldric edge back to the door.

"Idiots!" Apollon spits on the floor. "The lost profit will come from your hides. Now watch for Salvius, the slave broker."

Blood drips from a cut on my forehead.

Kassandra saunters past as if I don't exist. "Apollon, you must calm yourself before our important guest arrives."

She refills his goblet, whispers in his ear, and runs her fingertips along his shoulders. Her gaze falls on me. "What have we here?"

With my shoulder throbbing and my gut aching, I wonder if I might die. Maybe I'd prefer death to the terrifying unknown.

Apollon pulls Kassandra close and places his plump hand on her hip. At least her eyes don't sparkle like they did when we were together.

He pats her. "Clean him. He won't cover his debts, but I want the best price possible." Kassandra emits the laugh that entranced me and leaves through the same door she entered.

The best price. "Please, Apollon. Don't sell me!"

"Certainly. Once you pay the great deal of money you owe me, you may go."

I hang my head.

"That's right! You have no money and nothing to sell. You are the only valuable you own."

"You can't make me a slave!"

"The law says otherwise. I can either sell you or make you my slave." Kassandra returns with a basin and towel, and kneels beside me. "But the latter would be complicated."

"Go away." I moan and turn my head.

"Don't be foolish." As she sponges off blood, I try to ignore her closeness, her musky scent, and her familiar touch on my face.

"Let him do it himself." Apollon's command sounds like a growl.

"How? He's bound!"

When Apollon snaps his fingers, Haman unties me and Kassandra moves to a dark corner. I wash as best I can.

"Salvius is here," Aldric says.

"Fix him, quick!" Apollon hisses, and Haman props me on the stool, roughly drawing my cloak around my shoulders.

I moan.

"Shut! Up!" Apollon's anger scares me as much as the tall man draped in gold chains who enters. Strutting as if he's on stage, he swirls his billowing maroon cloak to great effect.

"Peace, Apollon."

"Welcome, Salvius."

"I came as soon as I received your message. And don't worry, if my first client isn't interested, I have another whose slaves are dropping like flies. With this drought, they're difficult to replace. He may even pay more than usual."

"Whatever fetches the highest price, Salvius. This scoundrel owes me a fortune."

"Well, let me inspect him." Salvius circles me like a vulture. "His face!" He tsks. "It won't matter, anyway. He's too old."

Apollon's face clouds with anger. "What do you mean?"

"My client keeps a few boys. Boys, Apollon."

"What do you mean?" Desperation wraps icy fingers around my heart as I try to protest. "I would never do such a thing. I'd rather die."

"If dying would pay back your debt, I'd accommodate you. But you'll do whatever gets the most money."

I turn to the flesh merchant. "I won't cooperate! I'll fight!"

"That's interesting." Salvius's eyes gleam. "I believe some men prefer a little, shall we say, sport."

I retch all over Salvius's cloak. Bile splatters onto the stone floor as the trader avoids my second hurl, then turns to slap me so hard I fall head first onto the stone.

Water hits my face!

Sputtering, I try to sit up. Apollon fires orders. Kassandra runs to fetch more water. Salvius grimaces at his spoiled garment and chides Apollon about damaged goods.

Leuthar announces, "Marcellus for Apollon and Salvius."

"Get him up!"

Aldric hoists me onto the stool, but I sway.

"Don't let him fall!"

Stepping behind me, Aldric supports my back with one hand.

And there is no other god besides me, a righteous God and a Savior; there is none besides me. Turn to me and be saved, all the ends of the earth! For I am God, and there is no other.[3]

"Save me, Yahweh," I whisper.

"Come in, Marcellus." Salvius greets his client.

"Your message sounded urgent." Draped in an off-white toga with the purple border that marks him as a magistrate, a man with a wreath of short blond hair enters. His blue eyes wander from Salvius's stained cloak to me. After scanning me up and down, he wrinkles his nose. "This is what you call a perfect product?"

Salvius points to Apollon. "A rough time getting him here, I believe. But once he heals, he'll be handsome again. And these bruises represent the boy's fight."

Bile again rises in my throat as Apollon motions Aldric away. Though lightheaded, I remain seated.

Marcellus lifts my chin with his cane. "Where are you from?"

I blink and gulp.

"Answer me. Do your people mutilate men?"

"Wh-what?"

"Idiot." He glares at Salvius. "Is he circumcised? A Hebrew? Do I need to check for myself?"

"No!" I sputter. "Uh, yes! I'm circumcised." I don't know if that fact will help or hurt me, but there's no hiding it.

"I thought so." Disgust punctuates each word as he stands a breath away from Salvius. "Never offer me one so old, no matter how *handsome*. And never offer me a Hebrew or Egyptian. You're not the only slave trader in Ephesus."

"No, no, Marcellus. I'm sorry." Salvius rushes after him, offering apologies and explanations all the way out the door.

Holding my breath, afraid Marcellus might change his mind, I sense Apollon to my left. Before I can brace myself, his fist pummels my side, sending me to the ground again.

"Adonai, please take me now," I moan. But Adonai doesn't take me. Nor does He save me. Maybe He's busy elsewhere.

"If I don't get enough money from you, you'll pay your debt with a slow, painful death." Apollon hisses. "If you want to live, you best sell yourself to the next opportunity."

"It's hard to sell one's self"—I draw a rasping breath—"with cracked ribs and dripping blood."

"Argh!" He lifts me by my shoulders and shakes me until my ears ring and every nerve burns.

"My dear." Kassandra's gentle voice interrupts Apollon's assault. "His death would bring only fleeting pleasure. Come, let me give Jude wine so he can perform better and you can enjoy a more profitable return."

Apollon's grasp loosens and I crumple to the floor. "Fine."

"Adonai, please!" I draw my knees to my chest.

"Your God doesn't want you. No one wants you." Apollon walks away.

"Get up and act like a man!" Kassandra drops to her knees and orders me. "Now, drink this."

My stomach complains, but I keep the wine down. After another drink, my pain subsides a bit—at least enough to breathe.

"Wipe your face." She forces a rag into my hand. But when Apollon leaves the room, her expression softens and her volume drops. "Oh Jude, I'm sorry."

"Why Kassandra? Why do you help Apollon?"

"You think I have a choice?" She wrings out the rag, turning the water pink.

"You're his slave?"

Her eyes fill with tears. "Why else would I be here?"

Salvius escorts a towering man, almost as tall as Aldric, into the room. His dark, chiseled face, weathered and unsmiling, looks as hard as his muscular body. The scar running down his left cheek does nothing to soften his appearance. Though he walks with the bearing of a soldier, he wears a blue linen tunic that looks more like a household servant.

Kassandra leans close. "Jude, please try. No one chooses slavery. But it's better than death—" she helps me stand "—I think." Then she moves away without looking back.

I attempt to appear hard-working and dependable. I'll do almost anything to leave this office and never come back.

CHAPTER 39
MIRIAM

Meron
Sivan (May) AD 20

Turn to me and be gracious to me, as is your way with those who love your name.

PSALM 119:132

"Nothing like a large group traveling to increase laundry." I grumble and set a large pot to boil.

Someone giggles behind me.

"Rachel? Don't you laugh. It will take a week to wash all this."

"Let me help you. I'll set my cheese in the kitchen and I'll be right back."

While she's gone, I whisper, "Adonai, I sure wish You would have fixed Judah so they could've married."

Rachel helps me sort and clean laundry for over an hour. As we pause for a drink, she asks, "Have you heard from Judah?"

"No. Not a word in a year."

"I didn't expect you had, but it's hard not knowing. I keep praying that he starts seeking Adonai instead of himself."

"I've been wondering—well—you told me about a betrothal. But I've heard nothing else?"

In her soft, calm voice she states, "I'm not betrothed."

I reach across and take her hand.

"I'm content." She smiles. "But, please, let's talk of something else."

"I hear Rabbi Yakov's returned."

Rachel wrinkles her nose, and I laugh.

"He's not your favorite either?" Hadassah asks as she joins us, hands supporting her back.

Rachel puts her arm around Hadassah's shoulders. Rachel must be a good three inches taller. She's calm where Hadassah is giddy, and even-tempered where Hadassah is emotional. But they've become fast friends. "How are you feeling?"

"Oh, let's talk about anything but that."

"Rabbi Yakov?" We all laugh at that.

Rachel says, "I wish he didn't start so many arguments. My abba can't stand him."

"Well, our dinner conversations get loud whenever he's here," I add.

"Abba and Seth think as differently about him as two men can, I think."

"I wish I could stay and chat more, but I must deliver more cheese. Want to accompany me, Hadassah?"

"I'd love to, unless Miriam needs me."

"You get out of here. A walk will do you good."

Watching them leave, I pray again. "Lord, please knock some sense into Judah and bring him back to us. And while You're at it, could you make Rabbi Yakov mute so our table can be peaceful?"

"Miriam, Tirzah has her baskets for sale today." Ezra points ahead of us.

"Yes, sir. I see her. Someone should have told the poor blind woman that she's right next to the tax booth." Under my breath, I curse Ari.

"Purchase three baskets, please. Whichever you think best."

"Do we need baskets?"

He winks at me.

"Shalom, Tirzah! How are you this morning?"

"Ezra!" She holds out a weathered hand.

"Your hand is so cold, my friend."

Her smile lights up her face. "Oh, it's just old age. No matter the weather, I always need a blanket. Good thing I have one!"

She does, but the brown and white striped thing covering her lap looks like it started its life about the time of King David. In his tax booth, Ari removes his scarlet cloak and places it on a peg. The scoundrel. Ignoring the cold, old, blind woman right next to him! He should—

Ezra's bellowing laugh halts my thoughts.

"How about a trade? We have some blankets. Old, but without holes. Miriam, what do you think?"

"Whatever you say."

She turns unseeing eyes toward me and her smile lights up her face.

"Agreed, and thank you!" Her extended hand is icy to the touch. I'll bring a few date cakes back as well. Maybe some warm broth. "It's just a short walk home. I'll go fetch them now."

When I return with two blankets and a satchel of food, Master is still there. Wait! Is he talking to Ari?

Behind him, I clear my throat. "Sir?"

He keeps chatting. I bet he didn't even hear me, so I turn to the blind basket weaver.

"Try this, Tirzah. A blanket with no holes."

"Such a tight weave! What color?" She lovingly examines the blanket with her hands.

"It is green, though faded in some places."

"And fringe! And you brought me food? Adonai be praised."

With Ezra still deep in conversation, I buy a bag of peas from Gilah.

She points to Ezra. "What is he doing?"

"With him," I shake my head, "I no longer attempt explaining."

Again, I cough behind him, hoping to end this public display of talking to someone he should shun. I overhear Ari saying, ". . . though brisk collections mean high profits, lately, I feel restless. What's wrong with me?"

Fidgeting on his stool, he stacks and restacks coins. I could tell him what's wrong with him.

"I enjoyed your presence at my home," Ezra says. "Thank you for honoring us with your attendance."

"No one in this village counts that as an honor."

"I'm of this village, and I count it so."

Slapping my hand over my mouth I contain my guffaw.

"You seem a loyal husband to Joanna," Ezra continues, "and a caring father. You're a son of Abraham and created being of the Almighty."

"And a tax collector."

Ezra smiles. "Really? I had no idea."

They both laugh, but I wince when I catch Daniel and Mazal whispering as they stare at Ezra.

"Remember, Ari," Ezra says, "you don't have to remain a slave to your choices. You're permanently a member of the chosen people and will always belong to the Holy One who did the choosing. You're not required to belong to the Romans."

Ari bolts upright, but keeps his voice low. "I belong to no one. And I'll remind you that I can raise your rates with a flick of ink!"

Placing his work-hardened hands on his booth, Ezra leans forward. "We all belong to whom we serve, Ari. But regardless, you will always find a seat under my arbor. Please come visit."

A few quiet moments slide by until Tirzah calls, "Ezra? You still here?"

"Right here."

She hugs the blanket. "The warmth this provides—I can't thank you enough."

"A fair trade for your lovely baskets." Ezra turns around. "Miriam! When did you get back?"

I don't respond.

"We should get home, don't you think?"

"Grand idea, sir."

Ezra meanders the market, with a smile for each person. I almost run into him when he halts to ask Deborah, "How are your three boys?"

"Active!" The two youngest dance around her. "Levi enjoys bet hasefer more since Samson began attending."

"He's been a good friend to Samson, which has made school endurable."

Leaning closer, Deborah drops the volume of her voice. "And thank you for the food you faithfully send. Samuel seems to be improving, but without your generosity . . ."

As she clear her throat, Ezra says, "It's a pleasure. I know you would do the same for us."

My toe taps under my long mustard colored tunic. A multitude of tasks await, but I keep my face serene. I'm at Ezra's disposal this morning. And what a morning it has been.

CHAPTER 40
ELI

Meron
Tammuz (June) AD 20

Is Ephraim my dear son? Is he my darling child? For as often as I speak against him, I do remember him still. Therefore my heart yearns for him; I will surely have mercy on him, declares the LORD.

JEREMIAH 31:20

Drawing a deep breath, I rap on the doorpost. "Master Ezra?"

Light spills into the dark courtyard.

"Eli? It's late—is Hadassah all right?"

"I'm sorry, Master. We have an . . . interesting situation. A visitor."

"At this hour?"

"Yes, and I'd prefer to send him away, but maybe you would like to speak with him?" I drop my voice to a whisper. "It's Ari, the tax collector."

Ezra's eyebrows rise. "Well, well, well."

"Shall I bring him here?"

"Oh, yes! Right away."

"Sir."

Returning to the back gate where Ari lurks, I breathe a prayer. More controversy is not what our home needs.

"Come. I'll take you to him."

Staying close behind me, Ari avoids the yellow squares of light shining through windows.

After Ari slips through his door, Ezra steps into the courtyard. "Bring us some refreshment. And when you return, please stay. You're excellent at quiet observation, and I'd like you to make sure I fully remember what he says." Quietly, he closes the door.

What other man in our village, or any other village in Galilee, would open his door to a tax gatherer?

"ALL OF THIS is your fault, really."

"Mine! I can't imagine how." Ezra leans back.

"Well, you started it!" Ari swirls his cup. "Yesterday, I observed a starving beggar on the street, and suddenly I realized that I hunger for kindness just like he hungers for bread. For the first time in years, I long for people to welcome my approach instead of turning away."

"And I caused this?"

"Your ridiculous banquet turned me upside down. I don't even know why I attended. Curious to be invited somewhere, I suppose. But it was so joyful and generous, completely contrasting my drunken gatherings with the people who associate with me after dark."

I wonder if Ezra knows how many times Judah snuck out to Ari's house.

"For years, I've made peace with my choices. The Romans hate me because I'm a Jew, and the Jews hate me because I'm a tax-gatherer for the Romans. But I viewed their scorn as the price for the luxury my family enjoys."

"Over-charging and cheating the villages doesn't help, you know."

Ezra points to the gold rings on Ari's hand. "Your fine clothing announces your wealth.

"I know." He jumps up. "When Gilah started refusing to sell to my wife, I started adding extra to her bill. But last week, I couldn't. My life feels like. . . like. . ." He strides about the room, waving his arms. ". . . like a strong wind flaps it about, blowing my satisfaction away." His arms fall to his sides. "Along with every excuse and justification."

"That must be difficult."

"It's most inconvenient. I hoped that if I skimmed less off the top, or overcharged by a smaller percentage—" He sits and leans forward. "But when Malachi, who I've overcharged many times, approached the booth today, I actually looked into his eyes and felt nauseous."

"When we understand the pain our sin causes, it can feel overwhelming."

Ari snorts and leans against the wall behind his seating cushion. "When I returned from delivering my deposit in Sepphoris last night, I couldn't face my family. I despise how they share the hatred and ostracization that is mine. Our opulent home, with its mosaic floors and imported furniture, began to smell unclean."

Ezra searches through scrolls on his shelf and rolls his choice out on the low table where the oil lamp flickers. "David says, 'For when I kept silent, my bones wasted away through my groaning all day long. For day and night your hand was heavy upon me; my strength was dried up as by the heat of summer.'[1] Perhaps your choices accuse you? But realize this Ari, conviction reveals that Adonai's not done with you."

Rubbing his forehead, the tax collector sighs. "When Abba died, taking care of Eema and my sisters became my responsibility. I felt I had to take this job. Eventually, I started enjoying the wealth, enough to endure the derision of my old friends."

"And now?" Ezra asks quietly.

Ari hesitates long before answering. "And now I don't know what to do. Words from my childhood plague me."

"Like what?"

"Like, 'The Lord is my shepherd; I shall not want. He makes me lie down in green pastures. He leads me beside still waters.'[2]"

"Adonai takes care of you."

"Maybe before. But now, after I've wandered so far? I'm too sinful. Too broken."

"But the Psalm continues Ari! 'He restores my soul. He leads me in paths of righteousness for his name's sake.'[3]"

"Restored? Me? Everyone hates me."

Ezra's sonorous voice fills the room. "'Even though I walk through the valley of the shadow of death, I will fear no evil, for you are with me; your rod and your staff, they comfort me. You prepare a table before me in the presence of my enemies; you anoint my head with oil; my cup overflows.'[4]"

An owl hoots outside, and Ari lays his head on the table and mutters, "Would He even want me back?"

"'Surely goodness and mercy shall follow me all the days of my life, and I shall dwell in the house of the Lord forever.'[5]"

CHAPTER 41
SETH

Meron
Tammuz (June) AD 20

Your steadfast love, O LORD, extends to the heavens, your faithfulness to the clouds... How precious is your steadfast love, O God! The children of mankind take refuge in the shadow of your wings.

PSALM 36:5-7

A little before the second hour, I enter the synagogue. Leaning against the cool stone wall, I fortify myself for a sweltering day and try to pray.

Rabbi Yakov arrived last night and will certainly be here this morning. I still hope he will cultivate me as a disciple, even though I'm aware it's Barak's support that brings him to Meron so often.

I grasp my tassels and pray through the knots, but worries crowd in. For one, how are we going to survive this drought?

"Adonai, please bring rain."

I'm afraid the sheep are infested with worms.

"Please give us wisdom for our herds."

The olives are smaller than they should be by now. What if we can't produce enough oil?

"Creator of all plants, bless and grow our fruit."

Hadassah's slight frame grows more encumbered with the baby. Small ewes struggle, even die, when they give birth.

"Please help her, Adonai," I whisper. "And give her strength for the baby's birth."

How will Abba act with Rabbi Yakov?

"And please help Abba be a peacemaker instead of amplifying the division between him and Rabbi Yakov."

The creaking side door interrupts me. I'm not ready for people yet, so I attempt to blend in with stone and pray silently. *Oh, Most High, why do answers elude me? Please show me what to do.*

Whoever came in now stands before the bimah with his cloak pulled over his head and his tzitzit in his hands. I can't understand him, but his voice sounds familiar. Moans echo as he grabs his head and cries. "Oh, Lord, forgive me! I'm so sorry."

It can't be! This morning, Abba mentioned something about trying to help a lost sheep find his way back to the Shepherd. He meant Ari? That unclean, friend-of-Romans may *not* pray in our synagogue!

His cry pierces the silence. As he beats his breast, Ari bows deeper and rocks back and forth. "Oh, Adonai, I've sinned beyond counting. I've cheated . . . lied . . . stolen." A sob punctuates each admission. "But now I come to You and I promise, I promise—"

He sniffs and coughs and cries. Kneeling, he thrusts his arms toward heaven.

I can't want him back. His sin is too great. But this repentance? It astounds me.

"What can I promise? I have nothing to offer." He swipes his nose with his sleeve. "I don't deserve Your forgiveness, but is there mercy enough for me?"

After a long silence, I step closer, but halt when he whispers hoarsely. "Please forgive me. I want only You." Then he lays face down on the mosaic floor and spreads his arms wide. Slowly, his sobs fade.

The side door creaks again, and Rabbi Akiva enters. Seeing Ari, he halts and scans the room. When we make eye contact, his eyebrows raise and he points to the prostrate sinner.

A rustling at the front door announces Rabbi Yakov's arrival.

Rabbi Akiva mutters, "Oh no," and strides over to Rabbi Yakov's cohort. "Shh. A lost child of the covenant seeks repentance this morning. Please, let's allow him to continue his prayers in peace."

"What do you mean? Who is that?" Rabbi Yakov's finger extends from his black sleeve toward Ari.

Jair hisses. "The tax collector."

Rabbi Yakov steps back, while his disciples shake their heads and mumble amongst themselves.

"You cannot want such an unclean man here," he says to Rabbi Akiva. "Send him away so morning prayers can proceed as they should."

I rush over. I know Rabbi Akiva, and he would sooner lift Mount Meron and throw it into the sea than send away a praying, repentant man. "I'm sure we can work something out."

"We view sinners as David looked at himself," Rabbi Akiva says. "He prayed, 'Have mercy on me, O God, according to your steadfast love; according to your abundant mercy blot out my transgressions. Wash me thoroughly from my iniquity, and cleanse me from my sin!'[1] The Holy One's mercy washes away even this man's uncleanness, as it did David's great sin with Bathsheba."

Rabbi Yakov chuckles. "A rudimentary understanding of the text."

Rabbi Akiva bristles.

"Could we pray over here?" I point to the opposite corner.

Maybe Rabbi Akiva can slip Ari out the side? Yet, Ari lies on the floor, seemingly unaware of anything beyond his own prayer.

With a sniff, Rabbi Yakov moves as far from Ari as possible and the prayer circle forms.

"Hear O Israel. . ." we repeat the Shema in unison.

Lifting his voice, Rabbi Yakov prays. "Thank You, Lord, that You showed us Your way and that we follow it. You ask us to give, and so we give. We do not keep riches for ourselves or steal from others, as some people do."

I wince.

Rabbi Yakov bellows. "Thank you for showing us the gift of fasting and for giving us the strength to fast twice a week, even when it hurts."

His disciples nod.

"There's so much evil in this world. Bandits roam the hills, and prostitutes roam the streets. Your men and women consort with the unclean. They become unclean themselves."

Agreement reverberates through the room. Still Ari lies as if in a trance, with Rabbi Akiva standing guard over him.

"Thank You, Lord that we're not in league with the Romans. Thank You that we're not cheating our people and taking their money. Thank You that we're not bandits, or adulterers, or—"

Don't say it. Please don't say it.

"—tax collectors."

Strangely, I feel a sense of shame, though I can't point out a single incorrect sentence.

"Amen!"

Rabbi Yakov shakes his head. "We are here for only a week, Seth." He smiles coldly. "I'll be moving on after Shabbat. I've done my best here, but . . ." His points again to the prone tax collector.

I bow my head as the entourage scurries out after their rabbi.

Rabbi Akiva rests on a stool beside Ari, who, now sitting, wipes his face and beams. Rabbi Akiva pats the man's shoulder and continues the psalm he'd recited to Rabbi Yakov. "'Hide your face from my sins, and blot out all my iniquities. Create in me a clean heart, O God, and renew a right spirit within me.'[2]"

"Are there enough sacrifices on this earth to cover my sins?" Ari asks.

"The Holy One wants you to turn toward him. David committed adultery, even killed a man to hide his sin. But when he finally repented he said, 'For you will not delight in sacrifice, or I would give it; you will not be pleased with a burnt offering. The sacrifices of God are a broken spirit; a broken and contrite heart, O God, you will not despise.'[3] You must sacrifice in Jerusalem soon. But your broken heart brought you into His presence today."

I feel cold and warm and angry and joyful and repulsed and awed. If this tax collector isn't beyond forgiveness, is anyone?

"I've never dreaded synagogue on Shabbat before." I help Hadassah stand.

"Ari's repentance! No one talks of anything else. Everyone argues and uses one text after another to say we should forgive or we shouldn't."

"Even some of the Gentiles state opinions."

"How dare they!" Her tone mocks me, but I find her playfulness relieving. She even bounces on her feet, something I've seen little of for the last nine months. Smoothing the front of my chiton with her hands, she says. "I can imagine how the gathering at Barak's house went last night and I assume Rabbi Yakov argued for Ari's ostracization."

"Hadassah, are you sure you should attend synagogue?"

"You think I would miss this? Now, tell me what he said. I won't make fun. I promise."

"That we must consider him dead, and that dead people don't come back to life. The interesting thing is that some people who have rejected the rabbi's interpretations in the past are now inclined to agree with him. Ari's sins have hurt too many for too long. Are you ready?"

As we walk, I say, "You seem worried."

"I'm just thinking. Even Eli seems doubtful about Ari. And I don't want this to divide our community."

In the synagogue, I escort Hadassah to sit with Miriam. "Please make sure she is okay."

"As always," Miriam says.

The big room tingles with emotion, opinions, and near oppressive heat. *Oh, Most High, intervene or give me something to say to ward off this catastrophe.* But the discussion begins.

Not surprisingly, Abba supports Ari rejoining the community. He and Rabbi Akiva stand with the lost lamb.

"Adonai has always called our fathers to return," Rabbi Akiva states. "If He welcomes back those who betray Him, shouldn't we do the same?

Abba reads from the prophet Isaiah, "'Seek the Lord while he may be found; call upon him while he is near; let the wicked forsake his way, and the unrighteous man his thoughts; let him return to the Lord, that he may have compassion on him, and to our God, for he will abundantly pardon. For my thoughts are not your thoughts, neither are your ways my ways, declares the Lord. For as the heavens are higher than the earth, so are my ways higher than your ways and my thoughts than your thoughts.'[4]"

Rabbi Yakov's black and white robes, stiff and clean, with his tassels touching the floor, stand out from the muted colors the villagers wear. His voice rises above the murmuring crowd. "What's your purpose here, Ezra ben Lavi?"

"To repeat Adonai's words and learn His ways. To put them before my own thoughts, or yours, or anyone else, so I can live by them. 'Let him who boasts boast in this, that he understands and knows me, that I am the Lord who practices steadfast love, justice, and righteousness in the earth. For in these things I delight, declares the Lord.'[5] How does that read to you?"

Rabbi Yakov asks, "How should the words be rightly handled and divided?"

"In order to be understood. Do you think they should be changed to suit us?"

Minor arguments break out in groups of two or three. My worst nightmare: Abba arguing with Rabbi Yakov in front of everyone. I catch Eli's eye, but he looks as helpless as I feel.

Rabbi Akiva quiets the crowd. "Friends, 'When words are many, transgression is not lacking, but whoever restrains his lips is prudent.'[6] Let's have fewer words and more restraint."

Abba chuckles. Rabbi Yakov bristles. I grimace.

Malik shouts, "We don't want Rabbi Yakov to restrain his words. He speaks with great authority. We should listen."

Rabbi Akiva's smile crinkles his eyes to small slits. "Thank you, Malik, but remember, 'A fool takes no pleasure in understanding, but only in expressing his opinion.'[7] But there's hope because, 'Even a fool who keeps silent is considered wise.'[8]"

Abba laughs. Rabbi Yakov coughs. I groan.

The crowd erupts into laughter. Red-faced, Malik plops down and Kefir nudges him good-naturedly.

Abba will never back away from such an argument. Rabbi Yakov will never agree. No resolution will come today. No peace. No agreement.

The arguments might divide our community, as Hadassah feared, but they also divide me. Loyalty pulls against preference. Compassion combats correctness. Once again, I find myself stuck in the middle and torn in two.

I TOUCH THE MEZUZAH, kiss my fingers, and pray on the way out of the village.

"Shalom Seth," Asher stops on the road. "Quite an argument yesterday!"

"Yes." Face calm, I keep walking. I'd rather get lost in our wheat field than speak to anyone.

Yesterday, after synagogue, I'd been so angry with Abba that I couldn't talk to him. Hadassah, no longer cheerful, remained moody and silent all night, probably because she agrees with Abba and hates that I lean toward Rabbi Yakov.

"Watch out, Seth."

I'd been watching my feet so closely I hadn't noticed Rabbi Yakov in the middle of the road, surrounded by his followers.

He says, "We depart now for Nazareth. And even with its reputation, we hope we won't encounter more issues with tax collectors."

His disciples chuckle as more people gather about. Jair, my least favorite of his followers, adds, "Or elders who don't value truth and correct interpretation."

"You might disagree with Abba, as I do." I step toward him. "But, don't question his devotion. His heart and mind belong to Adonai alone. You should—"

"Seth! Seth!"

A dust cloud approaches with a barking Rufus close behind. Samson barrels into me and tugs my sleeve.

"Samson! Don't interrupt." My stare narrows at Jair's smirk.

"Seth! It's Hadassah!"

I blink.

“Come on! We gotta hurry!” Samson won’t stop pulling on my arm.

“Thank you, Samson,” I say with forced composure. “Tell them I’m coming.”

“But Seth!”

When I shake his grip off, Samson stomps his foot and runs back toward home.

Turning to Rabbi Yakov, I say, “I’m needed at home.”

“There are always needs, Seth. Devotion reveals itself during challenging decisions.”

Does he think I shouldn’t rush to my wife’s side?

“Shalom.” I stride away. But once around the road’s bend, I lift my hem and run!

CHAPTER 42
SETH

Meron
Tammuz (June) AD 20

Come and see what God has done: he is awesome in his deeds toward the children of man.

PSALM 66:5

A scream rends the night.

Hadassah! Terror grips my heart as Abba grips my shoulder.

Our neighbors push their way into the courtyard.

"What happened?"

"Is everything alright?"

No one answers them.

"Oh Adonai, be with her," Abba prays.

I can't think enough to pray. We wait. And wait.

"Waah!"

"Praise be Your name." Abba lifts his arms in praise.

"Good fortune to you," someone says from behind me.

But I feel nothing at my own child's first sound. Abba looks at me questioningly. I can only mouth, "Hadassah?"

We approach the room where women's voices murmur and I'm tempted to barge in. Finally, Miriam emerges, shoulders stooped. Eli rushes to her side, enfolding her in an embrace.

At the sight of blood smeared across her dress, my heart shatters. My legs feel wooden as I move toward the news I don't want to hear.

Abba says, "Please, tell us, Miriam."

"A boy." She steps toward me. "A baby boy."

"And Hadassah?" I croak.

Miriam cups my cheek like when I was small. "She's alive." Her face and wavering voice warn me not to rejoice. "She somehow survived that terrible ordeal."

"And now?"

"She's still in danger, but she is strong. So strong." Leaning into Eli, she dissolves into tears.

I stumble toward our doorway and hold my breath as the pieces of my heart reconnect. I haven't lost her. Not yet.

"Let's go see Eema," I say to Isaac, my son. His miniature face combines Hadassah and myself, her straight nose and my serious eyes. Or maybe, all babies look serious? Tickling him under the chin, I add, "You shouldn't have fought so hard against being introduced to this world. Then, she wouldn't still be in bed."

He squirms and whimpers before letting out a full cry. Protectiveness overwhelms me. Pushing open the door with my free hand, I enter our room where, hearing Isaac's cry, Hadassah sits up, groaning and stretching.

"You look pale."

"You would be too if you'd been lying inside for three weeks. But you look more handsome than ever, holding our son." Sucking on his hand, Isaac quiets.

I pull a stool as close as possible, kiss her on the cheek, and lean over so we can examine our miracle. "His cheeks are getting fat."

Tears threaten to wash over the dark circles under her eyes. "I wish I had enough milk." She sounds defeated.

"Huldah's happy to help you feed him. What matters is he's healthy. And you . . ." From all Naomi and Miriam told me, I came close to losing her. We're finally confident she'll recover.

"I know I'm not 'healthy', but I'm a little stronger every day. Promise." Her head sinks back.

"Rabbi Akiva performed the bris, but I fear traveling to Jerusalem for your sacrifice will be too much for you."

"No. I'm going!"

For the first time since Isaac's birth, her old fire sparks.

"Hadassah—"

She presses her finger to my lips. "We will do everything properly for this little son of the covenant. I've three more weeks to gain strength. We'll bring Huldah to help feed Isaac, and Tova to help me. But we shall go."

"The trip's complications are mounting."

"Please?" She implores me with her eyes, her expression, and even her clasped hands.

I attempt gruffness. "We'll see. And I'll decide. Me!" I point to my chest. "And you'll go along with it." When Isaac cries again, I regret being so emphatic. I place him into Hadassah's outstretched arms.

She bounces and soothes him with a song. When he settles, she smiles coyly. "Yes, my husband. Whatever you decide."

"Don't ask me to put you in danger." I place curl behind her ear. "I can't."

"Oh, Seth, thank you for loving me."

"How's young Isaac?" Abba asks as I join him under the arbor a week later.

Yawning, I reach for a hard-boiled egg. "Hungry—especially at night." Chewing, I try to recall through a fuzzy mind the tasks for today. "But with Huldah's help, it's getting better."

"Ah, new fatherhood. I thought I'd never sleep again." Abba leans forward. "But you will, I promise."

"He's only four weeks old, but I feel like I haven't slept for a year." I run my fingers through my hair. "I'm inspecting the grapes and olives to see how they fare in this intense heat. But I'm not sure I trust my mind. Would you go with me?"

Abba nods. "Absolutely."

After examining the vineyard, we both feel relieved with their growth in such a dry season. "The Most High be praised," Abba mutters. Heading to the olive grove, a deep yawn overtakes me right as we halt when bleating sheep fill the road, stirring up dust. I start coughing in the middle of the yawn, and I can't quit.

"Are you okay?" Abba claps me on the back. As the herd thins, we bump our way out the other side.

After a swig of water, I say, "Isaac was fussy this morning. I hope he's okay."

"An abba's concern for his son is a beautiful thing."

For the first time, I consider all that's happened from a father's perspective. "How did you bear it?"

"What?"

"Judah's betrayal. How did you continue?"

"Fatherhood gives you insight." Our sandals crunch on the road. "Love always makes a choice. As a father, I chose love. Right now, Isaac remains an innocent baby. But he carries Adam's spirit. He'll also struggle with sin. You should decide now—what will you do if he hurts you? Betrays you?"

When we arrive at the grove's border, Abba grabs my shoulders. "Seth, I know you thought I should have disowned Judah, given him nothing, and punished him. But that wouldn't align with how Adonai treats us." He gazes across the valley stretching below. "And I'm sure Judah changed my reaction to Ari's return to the fold, which feels like finding a lost child."

I cough and run my fingers over the smooth olive leaves. Ari's repentance is nothing like that, and Judah isn't a lost child.

"Your gentleness with Hadassah and Isaac warms me. It gives me hope. Fatherhood changes our hearts, multiplying our protectiveness and mercy. I hope I'm less of a mystery to you."

I attempt a smile and move to the next tree. Abba, less of a mystery? Not even fatherhood can accomplish that.

CHAPTER 43
JUDAH

King's Highway
Tishri (September) AD 20

Then when they are exiled among the nations, they will remember me. They will recognize how hurt I am by their unfaithful hearts and lustful eyes that long for their idols. Then at last they will hate themselves for all their detestable sins.

EZEKIEL 6:9 NLT

Over the last week, skittishness has replaced revelry. We stop earlier and in the most protected positions Gallus can find.

Tonight, Gallus found a spot nestled next to cliffs that offers a defensible position. He's doubled the guards and tripled the fires. Even with the extra precautions, tensions run high. Will bandits attack tonight? He seems to think so.

Entwined in my old cloak, I'm sitting as close to the fire as I can get, though the night is mild. I attempt to recall a psalm Abba hummed during trouble, but fear paralyzes my memory.

I think about Abba—my shelter in boyhood storms. Whatever I faced, faded in his presence. When did I stop running to him? Why had I rejected my home?

"How's Pavlos?" Prisca kneels beside his sleeping form.

"Not good. His fever seems worse and he won't eat. And I feared his cough would never quiet."

"And you?" Prisca rinses his rag in water and replaces it on his forehead.

"What?"

"How are you?"

"Wow, Prisca. You've never asked me that before."

"Nor you, me."

"True. I'm sorry. So, how are you?"

"I asked first."

"Me? Do you ask how is the fool who sits in this precarious position, protected by a few armed guards and a bunch of bumbling merchants instead of in the safe home he chose to leave?" I stoke the fire.

Prisca laughs. I've never heard her laugh. "Don't forget nearly starving."

"Yes. The starving fool. My foolishness mocks me."

"Well?"

"Well Prisca . . ." I shrug. "I guess I feel lost."

She warms her hands. "Me, too." Wind swirls through the encampment and shoots sparks into the black night. Next to us, buried in blankets, Pavlos snores.

Jerking upright, she peers into the surrounding darkness. "Are those torches out there?"

My breath catches at the sight of flickering lights in the distance. "I think so."

"Everyone up!" Gallus commands as he strides through the camp. "Take a torch to your assigned positions and make noise!" Few in our caravan are soldiers or able to fight, but we must try.

"Pavlos!" I shake him.

"Wake up!" Prisca pats his cheek.

Pavlos tries to sit. "What?"

"Remember how you told me bandits only attack in the dark? Well, it's dark!" I light our torch.

"I—I can't get up."

Prisca and I heave him to standing and support him from both sides. "How can you sleep?"

"Would it help if I panic?"

"Now's not the time for banter, Pavlos."

"We must hurry!" Prisca adds.

The three of us move forward to our assigned spot behind a boulder.

"When things calm down, I'll return with medicine." Then Prisca sprints to her spot.

I light two more torches stored there as Pavlos coughs. "Drink some water."

"Are they attacking yet?"

I set the torches where they blaze above the boulder. "No, thankfully. Does Gallus think we can fight with torches and our own fear?"

"Gallus is a brave man."

"I can't laugh and be afraid simultaneously, so don't say such ridiculous things."

"Oh Jude." He shakes his wiry gray head. "He is a stalwart man who has been hardened by life. How did he come by that scar on his face? Why does he have no family? How did he get from Ethiopia to Iconium? You're not the only one who wasn't born to slavery."

"I've never imagined Gallus anything but a belligerent taskmaster."

"Remember to think past your own nose." Pavlos taps his nose then settles against the rock.

"How are you so calm, Pavlos? I taste my fear, plus everyone else's. Everyone's, but yours."

"'In peace I will both lie down and sleep; for you alone, O Lord, make me dwell in safety.'[1] The Most High might keep us safe or He might allow us to give account this night. You should try quoting a psalm from your childhood. It'd help."

"Wish I'd thought of that."

"Peace comes from Him, not from circumstances."

People run past and torches flare, as men curse, and from somewhere a woman screams.

"Get some weapons!" Gallus bellows as his horse reels, sounding more like a military commander than an estate manager.

"Good. We don't have to fight with our hands," Pavlos says.

"I'll fetch ours." Running back up the hill, I join others crowded around the wagon of weapons. Two spears, a bow, and some arrows are thrust at me.

"Do you know how to use a bow and arrow?" I ask Pavlos when I return.

"Not really. You?"

"I had a toy as a boy." Gulping, I test an arrow on the bow.

"We face danger every day, but we don't recognize it." He pats my arm. "Why do we only ask where Adonai is when we're in trouble?"

"Well, where *is* He now? Why would He allow us to be attacked?"

"He's right where He's always been—wherever we are."

We settle beside our rock. In the torchlight, I examine Pavlos, peace emanating from every wrinkle on his face.

"You should be angry at Adonai. But you speak as if He accompanies you in slavery. How have you never lost faith?"

"Oh, I've lost faith. I just found it again. And lost it. And found it —" His cough takes over and I hand him the waterskin.

"Then why aren't you afraid?"

"You think I'm not afraid? I don't want to be speared by some brute."

"That makes me feel better."

"Glad I can help. Wake me when I'm needed."

"Everyone! Stay ready!" Gallus yells as he gallops about the camp.

I shift to be able to peek over our rock. A few more lights flicker in the desert, but other than that, all is black.

Over an hour of watching and thinking later, I look up to the stars and realize that even more than the bandits, I fear never understanding how Pavlos walks in peace and hope regardless of his circumstances.

"Please, Pavlos, I must know." I shake him.

"What?" he says with a yawn. "Know what?"

"Even if bandits attack, I don't care. In fact, I no longer care if

Apollon double crossed me or even why Seth always got mad at me. Nothing else matters."

"Well, that's a change. But, other than what?"

"If I die tonight or, worse, get captured, I want to know your secret."

"Secret?" He draws in a wheezing breath. "Judah, you left your home to search for something else—wealth, position, women. But none of that satisfied. Then you lost everything and became more miserable. By the time you came to me, you only wanted food. But even a full belly can't make you happy. You had that at your father's and in Ephesus. But were you contented?"

"No. That's what I mean. You live with a joy I don't understand."

"You—" A coughing fit takes over. After he calms, he says, "You want freedom now, right?"

"Yes, but don't you?"

"That won't be enough either."

"What do you mean?"

"You started out free!" He blurts, drinking some more.

"That's true."

"You may not understand, but you know how to be content."

"No, I don't!"

"What does your name mean?"

"Um—praise?"

"When you stopped praising and focused on what you *didn't* have or what *others* did wrong, that's when you lost your way."

"I'm not sure I understand." I glimpse over the boulder. "What was your name as a boy?"

"I thought we were talking about you."

"Please?"

"Like several boys in my village," he utters softly, "I bore the name Lazarus—which means?"

I struggle to recall. "God is my helper?"

"Be assured," he smiles weakly, "He's your helper like He's always been mine."

In the camp, everyone stays rooted to their assigned positions.

"Judah," he whispers as I draw close, "you forgot to praise. Your abba raised you with Adonai's words as close as your daily bread. You learned them, but you rejected their wisdom. You experienced Adonai's trustworthiness, but you trusted the world and it ate you up." He catches his breath, but I don't move. "Your father loved you, but you preferred people who used you, and rejected the truth you knew in search of something you liked better."

He draws a few slow breaths. "In your good circumstances you blinded yourself to Yahweh's hand. But I see Him everywhere." As Pavlos wheezes and coughs, I prop him up. "What matters is where I focus my eyes and plant my feet. Mine stand on my Rock. 'He drew me up from the pit of destruction, out of the miry bog, and set my feet upon a rock, making my steps secure.'[2]" His pause lengthens until he finally says, "He helps me, so that's where I stay, and therefore bandits don't frighten me. At least not too much."

I wrap my cloak about him.

"And that's where I lie now, on my Rock, so I can sleep. Which I would really like to do right now. Okay?"

"Sure, Pavlos."

Trying to swallow all he said, I strain my eyes into the darkness. More torches flicker in the distance. Can I feel secure here? Can I trust Adonai?

That outlandish proposal makes me laugh, but deep inside I hear a whisper, *Trust Me, even here.*

Words Abba taught me as a child sweep over me like a wave, washing my mind, and suddenly I know. I know to my marrow that Pavlos is right. Abba is right. Adonai is true.

But what do I do with this revelation? Has clarity come too late?

Tears fill my eyes.

"What do I do?" I ask the dark.

I recall sitting with Meoklis asking him the same question and receiving the answer that wrecked my life. But for the first time, I don't blame him. I destroyed my life by choice.

"What do I do?" I say louder.

Pavlos pats my arm.

"You need something, Pavlos?"

"You know what to do." His raspy voice sounds distant. "'. . . Call upon me and come and pray to me, and I will hear you. You will seek me and find me, when you seek me with all your heart. I will be found by you, declares the Lord.'[3]" Pavlos grasps my arm with surprising strength. "' . . . I will restore your fortunes and gather you . . .'[4]" Another cough racks him, but he strengthens his grip. "'I will bring you back . . .'[5]"

When I wipe reddened spittle from Pavlos's mouth, his skin burns even hotter. "I wouldn't have survived without you." I hum a psalm until he falls into a rattling sleep.

Then, I close my eyes, and inch toward the Lord of my youth. I don't know how to start confessing all I've done. But, I might die tonight, and that makes me realize I'd better start talking to the One who has never left me, no matter how far I've run.

"Oh Adonai, I'm sorry . . ." Though I can't speak through my tears, my weeping leads me a step closer to Him.

RUBBING MY EYES, I awake to daylight. Last night's bonfires send lingering smoke to meet the morning mist, creating a haze.

"Pavlos, the Almighty protected us!"

"Judah," Pavlos whispers.

"Somehow Gallus's plan worked!"

"Judah—" He grasps my hand with frigid fingers.

Brushing the wiry gray hair from his wrinkled forehead, I discover he no longer burns. "Do you want water? Food? Let me fetch Prisca."

Pavlos holds me. "Shh. Water in a moment. But we have a little time." His voice sounds distant and raspy. "Judah, if you had freedom, what would you do?"

"Let me find help!" Fidgeting from one knee to the other, I pivot my gaze, searching for anyone.

His breathing becomes more labored. "What . . . would . . . you do?"

"I don't know! Why ask an impossible question?"

"If someone gave you freedom,"—a cough shudders Pavlos's body —"what would you do with it?"

"Fine—I'd go be a servant in my abba's home. I'd do what I do here but without starving and pigs. Now can I go?"

"Do you promise?"

"To find help? Yes, if you'll let me go!"

"No," Pavlos whispers.

I lean in closer.

"To go home."

"Please let me find help, Pavlos. Please!"

Pavlos grabs my hand with surprising strength. "'There is hope for your future, declares the Lord, and your children shall come back to their own country.'[6] Don't forget. Turn around. Go back. Trust Adonai again, Judah. Trust Him."

When a cough consumes him, I run. I haven't gone five steps before I collide with Gallus, who reaches for his whip. "What are you doing away from your post?"

"It's Pavlos—I think he's—he's dying!"

Gallus blinks rapidly, his hand releasing the whip. "Get Prisca and I'll inform Valerius."

Others follow me as I race to Prisca. "It's Pavlos! Please bring your herbs."

"Right away!" She rushes to her tent.

"Oh, Adonai," I sob, "if You still hear me, please help Pavlos. Please don't let him die. I'm sorry for everything. I know my prayers don't deserve to be heard. But if You hear me anyway, please!"

CHAPTER 44
SETH

Jerusalem
Av (July) AD 20

O my God, incline your ear and hear. Open your eyes and see our desolations, and the city that is called by your name. For we do not present our pleas before you because of our righteousness, but because of your great mercy.

DANIEL 9:18

"I'll open the door." Abba bounds up the stairs at the inn.

Yesterday, with great effort, we arrived in Jerusalem. Eli came to help us, as well as Tova and Huldah. It took us all afternoon to get settled.

This morning, we ascended the Temple mount. The beautiful Temple makes my heart beat with joy, even if built by heathen King Herod, and even when we worship Adonai while under Roman overlords. There we bought a lamb and a dove, and waited in the sweltering line for the priest to make the sacrifice. Now, back at the inn, Hadassah leans against the wall.

"Let me carry you." I pick up my exhausted wife, and for once she doesn't argue.

"How do you feel, Hadassah?" Abba asks as I lay her on the largest bed in our dim room.

"I'm grateful for the quiet." She wrinkles her nose. "And I wasn't prepared for the unpleasant smells of sacrifices."

"Haven't you experienced it before?" I fold her cloak.

Her hands clasp and unclasp. "I suppose they bothered me more this time."

When Isaac cries, Huldah takes him into the adjoining room.

"Well, get some rest," I sigh. "At least the sacrifices for Isaac's birth and your purification are complete." At the table I pour myself a drink in a metal goblet. When I look back at her, she's swiping tears away.

Abba throws me a reproving glance then says, "Hadassah, you were marvelous today." Catching my eyes, he nods toward her.

"What?" I mouth.

Hadassah sinks into the pillows, smiles wanly, and sighs. Abba pulls me back and whispers, "Say something kind to your wife."

"What do you mean?"

"Don't you think she behaved bravely today?"

I whisper back, "Yes, that's why I told her to rest."

"She needs kind words."

"She got them from you."

"She wants them from her husband."

"Why?" I whisper.

Abba looks to the ceiling and shakes his head. "Wives desire their husbands to admire them. The why is irrelevant."

"What are you two whispering about?" Hadassah sits up.

"Fine," I whisper back, and move to her side.

"Well?"

Abba clears his throat.

"About how you acted today—" I sit on the wooden bed frame, "—so brave, despite feeling poorly."

Her eyes warm and she reaches a trembling hand toward me. "Really?"

Maybe Abba remembers more about women than I thought.

Nodding, I hug her gently. "I'm proud of you."

"Thank you. I'm so glad we came, Seth."

"And I'm proud of all three of you, my children." Abba kisses Hadassah's forehead.

"Now," Hadassah pushes me, "I'll be a good girl and rest. You go enjoy your few days at the Temple, arguing to your heart's content."

"You know me well. Would you like me to light another lamp?"

"Please. And a drink would be wonderful."

Back on Jerusalem's bustling streets, I maneuver toward the Temple, where I hope to find Rabbi Yakov. Thinking of him, my palms sweat and that odd, tingling feeling that always accompanies nervousness sweeps over me. But I shouldn't be anxious.

Why are you restless, I chide myself, *when you're blessed beyond measure?* Struggling to recall where that question came from and why it needles me, I halt. The bleating of lambs fills my ears, and arguing rabbis bump me as they pass.

But I stand transfixed.

That's the question Abba used to ask Judah.

"Excuse me!" I work through the crowd to reach the Temple. Yesterday I'd spent all afternoon here. But this morning, Eli and I had to prepare for tonight's Shabbat. That took much longer than I'd thought. With just a few hours before Shabbat begins, I finally arrive.

Never mind—I'll participate until the last moment before sundown. Scanning Solomon's Portico, I spot a crowd surrounding Rabbi Yakov. I hurry over and jump into the argument, making up for lost time.

A few Sadducees join us and argue against any resurrection. I detest this sect. They pride themselves in running the Temple like they own it, displaying their wealth in their Sanhedrin clothing. To best them in debates gives me great pleasure.

As sunset draws near, men form groups to pray, and I see Abba beckoning me to join him.

"Seth!" I turn toward Rabbi Yakov. "Your arguments today, your grasp of the Word, and your interpretations make you formidable."

"Thank you." Warmth creeps up my cheeks.

"Certainly, your provincial Rabbi Akiva didn't teach you such understanding."

In fact, Rabbi Akiva taught me well. "Abba taught me Torah my whole life."

Rabbi Yakov's open demeanor closes. "Too bad he doesn't understand its application in relation to errant sons and tax collectors."

I nod.

"I hope you don't limit yourself to your father's lack of understanding."

How do I respond and obey the Fifth Command? From the corner of the Temple Mount, the shofar blows, announcing the beginning of Shabbat.

"Thank you for your concern, Rabbi."

"Shabbat shalom, Seth."

"Shabbat Shalom."

But I don't feel shalom.

I join Abba's group. "'Hear, O Israel: The Lord our God, the Lord is one. You shall love the Lord your God with all your heart and with all your soul and with all your might.'[1]"

The words flow from my mouth, but my heart begs, *Oh, Adonai, I want to love You with every part of me, but please show me how to obey You, learn from the rabbi, honor Abba, and be a husband and father. I implore You here, where You especially dwell. Please show me how!*

"HOW WERE your discussions with Rabbi Yakov?" Hadassah asks over the creaking of the axles.

"Fine," I say.

"Interesting," Abba mutters.

Eli urges the oxen forward.

"Did you see anyone you knew at the Temple?" She asks.

I shake my head.

"No," Abba says.

"Well, can you tell me when we'll get home?"

"Today," I say.

"Today," Abba repeats.

Eli flicks the oxen with a whip and says, "None too soon."

"What I don't understand is how the three of you have ridden on the same hard bench all morning without speaking a word! Eli, what did I miss last night after Shabbat ended?"

Smiling, he says, "Oh, they were just talking."

Hadassah laughs. "Okay, fine. I give up."

Heat waves over the fields we rumble pass, but I think the temperature between Abba and I is hotter. Even though our trip started well, last night, after Shabbat ended, he insisted on discussing Ari. Since that volatile conversation we haven't spoken.

I glance to the right. Abba's arms are crossed and his eyes distant.

To my left, Eli clicks the oxen forward. I bet he hates Ari as much as I do. He might even agree with me, though I doubt he'd ever tell Abba.

Abba turns toward Eli and I. "Eli, how do you think I should treat Ari?"

"Master, I'll support whatever you decide." Eli never takes his eyes off the oxen.

"Nice avoidance. I'm asking for your opinion, not your support."

Sitting between the two men, I swivel my head back and forth. If Eli would just be brave enough to be honest, it could help my argument. Hadassah leans closer.

"You're not talkative," Abba says, "but your words always contain wisdom. I want to know what you think."

After a long moment, Eli sighs and says, "I've hated him for so long, I'm having trouble changing my viewpoint."

"Do you hate him or what he did?"

"Isn't that one and the same?"

"Exactly," I chime in.

"Hmm." Abba sits contemplating, stroking his beard. Suddenly, he slaps his knees and we all jump. "That's the missing piece! I separate what he did from who he is, which could be difficult for the ones he hurt."

I groan.

Abba continues, as much to himself as us. "No one wants to be remembered for their worst actions. So, how can we forget on purpose?"

"Well, that's a question I've never heard before." Eli turns the oxen at a village and stops near the well, dust billowing around us.

"But Eli, 'the Most High doesn't deal with us according to our sins, nor repay us according to our iniquities . . . as far as the east is from the west, so far does he remove our transgressions from us.'[2]" Abba's baritone resounds though the narrow streets and a man leans out a window and stares our way.

I climb over Abba and draw water.

Hadassah's continues the Psalm from the cart. "'As a father shows compassion to his children, so the Lord shows compassion to those who fear him. For he knows our frame; he remembers that we are dust. . . . But the steadfast love of the Lord is from everlasting to everlasting on those who fear him, and his righteousness to children's children.'[3]" She stands and pats Abba on the back. "So, you and Seth argued about Ari?"

Eli joins me.

"Do not bring my wife into this!"

"I merely continued the psalm Abba began." Hadassah climbs down. "How's that bringing me in?"

Tova takes over filling our water vessels, and Eli waters the oxen. With a grumble, I check the animals' harnesses. Continuing a Psalm indeed.

The aroma of fresh bread sails past and Abba purchases loaves from a nearby stall. While Hadassah takes Isaac, Huldah retrieves some cheese. Silence reigns over the munching group, but Abba wears a far-off expression and chews slowly. I try to hurry everyone, before another argument arises.

Abba draws a deep breath. "'Come now, let us reason together . . . '"

I wasn't fast enough.

"' . . . says the Lord: though your sins are like scarlet, they shall be as white as snow; though they are red like crimson, they shall become like wool.'[4]"

"What is your point Abba?"

"I'm just trying to figure this out. If we can't forget, what if we tried to see the white of someone's repentance more than the scarlet of their sins?"

My face feels scarlet as I rub the pulsing vein in my forehead. "May I get my wife and baby home, out of the heat?"

"Certainly. But think about my question."

At a coo from Isaac, Hadassah twirls him, holding him high. He rewards her with his first, full-bellied laugh.

At the sound, I laugh. Abba laughs. Even Eli laughs.

Isaac hiccups and waves his arms as Hadassah tickles under his chin. His baby grin ends in a yawn.

Eli checks the axels while I help Hadassah and Isaac get settled.

"Are you ready to get home?" Hadassah asks as I hand her Isaac.

"Yes and no. I dread Ari and all the complications his repentance creates."

She grasps my hand. "Let's make sure one of those complications isn't us!"

CHAPTER 45
JUDAH

King's Highway
Tishri (September) AD 20

Out of my distress I called on the LORD; the LORD answered me and set me free.

PSALM 118:5

"Pavlos, I demand you get better." Valerius's gruff voice quavers.

"I'm sorry, Master, but not even you can order this away." Pavlos coughs and splatters blood on the master's embroidered grey cloak. He gasps for air. "The—the money I've saved,—"

"Yes, you're a free man anytime you want. As soon as we get home. I'll even pay you handsomely to stay on."

"I'm about to be more free," he draws a wheezing breath, "than is possible in this world."

I was foolish to cry out to Adonai. He must not control this world that takes every good thing and destroys it.

Pavlos's voice rattles. "Master, promise me that you will transfer my money to purchase Jude's freedom."

"What?" Blinking rapidly, I turn to Valerius. His gaze skewers me.

"Master," Pavlos grasps Valerius's hand, "promise me. Release him now. Let him go home to Judea."

"You'd deprive me of two servants?"

"But with money to purchase another. So please"—Pavlos grabs Valerius's cloak and pulls himself closer—"please!"

Valerius shakes his head, but says, "How can I deny you this?" Pavlos's shaking hand drops.

Weeping, Prisca wipes my mentor's face and kisses his cheek. "Thank you. For everything."

"Try to see the good, sweet one."

A sob breaks out of her.

"I promise—" Prisca grasps his hand as he struggles to breathe. "—it is always there, even when life is difficult."

Next, Gallus kneels beside Pavlos, looking forlorn. "I—I've never known a man like you."

Those are the first kind words I've heard the brute utter.

"You're a good man, Gallus, even if you hide it from everyone." Pavlos pats his muscular chest. "Stop living in the pains of the past. Look to life ahead."

"I'll try." The overseer wipes blood from the corner of Pavlos's mouth and then walks away.

"Master, I—" I approach Valerius. "I had no idea! I swear."

"Did you know he insisted that you accompany this caravan?"

"No."

"I suppose I believe you. He planned it all," he chokes, "though maybe not the dying part."

Kneeling beside my friend, I grab his gnarled hand, my tears washing his callouses. "Pavlos, please! Not even my freedom is worth losing you."

"Adonai's done a work in you, I think." Pavlos manages a small laugh.

"No, He hasn't! I just cursed Him for not healing you."

He squeezes harder. "And last night you called on Him. Yes?"

"Yes. But if I can't last twelve hours, how will I continue with Adonai if you're gone?"

"Twelve hours is progress. Anyway, He's healing me as we speak." His breath sounds shallow. "Now, you go do one right thing. And then another. And then another after that. You know what's right. You know. He's with you."

"Oh, Pavlos, Adonai doesn't listen to me. Becoming a servant for my father feels as likely as a mirage giving water."

Pavlos barely reaches a whisper. "He always listens, Judah. I redeemed your life. Use it well. Use it for others." With a grimace, he groans. "Go, Judah. Go tonight, before Valerius changes his mind. And don't forget, the Most High answered your prayer for my healing. After my last breath, I'll be whole. I'll be home."

As I stroke his weathered brow with the cloth, my grief flows, just like everyone clustered about us. "Pavlos, you opened my eyes to see myself." I sniff. "What will I do without you?"

"Keep asking the Most High to help you see. He'll show you the way." His voice is barely audible. "Now, sing me home."

I know what Pavlos means—a home where I can no longer reach him. But, as with everything in my life, I remain powerless to change it.

"Sing, 'Though I walk through the valley of death—'"

He wheezes, and I continue the song from my youth. "I'll fear no evil . . ."

As I finish the psalm, his face relaxes and he stops breathing. Peace replaces his grimace.

"Goodbye, my friend," I say, and I imagine him walking without a limp into complete freedom.

I shall not die, but I shall live, and recount the deeds of the
LORD.

PSALM 118:17

"ARE YOU REAL?" My voice cracks as I inch forward.

Either a well stands in front of me or my muddled mind imagines it. Hope gives enough strength to my weary feet that I stumble forward.

The smooth wooden lever I grasp is real. The wet waterskin I draw is real. And, praise Adonai, the water dripping from it is real, cool, and refreshing. I drink deep, the stream cooling my insides and splashing my front. My broken lips sting, but I don't care. Holding my last gulp, I wait for my mouth to no longer feel like the parched desert I've stumbled through for the last week.

My thirst almost drove me mad.

I didn't believe I'd ever arrive back in the Land again, much less drink Galilean water. Life as a slave on a caravan tortured me. Life as a free man without a single mite to buy a loaf of bread almost killed me. At first, I feared bandits, but my bedraggled state must not have seemed worth their effort. I stumbled forward the last few days, close to delirium. One word propelled me onward—home.

As water seeps into my fingers, toes, and mind, I operate the lever and fill my waterskins. Able to think again, I examine the tiny village perched on Galilee's northern tip, hoping for a place to sleep. Evening approaches and villagers hurry from hill and field to their homes. Home. Walls and love and security and belongingness. Do people realize the gift of normality?

"Stranger, you look done for." An elderly man, tassels hanging below his tunic, hobbles over. "I own little, but I share what Adonai's given. Would you like shelter in my barn? And a bit of my Martha's bread?" Kindness lies in each smiling wrinkle.

My mouth waters and I nod. I move to join him but my legs refuse.

"Here, let me help you. Lean on me. You're young to be in such desperate straits."

"Thank you," I croak.

With his arm around me, I limp toward his home. Tonight, I rest in safety and shelter. Maybe I'll survive this trek after all.

As I've made my way south through upper Galilee for the past week, starvation and filth still cling to me. I rinse in streams when I can, but most are muddy trickles. And though the drought has not struck as severely here, very little remains in the corners of the fields. When I can't glean, I beg.

Tonight, I sleep in Mount Hermon's shadow. The land smells and even sounds like home. The day after tomorrow, if I push, I will step back into everything I fled.

Yes, I miss home, from my shaggy, dirty head to my cracked, calloused toes. But fear matches my longing. How can I face the village in this failure, filth, and loss?

Rolling over, I turn my back to the communal fire of other poor travelers. Our numbers provide safety. We don't talk to or trust each other, but we also have nothing worth stealing. The evening chill sets me shivering and I wrap myself in my brown cloak, now more holes than fabric, as much as possible. It reminds me of Pavlos and again I wonder at his gift of my freedom.

I whisper to the cricket humming under a leaf. "I wish he was with me tonight."

Behind me a little boy chats with his abba, and I recall a night, long ago. Just a boy, I nestled against Abba as he told me a story about Adonai pointing Abraham's face toward the stars.

He pointed to the night sky and said, "Son, do you remember the time Abraham complained to the Most High?"

"Father Abraham complained? To Adonai?"

"Yes! He got discouraged. Abraham and Sarah felt too old for Adonai's promised son."

"He complained and got discouraged?" I'd never imagined the patriarch anything but faithful.

Abba squeezed me. "Of course. Yahweh always works with imperfect people. Can you think of a perfect one?"

I tried. King David? No, he sinned with Bathsheba.

"I know!" I puffed my chest out. "Enoch."

Abba's laughter filled the night. "Good job, my son. Though we aren't told he was perfect. Now, count the stars. That's what our Heavenly Father told Abraham. Look up. Number the stars."

I gazed from one horizon to the other. "I couldn't count them if I took all night."

"They're beyond numbering. That's how many people Adonai promised would come from Abraham and Sarah. And His promises for us—for you—are beyond counting. He's faithful, compassionate, and merciful.

"But many years remained before Isaac's birth. Only the Creator received credit, because Isaac was a miracle, like every promise fulfilled in our lives. Do you understand?"

"I think so."

"When Adonai feels far away, and you feel discouraged, look up. Try to count the stars, and remember that's how many promises He has for you. And He keeps His promises."

Abba wrapped me in his warm cloak while I counted. Eventually, I fell asleep, and he carried me home.

A snore from the traveler next to me interrupts the memory. Just as well—I must sleep to have enough strength for what I face. I long for and dread home. Long for and dread Abba, the village, Eli and Miriam, Rachel, and especially Seth. Peace and sleep feel impossible.

So I gaze up.

"One, two, three . . ."

Does counting stars still work?

". . . twenty-five, twenty-six, twenty-seven . . ." My breathing slows.

Do any promises remain for me?

". . . thirty-nine, forty, forty-one . . ." My eyelids flutter.

". . . fifty-four, fifty—"

Into my dreams, Abba approaches, reaches down, picks me up, cradles me in his powerful arms, and carries me home.

CHAPTER 46
MIRIAM

Meron
Tishri (September) AD 20

He heals the brokenhearted and binds up their wounds.

PSALM 147:3

"I should be stronger by now." Hadassah groans as she stretches her back.

I grab the basket from her hands. "So you harvest pomegranates and process figs to prove it?"

"I want to do something. Please don't be vexed with me. Not you, too."

"Seth?"

She bites her lip.

"I imagine he feels frustrated at his inability to fix you. Patience isn't his strongest skill."

She stares at me with a crooked grin.

"Yes, yes. I'm not so great at it either!" I steer my young mistress toward a chair in dappled sunlight. "You need to sit and rest."

Sinking down, she sighs.

"There's no reason to wrinkle your face like a prune." I shake my finger at her. "Someday, sooner than you think, wrinkles won't be a choice." She doesn't laugh.

Huldah places Isaac, asleep and snuggled in a basket, beside his eema. Hadassah dashes at a tear. "At least someone can feed him." Tear after tear courses down.

After I direct the servants processing pomegranates, I place a bowl of the scarlet seeds on Hadassah's lap. "These'll help you."

Hadassah nods and methodically eats.

The women around the table labor, gossip, and laugh. Hadassah no longer moves, and I hope she sleeps. I gather the pomegranate rinds to make medicine for stomach complaints.

When the baby stirs, I whisk him up. "Aren't you a handsome little man," I say, admiring his long, dark lashes and sparkling countenance. "So much like your eema."

"Do you think so?" Hadassah asks with a yawn.

"Yes. And something else." I glance around the courtyard before leaning close. "He looks like Judah."

Hadassah's eyebrows rise. "Really?"

With a nod, I swallow the uncomfortable lump I associate with the boy who ran away, but never left my heart.

"Miriam, why does no one mention him? I want to know more, but Seth gets angry at his name. And I don't want to hurt Abba."

"We don't talk about him for the same two reasons." I hand Isaac to her. "Do you want to try feeding him?"

She frowns. "Okay."

I kneel at her feet and place my hands on her cheeks. "I'm going to tell you something, and I want you to prepare yourself."

"Oh, dear. Seth warned me about your scoldings. But in all this time, you've never given me one."

"You experienced a difficult pregnancy and a horrible birth. Your body struggles to heal, and you need help to feed this baby."

"I thought traveling to the Temple—fulfilling the requirement—would help!"

"You have a child, something I longed for my whole life but the Holy One never gave to me. Your hard time will pass if you stop fretting and blaming yourself. Be grateful for Huldah's abundant milk. Tova and I want to help you, and we never find you a burden. Guilt and sorrow make your healing slower. Hadassah, you hold *life* in these hands." I encompass her arms which cradle Isaac. "Stop worrying about what you can't do and celebrate this."

She lays her head on my shoulder and I let her cry until Isaac rebels against being squished between us. His arms flail as he cries. We giggle through sniffles.

Hadassah nuzzles Isaac. "Oh, I miss laughing."

"I miss hearing you laugh. And I bet Seth does too. After all, he named his son after you. Isaac—laughter."

"Thank you, Miriam." Hadassah kisses Isaac's cheek and straightens her shoulders. "I'm an official family member now."

"Our family needs you, so rest and get better. I can harvest pomegranates, press figs, and dry grapes on my own. But you're the only one who ignites a light in Seth's eyes. And you're the only eema this boy has."

CHAPTER 47
SETH

Meron
Heshvan (October) AD 20

But you shall remember that you were a slave in Egypt and the LORD your God redeemed you from there; therefore I command you to do this.

DEUTERONOMY 24:18

"Seth, why are you angry? I'm talking with you, not disagreeing."

"Ha! Thinking differently than me isn't disagreeing?"

As Hadassah lays Isaac in his basket, she whispers, "I understand you disagree with Abba about Ari. But Ari's wife wasn't a tax collector. Since her husband repented, Joanna sold her fancy clothes and gave the money to the poor. She sacrificed in Jerusalem, along with Ari and their children. Yet, the women here still shun her. It's wrong and unforgiving."

"I have little time for this today. But Lavinia says—"

"That woman has an asp's tongue."

"Hadassah! She's important!"

"She's hateful."

When Isaac fusses, she pats his back. "Anyway, what makes her important? Because Barak is an Elder? You know, he's horrible too. Besides, she gossips and breeds dissension."

"I don't want you to befriend Ari's wife—"

"Joanna."

"All right, Joanna. Don't befriend her. That's final." I gather my things to escape from this room and this conversation.

"I won't be unkind to her. And I won't ignore her."

"You are still recovering and don't need more burdens. Don't invite her into this home."

Isaac asleep, she crosses her arms and taps her foot. How is one so small, so formidable?

"I mean it, Hadassah." I speak louder than I mean to, and Isaac fidgets and cries.

"Oh, Seth, I just wish—"

"No more. I must leave now. I'll return tonight, but not to resume this discussion. It's closed."

Her face tells me she isn't done.

"Shalom, Hadassah." Grabbing my satchel, I kiss her on the cheek and rush out before she can add more. I join Matthias, who loads food and waterskins onto our donkeys.

"Bye, Seth!" Samson yells from the barn entrance.

"Try to not get in trouble today."

"I always try not to, but it happens anyway." Samson scrunches his nose and Rufus whines at the boy's side.

"Try harder."

"Well, I'm going to the tower this morning with Ezra and Eli. I don't get in trouble much when I'm with them."

"We can hope. Goodbye, Samson."

"Shalom!" He races out the back gate, Rufus at his heels. Trying hard, indeed.

I want to leave before Abba sees me, because like Hadassah, he'll encourage me to welcome sinners back to the fold, and I can't tolerate anymore. Not today.

Touching the mezuzah, I proclaim under my breath, "Adonai will guard my leaving and returning from now and ever."

I need that guard today. I also need ideas on how to make things clear when I get back. Certain things must never change, like considering traitors dead to us.

CHAPTER 48
JUDAH

Meron
Heshvan (October) AD 20

You have led in your steadfast love the people whom you have redeemed; you have guided them by your strength to your holy abode.

EXODUS 15:13

Morning light wakes me to the day I've anticipated and dreaded since I took my first step across the desert. I shake out my filthy clothes. At least my brown chiton has faded to the same color of the dust that coats it. After I fill my waterskin, I wash my face.

"Putting it off won't make it easier!"

With that, I head across the valley toward Meron, chewing a few olives left from yesterday's gleaning. Miriam's bread invades my imagination, but I shove it away. She's more likely to give me her back than her bread.

Wrong expectations will make this worse.

By late morning, I reach the crossroads and take the right turn leading to Meron. My heart feels like it might jump out of my chest and I start sweating even though it isn't hot. I draw my tattered headscarf over my gaunt face, fix my eyes on the ground, and begin my ascent home.

"Do you have a stone to sharpen my hoe? I can't even break up the ground." Kefir's voice floats from the field.

"Why do you never prepare your tools before you get to the field?" That sounds like Malik.

Hearing voices I recognize causes panic, starting from my toes, to rise until my ears buzz. What am I thinking? I can't enter through the city gate! I should wait until nightfall and slip in through our back gate.

I jump down into a wadi beside the road. Staying low, I circumvent the fields until I reach a copse of terebinth trees. My breathing is hard and ragged. I must be mad to attempt this.

Crouching behind the trees, doubt attacks me. Once I ask Abba to be his servant, his answer will be final. If he rejects me, I'll be a homeless beggar, continuing my current abominable existence.

Fear holds me back. Hope pushes me forward.

"Oh, Adonai," I dare to pray, "could you help a sinner like me?"

CHAPTER 49
ELI

Meron
Heshvan (October) AD 20

Behold, the eye of the LORD is on those who fear him, on those who hope in his steadfast love.

PSALM 33:18

Samson races up the tower ahead of Ezra and me, taking two steps at a time. He loves to stand high above the valley and check for bandits, travelers, and wayward lambs. What did we do before he came?

"What do you observe, oh fast one?" Master pants and wipes his forehead, flapping his robe for some air.

"You think I'm fast?"

"As a rabbit. Makes me long for younger legs."

Samson grins.

"Something funny?"

"When I imagine you as a young boy"—he chortles—"you still have a gray beard."

Laughing, Master inhales and fans his face. "I love the aroma of fresh turned fields. It smells like new life."

Samson mimics him, sniffing deeply.

"All right, rabbit. Tell me what you see."

Samson scans the horizon, naming the hills and towns as Ezra has taught him.

"What's that?" Samson points to the left.

Turning, Master squints into the distance. "Where?"

"Way out there, behind those trees. Looks like a person. Think he needs help?"

"Where? Who?"

"See Kefir plowing? He's on the other side."

After a moment, Master stiffens. "Could it be?" He whispers. "Could it actually be?"

CHAPTER 50
JUDAH

Meron
Heshvan (October) AD 20

Open to me the gates of righteousness, that I may enter through them and give thanks to the LORD.

PSALM 118:19

From my vantage point, I glimpse my home's second story among Meron's clustered buildings. Across the field stands the completed tower—a monument to my foolishness. There are even people on top. My failures surround me.

I shouldn't have come back here.

"You! What are you doing back there?" Someone, I think Kefir, calls from the field.

Fear grips me, as strongly as the night Apollon sold me. When these villagers recognize me, they will beat and ridicule me to the full extent of their satisfaction.

And I deserve it.

Why did I think this would work? Did heat and starvation delude me? Or did Pavlos's dying words and my desire to come home blind me to reality?

A few men approach, field implements held aloft.

"Who are you?"

Even in my current state, they'll recognize me. I must leave. Now.

CHAPTER 51
ELI

Meron
Heshvan (October) AD 20

But you, O Lord, are a God merciful and gracious, slow to anger and abounding in steadfast love and faithfulness.

PSALM 86:15

Master leans so far over the tower's edge, I grab his robe.

"Oh, Adonai, giver of all good gifts," he says, "please let that be him!"

"Who?" Samson stands on his tiptoes.

While Master shields his eyes from the sun, I follow his gaze to the man still a long way off.

"Do ya know that ol' beggar?"

"It is!" Clapping, Master hops as if granted the young legs he wished for. "It's him! He's returned!"

He flies down the stairs even faster than Samson climbed them.

Samson gawks at me. "I've never seen Ezra run. Ever."

"We'd best go after him!"

We descend and scramble across the fields. I cringe as Master gathers his clothing and exposes his legs. Miriam would fall over dead.

But even more surprising is the speed of those old legs. I can't catch him.

"He's home!" Master bellows. "He's home!"

Samson passes me. "Sorry, Eli—I think Ezra needs me!"

CHAPTER 52
JUDAH

Meron
Heshvan (October) AD 20

But now thus says the LORD, he who created you, O Jacob, he who formed you, O Israel: "Fear not, for I have redeemed you; I have called you by name, you are mine."

ISAIAH 43:1

I'm as much a fool as when I asked for my inheritance. I must escape!

"Judah!"

The crowd moving toward me stops, glancing toward the tower.

I gulp and rub my eyes.

"Judah! Ju! Dah!"

Abba—my venerable, reverent, holy Abba—runs toward me. Runs! His clothes whip in the wind, and his headscarf flies off. Flinging his arms wide, he calls me by name.

Dozens of people jog after Abba—not just field workers, but villagers streaming from Meron. Men and women. Young and old. All asking questions at the same time.

"What is Ezra saying?"

"Do you know that man?"

"Ezra, why are you running?"

My eyes blur as love races toward me. Overcome, I fall to my knees and bow my head.

"It's Judah!" Someone yells.

"Judah's back!" Another cries.

The throng presses in around me, but Abba forces through. Before I can process his actions, he bends down, picks me up, kisses my cheeks, and proclaims, "Thank you, Adonai! Thank you, Holy One, for ruling men's hearts!"

I bury my dirty face in Abba's shoulder, inhaling his clean, wooly, Meron scent. I can't comprehend his welcome.

Wait! What was I going to say? I rehearsed over and over. Why can't I remember one sentence?

Murmurs ripple through the crowd.

"You're welcoming him back, just like that?"

"What about his punishment?"

Finally, my words return. "Abba, I have sinned against heaven and against you. I am no longer worthy to be called your son."

I stop. Tears sparkle in his eyes. I can't request a hired position. Abba just took on the judgment and humiliation I deserve. I can't ask for a single thing.

"You came back!" He plants another kiss and faces the crowd. "My friends, Judah's alive. He's found!" With a flourish, he pulls me forward, removes his green robe, and wraps me in it. "Bring shoes and my ring for him." He orders someone to his left.

"Yes, sir."

That's Eli's voice. I must apologize to him as well. I must apologize to so many.

"My son has come home!" Abba shouts to the onlookers. "Join us tonight. We'll prepare the fattened calf to celebrate."

As I pass through the crowd, I hear voices of surprise, anger, and confusion. But I'm guarded by Abba, who supports me as we walk home.

Friends and neighbors from a past life run ahead of us. A boy with wild curls stares from me to Abba several times before sprinting toward Meron screaming, "Miriam!"

"Judah's back," echoes up the hill, followed by, "and Ezra welcomed him home!"

I LEAN ON ABBA, light-headed from shock at this extravagant love. I never imagined being escorted through the front gate.

Passing the doorpost, I reach out a shaking hand and touch the mezuzah.

"The commands and the promises remain yours, son," Abba whispers.

Supporting me with his arm around my waist, we proceed into the courtyard.

Rufus licks my hand. Baking bread fills my nostrils. Methuselah's jangling harness resounds in my ears. Home.

Then, we halt. Miriam stands a breath away. Face frozen. Hands over her mouth.

We stare at each other, everyone in the courtyard watching. Is she glad or sad or mad? Too many emotions run into each other and fight to control her expression.

Dropping her hands to her hips, she states and asks, "You're back."

I nod.

"You're staying?"

I look to Abba.

"Absolutely!" Abba exclaims. "And we're throwing a party tonight to celebrate."

Miriam's eyes fly from Abba, to me, and back again before a smile spreads across her face. "Well then, since I smelled you before I saw you, I'll arrange a bath and clean clothes. And some decent food. When's the last time you ate?"

Miriam claps and begins handing out orders, love flowing through her busyness.

Eli joins us, shoes and ring in hand. She asks, "And we're hosting a party tonight? Nice to know, since there might be a thing or two to prepare." I missed her sarcasm. "Have you invited the whole village?"

Abba grins.

"Anybody showing up, or we just entertaining vagrants again?"

Abba shrugs. "I suppose we'll see."

"Humph," Miriam says. "Eli, who's available to help?"

The couple confer, with Abba interjecting. Before Miriam bustles off, she comes back and cups my cheek with a worn hand. "Oh, Judah." Then, she gives a quick pat and rushes off.

Our courtyard tilts, and my head swims. Before I know what's happening, my knees buckle.

Abba swings his supporting arm around me. "Eli, please escort Judah to his room. Leave the preparations to someone else."

Abba looks through my eyes to my heart. "Thank you for coming home. I'll come to you after you've had time to rest." Kissing my dirty cheeks again, he hurries off.

"Come. I'll help you," Eli says, putting his left arm around my waist.

Leading me across the courtyard, he takes me to my old room, now open with a lamp on the stand. A groan escapes as I sink onto a stool. Wine, water, and bread appear, and Eli pours water and a touch of wine into a stone cup.

"Here, drink this slowly. You look like you haven't had much for a while. "

I grasp the cup with a shaking hand and try to not drink in one gulp.

"If that stays down, I'll give you more."

The wine, though weak, hits me, and I lean against the wall. Eli tears off a piece of bread. "Chew this well."

I breathe the aroma of Miriam's bread into my soul. Tears mingle with dirt on my face.

"Take your time."

Activity hums outside, but Eli's smooth voice and quiet demeanor make my room a haven. My room. I never dreamed it would remain available for me.

"Here's some more wine."

I sip and take another small bite. Large water pitchers arrive.

"Ready to bathe?"

I finally look at Eli, a man I've respected my whole life. "Eli, I . . . I'm sorry . . . I . . ."

His hand rests on my shoulder. In his dark eyes, I see forgiveness. I've missed him. How valuable to be with people I trust.

With a grunt, I stand and gingerly remove Abba's beautiful robe. Then I shed my rags, but hold onto the rough brown cloak. Maybe I should keep it as a reminder of my folly, or to remember Pavlos and the provision the Holy One gave at my lowest.

"May I have that?" Eli asks.

"The man who gave me this . . ." Swallowing a lump, I add, "I wouldn't have survived without it. Or him." I hug the cloak tighter. "May I keep this?"

"If you want." He puts it to the side. "Though I hope it survives Miriam washing it."

As Eli pours water over me, dirt gives way to the flowing stream. With hard rubbing, I pry loose grime that has resided in my arms and knees for some time. After two rinses, I smell fragrant oils. Transporting from lost to found is all that surpasses transforming from filthy to clean. I cannot explain this restoration.

"Here's a cloth to wipe and dry. And I have oil to anoint you when you're ready."

Afterwards, I slip a wool tunic, the color of goat's milk, over my head, breathing in home's clean softness and Miriam's good soap.

Crash!

"Watch where you're going!"

"We need more cushions for people to sit on!"

"The banquet," I groan. My peaceful domain flees.

Eli shakes his head at the clamor outside. "I believe you should eat and drink more. Still slow. It will strengthen you for tonight."

"I don't know if I can face anyone else, let alone the whole town!"

"I know."

Eli has always said so little and known so much.

After a quick knock, a voice announces, "Broth!"

"Thank you, Tova. Drink this, Judah. It will fortify you better than wine."

The salty soup tastes better than any fine meal laden with sauces.

"Your abba wants you to rest before the banquet, so please try to sleep." He hesitates at the door. "I'm glad you returned, Judah." His voice breaks. "I truly am." He exits before I can respond.

Worries besiege my mind. I'll face all of Meron tonight? Will Rachel be there? And what about Seth? No one has said a word about him. I can't fathom how he'll respond. Before long, however, the warm bath and nourishing broth create a forceful weariness that drives me to wrap in a clean blanket and sink onto my familiar bed.

I WAKE from the first deep, pleasant sleep in a year and rake fingers through my long hair, no longer knotted and dirty. My stomach aches at the delicious aroma of roasting meat. Upon hearing tambourines and lyres in the courtyard, dread makes my stomach hurt worse.

With a knock, Abba brings in a lamp. "My son!" He hands me a bowl. "Here's some more broth. And Eli wisely insists that you not eat much tonight. You shouldn't get sick from your own party."

I swirl the liquid and watch the circles form.

"You look worried."

"Abba, do you think this party's wise?"

"Yes, son, I do."

"But—,"

"Look, I cannot keep you from everyone's opinions, but I can remove any doubt about my response. The quicker we display restoration, the sooner everyone adjusts. Now, what else worries you?"

"That scene near the tower . . . If it hadn't been for your covering . . ." I shake my head.

"And you're still under that protection tonight."

"I . . . I . . . um . . ."

"What, Judah?"

I haven't yet made eye contact with him and I sink my head into my hands. "Your open arms, your robe, your ring, a party welcoming me home—I don't understand your response. It's impossible."

"If I yelled and punished you, would you understand that better?"

"Strange, but I think that'd be a relief." My laugh lacks humor. "Receiving what I deserve would assure every one of punishment. But this? This acceptance? This love? I can't fathom it, so I'm sure no one else does."

Walking to the window, I stare at the pink sky. The tower—my failure and Abba's completion—stands silhouetted against the fading horizon. My voice drops. "I know my unworthiness. Abba, if you knew all I've done--"

"You think I don't? I knew when you left here, you turned your back on Adonai, threw off all restraint, and moved to a pagan city. I comprehend the consequences."

"But there's more. How can you forgive the pain I brought you? The financial loss? The shame you've endured? I imagine the village didn't make things easy on you."

"No, they didn't." But then he chuckles. "Oh, the things you missed. Surprising banquets and rescued orphans and repentant tax collectors. I've enjoyed a fruitful time. Unusual, but fruitful. The Lord always redeems what the locusts devour.[1]"

Guilt crushes me as each kind word increases its weight.

"Please face me, son."

I returned to be a servant. But son?

"I can't—" I bend over double as a sob breaks. Once I start, I can't stop. Grief heaves out of me as moans I cannot contain erupt. I grieve for lost innocence and wasted fortune. I grieve for Pavlos. But mostly, I grieve for the sorrow I caused my loving Abba.

"Judah, look at me."

What can I do? Abba, who comes between me and the angry mob. Abba, who draws me back into the family without explanation. Abba, who declares a feast in my honor. This man cannot be disobeyed.

So I face him, shoulders slumped and head bent as low as possible while meeting his eyes.

Abba closes the distance and lifts my chin in his familiar, strong hand. With a quick breath, I dare a sip from his well of deep, condemnation-free love.

"I'm sorry for everything, Abba. Can you forgive me?"

"I forgive you, Judah."

"How? How can you love me still?"

Abba grasps my shoulders, "Oh Judah, you're surprised at my love? That I ran to you? Don't you know why? I study the Holy One, the One who loves me with an everlasting love. My Protector rides through the heavens to my aid. He gives me a place to dwell, and His everlasting arms always sustain me.[2] I learned love from Him."

Security like a wool blanket during a desert night envelops me through Abba's strong arms. I lay my head on his chest. "What about Seth? How has he responded to my return?"

"He doesn't know yet." His voice drops. "He should be home soon, so he can join our celebration."

"And you think he'll celebrate?"

"That'll be his choice to make, just as you must choose how to proceed from here. How will you treat him? How will you follow the Most High?"

"Well, I feel cleaner on the outside. But my insides?"

"True. But do you remember King David's cry when he sinned with Bathsheba? He said, 'Against you, you only, have I sinned.'[3] Your greatest sin has always been against the Holy One, Judah. Confess to Him. He cleanses your heart with His steadfast love and abundant mercy. No one else can."

"A man named Pavlos spoke Adonai's words to me when I was at my lowest."

"What an answer to prayer!"

"Yes, you would've loved him. At times, I wondered if he was an angel. But he was definitely flesh and blood." I shudder at the memory of a red puddle in desert sand. "He told me when I got home, I should remember the psalm, 'I will give thanks to your name, O Lord, for it is good. For he has delivered me from every trouble . . .'[4]"

"Only the Most High delivers. Oh, Judah, I feared you dead, but here you stand, alive. Soon we'll go to the Temple for a sacrifice. But tonight, you walk in my joy. Sit by my right side as we celebrate that though you were lost, now you are found."

His joy lessens my fear. "Put this on." Abba unfolds his beautiful robe. "Tova worked the stitching, and it's perfect for tonight."

Uncertainty clings to me, but I find the robe's weight comforting.

"Come, Judah. We have a party to host!"

CHAPTER 53
JUDAH

Meron
Heshvan (October) AD 20

I will tell of the decree: The LORD said to me, "You are my Son; today I have begotten you."

PSALM 2:7

"Friends. Friends!" When Abba raises his hands, laughter ebbs and conversations quiet. All eyes turn to Abba, and I'm grateful to have somewhere to stare.

"Thank you for coming—this time." Did he just wink?

Some guests fidget and others laugh, which seems strange.

"My friends and neighbors, your presence increases our joy and blesses our banquet. Unfortunately, Seth, our host, is delayed. Let's begin and hopefully he'll join us soon."

Agreement rises from all sides. Roasting meat, a rare treat, calls to every belly. Maybe that's why so many attend?

"Before we eat—" Abba chuckles at the slight moan that ensues. "I promise to not speak long, though 'my heart overflows with a pleasing theme'[1] tonight."

"Well said," a voice from the crowd adds, and another concurs.

"Why do people talk when there's food to eat?" Samson complains from beside me.

"It always seems to happen," I whisper back. "And the better it smells, the longer they talk."

The boy smiles, but looks at me doubtfully. Eli told me about Samson, and his story intrigues me.

"Tonight, we celebrate Judah's return," Abba continues. "As our Heavenly Father called us, His people, to return throughout history, so I have longed for my son to do the same."

I pick at my sandals.

"Let us thank the Eternal One who fulfilled His words to my son. As the prophet Ezekiel spoke, 'For I will take you from among the nations and gather you from all the countries, and bring you into your own land.'[2] So He gathered Judah and returned him here."

"Amen," echoes from every corner.

"The prophet continues, 'then I will sprinkle clean water on you, and you will be clean from all your uncleannesses, and from all your idols I will cleanse you.'[3] So Judah is cleansed."

"Good thing. He stank," someone calls. Laughter rings. Scanning the crowd, I find enjoyment, not ridicule, and I chuckle. Cleanliness restores me. Laughter makes me feel human.

"True!" Abba laughs. "Before we eat the wonderful food Miriam's prepared, let me pray. May the rest of the prophet's words be fulfilled in Judah, and in us all, for we also need the new heart He promises."

Abba takes bread and breaks it. A hush falls over the party, and Abba's words take on their own heartbeat. "'And I will give you a new heart, and a new spirit I will put within you. And I will remove the heart of stone from your flesh and give you a heart of flesh. And I will put my Spirit within you, and cause you to walk in my statutes and be careful to obey my rules. You shall dwell in the land that I gave to your fathers, and you shall be my people, and I will be your God.'[4]"

I want that.

"Amen," Rabbi Akiva says.

Platters flow from the kitchen, but I start to feel like I'm back on the rocking ship. I understand Eli's advice to eat only a little. After a small sip of wine, I spoon a bit from each platter that passes.

"You sick or something?" Samson heaps roasted meat onto his plate.

"Since I haven't eaten much lately, Eli told me to be careful."

"Oh. Eli knows everything."

"He just might." I smile at his reverent tone. "Do you like Eli?"

"Did the sun make you crazy? Sure I do! And Ezra. Even Miriam." When I laugh, Samson mutters, "She's not so bad, once you get used to her."

"I agree, Samson. I missed them all immensely."

"Then why'd ya' leave?"

"Funny, but sitting here, I can't remember. But whatever my reasons, they were wrong."

"Humph." He stuffs more meat into his mouth.

Hadassah, Isaac on her hip, sinks between Abba and me. "Slow down, Samson. There's plenty." She smiles warmly. "I'm so glad you're back, Judah."

"As am I, Hadassah. Isaac is a fine son for you and Seth."

She kisses his forehead and he waves his arms like he wants to take flight. "We're grateful. And Miriam says he looks like you." She lowers her voice. "Though I didn't mention that to Seth."

"Smart woman."

"It's Seth I came to talk about." She turns to Abba.

"And what do you think of Seth's wife?" I whisper to Samson.

"She's great! I don't know how Seth got her—" He looks around nervously.

"I wonder the same thing." I smile. "I'm glad he got around to marrying her. I hoped she'd soften him."

A laugh tries to escape past Samson's huge bite. I transfer meat from my plate to his. After three more huge bites, Samson draws his eyebrows together, pets Rufus, who lies between us, and says, "I was scared when you came back."

"What do you mean?"

"Well, if you're here, maybe they won't want me no more. Maybe I'll be in the way now."

"Oh, Samson, I'm sure that's not true."

"It's not." His earnest hazel eyes alight. "After Eli took you to clean up, Ezra hugged me and said, 'First Adonai blessed me with you, and now with my son's return. Can you believe how good He is, Samson?'" His shoulders rise to his ears. "I'm just Samson ben Nobody. I don't know why he thinks I'm a blessing. But it makes . . ." He looks up, like he might find the words floating above him. Rufus licks his toes. "It makes even my toes happy."

I like this kid. "Tonight, my toes feel happy too." I scratch between the dog's ears. "Rufus, at the table? How do you keep Miriam from running him off?"

Rufus licks Samson's sticky fingers.

"He's my friend."

A new voice joins the conversation. "A true friend is hard to find."

Joseph stands beside me.

Samson elbows me. "You'd better stand and say hello. Ezra's always telling me to welcome guests."

Clearing my throat, I rise. "I—" I clasp and unclasp my hands. "Joseph—" I cough.

"You have something to say?"

"If I can get it out! But, before I apologize, which I will, I should say, you were right. I was wrong." My voice croaks as I hold out both hands. "I'm sorry, Joseph. I'm so sorry."

He slaps his forehead with his hand. "Wow, you have changed. I'll remember this forever—the first time you admitted I was right." Joseph's laugh, as well as his arms, draw me in, and we slap each other on the back. I'll tell him more, probably everything. But for now, we revel in being together.

Samson squeezes around our reunion and eases away from the table.

"Did you eat anything besides meat?" Joseph asks him.

"Why would I?"

"Making your escape?" I ask.

"Yeah, I'm goin' outside. You can have my cushion, Joseph!"

"You'll like him," Joseph tells me.

"I already do." We recline at the table and I eat some grapes. On the other side of the courtyard, Rachel serves guests. I know I should look away, but I can't.

Joseph nudges me. "Looks like some things haven't changed."

"Never. Did she marry?"

After an agonizing silence, I turn to him.

"I think I should find out more about your time away before I answer."

"Come on. If Asher refused me before, then I have no chance now. I just want to know."

"Hmm." He dips bread into oil. "No, she did not. There was a rumor of her betrothal, but nothing came of it."

When I catch her looking at me, she turns and scurries into the kitchen.

Abba leans over. "Isn't it wonderful, Joseph?"

"A miracle from heaven, sir."

They smile as if harboring a secret. I dare more drink and take a bite of meat while I wonder at all the new relationships and happenings while I've been gone.

CHAPTER 54
SETH

Meron
Heshvan (October) AD 20

"If your people Israel are defeated before the enemy because they have sinned against you, and they turn again and acknowledge your name and pray and plead with you in this house, then hear from heaven and forgive the sin of your people Israel and bring them again to the land that you gave to them and to their fathers."

2 CHRONICLES 6:24-25

Again I'm greeted with a surprise banquet in our courtyard? Again I'm greeted by Samson chasing boys, whooping and hollering?

"Samson!"

"Seth?" Samson skids to a stop. "You always show up when I'm having fun, and you always make me stop!"

"What's this? Beggars again? I smelled roasting meat before I entered the village!"

Samson leans over to his friend. "Levi, go get Eli." Wide-eyed, Levi escapes.

"Well?"

"Judah came home!" Samson says with triumph. "He's skinny as an old grapevine after the leaves fall off, and was dirtier than I was before I came here."

A guttural moan rumbles from deep inside me, and before I can contain it, it escapes. I throw my head covering on the ground. "Judah? Came back?"

Samson backs away.

"And he came back a beggar? No rich merchant's caravan attended him, I assume?"

"Ezra's so happy!" Words tumble as he steps toward the gate. "He killed the fattened calf and invited everyone to dinner. They even came this time!"

My forehead pulsates, its pace increasing with my heart rate.

"Seth." Eli approaches close enough to whisper. "Your father's been eagerly awaiting your return so you can take over host duties."

I do *not* whisper. "Abba wants me to host the thief who lost a third of our estate? He expects me to dine with that unclean, unwashed, degenerate dog?"

"He's washed. I saw to it myself."

"Is that supposed to satisfy me?" I shake my fisted hands. "He doesn't deserve this!"

"No, he doesn't."

"Tell Abba I'm here." I poke his chest.

"You dishonor him by calling him out? Again?"

"Don't question me."

Eli stays rooted to the ground.

"Get him. Now."

"As you wish."

CHAPTER 55
MIRIAM

Meron
Heshvan (October) AD 20

But You, O LORD, do not be far from Me; O My Strength, hasten to help Me!

PSALM 22:19

"What can I do next?" Rachel rushes into the kitchen. "And my, but don't you look happy!"

"Well, if I were like Moses's sister, the first Miriam, I would take a tambourine and lead our courtyard in song and dance. I can't remember the last time I felt this joyful!" I hug her tight.

"It seemed s like a miracle."

"Just listen to the conversations." We stand in the open doorway. "His homecoming is the balm our community needed. Over there, Rabbi Akiva, Ari, and Daniel are laughing together!"

"How wonderful. They can lay aside their disagreements, for at least one evening. It helps that Rabbi Yakov spreads his teachings in another poor village tonight." She winks and I laugh.

Hadassah, Isaac tied on her back, returns an empty platter.

Rachel tickles Isaac and grabs the platter. "You shouldn't be working! What can I take out next?"

As Rachel offers fruit to different tables, Hadassah lays her head on my shoulder. "Just look at Judah, wrapped in Abba's robe and reclining next to him! They look so happy."

"Mmm-hmm."

"What?"

"Oh, nothing."

"Tell me!"

"I'm just observing Judah stealing glances at Rachel."

"Really?"

"And she's extra careful to avoid his gaze."

"You sound like you wish they were together."

"They've been meant for each other since the womb. Though it's hard to imagine Asher ever agreeing to Rachel marrying him after what Judah's done."

"That's sad."

"It's Judah's fault, I suppose." I dust my hands off. "Have you seen Eli? I need his help with some heavy pitchers."

"Not in a while—wait, isn't that him entering through the front gate?"

He and I make eye contact and my smile fades. I hand a small jug to Hadassah. "Please take this to Rabbi Akiva."

"Sure."

I beckon Eli to a secluded corner. "Eli, you look like Samson the Judge after they cut off his hair. What's wrong?"

"I rarely hate my job."

"What do you mean?"

"That I'd rather do anything than what I have to do next."

"What do you have to do?"

Eli presses his hand to his forehead and takes a deep breath.

"Well? Tell me!"

"Seth's outside demanding that Master come to him."

I lean against the wall. “Not again.”

“I must tell Master and I’d rather cut off my right hand.”

“One reconciliation and one rejection. What do you think Ezra will do?”

“After the extraordinary ways he’s acted today, I won’t guess. Will he reject Seth, as most would expect, when he’s restored Judah to sonship, which no one anticipated?”

Eli leans out from the stack of barrels we hide behind. “Look at him laughing.” He draws back. “Should I tell him or go shovel out the sheep pen?”

For a moment, I massage his shoulders. “You’d best get it over with. Seth will grow more unpleasant the longer he waits.”

Hanging his head, Eli whispers a prayer. I lay my hand on his back, trying to infuse him with my support. After a moment, I pat his back smartly. He requires support and prodding—in equal measures. “Get it over with.”

Eli strides forward, and I follow right behind him. At first, Ezra smiles. Then he swings his legs away from Judah and whispers. “What is it?”

Eli squats next to him. “Seth is at the gate.”

“He isn’t joining our celebration?”

My heart constricts.

“He refuses.”

“Oh, Seth.” Master deflates. “He won’t enter into joy, even now.”

“He stays outside the gate. What message should I deliver?”

“You’re brave and loyal. But I’ll go to him.”

“Are you sure?”

“You don’t think I’ve humiliated myself enough for one day?” He shrugs. “Help me up. I have more Abba-work to do.”

“I will get Hadassah, Master,” I say.

“Thank you, Miriam. That may prove helpful.”

“Is everything okay?” Judah asks. “Do you need me to do something?”

“Yes, I need you to host our guests, to drink in Adonai’s pleasure, who celebrates the found, and to rest in my pleasure, because my heart healed when you appeared.”

Judah's loving face makes my heart catch.

As Eli and Master make their way through the merrymakers, people reach out a hand or raise a glass to Ezra. Others point and whisper about Ezra following his servant. It won't take long for them to realize what's happening. One son returns home, and the other refuses to come in.

Oh, Adonai, help!

CHAPTER 56
SETH

Meron
Heshvan (October) AD 20

I will give them a heart to know that I am the LORD, and they shall be my people and I will be their God, for they shall return to me with their whole heart.

JEREMIAH 24:7

Pacing back and forth, I notice Samson still standing by the myrtle. What a nosy, scruffy orphan. I will deal with him later.

At last Eli escorts Abba through the gate. I'm breathing so heavily, I can't speak.

"Seth, please come take your place as host," Abba says with pleading eyes. "Your brother's been found. Let us celebrate as a family."

My face burns so hot, I fear I'll burst like an overripe melon. "I won't dishonor Adonai by eating with that reprobate!" If I could just catch my breath, I might regain control.

"Please, son."

"And you put your robe around him?"

"Yes, and placed my ring on his finger."

"You did what?" Shaking my fist to heaven, I yell, "You invited him back into the family? Did you also give him another third of the fortune?"

"'I will gather them from all the countries . . . I will bring them back to this place, and I will make them dwell in safety.'[1]" Abba extends his arms, palms up. "Adonai always desires undeserved returns. Shouldn't we do the same?"

"You quote the Holy Word to justify someone we should consider dead? And I already know he lost everything. He came home with nothing."

"Yes."

"No doubt, your son wasted his inheritance on drunken nights and godless prostitutes, yet you throw him a party?" My arms fling so wildly, they feel disconnected from my body.

"Yes."

"He doesn't deserve it!"

"No, he doesn't."

I kick a rock which scuttles in Samson's direction. "Then why? Explain to me *why* you lavish extravagance on his undeserving hide?"

"Do you want what you deserve?"

I halt. "What did you say?"

"You think you deserve your life? You deserve to be born Jewish? Into affluence and position? Blessed with a home that's taught you Torah?"

"I *choose* to obey Torah."

"So does Eli, but he's a bondservant. So does Timaeus, but he lives in the hills as a shepherd, honorable yet disrespected, raising his son to do the same. Your blessings far outweigh your efforts."

Taking a step back, I almost trip.

"Please, Seth." Hadassah's voice startles me. "Come join our family and friends in this beautiful celebration."

"Naturally, you don't support me." I point at her. "Instead of agreeing with me as you should, you take Abba's side—like you always do." I resume my pacing. "Everyone's crazy. Why can no one see?"

"Seth, I'm on your side!" Her pleading stokes my anger. "I want you to experience the joy that forgiveness allows."

"You want me to forgive? You have all gone mad!" Glancing around in disgust, I catch Samson peeking from behind the bush. "And why are you here? You are not part of this family!"

The boy steps out of his bush. "You're stupid!"

"How dare you!"

"Maybe I'm not part of this family! Maybe I've been alone forever. But here"—he gestures to our compound—"people are nice, even when I don't act so good. Being wanted, being invited to the party, being with everyone—" His voice catches, and his fists rub his eyes. "I never thought Adonai noticed or cared. But now?" He rubs his eyes again. "And you've had it your whole life! And you got a brother back! And, and . . . and you're stupid!"

I consider grabbing a switch from the tree.

Abba plants a kiss on his head. "You are a part of our family, Samson." Then he faces me. "Seth, you need to forgive Judah for leaving. And for some offenses that occurred even before that. Your anger bars your heart and keeps you from fully enjoying your marriage or your relationship with me, much less restoring your relationship with Judah."

I feel like Abba slapped me. "You celebrate this sinner, but you've obstructed every opportunity with Rabbi Yakov. When have you celebrated my friends? When have you given me even a goat for those I prefer?"

"Seth!" I ignore Hadassah's open-mouthed stare.

Opening his arms, Abba looks like the tower he built, strong and reliable. Part of me desires to run into those arms and find shelter from this storm of hate. But every strain of music and whiff of meat reminds me of the injustice.

"My son, my son, everything I have is yours." Abba steps toward me. "Everything. Especially my heart, which I desire to resemble Adonai's heart. 'And they shall be my people, and I will be their God. I will give them one heart and one way, that they may fear me forever, for their own good and the good of their children after them . . . I will not turn away from doing good to them . . . I will rejoice in doing them good, and I will plant them in this land in faithfulness, with all my heart and all my soul.'[2]"

"No! It is Adonai and my devotion to Him that keeps me from polluting myself." Isaac's whimper filters into the silence, and I glare at Hadassah.

"Oh, Seth." She shakes her head. "I wish you understood what love means."

Torchlight dances across our group. Abba, his arms still open, stands a breath away from me.

"What have I withheld?"

As I try to formulate a response, Eli places his hand on Samson's shoulder, hopefully to escort him away. But the pair lean against each other.

"I give you everything," Abba says. "My possessions. This home. The groves, vineyards, and sheep. Everything is yours. But even more, all my heart is yours. I hold nothing back."

His arms stand open. Mine cross over my pounding heart.

"Seth, the lost is found, and the dead is alive. So we rejoice. But until you join that celebration, it will never be complete. Run into my arms, which are open to you now and always."

Inside the gates, laughter resounds. Here on the street, the donkey shuffles and the torch crackles.

"The choice is yours."

Finally, I move. I pivot and walk away. Away from home. Away from my family. Into the dark.

Behind me, I hear Abba say, "I'm here, Seth. I'll always be here."

CHAPTER 57
JUDAH

Meron
Heshvan (October) AD 20

Then I will give them one heart, and I will put a new spirit within them, and take the stony heart out of their flesh, and give them a heart of flesh, that they may walk in My statutes and keep My judgments and do them; and they shall be My people, and I will be their God.

EZEKIEL 11:19-20

Eyes still closed, I inhale. Bread. Mountain air. Sheep.

"Please let these smells be real," I whisper.

I peek open one eye. I'm in my room in Meron.

"Thank You."

Walking about the room, I trace my polished table and admire the patterned tapestry on the wall above it, the earthy colors matching my striped blanket. On a peg, next to the doorway, hangs Abba's robe. Next to it, I find a new undergarment with tzitzit tied to each corner. Stripping off my tunic, I lay the soft wool over my shoulders and grasp a tzitzit, trying to make sense of my restoration.

After drinking from the bucket of spring water, I dress and brave opening my door. Samson scurries across the courtyard, irritating Miriam and the chickens, while Tova withdraws bread from the tannur and Matthias herds sheep toward water. Under his arbor, Abba speaks with Hadassah.

I'm about to join them— Rachel! Balancing her cheese basket, she glides toward Miriam when our eyes meet.

"Oh!" She trips, but manages to regain her footing.

Last night, I thought she looked even more beautiful than I remembered, and in the light of day, I'm sure she does. Now, nothing stands between us but the courtyard and all my mistakes.

"Shalom," I say to her, attempting normality.

At least her cheeks color too. "Shalom, Judah." She rushes into the kitchen.

Even if she hasn't married, I don't deserve to look at her, much less dream about her. Like in David's psalm, "For my iniquities have gone over my head; like a heavy burden, they are too heavy for me."[1]

My sins remain heavy, even with Abba's forgiveness. Maybe I should steal away into the fields or orchards.

"Judah, is that you?"

"Coming, Abba."

Under the arbor, Hadassah laughs as Abba tickles Isaac.

"How do you enjoy being a Saba?"

"My best role yet." He jostles Isaac on his knee.

"And Isaac adores his Saba!" Hadassah pushes a plate of dried fruit and a fresh fig toward me. "Eli's forcing us to ration your food, but you can have this."

"The smell of Miriam's bread woke me. Good thing he's limiting my intake."

"Chew slowly," Abba reminds me.

I make faces at Isaac whose giggles fill me with joy. When the happy sounds turn fussy, Hadassah swoops him up. "I think someone needs to eat. Let's go find Huldah, little man."

Once she's gone, I ask, "Huldah?"

"We almost lost Hadassah during the birth, and she's still regaining her strength. Huldah is her wet nurse."

"Seth, a father. Hard to imagine."

A cloud passes over Abba's face.

"Abba, I'm sorry."

"Judah, you've apologized and been forgiven. Accept that."

"This apology is for how my return created discord between you and him. You looked so sad last night. I caused that. If I hadn't asked for my inheritance, run off, and lost everything, then Seth wouldn't have done or said whatever he did."

Abba chuckles sadly and looks at his hands. "You only exposed what was already there."

I search for something, anything, to say.

"I view Seth through the same eyes I view you. I've waited much longer than the time you've been gone for your heart's return. We had moments we seemed close, but you grew determined to throw away what you had in order to find something you hoped was better."

The sticky fig lodges in my throat.

Abba's warm hand grasps mine. "But last night, I looked in your eyes and saw your soul, as well as your body, had returned."

"I just hoped to become a hired hand. To sleep in the barn and work in your fields."

"You are my son, not a servant. So lift your head. Walk in forgiveness."

"I now understand the psalm that says, 'I am utterly bowed down and prostrate; all the day I go about mourning.'[2]"

"Sin's a heavy burden to bear."

"Or, how about, 'my friends and companions stand aloof from my plague, and my nearest kin stand far off.'[3] You stand close, but Seth reacted like I feared. I never understood David's pain until now."

"Let's take a walk." He calls across the courtyard. "Samson, would you like to join us?"

With a whoop, Samson runs our way.

As we ascend the path, Samson hunts for bugs, Abba greets neighbors, and I examine my shoes as villagers greet us. "Shalom!"

I'm grateful when we reach our vineyard. Abba steers us toward a section where a vinedresser prunes. Trimmed branches lie to the side.

Abba picks one up. "This branch didn't produce fruit, so the vinedresser cut it off for us to burn. But, Judah, look." Abba points to the original vine. "The vine remains, and because we cut the lifeless parts away, next year it'll be more fruitful than ever."

I scratch my head.

"Did you show him my vine?" Samson displays a beetle on his finger.

"You show him."

Samson beams, leading me to a branch tied into the trunk. "There! Last year Ezra, grafted this and said, 'This is like you.'"

Hope pokes at my shame. Tousling his hair, I wink at Abba. Maybe orphans and foolish men do have second chances.

As I sift a handful of the familiar soil through my fingers, I try to ignore a growing lightness in my head, but when I trip for the second time, Abba says, "Time to return and rest."

As we descend, a cool breeze refreshes me, and Samson's mimic of Rabbi Yakov leaves me breathless from laughter. I hope I never have to meet the man.

"Something smells amazing." As we enter the courtyard, my stomach grumbles.

Abba lays his arm on my shoulder. "I'm glad you're hungry—"

"Matthias!" I've never heard Seth yell so angrily at a servant. "Why haven't you prepared the lambs' ointment like I told you! What's wrong with you?"

We all gape at Seth.

"He would never yell at anyone like that if—it's my fault." I say.

"We are responsible for ourselves." Abba turns toward me. "He can't blame his sins on you anymore than you can blame yours on him."

"But my coming back must feel like an earthquake to his world."

Visibly breathing hard, Seth's gaze swivels to us. His eyes narrow and then he turns his back to us.

"Have you ever wondered how the Holy One feels when we, His people, turn away?" Abba asks.

"What do you mean?"

"'But they refused to pay attention and turned a stubborn shoulder and stopped their ears that they might not hear.'[4]"

"Seth is angry with me, not you."

"Seth rejects you, out of judgment. He rejects my acceptance of you, in the name of the Most High, as if Adonai instructs him to turn his back on his own family. But, remember, the Holy One always calls His people back, promising forgiveness and reconciliation. I've waited for both my sons. One returned." He hugs my shoulders. "One hasn't. Should I stop waiting?"

Abba envelops Samson with his other arm. "Let's pray Seth's heart soon returns so our family can love and enjoy one another fully. Until then, we wait."

"I hate waiting," Samson declares.

Abba laughs. "It's not my favorite thing either. But here's a verse, oh impatient one. 'So you, by the help of your God, return, hold fast to love and justice, and *wait* continually for your God.'[5]"

CHAPTER 58
JUDAH

Meron
Heshvan, (October) AD 21

Teach me your way, O LORD, that I may walk in your truth; unite my heart to fear your name. I give thanks to you, O Lord my God, with my whole heart, and I will glorify your name forever. For great is your steadfast love toward me; you have delivered my soul from the depths of Sheol.

PSALM 86:11-13

A cool wind rustles the leaves, and the hint of rain still lingers on the breeze. Plants that appeared dead all summer now sway, green and flowering. Standing on the edge of my cliff, I inhale clean air and thank Adonai for the rain that restores our dry land.

Running my finger along the soft leaves, I marvel at how brittle and dry my heart seemed just one year ago. I feared it could never again beat without breaking. "Thank you, Most High, for healing me so I can love and mourn and praise and cry out to You. And thank you for bringing me home."

How I wish Pavlos could see me now.

"'This is the day that the Lord has made; let us rejoice and be glad in it!'[1]" Raising my arms, I call out to the birds above and lizards below, "And today, rejoicing is easy because it's the day I will lead the procession to Rachel's home."

Descending toward the village, I hear Miriam before I enter our gate. "We need two more tables over there." Our courtyard bustles with the marriage banquet's preparations.

I can't decide if Samson is running from one side to the other in search of something to do, or to just run off his nervous energy. Near the arbor, Hadassah chases Isaac, looking haggard and weak.

"Come here, little man." I grab Isaac from behind and throw him into the air. He squeals in delight. If I'd never returned, I never would have known my nephew. What I would have missed!

"Oh, thank you, Judah."

Hadassah's breathy response causes me to examine her. Though we don't speak of it, I know from Abba that she and Seth recently lost a child to miscarriage. Not only has her energy been absent, but so has her smile.

"Why don't you go rest? I have a little time." I swing Isaac to my shoulders.

Pounding my head, he chants, "Du-da! Du-da!"

"Uncle 'Duda' loves you too, buddy."

"I can't leave all the preparations to Miriam!"

"She has plenty of people to boss around. At least sit." I lead her toward the arbor. There, Abba and Eli confer quietly with drawn faces and low tones.

"What trouble threatens on my wedding day?"

"Yes," Hadassah says. "There should be no unhappy talk today." Lowering herself onto a stool, she sighs, props her arm on the table, and rests her cheek on her fist.

I sit beside her. "Are you okay, Hadassah?"

Isaac kicks his chubby legs and yells, "Down!"

"Down, please, Isaac," Hadassah corrects.

"Down, peez!"

Abba says, "My dear, I agree with Judah. You look done in. Miriam's ginger and mint tea usually helps you, doesn't it?" At her slow nod, Abba continues. "Eli, could you bring some refreshment?"

"Right away. And I think Isaac and Samson can help keep each other out of trouble for a bit. Come with me, young Master Isaac." Squealing, Isaac sets off at a tottering run across the compound toward Samson, with Eli hurrying to catch him.

Hadassah places a hand on my arm. "I'm sorry, but Seth won't attend the wedding. I tried, but he refuses. He left early this morning to stay with my cousin in Safed for a few days. He's another follower of Rabbi Yakov."

I wonder if she realizes her nose wrinkles every time she says the rabbi's name.

"I'm sad, but not surprised. I didn't expect him to come." I trace my finger along a worn groove in the wooden table. "Is that what you and Eli were talking about, Abba?"

"Eli thinks I should deal with Seth." Abba paces slowly, clasping and unclasping his hands.

"Deal with him?"

My sister-in-law lays her head on the table.

"His rejection and disrespect continues. Eli's noticed that Seth's refusal to accept you back into the family causes division in our household. Do the workers and servants obey him or me?"

"What do you think?"

Abba looks around the compound for a long moment before lifting his hands. "Why should I stop waiting on Seth when I waited so long for you?"

"Oh, Abba."

As the three of us ponder in silence, the musicians arrive to warm up and servants bang boards onto supports for temporary tables.

"At least the roasting goat smells delicious!"

With a few quick pats on my knee, Abba smiles broadly. "That's right! Today is for celebrating! Are you ready?"

"I've been ready since I was eight-years-old."

"Then let's focus on the joy before us and pray for Adonai to work in Seth's heart. He's managed to soften harder hearts than his."

I laugh. "Not only mine, but Asher's. I'm so grateful he *finally* agreed. The Most High certainly accomplishes great things!"

"Amen!" He hugs me tight. "Let's bring your bride home."

MUSIC, laughter, and conversation surround us as yellow torchlight dances on the courtyard's stone walls. I turn from all of it to stare at Rachel with unabashed brazenness. She's my wife. I can look at her all I want, though it will require much gazing before I satisfy my thirst for her lovely face.

Without looking my way, she leans over. "You're staring again."

I brush her shiny black hair behind her ear. "Yes."

"Any idea when you might stop?"

"In about forty years."

Her laugh tickles my heart. "By that time, I'll be wrinkled and gray. 'Beauty is vain,'[2] as you well know."

"'But a woman who fears the Lord is to be praised.'[3]" I complete the proverb. "Your beauty runs far deeper than your skin, so you'll always enchant me. Anyway, a large part of my heart always belonged to you. Today, it finally receives its dearest wish."

"Oh, Judah, I love you." Her radiant eyes shimmer, and her beautiful mouth smiles. She grasps my hand, lifts her free hand, and prays. "Adonai, 'You are good and You do good,'[4] and I thank You for answering my prayers for Judah's return to You and to me." Her voice catches. When she squeezes my hand, I find tears streaming from her closed eyes.

I squeeze back and add, "I thank You, my Most High King, and praise You for being, 'merciful and gracious, slow to anger and abounding in steadfast love and faithfulness.'[5]" Leaning my forehead against hers, I whisper, "And thank You for this woman's faithful heart. May our home bring glory to Your name."

Locked together by hands and hearts, we don't move. I am again, like so many times in the past year, astounded by the extravagant forgiveness showered on me by Adonai, my family—well, at least most of it—and my friends.

"You are content?"

"Beyond content." I start laughing.

"What's funny?" The quirk of her mouth is so cute.

"Me! That I'm so stubborn I had to travel all the way to Ephesus, lose everything, and become a slave, to pound into my thick head that all I needed existed here. Here, in Abba's embrace, in your heart, and especially in my Heavenly Father's refuge."

"Well," she leans against my arm and lays her head on my shoulder, "though it felt like it took forever—"

With a chuckle, I kiss the top of her head.

"—I'm grateful you finally figured it out!"

"Me too, my love. Me too."

Finally, I am home.

ENDNOTES

Chapter 1

1. Psalm 9:9

Chapter 3

1. Joshua 24:15

Chapter 4

1. Proverbs 18:22a
2. Proverbs 17:17

Chapter 6

1. Numbers 15:39-40
2. Psalm 121:4

Chapter 7

1. Psalm 90:12
2. Psalm 90:13
3. Psalm 90:17

Chapter 8

1. 1 Samuel 15:22b

Chapter 9

1. Proverbs 18:10
2. Genesis 2:2b

Chapter 10

1. Proverbs 17:25

Chapter 11

1. Proverbs 27:7
2. Psalm 62:5-6
3. Jeremiah 15:16
4. Psalm 36:7a
5. Psalm 28:7a

Chapter 12

1. Isaiah 26:3
2. Deuteronomy 6:4-5

Chapter 13

1. Psalm 116:8-9

Chapter 15

1. Numbers 6:24-2
2. Genesis 31:3

Chapter 16

1. Amos 5:8
2. Psalm 8:3-4

Chapter 18

1. Ecclesiastes 4:9
2. 1 Chronicles 16:34
3. Hosea 6.6
4. Psalm 26:5

5. Jeremiah 8:18

Chapter 21

1. Proverbs 20:1

Chapter 22

1. Psalm 36:8
2. Jeremiah 11:8
3. Psalm 1:46:1-2a
4. Jeremiah 3:22
5. Jeremiah 3:12

Chapter 23

1. Proverbs 6:30
2. Song of Songs 5:16b
3. Song of Songs 2:10-12a

Chapter 24

1. Deuteronomy 22:11

Chapter 25

1. Song of Songs 1:3a
2. Deuteronomy 24:20

Chapter 26

1. Deuteronomy 6:4-5
2. Proverbs 15:22
3. Proverbs 13:11

Chapter 28

1. Jeremiah 11:5b

Chapter 30

1. Proverbs 22:9
2. Proverbs 19:17
3. Psalm 18:2

4. Hosea 12:6

Chapter 31

1. Psalm 147:17b
2. Proverbs 17:9

Chapter 34

1. Proverbs 17:22
2. Jeremiah 31:20b
3. Leviticus 25:35
4. Deuteronomy 15:7-8
4. Psalm 103:12
5. Psalm 103:13
6. Isaiah 44:22

Chapter 37

1. Psalm 139:7

Chapter 38

1. Proverbs 27:12
2. Proverbs 21:5
3. Isaiah 45:21b-22

Chapter 40

1. Psalm 32:3-4
2. Psalm 23:1-2
3. Psalm 23:3
4. Psalm 23:4-5
5. Psalm 23:6

Psalm 41

1. Psalm 51:1-2
2. Psalm 51:9-10
3. Psalm 51:16-17
4. Isaiah 55:6-9
5. Jeremiah 9:24

6. Proverbs 10:19
7. Proverbs 18:2
8. Proverbs 17:28a

Chapter 43

1. Psalm 4:8
2. Psalm 40:2
3. Jeremiah 29:12-14a
4. Jeremiah 29:14b
5. Jeremiah 29:14c
6. Jeremiah 31:17

Chapter 44

1. Deuteronomy 6:4-5
2. Psalm 103:10, 12a
3. Psalm 103:13-14, 17
4. Isaiah 1:18

Chapter 52

1. Joel 2:25
2. Deuteronomy 33:26-27
3. Psalm 51:4a
4. Psalm 54:6b

Chapter 53

1. Psalm 45:1
2. Ezekiel 36:24
3. Ezekiel 36:25
4. Ezekiel 36:26-28

Chapter 56

1. Jeremiah 32:37
2. Jeremiah 32:37-41

Chapter 57

1. Psalm 38:4

2. Psalm 38:6
3. Psalm 38:11
4. Zechariah 7:11
5. Hosea 12:6

Chapter 58

1. Psalm 118:24
2. Proverbs 31:30a
3. Proverbs 31:30b
4. Psalm 119:68
5. Exodus 34:6

ACKNOWLEDGMENTS

Thirty years ago, I sat in a church on a Friday night in Dayton, Ohio and listened to the late Dwight Pryor (jcstudies.com) teach on how to understand the Prodigal Son by looking through Middle Eastern eyes. Enthralled, I could imagine the scenes he described playing out in my mind. I told Dwight that night, “I will write this!” Of course, other than deep dreams of becoming an author someday, I had little understanding of the work a novel required. But, how hard could it be?

Thirty years later I know exactly how Herculean the novel-writing task is. I could never have persevered without mountains of help. When I pause now to acknowledge the people who walked beside me in these decades in between, and helped me get across the finish line, I tremble. What if I forget someone? How can I possibly pen an appreciation without writing a novel-length thank you?

So it is with fear and trepidation that I attempt this.

First, I thank all the members of Hill Country Christian Writers Critique Group. They saw the early pages of this novel and encouraged me to keep going. Also, I’m more proficient at this craft—that I’m still learning—because of their critiques along the way. I would never have written my first book without HCCW. And without my first completed, I would never have written this book. Judy Watters, who started and steered the group, deserves special acknowledgment.

Next, I want to thank all the teachers at writing conferences and online seminars. I was the girl on the front row, scribbling notes as fast as I could. Thank you to the agents at the conferences who ultimately rejected me, but still encouraged me to keep going.

The Lanier Theological Library in Houston, Texas provided incredible resources into 1st century life I could never have found anywhere else. Besides, it provided an environment that can do nothing but make me more productive. Thank you, Mark Lanier for investing in something that benefits so many.

My editor, Ambria Salletmayer, took my manuscript, which I thought just needed a few polishing touches, and skillfully, and sometimes brutally, pointed out all the flaws. She suggested and taught and encouraged me. Finding Home would not be the novel it is without her skillful editing pen. Any faults that remain are my own.

This book would not have been edited and developed to the level that it is without the wonderful people who supported my KickStarter campaign. On the page following the Acknowledgments page, I have listed their names. Thank you from the bottom of my heart!

Friends and strangers joined me as beta-readers and offered invaluable feedback. More friends and strangers joined my launch team to help me take this story to the world. Thank you for your generosity and willingness. I appreciate your help more than I can express. Heather Boyle gave the book a final proofread and Michelle Nezat made my book trailer without me asking and far better than I could have ever pulled it off. Thank you!

And then there is my precious family.

To my parents, James and Diane Kleypas, to whom this book is dedicated— I could only understand the extreme love of the Father because I first experienced it in our home. Thank you for your unending support and encouragement along the long road of producing this book.

To my children's spouses: Virginia, Mishael, Giana, Nathan, Andrus, and Daniel— thanks for joining our crazy crew with acceptance and love. Our family is better because you are a part of us.

To my adorable and amazing and brilliant grandchildren: Olivia, Isabella, Emiliana, Noble, Nathan, James, Travis, Ivy, Austin, Judah, Vesper, and Harper— the light of your souls bring hope to the world and make my life a million times better.

To my children: Caleb, Luke, Aaron, Grace, Leah, Hannah, and Abigail — without you I wouldn't have known the depth and breadth of a parent's love. Y'all have my whole heart. Without you I also wouldn't understand grace because you met me time and again with open arms regardless of how tired or crabby or hangry I became. Thank you for believing I really would eventually finish this book.

To my honey, my man, and my one and only— Nathan, you have patiently listened to me talk about this novel for thirty years. You've supported my pursuit of figuring this thing out. You've made me delicious breakfast tacos day and night, and never made me feel bad when I failed to think of what to fix for dinner. You've funded my efforts and you've encouraged me when I wanted to quit. Thank you doesn't begin to express how I feel or what I want to say.

And lastly, to my loving Heavenly Father who loves me with an everlasting love. This is Your story. You are the Author as well as the Hero. You are the One with arms open and love flowing, ready to forgive. You search the horizon and when I am still a long way off, You run to save me. I love you, Lord.

KICKSTARTER SUPPORTERS

Janay Abale
Jessy Alvarado
Bethany Baird
Adam Bell
Lisa Bell
Shelly Billingsley
Heather Boyle
Ashley Bradley
Bill Brockmeier
Carrie Catalani
Carole Clark
Kristen Clark
Marilyn Cluck
Laurie Christine
Susan Dehnel
David Dixon
Amanda de Koning
Judy Easley
Kristin Flanagan
Susan Fry

Julie Garner
Debra and Ed Gill
Joy Gruben
Dawn Hall
Kelly Harris
Janie Harrison
Lindsey Hayden
Mary Hess
Mindy Hite
Jennifer Hoffer
Bethany Horsman
Sheryl Hurlin
Don and Patti Johnson
Jacqueline Jones
Jim and Diane Kleypas
Carolyn Leiloglou
Richard Lesko
Leah Macias
Sarah Wells Macias
Monica Marin
Sharon Martin
Veronica Martinez
Mary Miller
Charlotte Mims
Elisabeth Muchiri
Sarah O'Hayre
Vonda Parker
Christine Pleiman
Susan Rath
Dede Reck
AJ Rohrer
Kayla Rohrer
Glenda Shaw
Debbie Shea
Rebecca Siedschlag
Lorrie Singer

Brittany Smith
RaShell Southerland
Laverne Stanley
Sharla Taylor
Angie Their
Rose Thiessen
Thomas Umstattd Jr.
Nancy Wallace
Cherie Wais
Karen Walthall
Susan Wash
Ruth Wedemeyer
Elizabeth Wells
Geneva Wilson

ABOUT THE AUTHOR

Susan Macias loves words, and employs them to make much of Jesus and point others to their loving Heavenly Father, whether in her books, her blog, or on her podcast, *We're Not Done Yet*. Her award-winning book, *Unceasing*, calls parents to abandon worry so they can dive head-first into powerful prayer. Her devotional, *Putting Jesus On*, reveals the wealth of our identity in Christ.

Married to Nathan, her sweetheart for 40 years, she is mom to seven, grandma to twelve, and most importantly daughter of the One True King. She lives life free of gluten and full of caffeine, while focusing on her grandchildren, and finding time to write and speak about Jesus.

For more information about the writing of Finding Home, as well as additional resources, check out susankmacias.com/finding-home.

You can find out more on her website, susankmacias.com. And she shows up now and then on social media under, Susan K Macias.

ALSO BY SUSAN K MACIAS

UNCEASING: A PARENT'S GUIDE TO CONQUER WORRY AND PRAY WITH POWER

Discover the secrets of powerful, heaven-moving prayer that blesses your kids and overcomes your worry!

With *Unceasing*, you will learn how to start offering powerful prayers that will free you from anxiety and give you joy in God's work in your kids' lives.

Using Philippians 1:3-11, *Unceasing* gives you clear, actionable steps to start offering powerful prayers.

As you apply the truths in this book you will feel the burdens lift while you watch in amazement as the Lord works in your child's life.

PUTTING JESUS ON: MY IDENTITY DEVOTIONAL

How can you walk confidently in your God-given identity? Our enemy wants us to live naked, regretful, ashamed, and fearful. Jesus, on the other hand, offers us glorious attire.

He gifts us a rich identity so that we can clothe ourselves in joy and peace. When we wrap ourselves in the identity Jesus provides, we stand ready and willing to follow where He leads.

Do we put on Jesus and wear His identity or are we going exchange His precious wardrobe for the shabby rags the world offers?

This devotional gives you the ability to put Jesus on every day, living as He designed you to live.

31 DAYS PRAYING FOR MY DAUGHTER: PRAYER JOURNAL

This Scripture journal will lead you on an exciting 31 day journey of prayer.

Each day's prayer is drawn straight from the Bible and the interactive journal gives specific guidance and questions to empower your prayer, while leaving room for you to personalize it for your own daughter.

There is nothing more valuable that you can do than pray for your daughter and this journal will help you pray with power and conviction!

Made in the USA
Columbia, SC
17 February 2024